Kolymsky Heights

Lionel Davidson

Kolymsky
Heights

St. Martin's Press / New York

Design by Jaye Zimet

Maps © 1994 Mark Stein Studios

Library of Congress Cataloging-in-Publication Data

Davidson, Lionel
Kolymsky Heights / Lionel Davidson.
p.   cm.
ISBN 0-312-11407-9
I. Title.
PR6054.A87K65   1994   94-28812
823'.914—dc20   CIP

First published in the United Kingdom by William Heinemann Ltd.

First U.S. edition: September 1994

10 9 8 7 6 5 4 3 2 1

For Frances

Prologue

How long, dear friend—how long? I await you with eagerness! So much has happened, so much I must not forget, that I use this time to make an account. And to offer a warning. Everything that follows you will find very strange. For now—just follow the sequence.

Soon after our last meeting (you remember *when?*) I returned home and took a short holiday with my wife in Pitsunda on the Black Sea. There, there was a motor accident. My wife was killed, I myself badly injured. I spent some weeks in hospital and more in a sanatorium, a victim of severe depression. My friends, my colleagues, all urged a return to work. I returned to work but could not work. My institute was nothing to me, my former interests of no further interest.

This depression was diagnosed as "clinical," and I was thereupon transported to a clinic! There I received various treatments, none of avail; and there presently a certain academician began paying me visits.

This academician was only vaguely familiar to me, yet it was soon apparent that he had the liveliest and most knowledgeable interest in my affairs. He had fully consulted my doctors, was aware of my domestic situation and of course of my publications. In a series of conversations he assured himself that I was still alert in my field. And he made me a proposition.

A research station in the north, he said, needed a new director. Its present head was in a precarious state of health and had not long to live. The work conducted by the station was of the greatest value, and a committee had sat for some time considering possible candidates, aided by members of the "state organs"; from which I deduced that there must be a security aspect to the work. This he confirmed, and went further.

That part of the work that interested the "organs" would not, he said, meet with approval in all scientific circles—this was perfectly understandable and a valid reason for refusal. He had no knowledge of it himself but understood it to be similar to the studies at Fort Detrick in America and Porton Down in England, which is to say the research into materials for chemical and biological warfare.

The next negative aspect was no less important: The appointee to the station would never be able to leave it. For a return to normal life had been deemed impermissible. This was not to say it was a life of imprisonment. Far from it. But this drawback should be weighed in my decision, along with two others: the location of the station and its meteorological conditions (by which I understood that it was in an isolated place with very bad weather).

After this, all the aspects were very positive. Living conditions at the station were not merely good but luxurious. On the professional side, the budget was almost unlimited: At least, he had never known the committee to refuse any request by the present incumbent. (And since he is safely dead I will name him: L. V. Zhelikov was that incumbent.)

As with the budget, so with the research program. It was virtually boundless, going far beyond the military applications. He talked extensively on this subject—in particular of a field of especial interest to me. And on his final leaving told me one thing more. All previous appointments to the station had been subject to rigorous vetting. This was principally to determine whether the candidates were psychologically suitable for the life. Many were judged not to be, and even of those selected there had been a percentage of failures. For these unfortunates there was nothing to be done. They could not leave, of course; they had to remain, unhappily for life.

In my case such vetting would not be necessary. But he said I should bear in mind the position of the "unfortunates"; that he would not be traveling to see me anymore; that after thinking the matter over carefully I should simply send him a card saying yes or no. And I said I would do this.

I said I would do it and I sent him the card, saying yes; although in fact I had given it no thought at all. As soon as the words were out of his mouth I had known I would accept. My reasons were simple. My present malaise, I was certain, would not continue. Life resumes, as it always does. I was just as certain that I must now devote what was left of it to that special subject he had mentioned. And too, there was the "isolated place with the very bad weather." Siberia, of course.

For now I say that I sent the card, and six weeks later, very precipitately, with barely time to take leave of my friends or say where I was going (for I did not know where I was going), I traveled under escort to the research station.

There I learned the reason for the precipitancy. Zhelikov had days to live. He was riddled with cancer. He sat in his magnificent underground apartment, the apartment I sit in now, in the mobile chair-bed he had designed (his electric chair, he called it), in a state of considerable pain, exhaustion, and impatience. He had taken none of his morphine drugs that day, in order to keep his brain clear. Almost at once he began giving detailed instructions on how I should deal with a problem that had arisen that very week.

The problem was the collection of a mammoth. Many of the extinct beasts have been found in these parts, of course; the need always being to arrive on the scene before the native hunters, who eat them (and additionally conduct a tidy trade in ivory carvings). Some short time before, the government had prohibited these practices and had made it an offense for a finding not to be reported. This had no effect on the tribesmen, who do not ''tell'' on each other, but a significant one on building operations. Among large construction crews there is certain to be gossip, so finds are reported at once—and at once followed by standstill orders until properly inspected.

It is not the only significance. Hunters' finds have been in caves or other surface locations, the animals having died naturally, with a slow dispersal of body heat and inevitable degeneration of the soft tissue. There was nowhere a complete mammoth, quick-frozen so to speak, with its soft tissue intact. What excited Zhelikov now was the probability that he had such an animal within his grasp.

At a sea cape to the north of the research station a site was being prepared for a large installation. During excavation the ground had given way disclosing a crevasse. In the crevasse was a ledge, and on the ledge a mammoth. It was encased in ice. Evidently it had fallen— and fallen a long way, to immediate death. A quick-frozen mammoth!

In a fury of impatience, Zhelikov insisted that I go at once to the crevasse. Too sick to travel himself, unwilling to rely on his assistants, he had been awaiting me for four days. For two of these days I had myself been traveling, and was now almost terminally weary. Yet such was his force of character that, not two hours after my arrival, he had driven me out into the cold again; and to a most fateful mission.

At that time of year (it was February) our region has almost twenty-four hours of darkness and a mean temperature of minus fifty degrees. It is also subject to very violent, very localized, gales. We flew into one after half an hour, and although the helicopter was a large and robust machine it was so battered by flying ice that the pilot was forced into an altitude far above visual contact with the ground.

Over the site itself we switched on all our lights and were informed by radio from the ground that they had switched on theirs, but we were quite unable to see each other. The pilot cautiously descended, catching a misty glimpse of the lit-up diamond pattern, but felt his rotor blades come under such an onslaught that he rapidly ascended again, asking what he should do.

Zhelikov's chief assistant and the technicians in our party gave their opinion that the attempt should be abandoned, and they advised an immediate return to the station with our remaining fuel. By radio I asked Zhelikov for a second opinion—in no doubt what it would be. And was not surprised. That obsessed man, hanging onto life for one reason only, told us not to waste precious time and ordered that one attempt—"a good real attempt"—should be made to land. After the beast had been recovered we should *then* delay a return until the weather improved.

The pilot scowled, gritted his teeth, and dropped again through the furious bombardment, seesawing violently over the pattern of lights before setting us precariously down. Even on the ground we were so rocked about that we had to wait, strapped in, for vehicles to take us the two hundred meters to the residential hut.

Here there was a tremendous blaze of heat and light, the sheet-metal stoves glowing cherry red, the construction workers lounging on their bunks in undershirts. They came bounding at us like eager dogs, Zhelikov's standstill order having kept them hanging about for the best part of a week.

Without being relieved of my furs, or my hat even, I was at once made to look over the technical drawings of the exposed crevasse and of the ledge where the mammoth was lodged; and within minutes was back outside again and being hurried toward it in a "snow tank."

A saucer-shaped depression had been excavated at the construction site, rather steeply stepped down at the center, where the crevasse had been exposed. This was surrounded by short pylons, upon which were mounted the floodlights that normally enabled work to proceed twenty-four hours a day. A crane had been rigged with a double bo-sun's chair, and in this I and Zhelikov's chief assistant were hastily strapped and lowered, first into the depression and then, more cautiously, into the crevasse.

Above, it had been impossible to speak in the tremendous volume of howling and shrieking, but as we descended the noise diminished in the crevasse itself to a mere distant fluting. We were soon conversing in normal, even soft tones, for the narrowness of the glassy chasm did not incline one to loudness. I carried a flashlight, no floodlight reaching here, and the assistant (whom I will call V), a communications set.

We dropped slowly to the ledge, at first visible only as a long uneven hump of ice, and with V giving instructions on his set had ourselves swung to the left and the right and then below while we examined by flashlight the structure of the ice and the dim shape of the animal entombed in it. It had fallen on its left side, its limbs inward toward the cliff, so that only one of its tusks, and no part of its trunk, could clearly be made out. Very little *could* be made out except its approximate size, some two and a half meters long (which marked it as a juvenile beast) and the characteristic upward slope of its receding quarters to the bulge of its abdomen. The sandwiched layers of ice, about seventy centimeters in depth, allowed only the most opaque view from above, but in a narrow window of clear ice at the side it was possible to see strands of the animal's shaggy coat.

We swung there and back, above and below, while V, an expert in the properties of ice, took careful note of the faults and stresses of the crevasse and suggested amendments to Zhelikov's recovery plan. Then we had ourselves hauled up and gave the orders for work to commence.

Two teams were lowered into the crevasse carrying steam lances and hooks, and within a couple of hours had successfully cut away and raised the immense block of ice, which was then bound up in the tarpaulins and chains we had brought with us. This work, in the constant fury of wind and ice, was completed with the greatest difficulty, and was no sooner done than the storm itself ceased, leaving complete frigid calm—as is the way in these regions.

We at once boarded the helicopter, hovered while the load was attached and the rotors cautiously took the strain, and then took off. Thus, flying close to the ground and very slowly—in ceremonial slow motion, almost as if at some great state funeral—we carried the animal back to the station.

We carried it back and maneuvered it to the prepared position in the tunnel. And had not long removed the tarpaulins when Zhelikov appeared, driving erratically down the ramp in his chair.

In our absence the old man, wasted by pain, had forcibly been given drugs. Left alone in his room, in a state of semiconsciousness, he had nonetheless caught wind of our arrival and "escaped." He now began driving around and around the block of ice, vainly trying to raise himself to view the animal. V and I assured him that nothing apart from a tusk was to be seen. But in his befuddled anxiety he suspected that we were concealing something—that the block had been fractured in the course of removal and the mammoth damaged. We insisted that this was by no means the case, but still could not satisfy him.

The indomitable small figure, muffled in furs in the frozen tunnel, seemed to have shrunk further while we were away. His head was no bigger than a grapefruit. But still he tried to impose his will. He insisted angrily that no attempt whatever should be made to repair the damage until his planned program of X rays and photography of the animal in position had been carried out. And this had to be carried out immediately!

V and I were so exhausted we almost told him the secret there and then. And were mightily relieved when his doctor and an attendant hurriedly appeared and spirited him away. For some moments afterward we gazed at each other, knowing that the shock of it might have killed him on the spot.

In the fine and even lighting of the tunnel a far better view was obtainable through the window of clear ice. Some bits of frosting had been knocked off, and the shaggy coat of the animal was clearly visible inside. It was not the coat of a mammoth. It was that of a bear. Bears were not extinct—were indeed very plentiful. The whole body of science held that they had not changed their form in millions of years. Yet what we appeared to have here was a bear with a tusk.

But still we left it for the night.

I slept the sleep of exhaustion, and early next day supervised the X rays and photography. Zhelikov slept on, heavily sedated. The first plates were developed in minutes, and I imposed immediate secrecy on the small team involved until Zhelikov himself, after suitable preparation, could be informed. But this was not to be. That doughty fighter, in the front rank of scientists, did not return from wherever he had gone; shortly before noon his mantle passed to my shoulders, and with it the problem of the animal in the tunnel.

In subsequent days I had it photographed again and again, from all angles and by the most advanced means. But from the very first plate the facts had been clear. We had not been wrong about the coat of

the bear, or about the tusk. Yet it was not a bear with a tusk; and animals other than bears wear the skins of bears.

This animal was human; it was female; it was 1.89 meters tall (six feet two and one half inches); it was in the thirty-fifth week of pregnancy, and it had given birth before.

These latter facts and some others I of course established later, yet I will state the leading ones now.

Sibir (as we call her, the sleeper) is a handsome, indeed a beautiful, female, of fair complexion and finely set features. Her eyes are gray, very slightly slanted—the only "mongoloid" feature, for there is no mongoloid fold to the lids—and her cheekbones are high, somewhat flattened. One would say, in short, that she is of Slav type, if such terms had meaning, which of course they do not. She predated the Slavs and all existing peoples by tens of thousands of years; for her moment of death was near to forty thousand years ago.

By our best reckoning she was in her eighteenth year when she fell into the crevasse and broke her neck. She had eaten a recent meal of fish, and had more with her in a large deerhide bag. The bag had been on a sled, which she was drawing, and the tusk (one quarter of a tusk, the terminal curved portion) was attached to the sled as one of its runners; its twin had evidently broken off and fallen farther into the crevasse on impact. The force of the impact had dislodged the load on the sled and distributed it around and above her upper body, giving the impression of bulk and length we had noticed.

She had fallen on her left side, with the left arm (she was a left-hander) outstretched, perhaps in an attempt to protect her unborn child. This child, responsible for the pronounced bulge, would have given her a difficult delivery in any case, for its head was very large, its father plainly of Neanderthaloid stock (not the specialized Neanderthal of Europe but the earlier, more generalized form with higher vaulting to the skull—its European successor being in this respect a throwback; evolution does not proceed along straight lines).

Apart from the broken arm and neck she was uninjured. She had frozen rapidly, brain damage being minimal. And she was perfect. And also perfectly whole: lips, tongue, flesh, organs (her digestive ones indeed arrested while at work on the fish) all healthily fresh: quick-frozen. There was even saliva in her mouth. Apart from her height she seemed in all respects of absolutely modern type. And yet, in all respects, she was not. Of which, more later.

Now two things must be said. Of all inhabited lands on earth this region, of prehistoric ice, is the only one where such a find could be made. Next, it was made at precisely the moment when use could be made of it—although our operations have been very careful and she is barely blemished. I cannot bring myself to disfigure her.

I look at her often. She is still in my tunnel, serene and detached in time, forever in her eighteenth year. You will see her. So, the end of one long chain of chance and the beginning of another—this most momentous other, the reason you are here.

I do not doubt, in connection with your present location, that you will have many things to tell me. Well, I await them.

And now to begin.

One

The Postman and the Professor

1

At ten to nine on a June morning, a shining and brilliant morning that promised a day of great heat, a lady of sixty-three cycled through the streets of Oxford.

She cycled slowly, corpulent and majestic as some former queen of the Netherlands, sun hat bobbing, flowered dress billowing. Up and around churned the floral thighs until, turning into the High, they were arrested by a slowly changing traffic light. She swooped at once off her saddle and applied the brake—applied it a moment too late, so that her broad-sandaled feet went pit-a-pat in small skittering hops as she wrestled with the machine.

Bad coordination. Oh, *schrecklich, schrecklich.* Everything today was frightful, not least her head. She took the opportunity to remove her hat and fan the head, also to pull at a clinging portion of skirt and shake that about too.

Her sister had advised her to stay in bed today. Out of the question. With retirement age three dangerous years behind her, she could not allow a cold in the head to keep her in bed. Her employer would not be staying in bed. And other people were after her job. . . .

The lights changing, Miss Sonntag ascended once more and pedaled regally on. In the city of bicycles there were not today many bicycles. The university was in its Long Vacation, but her professor was not yet on vacation. Until he went—which would not be before the River Spey showed more salmon—there would be no time off for her. *Ach!*

Brasenose passed, and Oriel and All Souls. She turned in at the close as the clocks all began chiming nine. The little forecourt was airless and deserted, no bicycles in the bicycle stand. She chained her own and went wearily inside. The caretaker had sorted the mail and separated the professor's with an elastic band. She took her hat off, and sneezed.

The air in her room was stale but chill. She tried to turn the air conditioner off but couldn't, and opened the window instead. Then she switched the electric kettle on and looked for the post. She could not see any post. But she had *somewhere* seen some post. Her head was so thick with her cold she couldn't remember where. In the hall, perhaps, where it had arrived? She went out and searched the hall. No post.

The kettle was whistling, so she went back in and made herself a cup of coffee and hung up her hat. Underneath the hat, on the chair, was the post. She gazed dully at it and blew her nose. Then she drank some coffee and started work, and almost at once was interrupted by the telephone. She answered it, continuing to straighten out letters and toss the envelopes into the bin, and had completed them all before hanging up. This was when she realized that something else was wrong with the post. There were six foreign envelopes. There were only five foreign letters.

She shuffled the letters blankly about, and then looked on the floor and in the bin. In the bin were the six foreign envelopes, and ten British ones, all empty. She saw this was going to be a totally bad day. She also saw that her boss had arrived. His long stooping form had tramped past the glass panel of her door. She sat back on her heels and considered her sister's advice. Then she pulled herself together and in an addled way began matching letters and envelopes to find out which was missing.

There were ten British envelopes and ten British letters; three American envelopes and three American letters; two German envelopes, two German letters; one Swedish envelope, no Swedish letter. She looked at this envelope again. It was a tatty one. The address was written on a slip of tissue paper and stuck on with Sellotape. Nothing was in it. After a while, unable to understand anything anymore, she merely took everything in to the professor and told him they were a letter short.

The professor looked up at her, mystified.

"A letter short, Miss Sonntag?"

"This envelope has no letter."

He had a look at the envelope.

"Göteborg, Sverige," he said. "What is there at Göteborg, Sverige?"

"The university, perhaps?"

"With absentminded professors, perhaps?"

This thought occurred to her just as he said it, and she cursed the cold in her head. At another time she would have had the thought first and left the envelope where it was (as, it was later thought, she had probably done at least once before). Thickheadedness had sent her hunting through the accursed bin.

Her head was no less thick but she said stolidly, "This does not seem to me a professor's letter. I mean, naturally there *is* no letter, but—"

"That's all right, Miss Sonntag."

The professor took his jacket off. His unusual head, large and knobbly and extending in various unexpected directions, was bald as an egg. It was glistening now. "It's awfully hot in here," he said. "Is the air conditioning going?"

"Oh, yes." Miss Sonntag sneezed defensively into a Kleenex. "It is keeping my cold going." She watched him wind his glasses around his ears and examine the envelope more closely.

The address was written in ballpoint in shaky block letters:

PROF G F LAZENBY

OXFORD

ENGLAND

Professor Lazenby looked at the back of the envelope and then at the front again. Then he held it up to the light. It was a flimsy airmail envelope and he looked through it. Then he looked inside and after a moment withdrew a tiny strip of tissue paper partially stuck to the bottom.

"Well! I did not see this," Miss Sonntag said.

"Quite all right, Miss Sonntag."

There was nothing on the paper. He upended the envelope and carefully tapped it.

"You don't think there was some powder in there and I have thrown it in the bin?" Miss Sonntag said, alarmed.

"We can go and look in the bin."

"Well, I will do it! Naturally. I am just so sorry. It has not occurred to me—"

They both went and looked in the bin. They removed the envelopes, carefully tapping each inside the bin. They removed all the envelopes, but there was no powder in the bin. There was just, at the bottom, another strip of tissue paper.

At that moment Miss Sonntag remembered that the phone had rung as she opened the first envelope, and that the first envelope had been the Swedish one, which naturally had been the first to go into the bin. She began explaining this to Lazenby but he only said, "Quite all right, Miss Sonntag," and they both went back to his glassed-in room off the main lab. A few graduate students were by this time at work in the lab; it was the department of microbiology.

Lazenby inserted himself into his chair and loosened his tie. Then he looked at the two bits of paper and smelled them. "These are cigarette papers," he said. He held one up to Miss Sonntag and looked at the envelope. "The address is also on a cigarette paper," he said.

"Well! I don't know about this. I don't know what I am to do," Miss Sonntag said faintly. She couldn't smell anything on the paper.

"How about getting me a cup of coffee?" Lazenby said. "Also . . . maybe . . . that fellow from Scientific Services. You've got his number." He was looking sideways along one of the papers. There was nothing on it but he had an idea something was in it. There was a suggestion of indentations on the surface.

"Of course. At once, Professor. But I wish to say," Miss Sonntag said formally, "that without this cold in my head I could not have made this mistake. It is not something—"

"What mistake? *No* mistake, Dora," the professor said kindly, and also accurately. "It was acute of you to spot this. Most thorough. I admire it."

"So? Ah. Thank you. Yes. Coffee," Miss Sonntag said, and fairly hurtled through to her own room, her cheeks pink. She couldn't remember when he had last called her Dora. Her sense of smell had miraculously returned. She smelled flowers everywhere, also her own lavender water, and through the open window all of glorious Oxford.

Three sugars in his coffee. She spooned them in, still glowing at recollection of the tribute to her thoroughness. Then she recollected the other thing he wanted. The man from Scientific Services.

2

The man from Scientific Services was an old student of Lazenby's who remembered him chiefly as rather a sketchy performer at his work but a useful bluffer when experiments went wrong. He had gone down with a disappointing third and got a job with the old Ministry of Agriculture and Fisheries. From Ag & Fish he had gone somewhere else, and after that Lazenby had lost touch with him. He had surfaced again, urgently soliciting help and inviting the professor to lunch, a few days before Lazenby was due at a conference in Vienna. Although having much to attend to, Lazenby could not well resist a plea from an old student; but he had been greatly surprised at the opulence of the meal laid before him. During the meal the old student invited him, as Lazenby understood it, to become a spy.

"Oh, nothing like that, Prof! Much too strong a word."

"You want me to report on what people say to me in private in Vienna?"

"Not personal things, of course not. *Programs,* costly *budgeting* things. There's an *immense* amount of duplication going on. Cannot be good for science, Prof."

"I find that someone is duplicating my work and tell *you?*"

"Someone else might find it and tell us. Then Scientific Services would tell *you.*"

"Scientific Services is a government body?"

"A *sort* of government body."

"I see." He had heard of this sort of government body in America. There they called it the CIA, and many American scientists did indeed assist it, as he knew, in the ways mentioned. Lazenby hoped to God it wouldn't catch on in England. "Well," he said. "Thank you for the meal, Philpott. I have enjoyed it."

"Give us a try, Prof! Let me send you some stuff in your own field."

"By all means. Who gave you it?"

"Oh, people you know. All top class."

"Why didn't they give it to me?"

"Didn't spot the significance, I expect. It needs putting together, you know. Scraps here, scraps there."

"Yes." Scraps. Smelly. "Well, I shall be very interested," he said.

"You will be, Prof. I promise you. Most useful stuff, particularly at budget time. All our contributors say so."

"And will I continue to receive the useful stuff," Lazenby asked, "should I decide not to be a contributor?"

"Good of the country, Prof."

"The country?"

"Science." Philpott blinked. "Knows no boundary. Taught me that yourself. Republic of Science. The fact is—stray items, of no use to the other chap, do turn out to be of the greatest use to *one.* Happens very frequently. Honestly, Prof, they *all* do it."

"Who do?"

"Foreigners. They *expect* one to do it. Would be highly surprised to learn you weren't in touch with someone like us already. I assure you!"

"Well. I will accept your assurance. And the stuff," Lazenby gravely told him.

And to his surprise it did turn out to be useful. Scraps, as Philpott had said, but skillfully put together. And showing indeed possible duplication of some projected work. Not much, but enough to give him pause.

With only a small feeling of guilt he had acceded to Philpott's request. Not grossly violating any confidences. Just scraps that might prove of interest to some other chap in the republic. And these scraps, too, had come back to him, interwoven with others, in the bulletins that periodically arrived from Scientific Services. They arrived not by post but by courier, accompanied by a note suggesting an early reading, and a request that the material should not be photocopied.

On one occasion, when a bulletin had been mislaid for some weeks, unread, Miss Sonntag had been astonished to find that all the words on it had disappeared. To prevent a recurrence of the mishap she had photocopied the next bulletin. The photocopy had come out blank, and the original itself had gone blank. It was the recollection of this— and the ways of foreigners—that had brought Philpott to mind when Lazenby gazed at the cigarette papers.

Lazenby met his old student for a drink at the Mitre. Philpott had urgently requested the meeting either at the institute or in London. Lazenby had no intention of running up to London and didn't want him at the institute. The Mitre was a much more discreet venue—few tourists yet on the scene, and all the students away. They sat quietly in a corner while Philpott produced, one after the other, various papers from his briefcase.

One was a photo of the envelope and the bits of cigarette paper; another an enlargement of the address; and some others showed treatments that had been applied.

"The envelope and the sticky tape are Swedish," he said, "but the ballpoint isn't. The cigarette papers are Russian. We believe a sailor posted them. We believe he was given the cigarettes and told to slit them and remove the tobacco, and then put the papers in an envelope and send them off. The address was written on this third paper. It was there in faint pencil and you probably didn't notice."

"I didn't," Lazenby admitted.

"Well, it was there. The pencil lead is Russian, too. What probably happened is that something was inscribed on one layer of paper in order to impress it on another underneath. The ones underneath were wrapped as cigarettes and given to the sailor—presumptive sailor— together with this other for the address. This one he had to tape to the envelope and then trace over the pencil with ballpoint."

16

"Well now. Very clever."

"Yes. This is what came off the cigarette papers."

Lazenby looked at the enlargement. The indentations had been enhanced in some way and revealed a string of figures:

18 05 22 (01 18 01-05)   04 05 21 (31 27 12-15)
10 05 18 (46 10 49-52)   16 19 01 (18 11 13-14)

There were several lines more.

"What is it?" he said.

"You'll see it breaks into segments, each starting with a group of three numbers. Forget the bits in brackets. The first lot is eighteen, five, twenty-two; then four, five, twenty-one; and ten, five, eighteen . . . It's alphabetic code, English alphabet—that is, one stands for A, two for B. You'll see how it works out."

Lazenby tried for a minute and got lost.

"The first group is R-E-V," Philpott said, "the second J-E-R, the third D-E-U, and so on. They're books of the Bible. The bracketed groups give chapter and verse, and the hyphenated portions identify the words required. Here it is."

Lazenby looked at a new sheet.

I am he that liveth/ I am yet alive/
in the north country/ in dark waters/ in
the waste howling wilderness/ Wherefore
do you not answer me?/ Behold new things
do I declare/ The eyes of all/ shall be
opened/ Send me therefore the man/
understanding science/ of every living
thing/ Let me hear thy voice concerning
this matter/ the first day at midnight/
Voice of America.

"The Voice of America is in the Bible?" Lazenby said, bemused.

"Well, no, it isn't," Philpott confessed. "That group just came out as 'VOA' and there was no book for it. It is quite plain in context, though."

"Ah. The same with science, is it?"

"Science? No, that's the Book of Daniel." Philpott consulted another sheet. "Yes, Daniel one, verse four."

"Good." Lazenby finished his drink. "That is a very good thing to know," he said.

"Have you any idea what this is about, Prof?"

"None at all. Tell me yours."

"Well." Philpott frowned. "We believe it's from a Russian scientist, a biologist, someone in a life science, anyway. He evidently knows you, or of you. He has tried to reach you before. He's come up with something he thinks a lot of. He wants you to let him know if you got it and understood it. He can get the Voice of America. That, more or less, is what we consider it means."

Lazenby thought about this.

"Have you considered the man might be a nut?" he said.

"He's gone to rather a lot of trouble, Prof."

"Nuts do go to a lot of trouble."

"Quite. This one would be a Jewish nut, incidentally, or one of Jewish extraction."

"Because of the Bible?"

"Because of his thumbs. He left two good prints on each of the papers."

"You can tell a Jew by his thumbs?" Lazenby said, staring.

"There is apparently something called a Jewish whorl. The Israelis are expert at it. Yes, Department of Criminology," Philpott said, checking. "Tel Aviv. Rather keen on spotting a Jew from an Arab out there. Genetically it's a dominant, so even with an ethnic mix it tends to come through. The interest here being—you'll see he seems to be stressing that he's alive, as if you might suppose he isn't. What we're hoping is that you might recall a Jewish biologist who has dropped out of sight for some years. We think he *has* met you. He's certainly addressing you very directly, as if he thinks you will know him. Which would mean he's traveled abroad to conferences and so forth, since you never yourself visited the old Soviet Union."

Lazenby tried to think when he had told Philpott that he had never visited the old Soviet Union. He decided he had never told him this.

"I'll think about it," he said.

"We'd be very grateful. Some preliminary work has been done, actually. I wonder what you know about these people." He handed over a list.

There were ten or so names on it, all distantly familiar to Lazenby; all in biological sciences.

"A thing I know about Stolnik," he said, perusing it, "is that he's dead. Some years ago, I believe."

"Yes. We have the obituaries. I shouldn't worry too much about that. If the chap has *had* to go out of sight."

"Ah . . . Well, it's all a long time ago, of course," Lazenby said. It was a very long time. He had thought most of the men on the list were dead. One of them had certainly had a serious motor accident. "I expect I met them all."

"Might they appear in your diaries?"

"I don't keep diaries."

"Miss Sonntag's, perhaps—appointment diaries?"

"When from?"

"Upwards of five years? Maybe ten."

"Highly unlikely. What would you expect to find there, anyway?"

"Meetings. Which we might be able to reconstruct. Perhaps some mention of the other chap."

"Which other chap?"

"He wants you to send him one." Philpott found the place for him. " 'Send me therefore the man understanding science—of every living thing.' . . . Another drink, Prof?"

"All right, very small. With a great deal of soda."

Philpott got the drinks. "The feeling is," he said, settling himself, "that it must be some *particular* chap. Whom you have jointly met, or discussed. Feasible?"

"Yes. I suppose it is."

"Might there be anything in your *correspondence?*"

"In ten years of *letters*—"

"Well, we could help there, of course," Philpott said.

Lazenby drank a little, musing.

Philpott, although not a big brain at science, had never struck him as a total idiot. It must surely be obvious to him that a prankster was at work here.

"Philpott," he said, "why do you suppose anyone should choose to write to me on cigarette papers?"

"As the only choice—if it was—it isn't such a bad one. An advantage of a cigarette is that, if apprehended, you can smoke it."

"Yes. Why bother writing in code on it, then?"

"In case you are apprehended, and *can't* smoke it."

"The code didn't seem to give your people much trouble, did it?"

"Once they spotted it was the Bible, no. People not brought up on it aren't so likely to do that, of course. Also the Russian Bible isn't the English one—different book names, I believe, and some other kind of ordering for chapter and verse. In any case, belt and braces. He's a careful fellow."

"Hmm." Lazenby mused again. "Send him a man," he said. "*How* send him a man?"

"Well, the American view there—"

"What American view?"

"He wants answering on the Voice of America. Radio station. The

Americans run it. . . . Anyway, *their* view is, find the man and you have probably found the how. He will know how.''

"You don't think it would be more sensible for him to send some cigarette papers *to* that man?''

"I do. Much more sensible," Philpott agreed. "It leads to a view either that he doesn't know where that man is or doubts that he has your contacts.''

"Nobody to show cigarette papers to?''

"Exactly.''

"Yes.'' Lazenby gazed again at the papers. It was plain that any question he cared to put would meet with a ready answer. There *were* some other questions but he decided not to put them. The River Spey awaited in a few days, and nothing—in particular nothing as crazy as this showed signs of being—was going to interfere with it.

"Might I ask, Prof," asked Philpott, "if I could get at your archive right away? Spread the load—if you had no objection.''

"I would have every objection. Of course you can't, Philpott.''

"Ah . . . Miss Sonntag, then?''

"I'll ask her. What is it you want, exactly?''

"Anything from the men on this list. We think he must be one of them.''

"Why?''

"They have all had some contact with you at one time or another. And they are now all out of circulation. They aren't hospitalized, not over this period of time. They haven't retired. Not drawing pensions, at any rate. And they're not dead, barring a couple of doubtful cases. Almost certainly they are working at something.''

"Yes? Who says all this?''

"The Americans. Far and away the best at it," Philpott said, nodding. "And with an outstanding biographical department—exceedingly detailed and current. For instance, they know the locations and the senior staff of all establishments in the business of—well, in various kinds of business. This man is not at any of them. He must be at some other, which they *don't* know about. And that bothers them. It bothers them very much. They want to liaise on it urgently, the moment we have something to show.''

"Yes. I see," Lazenby said, frowning. What he principally saw was a time-waster of prodigious proportions, here, if allowed to develop.

"Can Miss Sonntag get at it right away?''

"I will certainly ask her.''

"There's a time element, actually. And also another question. Has something like this ever happened before—that is, some other envelope that has turned up with apparently nothing in it? It probably wouldn't have been from Göteborg. More likely Rotterdam or Hamburg, Rotterdam the likeliest.''

"I could ask that, too. Why?''

"I can't tell you that now. I will as soon as I am authorized—together with a great deal of other information. Of course, if you have any thoughts yourself, Prof, I hope you will contact me right away.''

"Certainly, certainly, Philpott,'' Lazenby said, and allowed the subject to drift at once out of his mind. There would not *be* any other thoughts, he was quite clear on that. Secret codes, unknown establishments . . . All that, they could get on with very well by themselves.

And this, as a matter of fact, they were doing.

3

The unknown establishment was assumed to be biological and its work to do with military biology. This was the first point of interest for the CIA and at their headquarters in Langley, Virginia, eight miles from Washington, a team of specialists was engaged in hunting it down.

They started by assuming that it must have independent sources of water and power; also chemical stores, animal pens, cleansing stations, and various kinds of security arrangements. All this needed people, and places for them to live, and some means of access, probably a landing strip. Above all, it needed isolation.

The "waste howling wilderness'' of the "north country,'' evidently Siberia, remained even in modern times unmatched for isolation. Its forested area alone was one and a third times the size of the United States. Over the land lay deep snow and ice all winter, and quaking bogs in summer. This made for a road system so rudimentary that transport went mainly by air or river, with access to security areas available only on official permit.

This provided the first problem. If the place was so hard to get at, why should the unknown correspondent suppose anyone from outside could get at it? Just as important, how had he got anything out of it himself?

Specialists in global transportation put up a possible answer to this. The Siberian inland waterway system was very extensive. Two rivers in the northwest alone, the Ob and the Yenisei, had some dozens of ports with several others under construction. The reason for this was

NORTHERN ASIA

ARCTIC OCEAN

*LAPTEV
SEA*

*EAST SIBERIAN
SEA*

75°—

Ambarchik
Pevek

*Cape
Schmidta*

Tchersky

Kolyma River

Bilibino

*Cape
Dezhnev*

CHUKOTKA
PENINSULA

Lena River

BERING STRAIT

S

I

A

Yakutsk

Magadan

60°—

*BERING
SEA*

*SEA OF
OKHOTSK*

45°—

Vladivostok
Otaru

PACIFIC OCEAN

Nakhodka

SEA OF JAPAN JAPAN

KOREA

Niigata

*YELLOW
SEA*

Tokyo
Yokohama

Nagasaki

| 0 | 400 | 800 |

Scale of miles at 60° north latitude
Mercator Projection

30°—

the extension of the huge natural-gas deposit, the biggest in the world, which lay between the two rivers. As Russian oil production declined, the gas was due to replace it, both for internal energy and for external trade. For both purposes the product was vitally needed; and, as satellite observation showed, work was going on around the clock to get it.

To finance the project (which included a tunnel to west Europe three thousand miles long), massive foreign loans had been negotiated. The loans would be repaid in gas and were being supplied in the form of equipment. The amount of equipment was staggering. Apart from the rigs and drilling gear, there was all the piping to go inside the tunnel. There were giant compressors and pumping stations at intervals along it. There were thousands of earth-moving machines, tens of thousands of tractors.

In the lively scramble for orders, Western shipping companies had not been backward. The equipment for the original field had been carried largely by ships of the old Soviet Union, but for the new deal the managing consortium had specified that new equipment, wherever possible, should be transported in vessels of the countries supplying it.

The countries supplying the new equipment were Germany, France, Britain, Italy, and Holland. Ships from all of them were now ferrying loads along the Arctic sea route. Russian icebreakers were guaranteeing the route from early June to early October, the latter date varying with the ice pack, a fact that led the experts to a prediction.

It was now the first week of July, and the ice was building early. The prediction was that nothing could be expected from the unknown correspondent after the end of August. Western shippers, reluctant to hazard their vessels even in a "guaranteed" September, were handing this slice of business to Russia's own merchant fleet. It was not thought that a member of this fleet had posted the message. A foreign seaman, more familiar with foreign ports, and with greater privacy to fiddle with ambiguous cigarettes, had done it. He would not therefore be doing it after August.

But this raised other questions.

The ports opened to the foreign vessels were Dudinka and Igarka on the Yenisei, and Noviy Port and Salekhard on the Ob. Because they were guaranteeing a quick turnaround at these ports, the Russian authorities had provided no shore facilities for foreign crewmen. None of them was allowed ashore anyway.

If sailors were not allowed ashore, how had one of them got the message?

Tentative answers were provided for this, too. An intermediary had

NORTHERN ASIA

ARCTIC OCEAN

LAPTEV SEA

EAST SIBERIAN SEA

75°

● Ambarchik
● Tchersky
● Pevek
● Bilibino

Cape Schmidta

Cape Dezhnev

Kolyma River

Lena River

CHUKOTKA PENINSULA

BERING STRAIT

S I A

● Yakutsk

● Magadan

60°

SEA OF OKHOTSK

BERING SEA

Vladivostok ●
Otaru ●
Nakhodka ●

45°

PACIFIC OCEAN

KOREA

SEA OF JAPAN

JAPAN

Niigata ●

YELLOW SEA

● **Tokyo**
Yokohama ●

Nagasaki ●

0	400	800

Scale of miles at 60° north latitude
Mercator Projection

30°

the extension of the huge natural-gas deposit, the biggest in the world, which lay between the two rivers. As Russian oil production declined, the gas was due to replace it, both for internal energy and for external trade. For both purposes the product was vitally needed; and, as satellite observation showed, work was going on around the clock to get it.

To finance the project (which included a tunnel to west Europe three thousand miles long), massive foreign loans had been negotiated. The loans would be repaid in gas and were being supplied in the form of equipment. The amount of equipment was staggering. Apart from the rigs and drilling gear, there was all the piping to go inside the tunnel. There were giant compressors and pumping stations at intervals along it. There were thousands of earth-moving machines, tens of thousands of tractors.

In the lively scramble for orders, Western shipping companies had not been backward. The equipment for the original field had been carried largely by ships of the old Soviet Union, but for the new deal the managing consortium had specified that new equipment, wherever possible, should be transported in vessels of the countries supplying it.

The countries supplying the new equipment were Germany, France, Britain, Italy, and Holland. Ships from all of them were now ferrying loads along the Arctic sea route. Russian icebreakers were guaranteeing the route from early June to early October, the latter date varying with the ice pack, a fact that led the experts to a prediction.

It was now the first week of July, and the ice was building early. The prediction was that nothing could be expected from the unknown correspondent after the end of August. Western shippers, reluctant to hazard their vessels even in a "guaranteed" September, were handing this slice of business to Russia's own merchant fleet. It was not thought that a member of this fleet had posted the message. A foreign seaman, more familiar with foreign ports, and with greater privacy to fiddle with ambiguous cigarettes, had done it. He would not therefore be doing it after August.

But this raised other questions.

The ports opened to the foreign vessels were Dudinka and Igarka on the Yenisei, and Noviy Port and Salekhard on the Ob. Because they were guaranteeing a quick turnaround at these ports, the Russian authorities had provided no shore facilities for foreign crewmen. None of them was allowed ashore anyway.

If sailors were not allowed ashore, how had one of them got the message?

Tentative answers were provided for this, too. An intermediary had given the sailor the message. The intermediary must have had time to establish a relationship with the sailor. The sailor had to be a regular on the route. However regular he was, the only local citizens he could meet were those allowed on his ship—in the normal way, port officials or dockworkers. But the area was a security area, which neither port officials nor dockworkers were free to move in and out of at will. The intermediary had to come from outside. He had to have access to the ship—and also to the research station. What kind of intermediary could this be?

The experts proposed a transport worker. The foreign ships were not leaving Russian ports unladen. Some carried specialist return cargoes, of a kind that might afford access to the ship of a specialist worker. A closer examination of the ports concerned showed Dudinka, on the Yenisei, as the likeliest to have specialist return cargoes. Dudinka was the port for Norilsk, a large mining and industrial center, and its main business was nickel and precision nickel-alloy parts.

A report was called for on the handling of nickel-alloy parts, and meanwhile three working propositions were set out:

1. The message had been posted by a sailor who regularly worked the Arctic route.
2. It had been given to him by an intermediary with access to his ship.
3. The intermediary was a specialist worker whose duties allowed entry to the research station and to the port.

These propositions (every one of them accurate, as it turned out) were then addressed very vigorously.

"Let me hear thy voice concerning this matter the first day at midnight, VOA," the unknown correspondent had asked. The Voice of America was a wholly owned subsidiary of the CIA, so there were no problems with this one. The first day, in biblical terms, was Sunday, and the VOA had a taped religious program that went out then. A substitution was made and a man with a powerful voice preached a sermon on communication and identity. He used Exodus, 12:3—"I have heard thy voice"—and also Samuel, Joel, and Esther: "Where art thou?"; "Who art thou?"; and "What is thy request?"—and he said these questions needed plain answers from everyone, particularly those in the waste howling wildernesses of life.

* * *

25

On the message itself were the prints of the man who had written it, and who had evidently rolled the cigarettes. They were on the address paper, too, but not on the envelope or the tape. On all these appeared another set of prints, some very smudged and fragmentary, but similarly traceable to a single source, evidently the sailor.

For the reasons agreed, the sailor had to be a regular on the route. He was the postman. His regularity had to be relied on. From the internal evidence of the message—"Wherefore do you not answer me?"—he had been used before. It was not possible to say when he had been used before, or where he had posted the message before. But it was known where he had posted it this time.

The global list of ship movements showed three vessels from the Arctic as having been in Göteborg around the date of the postmark. One of them, a Japanese tramp that had merely used the Arctic as a cheap delivery route for a random load to Western Europe, could be discounted; but the other two, a Dutch ship and a German, were of greater interest. Both were in regular service on the Siberian run, and the Dutchman had returned with a cargo of nickel parts.

Göteborg was not a regular stop for this ship, but part of its nickel had been consigned there, and it had put in to the port for twenty-four hours: ample time for someone to slit cigarettes, buy an envelope, and post the letter. This ship had then sailed for Rotterdam. The German had gone to Hamburg.

CIA officials in Holland and Germany were instructed to obtain, by any means possible, fingerprints of the crews of both these ships. But it was known already that the Dutchman had come from Dudinka. The origin of its cargo was not in doubt either.

Between Dudinka and the nickel mines of Norilsk was a road forty-five miles long, and the cartographic department had every inch of it mapped. Most of Siberia was similarly mapped. The maps came to them from the Defense Mapping Agency Aerospace Center at St. Louis, Missouri, and they were updated every few weeks. They showed not only geographical features and roads but the progress of all building works, both above and below ground.

The area around Norilsk was covered with a network of minor roads linking its industrial center with outlying districts. The roads were well maintained, summer and winter, and heavily used.

Although the complex was large—the largest in the Arctic Circle—it was still only a dot on the vast expanse of taiga surrounding it. Much of this area had been under regular surveillance for years, large numbers of "objectives" being in it. The purpose of most of them was known, but a few still remained in doubt. These were the ones that came under scrutiny now.

The major requirements for the secret establishment were still as specified; but in analyzing satellite photographs a few other features were added. It had to have buildings whose precise function was still uncertain. It had to have barracks, probably with separate areas to accommodate scientific, maintenance, and security staffs. And it had to have a road, to accommodate the transport worker.

Shortly afterward, in a flurry of activity, St. Louis was being pressed for further information: analytical material, to determine the mineral content of two lakes in the area, and gazetteer material to support the words "dark waters" as a local name for them.

4

Miss Sonntag, while this work proceeded, was getting on with her own.

Something had come to mind after her cold. She had an idea that an envelope without a letter had appeared once before—she did not exactly remember when. But she didn't associate it with Sweden. There was not much correspondence with Sweden. Her impression was that it was from Holland. In the same post, if she was not mistaken, there had been a number of circulars from there—academic book promotions from Amsterdam or The Hague or Rotterdam, most addressed with bits of stuck-on paper. Quite often these mailings were duplicated. She had thought that one was duplicated. Nothing in the envelope and she had shot it into the bin and thought no more about it. But after her cold she thought about it.

She had mentioned it to Lazenby, and seemed to catch him by surprise.

"*Holland,* you say?"

"I think Holland."

"Ah . . . Rotterdam, would you think?"

"I can't be certain Rotterdam. Perhaps Rotterdam."

"Well, I was supposed to . . . Hmm. I wonder," he said, and was thoughtful for a moment. "When are you off, Miss Sonntag?"

"Off? On holiday? Next week," she said in surprise.

Next week was the middle of July, and every year she went off on holiday then; this year to Florence, with her sister, Sonya, a retired nurse. The flight was booked and the pensione was booked. "If it is quite convenient," she said, anxiously.

"Oh, yes, rather. Still . . . ," he said, and produced a list. "I wonder if there'd be time for you to look out some letters. It shouldn't take for*ever*."

It didn't take forever, but it took four solid days, and it took place in the basement. And by the time she got down to it she had the building to herself, even Lazenby having gone off. He had left her his telephone number on the Spey.

He had not mentioned why the letters were needed, but evidently it was his work on cell structures at low temperature. The low-temperature aspect, which was the only subject of correspondence with the Russians, he had given up eight years ago. Everything before eight years ago was in the basement.

The basement was exceedingly dusty, and ill-lit and hideous. Hundreds of thousands of papers were there, in spring-lock boxes: lectures, reports, lab books, all mixed in with the correspondence. These days she kept an index of everything, but the only index for this heap of archive was what was on the box labels—dates and subject categories. That was what he had wanted when she had joined him fifteen years ago.

At that time his wife (his former secretary) had just died, and he had had the institute for only a year. And in the very earliest box Miss Sonntag had come, with a pang, on condolences from foreign colleagues. They had been written to the institute; always a private man, he had not encouraged correspondence to his home. With the years he had become, if anything, even more private—detached, sardonic. But never with her. With her he had always been warm, playful. In the early years indeed she had wondered . . . she had still been in her forties, he was not a *young* man, quite bald even then . . . But that was all nonsense. It was nonsense, but yet she thought with a pang of this also.

And meanwhile read on, very diligently, abstracting a paper here, a paper there. These she read out to Lazenby every night at his hotel on the River Spey. She had read out twenty-four by the end.

"I have gone through two years more, Professor, after the last," she told him, "and found nothing. Do you wish me to continue?"

"No. That will be the lot. That fellow can have them now—the personal ones included. Tell him to send a courier. I suppose nothing of the—of the other kind has turned up in the post, has it?"

"No, nothing."

"Hmm. You are going off when?"

"In two days. Unless you want me," she said, with extreme caution, "to wait on until you come back?"

"No, no. I'm coming now. Nothing doing here. No fish. But you've done a grand job, Dora. Really very good of you. Many, many thanks indeed, Dora."

Dora, Dora! She put the phone down, with mild rejoicing, and forgave him the four days in the basement.

Then she took off to pack her sandals and other sensible shoes; and for the rest of July walked about Florence with Sonya.

Nothing happened while they were away. No messages turned up in the post. Nothing of value had come from the basement.

By the end of July plenty of answers had turned up at Langley, and they were bad answers.

No vessel at Dudinka had been boarded by anyone but port workers. No special handling was needed for nickel-alloy parts. No fingerprints supplied by the station chiefs in Holland and Germany matched the ones on the envelope. And no name resembling "dark waters" was known for the two lakes near Norilsk, which furthermore were bituminous and of no use as a water supply.

All this was discouraging, and something obviously wasn't right.

In England, Lazenby had come early to the conclusion that things were not right. He had come to it actually in Scotland, listening to Miss Sonntag on the phone. He had let her read everything out, but even after the first few boxes he had known that something was wrong. There wasn't anything from Rogachev. Rogachev had been one of his earliest correspondents, and should have turned up early. But he hadn't. And as the boxes continued he had not turned up at all.

Lazenby had only the sketchiest recollection of the man: a red-haired fellow, jokey, rather too personal, and a drinker. Most of the Russians were drinkers, and Lazenby was not—a small Scotch occasionally, a glass of sherry. And they had got him drunk. At a conference somewhere. At night. He had a confused recollection of lurching down a street with a number of them, Rogachev making jokes. There was something else in the scene that was disreputable, but he couldn't place it.

This he did not manage to do until weeks later, back in Oxford, when he had to get up in the middle of the night. Advancing age made it necessary for him to get up in the night sometimes now. He was urinating away, half asleep, when the impression came back. Urinating against a wall. With Russians. All jabbering in Russian. Rogachev on one side of him and a young Asian on the other. The young Asian, when not talking Russian, had been talking a transatlantic kind of English, and talking about Siberia.

Lazenby knew this was important. A number of things seemed to come together here—of relevance both to the message and to the murky episode itself. He couldn't recollect more of the episode, and in the morning still couldn't. But it still seemed important, so he wrote it down. He didn't write anything about urinating against walls. That was personal and of no importance to anybody. But Rogachev obviously was. And the young Asian might be.

This happened in September, when it was known that no further communication was possible, but he completed his statement and passed it on anyway.

5

By September, the inquiry had ground down at Langley. It didn't stop but it settled where it had started: the biographical department.

In charge of it was a man called W. Murray Hendricks. He was an elderly lawyer who had been with the department since the mid-1960s, when a series of chaotic upsets to do with faulty cross-referencing (which had cost the country some billions in an unnecessary arms race) had brought about his rapid transfer from the Library of Congress. There he had been in charge of copyrights. Here he was in charge of lives. He was an orderly man with a mild manner.

W. Murray Hendricks, now able to examine all the papers calmly and without pressure, had come to three conclusions.

The first was that the relationship between the unknown correspondent and Lazenby was likely to have been social rather than professional. His assessment of Lazenby was that he was a remote sort of fish: Professional matters he might remember, social ones not. This one he didn't remember. It was probably social.

To be social with Lazenby called for qualities of warmth and gregariousness in the other party. Hendricks looked through the candidates on the list, the roster of those who had had contact with Lazenby, and found three warm and gregarious ones. Two of them, he saw, had sent Lazenby condolence notes on his wife's death—these had appeared in the twenty-four letters sent from London—but one of them had not. He looked this one up.

It was a Professor Rogachev—Professor Efraim Moisevich Rogachev—and the department held a useful file on him. It stopped abruptly. In examining where it stopped he saw why no condolences had been received; why there were, in fact, no letters at all from him. Lazenby's archive covered a period of sixteen years. This man had gone missing seventeen years ago. He had had a motoring accident at Pitsunda on the Black Sea. His wife had been killed and he himself injured. He had returned to work briefly but had then had something resembling a nervous breakdown, after which—nothing.

Hendricks looked up the man's activities before the accident. He found that the week before he had been at a conference in England, at Oxford. The department kept records of conferences, and Hendricks sent for this one. It contained a full delegate list and also reports on the conference activities. Leafing through, he saw that Lazenby and Rogachev had met there on at least three occasions: at a welcoming reception for the delegates; as fellow panelists in a seminar; and as members of a subcommittee.

Before this they hadn't met for three years—far too long ago to be relevant now, which brought him to a second conclusion.

Efraim Moisevich Rogachev was the likeliest man to have sent the message to Lazenby, and he had done so as a result of the meeting at Oxford.

The relevant meeting was probably the social one, the reception. Something had happened at it. Whatever it was, another person had also been involved. The message asked for another person. The person might merely have been mentioned, but it was more likely that he was there. He would be a Russian-speaker, and most probably a Russian. He was being asked to go to Russia. Without a fair knowledge of the place he wouldn't get far in it.

But if he was being asked to *go* there, he was evidently not there now.

Hendricks had a closer look at the Russian delegation. It was a strong one; twelve members. Three of them, he saw, had defected not so many years afterward.

Third conclusion. The man required had been present at the Oxford conference and was likely to be a Russian not now in Russia.

Hendricks had copies made of the photographs of the Russian delegates, together with brief biographical details. But before dispatching them to London he had second thoughts.

The mission that was being suggested was a hazardous one and needed a young man—at least not an old one. All the Russian delegates *were* now old. It couldn't be any of them. Just possibly it might be some other Slav who was present, a Pole or a Czech, Russian-speaking. But further reflection showed this to be unlikely, too.

Getting someone into Russia on clandestine business wasn't a difficult matter, but this was not a matter of simply sending someone to Russia, but to Siberia. And not simply Siberia, but a sealed area of Siberia. Quite a different proposition.

On the face of it, an impossible proposition.

Yet Rogachev thought it could be done. He thought he knew the person who could do it.

Several interdepartmental discussions produced a fourth and final conclusion.

A person who might get into a security area of Siberia was a Siberian person. More specifically a Siberian *native* person: non-Caucasian, mongoloid, Asian.

There was nobody like that on any of the Slav delegations, or on the Russian either. It left open some other kinds of delegation; but there was no certainty that this man was a delegate at all.

Hendricks decided on a wider sweep.

He ordered a check on *every* academic who had been in Oxford at the time of the conference.

This assignment, a large one, was methodically broken down. The period in question had been a Long Vacation, which let out the students and their normal mentors. The academic had to be of a certain age and type. His age, not more than the twenties at the time, suggested a well-qualified graduate or a research fellow. His type, Asian, suggested certain characteristics, perhaps even a name, that ought to stand out in some way.

The inquiry was thoroughly handled, as thoroughly as all the others had been, and produced results that looked just as barren. Some colleges had records of guest scholars of seventeen years before, but most did not. Halls of residence and bursars' accounts helped fill up gaps; but even when the name came up it attracted no attention and merely joined the others on the list that went to Hendricks.

From Hendricks it attracted immediate attention, and a series of howling and uncharacteristic curses.

He already had a stout file on this man.

He knew he should have thought of him long before; and he also knew that not much would be forthcoming from him.

He was brooding on the matter when Lazenby's statement turned up, and he nodded wearily over it. It was a jumbled recollection of a jaunt Lazenby had shared, time and location unknown, with Rogachev

and a young Russian of Asian appearance who spoke a transatlantic kind of English.

Hendricks was now in a position to supply both time and location, as well as the name of the young man, and a pretty ample biography into the bargain. But still he hesitated.

He could trace the wild young man himself. This would take time. But time was not something he was short of. Ships were now off the Siberian run and would not be back again before next June. Until then no message could come from Rogachev anyway.

He came to his decision, and on the following day set the new search in motion.

That was on September 30, and two days later, on October 2, another message arrived from Rogachev.

6

Miss Sonntag, at work with her paper knife, looked at the envelope, and her mouth fell open. Then she ran in to Lazenby.

He had a look at it, and at Miss Sonntag, and at the envelope again.

PROF G F LAZENBY
OXFORD
ENGLAND

After this they looked at each other.

The new message was more robust in tone.

*Go up, thou baldhead/ How is it that
ye do not understand?/ I want that man/
that speaketh the tongues of the
families of the north/ him that pisseth
against the wall/ As to my abode/ it
was written plainly in the beginning/
I dwell in/ dark waters/ Shew him all my
words/ that the people shall no more/ sit
in darkness/ nor like the blind/ stumble
at noonday/ Make speed/ Baldhead.*

"This one *does* ring a bell, Prof?"

"Yes. Yes, it does," Lazenby said.

"We thought that. But there are some points here of even more interest than the message."

These points were the postmark and the address. The postmark had been stamped at Ijmuiden, Nederland, and the address had been written with a Japanese ballpoint—its ink Japanese, of a formulation used only in Japan, for Japanese script, not exported. The analysis had been made after discovery that the only ship in from the Arctic at Ijmuiden had been Japanese. In Göteborg, at the time of the earlier message, there had also been a Japanese ship. On both messages the fingerprints were the same, and in both cases the ship was the same.

This ship had not been to Dudinka, or to Igarka, or Noviy Port, or Salekhard. It had sailed the Arctic from one end to the other, but it had not stopped at any of those places.

Wherever it had stopped, the ship was now moving again. It was steaming down the coast of Portugal and going home, where it would arrive in two months if unlucky, or nearer three if not. This was because it was tramping, and would put in wherever cargo offered—in general, to ports not served by regular lines.

This was what it had done in the Arctic also. But between the Arctic and its present route there was a difference. Wherever it put in now a Lloyd's agent was likely to report the fact. No Lloyd's agents had reported facts in the Russian Arctic. There its only listed port had been Murmansk, which had been its listed port in June too. But it must also have called at some port other than Murmansk, for the secret establishment could not be anywhere near there. Murmansk was the base for the Russian Northern Fleet, with extensive yards and service facilities. No biological plant would be sited in that vicinity, which in any case was under constant surveillance, all its objectives known, in no way a waste howling wilderness.

This opened up the rest of the Arctic for consideration, several thousands of miles of it; and it also opened up the inquiries in Japan.

From Japan the answers were good and informative.

The ship was one of a line of six tramps, and the Arctic run was a summer perk of the masters'. Only one of them had been taking it on for the past couple of years. The only regular business on the route was with Murmansk, and any other picked up along the way was the perk: It could be accepted or not at the captain's discretion. If he reported it, the owners took a share; if not, the crew did. The only sure information was the crew's, and they were not likely to give it.

But the ship was being watched, and inquiries would continue.

Wonderful, said Hendricks, and got on with his own. These were not going so well either.

By Christmas—*at* Christmas—the next news arrived. The Japanese ship had crept back into Nagasaki unnoticed. All the crew had crept off it, and away on leave. When they came back they were being dispersed and the ship broken up. For its engines were clapped out and its equipment was clapped out, and the ship was finished.

Hendricks passed a hand over his face. He felt like that ship.

He had at last received a reply from the wild young man. His own previous letter, one of a series, had been dignified and discreet. He had had it mailed in an area where the young man was thought to be at present. It was on plain paper and gave a local post-box number for reply. It said that the old friend mentioned earlier, from Oxford, England, was making a last attempt to reach him. The matter was urgent and personal, and a kind acknowledgment was requested by return for the present letter.

The kind acknowledgment came back on the letter itself. It was in red felt-tip and said FUCK OFF SPOOK.

Hendricks thought he could give up then. Nothing more would come, he was certain. The crew of a Japanese tramp would show no zeal to help a friendly intelligence agency. The young man was not friendly to any intelligence agency, and had not been fooled by this one.

But still he postponed the decision. Not much money was being spent, and he decided to consider the matter again in April, when the new budgetary year came round.

April came round, and he considered it again. In particular he considered Rogachev.

Not a bad record, but not outstanding; nothing at all out of the ordinary. He had done time in a labor camp in the fifties, but so had many other Russian scientists—it was a respectable thing to have done. Respectable, in fact, was the description for him, and biology his field—a teamwork field. If anything remarkable was going on in it, some whiff would surely have come from other teams by now. No other whiffs had come. Was it likely that an old man pushing eighty had come up with something on his own? It was not likely. Far more likely, the years of isolation had brought on childish delusions. There was something childishly gleeful in the tone of the messages.

Hendricks hesitated only briefly; then he closed the inquiry down: papers to be kept current for six months in case by chance something new did come up, although he didn't expect anything to come up.

But something did then come up. By chance something quite new came up.

7

The satellite came up over the Indian Ocean, and twenty minutes later it was over Siberia.

The satellite was one of a group of three delivered to the U.S. military by Boeing, a development of the company's Big Bird series. Each of the three had a telemetry package that allowed instantaneous relay, and each was in a slightly different orbit.

This one was in a polar orbit. Traveling north–south, it made a complete circuit of the earth once every ninety-four minutes. Its intelligence-gathering equipment was turned on only over the territory of the old Soviet Union, however. There it had to monitor upwards of five hundred land objectives.

An hour before another satellite had overflown the site, and there had been no recordable activity. But when this one came around, three hundred miles to the west of it, the fires were already burning.

At first the fact went unnoticed, for the satellite's current objective was a missile base. Of this it had to take four still photographs and ten seconds of video. All the stills were good, despite freckling along the right-hand edges, but the results showed no change and were merely saved for reference.

The video was different. Something was spotted moving in it. A loaded flatbed truck was moving. This was unusual at three o'clock in the morning, and attention was diverted to it to find out what it might be carrying through deep snow at that hour. For this reason some time passed before it was noticed that the right-hand edge of the video was also freckled.

Optical enhancement brought up the freckles as flames, and interest rapidly switched to the new development.

The location of the distant fire was soon established, as was its probable origin in an explosion: The flames were still shooting one hundred feet high. This was surprising, for the low-rated objective had not been known to house explosives. In earlier listings it had been marked as a weather station. Later analysis had shown the ground to be covered over a wide area with ventilators, indicating that work went on below ground, and too extensively for simple meteorology. The radio traffic and transport pattern showed no military significance, however, so the low rating was retained, but all visible structures were marked and thereafter updated. They consisted of a few concrete buildings, telegraph poles, generator housings, power pylons, and a fenced area of sheds, evidently used for storage, just off the landing strip.

The enhanced freckles were compared with earlier photographs, and some differences emerged. The largest concrete structure, apparently the dome of something below, had vanished, and so had the generator housings. Pylons and poles had been toppled, sheds blown down, and burning debris scattered over a wide area.

More optical work brought other images into definition. A thin threadlike line of beads, at first glance glowing debris, was detached from its background of flame and translated into a formation of men. They were standing in line, each with his hands on the shoulders of the man in front. They were bandaged about the eyes, and dressed only in underpants—their clothing evidently abandoned in flight from the burning buildings.

Slightly apart from this line was another man, also in underpants, but with no discernible bandage. This individual had something in his hands. It was not possible to see what it was, but a study of the video showed his head going up and down while those of the men in line turned toward him and away.

An anthropometrist was called in.

This expert's field was body movement and measurement; he concluded that what was in the man's hand was a list, and that a roll call was going on; and from the ten seconds of action that it was a rapid one, not surprising for almost naked men in fifty degrees of frost. But some aspects of it puzzled him, and he asked for further imaging work to clarify the effects of flame and heat distortion. The imaging work was done but it did not solve the problem. He ran a few tests to prove that what he was beginning to suspect could not be true. But it seemed that it was true.

The men who stood in their underpants in the Siberian ice had arms that were too long. There was something not right about their femurs, too, and the whole shape of their legs. The man reading the list and calling out the names was built the same way. And however the anthropometrist juggled the results, the way did not turn out to be human.

April was the month of this observation.

8

In April Lazenby was into a fish, and it was a magnificent one.

Last year he had caught nothing at all, but already this season he had had several splendid touches. The river was in spate, red-brown with peat and roaring like an engine. It was full of fish. The water boiled over the rocks, spray dashing high, and wherever he looked there were fish. The very air was full of them. He'd seen nothing like it! An incredible spring run!

He had tried all his normal flies, big sunk ones for the colored water, Thunder and Lightning, Childers, Ackroyd. And they'd gone for them, oh yes; some heart-stopping tugs. Tugs only, but they couldn't make out the flies in all the peat. For the fish to *take* it needed something flashier, a big old-fashioned Butcher, so he had tied one on, and right away had the rod nearly snatched out of his hands. The salmon had leaped, and dived deep, into the Long Pool. Lazenby backed up the bank now and scrambled along it, letting out line. He could feel the fish on the end, very strong, twisting and turning.

It was snowing slightly and already getting dark. But what a wonderful brute—thirty pounds if it was an ounce, maybe even forty! He couldn't leave it sulking in the pool, had to get it out of there and into fast water. But careful now. Getting dark. Beyond the deep pool he would have to clamber back into the river again. Racing water, slimy rocks. Careful. For now just keep pressure on him. Let him know he couldn't stay there in the pool. Out now, come on, out. Yes, he was out! Coming over the lip into white water—a gorgeous brute, silver, tail flipping, very strong, not long in from the sea.

Lazenby let him take line, keeping on pressure, slithering down the bank. He entered the water carefully, feeling his way between the rocks, the current dizzying. The salmon had commenced a long dash upriver and the reel was whirring. Good, let him run, just a little pressure. He steadied himself against a rock, got both feet planted firmly, and started playing him, real pressure, the rod bending. Now tire the brute.

Minute by minute he wrestled the salmon. For forty minutes.

He was as exhausted as the fish when he guided him gently into the shallows at last. He had the net there underwater, the long rod crooked under his arm so he could get both hands to it. He was so tired he nearly fell over the fish in the water. Then he had hauled it out and up onto the bank and he collapsed himself.

He pulled the Priest out of his pocket and dispatched the salmon and sat a while longer, panting. His gear was some way back, and when he reached it the light was too bad for him to see the gauge on his weighing hook. He got the fish, and his gear, back up to the car and drove to the hotel, and headed right for the fish room through the garage block at the rear.

There, with a slight disappointment, he found it went nineteen pounds.

"But yon's a beauty, Professor—fresh in! This here you can call a *fash!*"

"Yes, not a bad chap, is he?" Lazenby said modestly, and watched as his prize was sacked and labeled for the smoker's at Aberdeen before he went through to clean up and change. The passage led into the reception lounge and there, to his astonishment, he saw waiting for him Philpott and a grave fellow in a three-piece suit.

"Hello, Prof. I don't think you've met Mr. Hendricks—Mr. W. Murray Hendricks. He's got something very interesting for you."

9

Up in Lazenby's room, after dinner, Hendricks opened his briefcase.

Twenty hours after the first satellite, another one had overflown the site, its cameras specially switched on. The first Bird had captured its images from three hundred miles away at three o'clock in the morning; the second was directly overhead at eleven the same night. The fires were out, a gale was blowing, and masked figures in protective clothing were working under floodlights. They were working on the structure with the blown-off roof.

Military biology of *some* kind had been going on in the place, that was certain; despite the wind, a number of elements had been identified still escaping into the air. What had produced the explosion it was not possible to say, but the nature of the work in the establishment had certainly been very varied.

Lazenby was shown some shadowy prints: a jumble of wrecked equipment photographed through the hole in the dome. Transparent overlays with sketched-in lines helped to clarify the mess, but Lazenby still couldn't make it out.

A ducting system, Hendricks explained. It had been identified as part of a layout internationally designed ''P_4.''

''Ah, P_4. Not my field,'' Lazenby said. ''That's rather a high security label, the highest actually. It's a system for the containment of tricky bacteria—*E. coli,* I believe, normally. They use it to replicate cells, for gene splicing.''

''Yes, *E. coli* is what they were using, and it was for gene splicing,'' Hendricks said. ''This is the remains of a genetics lab—quite a large one.''

''Is it, now? What would they want with that?''

Hendricks probed in his briefcase again and showed him the photographs of the individuals in line. There were over a dozen prints now, some sections having been detached and enlarged. These images were also muzzy, but again overlays had been provided to outline the limbs.

Lazenby examined them. ''Apes,'' he concluded.

''No, they aren't apes. Not now.''

Lazenby peered again. ''Improved apes?''

''Yes, these can talk and read. This one can, anyway. He is reading a list and calling out names, and the others are answering him. It's clearer on the movie.''

Lazenby looked at him over his glasses for some moments.

''You're not supposing this is Rogachev's work?'' he said.

''Well, it's his place. There's no doubt about that. I can show you.''

He showed him a map. It was a section of a large-scale sheet of the Kolyma region—some thousands of miles, he said, from where they had previously been looking. Ringed on it was the spidery symbol for a weather station, and close by the weather station a lake. ''Blackpool'' had been handwritten over the lake.

He explained this, too. The name came from a book, one of a collection gathering dust in the department's library; the cross-referencing system, though improved, had not caught it.

Lazenby looked at the sheet of paper handed to him.

ON FOOT THROUGH SIBERIA
Captain Willoughby Devereaux
London 1862 [Extract, p. 194]

The water, enclosed in a basin of black basalt, has from a distance the appearance of ink, but is perfectly clear and in fact the purest in the area. It is known locally as Tcherny

Vodi (dark waters) but I preferred the homelier appellation of Blackpool; and at Blackpool I camped for some days before returning the thirty miles to Zelyony Mys (Green Cape).

"Here's Green Cape," Hendricks said, unfolding a further section of map. "It's a port, on the Kolyma River, exactly thirty miles from the lake. That's how Rogachev's cigarettes came out."

Lazenby looked from the map back to the prints.

"You think *this* is what he's trying to get out?" he said.

"No. I don't. What would be so secret about it?"

"This isn't startling enough for you?"

"Yes, it's startling. But more startling is why they've kept quiet about it for so many years. Also where it's going on. Would you experiment with apes in a place like this?"

"Well, the Arctic isn't their environment," Lazenby said.

"Right. It isn't. And this isn't just the Arctic. It's the most secret place they have—the remotest, the least accessible. There's hardly any information on it. On this place itself there's none. We knew nothing about it. Now *that's* startling. It's disturbing. We're pretty well up on Russian science. People change jobs, news gets around. But nobody has changed jobs here. That is, if you get a job here you evidently don't leave. And work has been going on in it for a long, long time, we can see that. Which raises another longtime question. What do you know of a fellow called Zhelikov?"

Lazenby looked at him. "Zhelikov the geneticist?"

"That's right. L. V. Zhelikov."

"Well, I knew *of* him. Who didn't? He was the favored student of Pavlov, the dog man. He'll have been dead, what—thirty, forty years?"

"Nobody knows when he did die. They didn't tell anybody. We think because he died here. We think this was his place, and Rogachev took over from him. Which would make it about seventeen years ago. You're right that Zhelikov went out of *circulation* some forty years ago. He was in a camp then, in the fifties. We think they let him out and offered him this, and he took it. Rogachev was in the same camp with him. Did you know that?"

"No, I didn't."

"Well, he was. They knew each other. Anyway, this place was here when *Zhelikov* arrived. At least forty years ago, and probably established a lot longer. After all, they wouldn't have sent a guy of his class up to Siberia to *start* something going there. Something must already have been going, probably involving animals, since that was his field. But not just animals. Animal work isn't secret. This is secret. It's very secret—they've put it in their most secret place. So yes, the pictures are startling. But more startling is what else is going on there. And why he's trying so hard to tell us about it.''

They looked at each other for some moments.

Philpott discreetly collected the papers and returned them to the briefcase. He took another one out.

"We need your help,'' Hendricks said.

"Well, anything I can do, of course—although exactly what—''

"Would you go on a trip for us?''

Lazenby stared at him, and his mouth dropped open.

"No, not Siberia.'' Hendricks's own small mouth curved wryly. "Somewhere else. We think we've traced the young man you mention.'' He held a hand out and Philpott placed an enlarged photo in it. "Would he look anything like this?''

Lazenby gazed at the photo. The young Asian of his nightmare evening stared sullenly back. Broad, high cheekbones, eyes glowering from under a heavy fringe of hair.

"Well—that *is* him!''

"Could you put a name to him now?''

"Raven!'' Lazenby said. The name had swum suddenly into his mind. A number of other things had also swum there. Whisky after whisky. Staggering down a road, the whole bunch of them. Red-haired Rogachev joking away. Then round a corner, up against a wall—a familiar corner, a familiar wall . . . It was Oxford, damn it! It had been in Oxford.

He looked up to find Hendricks and Philpott gazing at each other.

"Raven?'' Hendricks said. "You're sure of that?''

"Almost sure. Also a Goldilocks. There were several people . . . it was all very—confusing.''

"Goldilocks?'' Hendricks and Philpott were again exchanging glances. "Look, Professor, if you were maybe into nicknames, could Goldilocks have been *Rogachev*—a *red*-haired sort of fellow?''

"Nicknames, ah. Yes, I suppose it could be.''

"With the other fellow as Raven because he was *dark,* very dark, in fact black—his hair?''

"Possible. 'Raven' doesn't *sound* too Russian, does it?''

"No. This fellow isn't Russian. He's an Indian.''

"An Indian?''

"A Red Indian. Canadian. His name's on the back there.''

Lazenby looked at the back. The caption read: "J. B. Porter (Dr. Johnny Porter).''

"Doesn't the name mean anything to you?''

"I can't say it does, no."

"Riots in Quebec?"

"Oh, him. Well, I wouldn't have connected—"

"No. He doesn't look like that now. That's the way he looked at Oxford. We think that's where you met him."

"Yes, I think so too."

"Can you remember *how* you met him?"

"Well, during a conference. At a reception, I think. For the delegates."

"He wasn't a delegate. What was he doing there?"

"That I don't know."

"Did he seem to know Rogachev already?"

"I don't know that, either. They were just talking away about Siberia."

"About what aspects of it—do you remember?"

"Well." Lazenby thought. "Languages, people, I suppose. Physical impairment of some kind—blindness was it? Snow blindness, perhaps. Something of the sort. About Siberia, anyway. Rogachev had worked there, of course, and I thought this fellow some kind of native. They were talking Russian rather a lot, and he certainly seemed to know the place, so I assumed—"

"Yes, he knows Siberia. He's been there. There isn't any doubt this is who Rogachev wants. He won't talk to us. We think he might talk to you. Will you talk to *him* now?"

Lazenby stared at him.

"You don't *mean* now, of course," he said.

"We know where he is now. He's a difficult man to pin down. Now we've pinned him down. He'll be there for the next four days."

"Where?"

"Montreal."

"Montreal." Lazenby thought of his fish on the way to the smoker's. He thought of the whole river full of fish. "Well, damn it," he said, "I hardly know the fellow, really."

"That's all right," Hendricks said. "Nobody does, really."

Two

Concerning the Raven

10

The name on his birth certificate was Jean-Baptiste Porteur but from the age of thirteen he had become plain Johnny Porter.

He was a Gitksan Indian, one of the small bands affiliated with the larger tribe of Tsimsheans who inhabited the Skeena River area of British Columbia.

The language of the Gitksans was K'san, and only a smattering of it was understood outside the tribe. Few of the tribes were mutually intelligible. But almost as soon as he was talking, the young Jean-Baptiste could also talk Nisqa, the language of the Nass Indians. Not long afterward he had some Tsimshean, too. This was a language so unusual that linguists had been unable to relate it to any other on earth. The other tribes found it incomprehensible. By eleven he was fluent in Tsimshean.

It was this ear for language that took him, at thirteen, to the mission school—that, and a disagreement with his uncle.

Like all Gitksan males (and males of the affiliated tribes) he had to leave home at puberty and live with an uncle or some other male relative of his mother's. The society was exogamous—sexual relationships were prohibited between members of a clan. The taboo was incest-based and prevented an individual from sleeping with his mother or his sisters. For the society was also matrilineal: Descent came through the mother.

This meant that the children of a marriage became members not of the father's clan (which necessarily had to be different) but of the mother's. The mother and her children were all members of the same clan. They could marry into other tribes but not into their own clan within the tribes. This was of the first importance, and in matters of personal status clan came before tribe.

There were four clans: Eagle, Wolf, Raven, and Fireweed. Porter's mother was Raven, so he was Raven. At thirteen he went to stay with a Raven uncle. The uncle threw him out.

The disagreement arose over the boy's rebelliousness and his duplicity. (All Ravens are duplicitous. Raven is Trickster. He is very resourceful. He stole the sun and brought light to the world. He does good, but only by accident. He is very cautious. He takes nothing on trust. He is not to be trusted.)

Porter's uncle didn't trust him. Apart from not doing what he was told, the boy lied about what he did do.

Because of his facility with languages the uncle took him along whenever he had dealings with the Tsimshean or the Nass. He told him to keep quiet but to let him know privately what they said among themselves. The boy disliked this job and told him so, but was made to do it anyway. After being worsted in several deals the uncle knew that he had been lied to, and he beat the boy. This didn't make any difference, and the boy went on lying.

The situation was difficult. He could not go on beating the boy, for he was growing too fast. (His father was a Fireweed and Fireweeds grow fast. Fireweeds grow from forest fires; they are phoenix; their ancestress married a Sky Being, and they have a natural inclination toward the sky.) On the other hand, he couldn't keep a defiant boy in his house. Also he couldn't send him home. And it would dent his authority to ditch him on another relative.

He ditched him on Brother Eustace.

Brother Eustace was at that time the head of a mission school at Prince Rupert. He acquired boys mainly from the major tribes and would not often take a Gitksan. Discipline at the school was strict, and the boys were strapped if found speaking a tribal language. The aim was to detach them from tribalism; and it was hoped to achieve it more thoroughly when the school moved that year (for reasons of a financial trust) to Vancouver.

For the uncle the idea of having his nephew as far away as Vancouver was like a light in the darkness. But there were difficulties. Because of the removal no new entries were being accepted to the school. As a Raven he laid his plans with care. He went to see Brother Eustace. He asked him for religious tracts he could give to some weak people he had observed sliding into wickedness.

Brother Eustace was touched by his concern and gave him the tracts. The uncle thanked him, at the same time expressing the thanks of all progressive Indians for the mission's work in educating their young and removing them from temptation—in particular the removal to Vancouver, and all the extra work it would entail.

Brother Eustace sighed, and said it was a cross that had to be borne.

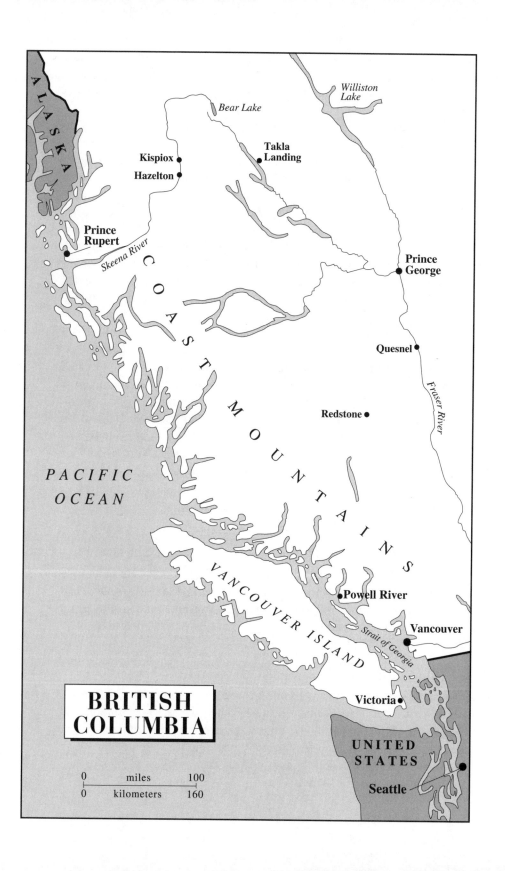

ALASKA

Williston Lake

Bear Lake

Kispiox

Takla Landing

Hazelton

Prince Rupert

Skeena River

C O A S T

Prince George

Quesnel

M O U N T A I N S

Redstone

Fraser River

PACIFIC OCEAN

VANCOUVER ISLAND

Powell River

Strait of Georgia

Vancouver

Victoria

BRITISH COLUMBIA

UNITED STATES

Seattle

| 0 | miles | 100 |
| 0 | kilometers | 160 |

The uncle sighed too, and he said the hardest job would be to stop the lads talking their native language. They would do it even more, far from home and feeling nervous. And Vancouver would be particularly dangerous.

Why would it be? Brother Eustace asked him. Why would Vancouver be dangerous?

Not Vancouver itself, the uncle said. Vancouver as a large sinful city. And not the language itself, but the foolish myths *embodied* in the language; which, as a matter of fact, did not sound foolish in the language. He explained this. He said that in K'san the Bible stories sounded even stranger than tribal stories. It was only in English and as a committed churchgoer himself that he had been able to distinguish the truth of Bible stories from the foolishness of tribal ones. For instance, in English Jesus sounded wonderful, but in K'san he sounded crazy. The boys had to be discouraged from even thinking in native languages.

Brother Eustace frowned and said the boys already were punished if caught speaking these languages.

And a good thing, too, the uncle said. But first you had to catch them. And to know what they were saying—not easy in a Vancouver dormitory. For a Nass would not tell on a Nass, nor a Tsimshean on a Tsimshean, and others could not understand their languages. He knew these devious people, and in dealing with them himself he had lately taken the precaution.... In fact it would be a very good idea if— But no. No, it wouldn't. It would be a bad idea, and too great a sacrifice for him.

Brother Eustace looked at him closely.

What sacrifice? he said.

Falteringly, the uncle explained. He happened to have a nephew who understood both Tsimshean and Nisqa as easily as K'san. The boy was naturally gifted in that way, and a wonderful help to him. He accurately reported what these tricky people said among themselves, and had saved him much time and money. Just at that moment it had struck him that the clever boy would be as great a boon to the mission as to himself. But no. He couldn't give him up. All the same . . . He didn't want to stand between the mission and such a useful aid. Or between the boy and a proper education. But still—

But still, Brother Eustace said, he would see this boy.

A week later Jean-Baptiste Porteur joined the mission school (and lost his fancy name for the no-nonsense Johnny Porter) and ten weeks afterward accompanied it to Vancouver. Six months later, despite high promise as a pupil, he left, by way of a window, sick of being strapped for not telling on his schoolmates.

50

He found himself in a quandary. He couldn't go back to his uncle, and he couldn't go home. He went to the harbor and hung around there, washing up in diners and bars, before coming to the conclusion that the only thing for him was to get on a ship. Shortly afterward, he found one that would take him and signed on. For the following three years, he sailed the world. There was regular traffic between Vancouver and Yokohama, and between Yokohama and everywhere else, so that for lengthy periods he did not see Vancouver again. But he was back in the port and walking in the street one day when a hand fell on his shoulder and he turned to find Brother Eustace.

"Porter? It *is* Porter, surely?"

The last time he had seen the hand, a strap had been in it. Now it was being held out to him to shake.

"Hi, Brother," he said, and shook it. He now towered over Brother Eustace.

"I am delighted to see you, Porter! I can't tell you how delighted I am! Whatever happened to you, my boy?"

Soon afterward, over a meal, he was telling Brother Eustace what had happened to him. And Brother Eustace in turn was telling him the reason for his special delight. It was providential, he said. It was an act of God. Porter had been the most promising boy in the school, and here, today, this very morning, he had been asked by the government to forward the names of promising Indian boys for special treatment, for an assured life of leadership and prominence, for higher education. He had been racking his brains, and here—Porter!

School, Porter thought, no.

I can't go back to school, he told Brother Eustace.

My dear boy, it isn't simply school! Not school! his old teacher said excitedly. You will need preparation, surely. Which I will be more than happy to undertake. The exam isn't the normal one but an assessment of intelligence, ability. You'll sail through it.

Well, Porter thought, he had sailed enough sea. He was now sick of the sea. Maybe this was worth a turn.

But he gave no answer then.

First he made a trip back to the Skeena River, which he had not seen for three years. The first thing he did there was to find his uncle and beat him up. He beat him thoroughly and methodically, without rancor—as any Raven would, simply repaying old injuries.

Then he visited his parents and told them his intentions, at which his mother, a well-known seer, went at once into a trance, exclaiming, "O Raven, Raven! You bring light to the world but will die in the dark. It will end in tears."

"Okay," Porter said.

He had often heard his mother pronouncing in this way, and common sense told him that people mainly did die in the dark and all things ended in tears.

Just two months later, on a date that happened to coincide with his seventeenth birthday, he enrolled in the University of Victoria.

At Victoria the preferred course for the new intake of Indians was forestry studies. Forestry was a major industry of British Columbia, and one well suited to future native management. At the muscle end of the business, large numbers of Indians were engaged in it already.

Porter became engaged in it. The first required subject was botany, which he liked well enough. But after a few weeks he discovered biology, and decided to specialize in that. Switching studies so early was discouraged, but care was being taken not to disaffect the Indian students, and his application was reluctantly approved. This was when his career took off. He learned with exceptional rapidity. He learned in all directions.

It took him no time to find out that although the meeting with Brother Eustace might have been an act of God, the reason for the delight was probably an Act of the U.S. government.

The U.S. government, in a settlement of claims with the Indians of Alaska, was planning a cash payment of half a billion dollars, plus a further half billion in royalties, plus 15 percent of the territory of Alaska. This bounty was to be administered through Indian corporations.

The Canadian government, with similar problems ahead, was thinking on different lines. Rather than separate the Indians, and pay them, it was better to integrate them. Full partnership in the commonweal was surely of higher value than dollars, or royalties, or title deeds to portions of Canada. To do the job successfully it was necessary to select the brainiest and immerse them in the value.

Porter appreciated the value, and knew why he was getting it, but for the time being he kept his head down in biology. Before he was twenty he took a first-class degree in it, and as the outstanding student of his year was urged to go at once for his doctorate.

Instead he dropped the subject and immediately began studying another, two thousand miles away, at McGill.

Although he was wayward, this was not a wayward action. There were good reasons for his choice. McGill was in Quebec, at the other side of the continent, but it had old connections with Victoria, which had indeed started life as a far-western affiliate of the older university.

But the main reason was Quebec itself, and Montreal. Ethnic issues were high on the agenda there—French separatism the principal one, but with Indian questions also to the fore. These were the questions he planned to study.

In his last year at Victoria he had started numbering Canadian-Indian claims against the government. There were 550 of them, few properly documented, all poorly prepared. In the absence of a written language, oral traditions had to be relied on, and the Department of Indian Affairs did not rely on them.

Porter addressed himself to this. He broke the problem into two. In the first part he aimed to demonstrate the reliability of tribal records, and in the second to get the ones relating to claims admitted as evidence.

He began reading anthropology. He not only read it but famously added to it. (His *Amended Syllabary of Tsimshean,* unique as an undergraduate publication, won him a gold medal.)

"Syllabaries," in the absence of any developed writing among the Indians, had been recorded for several of the languages. These sound-clusters had been taken down by anthropologists, none of them Indian. Porter was the first Indian at the work, and he soon found that many of his predecessors had had a tin ear. The languages were exceedingly complex, and a misheard click or vowel frequently altered, or even reversed, the meaning of whole passages.

He followed up with other publications, and learned more languages—all for his main work: a comparative study of tribal legends, designed to show their line-by-line similarities. For as it happened there were many similarities.

When he was a child it had not struck him as strange that the stories of the Gitksan, the Nass, and the Tsimshean should be so similar. They were grown-up stories that everyone knew; why shouldn't they be similar? But now it seemed strange. These tribes were almost unintelligible to each other. Yet their stories, which took hours or even days to recite, were identical almost to the smallest detail. Without writing, by word of mouth, they had been faultlessly transmitted from generation to generation over vast periods of time.

All this was useful evidence for the first part of his task, and he published it to acclaim. And before he was twenty-three had taken a First in anthropology also.

His energy at the time was prodigious, and his waywardness a byword. His supervisors found him impossible to control. In this period he became strongly politicized, and he also contracted a marriage—a sadly unfortunate one. And his movements were erratic. Before publication of *Comparisons,* his study of tribal legends, he suddenly took off to Russia for seven months—this the result of a letter from an institute there commending his earlier work and enclosing syllabaries of some native Siberian languages. The translations struck him as unreliable and he set out to learn the languages himself.

He returned to take his First, however, and as not only a prize student but now Canada's prize Indian, was offered a Rhodes scholarship to Oxford. He accepted at once, again for reasons of his own. (His young wife was now, tragically, dead, and he was on his own again.) More than ever he was immersed in his work, and a difficulty had surfaced in it.

Proving that tribal storytellers had good memories was not enough. What they remembered were stories. In official eyes the "claims" were also stories. The repetition of them, in however much detail, did not make them true. What was needed was other evidence, *written* evidence. A single piece of it that could match, detail for detail, the oral version of the Indians would not only authenticate that version but help to validate all the others he had researched. At the least, it could take matters out of the Department of Indian Affairs and into the courtroom.

The evidence he particularly wanted related to treaties made between the Indians and the British in the years 1876, 1877 and 1889. In the powwows preceding them, various agreements had been arrived at.

"These agreements," as a framed inscription in his room reminded him, "remain in the memories of our people, but the government is willfully ignorant of them." The inscription was a copy of a mournful resolution by a convention of chiefs. "Yet the obligations were historic and legal ones: solemn agreements. Indian lands were exchanged for the promises of the commissioners representing Queen Victoria."

Unfortunately the commissioners' promises did not appear in the published treaties, although the details relating to land had been quite exact. When the British later gave up direct rule in Canada, no promises turned up in the papers left behind. But they would be in *some* papers, Porter reasoned. Even to experienced colonial negotiators, the circumstances of a powwow were exotic enough to merit record—in notes, reminiscences, letters perhaps, which could still be moldering away somewhere in England. The question was, Where? Oxford was a likely place to start finding out.

He had been in the town three months when the letter arrived from Canada. His old professor of biology there wrote to say that he was coming to Oxford for a conference on June 29, and looked forward to seeing Porter. Which, on June 30, he did.

The event was a reception for the visiting scientists, and his professor had taken him along as a guest. "After all," as he told him, "you were one of us yourself, before you fell into error." And he had introduced him to other biologists.

Porter, at the time, was an aloof, disdainful figure of twenty-three. He was the tallest man in the room, and his hair was overlong. He wore it cut in a fringe over his striking eyes with the rest hanging straight and black like a helmet all around. At any gathering he would have been distinctive, and even at this international one he stood out. Yet it was not one of the welcoming hosts but one of the receptive guests who identified him first.

"A Canadian Indian?" said the twinkling Russian.

"Right."

"And from the northwest, I think. The Nass River?"

"Skeena River."

"Ah. Tsimshean."

"Gitksan."

"Gitksan—I don't know of. But all you northwesterners were late arrivals in that continent. You still look like our Siberians. You know of them, perhaps?"

Unsmiling, Porter replied with a burst of Evenk, at which the Russian held up his hands. "Bravo! But it's the *people* I know, my friend, not the language. You are ahead of me."

Porter was ahead of him in English, too. Although the Russian's vocabulary was good, he was once or twice at a loss for a word; and Porter supplied the word. He could even supply it in Russian, and this was the language they were speaking—his professor having left them to get on with it—when a third man, an Englishman, was hauled in to join them.

The name of the Englishman was Lazenby, and the most prominent thing about him was his own extraordinary head. The vast and gleaming cranium, knobbly and extending in various directions, was devoid of a single hair. It contrasted weirdly with Porter's own powerful array and was the reason the ebullient Russian had called Lazenby over. But they were soon discussing a variety of topics—the Russian's animation very infectious. Asiatic migrations, pigmentation, natural defects, blindness . . . In some way they were on to Siberia, and discussing it in a mixture of English and Russian by the time Rogachev (Porter had at last got the Russian's name) had located the whisky. Food had been amply available on the buffet tables, but not much to drink. And Rogachev had found the drink.

This was one of the things Porter remembered next day: that the Russian had found the drink, and could hold it. While the Englishman, reluctantly matching them glass for glass, could not; he was unsteady on his feet when they left, Rogachev jovially proposing that they stagger home together.

In fact the Russian was being accommodated in college and Porter's own college was in another direction. All the same they had walked Lazenby home, and on the way Rogachev had arranged another meeting with the young Indian, whom by then he was calling Raven, having learned his clan and deciding the name was apter for him. In the same spirit he had allotted other names to himself and to Lazenby. But it was Lazenby who had suddenly discovered an urgent need to urinate. And Rogachev who had discovered the wall. And there the three of them had stood, companionably watering it, one set of chances having brought them there and another set, later on, to recall the scene.

11

Lazenby flew to Canada on a Tuesday, but it was not a Tuesday in April but in July; and not to Montreal but to Vancouver, several numbing hours farther. And so many changes of plan had occurred in between that he was half out of his mind before he started.

The fellow Raven seemed to be *wholly* out of his mind.

He had university jobs two thousand miles apart. He seemed to attend to them when he felt like it. He cut lectures, left classes, disappeared into woods. Lazenby would have kicked him out years ago; except Raven (*Dr. Porter,* as they were calling him now) did not seem to be a person you kicked out so easily.

At Vancouver Lazenby was met by Hendricks and a young colleague called Walters who had been making arrangements for him. These Lazenby heard about over dinner at the hotel.

Porter, it seemed, was at a place called Kispiox. It was up north, near Prince Rupert on the Skeena River. This was his home ground—Tsimshean Indian country—and he was in the forest there. His movements were not known from day to day, but he was calling in regularly at the Kispiox post office.

"He's doing that twice a week, sir," Walters said. He was an abnormally clean young man with blue eyes and a blond mustache. "And he's very prompt. He picks up his mail right at noon, and answers it there, too. They all call him Johnny, he's a favorite son. I was up there yesterday, and I phoned this afternoon. He hasn't been

in this week, but tomorrow's Wednesday and that's one of his days. So I've fixed this, if you agree.''

He had fixed a small jet to fly them to a place called Hazelton, not far from Kispiox, which would enable them to get there before noon. In case Porter did *not* look in tomorrow, he had also checked out hotel rooms where they could wait for him the following day.

Every bone in his body aching, Lazenby considered these arrangements somewhat sourly.

''What time would that mean getting up?'' he said.

''Not too early.'' Walters smiled. ''It's only about five hundred miles, so if we're in the air by ten we'll make it. I have transport arranged at Hazelton. From the airport there it's just a drive through the woods to Kispiox.''

''You're coming, of course,'' Lazenby said to Hendricks.

''No, George, I'm not.'' The relationship had flourished a little between them. ''The fewer people the better. I only came to introduce this young fellow, your escorting officer. He's done all the work anyway. He's been around Porter for weeks.''

''Have you spoken to him?'' Lazenby asked the young man.

''No, sir, I haven't. My orders were to make no contact.''

''You make the contact, George,'' Hendricks told him. ''He's a very suspicious man with a big phobia about us—probably warranted. This ethnic thing of his is quite wide-ranging, and we've been observing him a long time. He's stirred up a lot of minority-group activity, not just Canada—it's worldwide. But he's on vacation now, and relaxed. The best thing is just to come to him and talk straight. Tell him what you know, and hope he'll listen. If that's all right with you.''

Lazenby closed his eyes.

The idea of ''making a contact'' with a very suspicious Indian five hundred miles into the Canadian wilderness was not more surreal than the other things that had happened to him today. He still seemed to be floating somewhere between the Atlantic and the Rockies, and more than anything he just wanted to get to bed.

''Yes. Fine,'' he said. ''Fine.''

So next day, the air again, in a small jet, buzzing north.

Mountains, lakes, forests drifted mistily below, veiled in rain. It was still raining at Hazelton, a dismal small airport with not much activity going on in it. The transport was waiting, however, a Toyota pickup, and they hurried into it.

They drove for some time on a hardtop road and then were off it and bumping and lurching along an old lumber track. Dense stands of spruce and hemlock dripped on all sides, and square stacks of trimmed logs, soaking gloomily in the dim light.

Kispiox itself, when they splashed into it, was not much cheerier. It lay in a large clearing, an Indian village with totem poles and frame houses and a white-painted frame church. Full washing lines were strung everywhere, clothes hanging like distress signals in the steady downpour. Apart from a few battered pickups there were no other signs of life.

The post office seemed to be a general store. It was empty apart from an old man smoking his pipe in a rocking chair.

"Hi," he said, peering. "You the guy was over from Rupert—Mr. Jackson, ain't it?"

"Right," Walters said amiably. "How you doing? I called up yesterday afternoon. You said Johnny would be in today."

"Oh well, shit!" the old man said. He took his pipe out. "I clean forgot that. I should have told him you was in. I wrote down a note about it. Went right out of my head!"

"He's *been* in?" Walters said.

"Telephoned. About couple hours ago. He's over at the Takla. Been there a few days, apparently. Hell, I'm sorry about that. Had him right there on the phone," the old man said. "You come over from Rupert special, then?"

"Hazelton. Did he say how long he'd be at the Takla?"

"Well, he wants his mail sent over. That takes two days. Has to go to Takla Landing, see."

"Where is Takla Landing?" Lazenby asked.

Walters was worrying his small mustache. "About fifty miles," he said. "Maybe sixty."

"Seventy, more like," the old man said. He was looking at Lazenby. "You English, mister?"

"Yes," Lazenby said.

"Thought that. Glad to know you." He was extending a hand and Lazenby shook it, observing for the first time that the man was an Indian. The big-boned face had quite a merry look, merrier than the recalled somberness of Porter's. He suddenly realized he remembered Porter's face quite well. "It's a shame you come special," the old Indian said. "Still, if you're only over at Hazelton . . . Maybe I can call him for you, leave a message? Since I forgot it before."

"No, don't worry about it," Walters told him. "He's staying at Takla Landing, is he?"

"No, he ain't staying there. The *mail* goes there. Then by floatplane over to Bear. That's where he is. Least, he said to readdress everything to Noreen's.''

"What's Noreen's?''

"North end of Bear. That's *Brown* Bear—the lake. Floatplane is the only way in. It ain't no trouble for me to call there. Only government money,'' the old man said merrily.

"Is it a logging camp?'' Walters asked, puzzled.

"No, Noreen's ain't a camp,'' the Indian said, amused. "She has that lodge down by the lake. Puts up a beer, chow, a few bunks—it's like for guys come up fishing. It wouldn't be no trouble at all,'' he told Lazenby, "for me to call and say you looked in. Mister what was it?''

"This is Mr. Brown,'' Walters said, "and it isn't even worth mentioning. He wanted a look at Kispiox anyway.''

"Nothing to look at, all this rain. Been raining for days,'' the Indian said. "It ain't raining at Bear. Johnny found that out. Think he's doing a bit of hunting, fishing there. Anything else I can do for you, then?''

"Sure, I'll take that note you wrote—could mix you up,'' Walters said.

The Indian found the note, behind the till, and they went back out in the rain, to the Takla.

The Takla was a chain of connected lakes and rivers stretching for 150 miles, and Takla Landing was somewhere over halfway up it. They left the pilot to wait with the jet there, and hired a floatplane.

Bear Lake was another half hour.

It was still not two o'clock when they touched down on it, the water very somber. On all sides the trees stood like a wall around the lake. They taxied up an inlet to the jetty, and when the engine stopped the silence was massive. It was very gray and still here but, as the old Indian had said, not raining.

"When you want to be picked up?'' the pilot asked.

"I don't know,'' Walters said. He mused. "You busy this time of year?''

"Well, fish are rising. Char and Dolly Varden, big ones, all the way up. People are coming in. I could wait a while for you if you want, see if Noreen can take you. That smokestack is hers, through the trees. But there's other places.''

"Okay, thanks. I'll leave the bags,'' Walters said, and helped Lazenby out.

The air was very heavy as they tramped through the trees, and there were swarms of midges about. But they did not have to tramp far. Noreen's was a rambling wooden structure with a broad porch and mosquito frames over the doors and windows. The hall inside was dark and empty, and Walters rang the bell on the desk.

Noreen came rubbing her hair with a towel, a round comfortable figure in dungarees, and she said she could take them, "long as you boys don't mind bunking up together."

Walters went out for the luggage while Lazenby, with some misgiving, was led to the room he was to bunk up in. He saw with relief that the beds were at least on opposite sides of the room, which was spacious and cedar-clad. "Plenty of cupboards," Noreen said. "This one here is for tackle, but no smelly stuff. That goes in the fish room. You over from England, then?"

Lazenby said he was and asked if a Dr. Porter was staying there.

"*Johnny* Porter?" Noreen said. She looked at him curiously. "No, he doesn't stay here. You looking for him?"

With a sinking feeling, Lazenby realized that Porter didn't seem to stay anywhere. The elusive shadow was always somewhere else. He felt exhaustion sweeping over him again. Already today he had taken off and landed three times, and plenty of afternoon still remained to pursue the phantom elsewhere about the lake. Except that, as a roar outside announced, the plane had just taken off.

He was explaining the matter of the mail when Walters returned with the luggage, and Noreen's face had cleared.

"Well, if he arranged that," she said, "I guess he'll be in. He does that—has mail sent on here. I don't mind. He's okay, Johnny. When you know him. You know him well, Mr.—"

"Lazenby," Lazenby said firmly. "Professor Lazenby." He had seen Walters's mouth open, and had not come to terms with "Mr. Brown."

"Nice to have you with us," Noreen said. But her eyes were on the luggage. "You boys not planning on any fishing, this trip?"

"Not this one," Walters said. "The professor here just wants to see Johnny—college business."

"Well, he won't be in till dark, if it's just for mail. And not till tomorrow, any case. Don't come till then. Can I fix you boys something to eat?"

They had a moody lunch; after it Lazenby took a nap, and woke up rather more cheerful. Noreen had indicated that if he was a fishing man he could take a rod and a boat tomorrow. This seemed such a reasonable way of filling in the time until Porter showed up that he took himself briskly off to inspect the lake.

A few boats were coming in before dark, and he was encouraged still further by the splendid specimens they brought with them. Enormous great things, species of trout, presumably the char and Dolly Varden. And rainbows, glorious jobs, he'd never seen such a size. No salmon, of course, in this landlocked water, but things were definitely looking up.

And looking up to such an extent that as he sat with a sherry in a nook off the bar—Walters having discreetly taken himself off to play pool—he saw that the remarkable locality did indeed have salmon. Strange salmon, kokanee, lake-dwellers. A type of sockeye, no doubt. Yes, so they were: sockeye. His eyes fairly goggled through the fishing magazines. Rainbows over ten pounds. Char to thirty. God alone knew what the kokanee went to. Spin, troll or fly . . . The flies also of great interest. Variations of patterns he had used himself to good effect on the Spey. But also others that might get an even bigger effect. He mused over Mickey Finn, and the Goofus Bug—"good floater, deadly on fast water." The Spey was the fastest water. He took note of the supplier of Goofus and was screwing up his eyes over the illustration when a voice spoke in his ear.

"You were asking for me?"

He spilled his sherry.

A face like a totem pole's made handsome was staring into his.

The cheekbones were high and flat, the eyes dark, penetrating, and unsmiling. The long figure was bent over him, a pair of hunting boots on one end and drawn-back glossy hair on the other. The wide mouth had a mustache on it now.

"Raven?" Lazenby said faintly.

"Hi, Goldilocks," Raven said; and in the same moment Lazenby recalled the Russian, and his too-personal jokes. *Go up, thou baldhead.* Oh yes. He, Baldhead, was Goldilocks! Very funny.

12

The Indian was taller than Lazenby remembered, and quieter than he remembered. He was very quiet indeed: a grave, composed figure, exceedingly reserved. They had dinner together, and Lazenby took stock of him across the table.

The youthful bull of the seventies had gone. His fringe was no more, and the heavy helmet of hair. It was drawn sleekly back now, lengthening the face and chastening it; an austere pigtail hung down the back. Only the mustache seemed to add a normalizing touch.

Lazenby set the ball rolling by asking him if he had met Rogachev again, and he said he had. He had met him again and talked with him again, two nights running—had talked both nights away, all on that same visit; but afterward he had heard nothing more. Yet he stayed silent during Lazenby's story, and made no comment when it was over.

Lazenby chewed at his own meal for some moments.

"Anything you'd like to ask me?" he said.

The Indian consulted a neat forkful of food.

"He wants me because I look like a Siberian, right?"

"That, and your other qualifications. But that, yes. I should think certainly."

"How does he suppose I could get there?"

"This man Walters knows about that. That's Walters of the *CIA*."

"Uh-huh. You have these . . . messages?"

"I don't, no. This CIA man has copies. Will you meet him?"

The Indian examined his forkful again, and ate it.

"Yes. I'll meet him," he said.

They found Walters having his dinner on a tray in the bedroom. He scrambled to his feet to be introduced; and he said he was honored to be introduced.

The Indian merely shook his hand, and said nothing.

"Well now," Walters said, as they were seated, "I guess we know why we are here. How do we feel about it?"

The Indian produced a small tobacco sack and rolled himself a cigarette.

"Are you the one in charge of the arrangements?" he asked politely.

"No, sir, I am not. I am here as an escorting officer, and I would continue in that role for you. But I can answer any general questions you have."

Porter lit the cigarette.

"You have some papers for me," he said.

Walters reached in a breast pocket and produced an envelope. There was a wax seal on it. The Indian looked at the seal, but merely inserted a thumbnail under the flap and tore the top off. Two numbered sheets were inside. He read one and then the other, and smoke began to issue slowly from his mouth. Then he read them again, and pocketed the sheets. His face hadn't changed.

"You know where I'm supposed to go?" he said.

"Yes sir, I do."

"And how I get there?"

"Yes, sir. I know that too."

"Tell me," Porter said.

Walters looked at Lazenby. "I don't know if you are authorized to hear this, sir," he said.

"Not at all. I am sure not," Lazenby said hurriedly, and rapidly left them; and in the room behind him Porter smoked as the plan was laid out for him.

When it was over he carried on smoking.

"Is there anything more I can tell you, sir?" Walters asked presently.

"I heard the plan for getting there. I didn't hear how I was to be dropped off."

"That part isn't fixed yet."

"Or how I get back."

"That isn't fixed either. Obviously it won't be the way you get in. But a number of options will be arranged for you, and you would have backup."

"What backup?"

"Operatives on the ground. You don't need to worry about that. I stay with you through training, and anything that isn't clear, I get it clear. That's right up to when you go."

Porter stubbed his cigarette out.

"This day-to-day job you've dreamed up for me out there. You know I've never done anything like it?"

"Yes, sir, I know that. In camp you'll be doing it in your sleep."

"What camp?"

"An operations camp we have, down south."

Porter considered this.

"This area of Siberia—I'd need to know it. If nobody has been there, how do I get to know it?"

"All I can say is that if you don't, you won't go. That applies to any stage of this operation. If you don't feel you can do it, you cut out—right up to the drop-off. Because at that point you'll be on your own."

"What about that backup?"

"Just then there isn't any. . . . But I can assure you there's no way you'll go in unless you'll feel one hundred percent at home in the place."

"With my own apartment."

"Yes, sir."

"I just turn the key and walk in?"

"That's what you do."

"In this sealed area where nobody's been?"

"That's right."

"What do the neighbors say?"

"You'll learn about the neighbors. We're working on it."

Porter thought about this.

"What information is there on the place?"

"It's being collected. Is there something special you'd want to know?"

"Sure, the slang, the dialect. What they talk about there. Knowing the languages isn't everything."

"Okay." Walters produced a small book and made a note. "I'll try and get it for you," he said.

"From this sealed area, you can get it?"

"I'll try."

Porter took out his tobacco sack again.

"Who are the operatives on the ground?" he said.

Walters smiled. "Even if I knew that, sir," he said, "I couldn't tell you. You know what you have to know. That protects the operation, and it also protects you."

Porter slowly rolled a cigarette.

"You know," he said, "I don't believe that without me you have any operation."

"Yes, sir, that's right."

Porter lit the cigarette. "Why the end of August?" he said.

"That's the date for getting you in position on time. The schedule is very exact. After that there's no point in getting you out there at all."

"Why do you want to get me out there?"

Walters smiled again. "I don't know the object of this mission at all. I do know we're the only ones that *can* get you there. But my orders are not to press you in any way. If you want to go, you go. But if so, I've got to know fast. Could you be available right away?"

"No. I've got to run down to Prince George," Porter said. "I'll be there until—maybe ten days from now."

"That's too long," Walters said.

"That's too bad."

"Can't you drop it? We really don't have that margin."

"I can't drop it. . . . Maybe I could cut it a little." The Indian thought a while. "This stuff you're going to get me—when would you have it?"

"In a few days, perhaps. Where are you staying there?"

"The general post office," Porter said.

Walters made no comment on this but merely noted it in his book. "Well, do I tell them to start?" he said.

The Indian paused.

"I'll see this stuff first," he said. "Tell me again—it's guaranteed I can pull out any time?"

"That's guaranteed."

"With no arm-twisting, no funny stories planted about me in funny places?"

Walters put his book away. "Look, sir," he said, "I know you have problems over contacts with us. It's certainly not in *our* interest to reveal them."

"Not at this time," Porter said.

"Not any time. We have other critical relationships. It would be counterproductive even to try."

"So long as we both know that."

"I think we do. Well, thanks for this meeting, anyway. We got over that one," Walters said smiling.

"Sure," Porter said, and for the first time smiled back.

"Well, now," Lazenby said. "What do you think?"

They had the room to themselves, and the Indian was carefully rolling himself another cigarette.

"I don't know. Maybe I'm being fixed," he said.

"Fixed? In what way fixed?"

"I don't know the way." He neatly licked the cigarette. "But I guess you know I'm a big pain in the ass out here. This government we have, they'd like me far away and in deep shit. But could they set up something like this, with *their* brains and resources? I doubt it. The CIA, now—that's a different story. So what is with them, I wonder?"

"Well, I don't think," Lazenby said, "that there is anything with them. I gave you a very fair summary, I believe, of events as I saw them for myself."

"You didn't see any events yourself." Porter lit the cigarette. "You saw what they showed you. All this rigmarole with satellites, lead pencils, ballpoints. You analyzed any of it personally?"

"Obviously I didn't."

"That's right. *They* did. Don't trust the bastards—governments, government agencies. They rig things, they fake things."

"You're not suggesting somebody faked all *this?*"

"Why not?"

"I didn't receive these bizarre papers from Rogachev?"

"You received bizarre papers from somebody."

"Then, if not Rogachev, that somebody was certainly a most gifted clairvoyant. There were things there that couldn't possibly have been known—things I barely remembered myself."

"Pissing up against the wall?"

"That, yes. Who else *could* have known it?"

"My roommate at Oxford? The guy I told next morning—the Yankee Rhodes scholar who went into their State Department? He couldn't have remembered the crazy story and passed it on to the Department of Spooks?"

Lazenby stared at him.

"You told somebody about it next morning?"

The Indian blew out smoke and shook his head. "No. There was no Yank. I merely illustrate a point, Goldilocks. Take nothing on trust. Many tricky dicks walk the trail. You want a drink?" He had taken a half-pint flask from his jeans pocket.

Lazenby gazed at this most cautiously.

"A very small one, perhaps. What is it?"

"Rye." He poured for them both into tooth mugs. "This is a weird plan they make for me, Goldilocks," he said.

"Don't tell me about it. I don't want to know."

"Okay." He took a long drink. Then he took the two papers from his pocket. "This the stuff they showed you?"

Lazenby examined the sheets. "Yes."

"What's it supposed to mean?"

"Well—what it says. That he obviously believes he has something important and thinks you can get to him."

"They discuss it with you, what it meant?"

"We puzzled over it, yes. We couldn't see any more than that. Can you?"

The Indian poured himself another drink.

"These are *very* tricky dicks," he said at last.

Lazenby watched him drink the rye.

"Tell me," he said mildly, "why you suppose anyone should go to such great labors to 'fix' you in a distant place."

"Scenarios?" Porter nodded. "Maybe they want somebody *in* that place. But nobody can get to it. So they look in the computer, and bingo, *I* can get to it. I'm just the girl. I have the looks, I have the patter. For what? God knows for what. To take something, bring something? You'd never know even while you were doing it."

Lazenby gazed at the Indian. The sudden loquacity, after his reserve at dinner, did not disguise an essential stillness about the man. There was an austere, watchful quality about him.

"Well," he said, terminating the discussion. "I've told you what I came to tell you. All I can add is that at one time I also thought it great nonsense."

"You believe it now, do you?"

66

"Oh, yes. Certainly."

"Would you go yourself?"

"I?" Lazenby stared at him. "*I* wouldn't. Good God, no!"

The Indian didn't say any more. He didn't even look at Lazenby. He just sat and smoked his cigarette. He did this until it was finished and then pocketed the bottle, and nodded, and went.

13

And two days later, job completed, Lazenby himself went, home. He watched most contentedly as portions of British Columbia receded at six hundred miles an hour.

What the Indian had decided to do he had no idea. A very complicated fellow, tricky. Suspected everybody of tricks. Up to plenty himself, of course. He'd decide nothing in a hurry.

In Prince George it was raining and the girl came in drenched, with a dripping umbrella and a bag of groceries.

"Oh, God, are you still watching that?" she said.

Porter's eyes hadn't left the screen.

"Quiet. The man is making a joke."

"He was making the joke when I left."

"That was another joke."

"Who *is* that little bastard? Why are you watching him?"

"He's a jolly little bastard. I like him."

The little man on the screen was very jolly. He wore high reindeer boots and was smacking them as he laughed. His male companions were also smacking theirs. The women's boots couldn't be seen, but they were all elaborately dressed and just as jolly, dark eyes sparkling under their center partings. They were taking part in a talk show.

"Is that Eskimo they're talking or what?" the girl said.

"Eskimo is *Inuit*. The people are also called Inuit. This isn't Inuit," he said. The tall blonde was an ex-student of his and should have known better. At the present time she should have known much better, for she was editing a book, his last, which was about the Inuit. "Go and take that bath," he said.

"You said you were going to take it with me."

"All right." Porter reluctantly switched the tape off. There were about twenty snippets on it, bits of newscasts, talks, chat shows.

Snatched by satellite evidently. No information had come with the tape. Just the tape. He'd watched it a few times and would watch it some more. He reached for his wallet and took out the much-handled messages again, comparing them side by side.

I am he that liveth/ I am yet alive/ in the north country/ in dark waters/ in the waste howling wilderness/ Wherefore do ye not answer me?/ Behold new things do I declare/ The eyes of all/ shall be opened/ Send me therefore the man understanding science/ of every living thing/ Let me hear thy voice concerning this matter/ the first day at midnight/ Voice of America.

Go up, thou baldhead/ How is it that ye do not understand?/ I want that man/ that speaketh the tongues of the families of the north/ him that pisseth against the wall/ As to my abode/ it was written plainly in the beginning/ I dwell in/ dark waters/ Shew him all my words/ that the people shall no more/ sit in darkness/ nor like the blind/ stumble at noonday/ Make speed/ Baldhead.

What the hell! Had they really not seen it, the CIA geniuses? Or had they manufactured it themselves? He still couldn't tell. Some stuff here was meant solely for him. Could they possibly have known what had been discussed?

He wasn't clear what to do. Drop the whole thing and go back to Montreal, east? Or find out more at the operations camp the young spook had mentioned, south?

He followed the girl into the bathroom, brooding. Sleep on it, and then decide. East, south, where?

Three

North by Northwest

14

On August 28 Porter arrived at Narita airport, picked up his bags, negotiated Immigration and Customs, and descended to the train. A car was waiting for him outside, as he knew. He had no intention of taking it. The airport express could get him where he wanted, which was Tokyo central station.

He made it by five o'clock, to find the rush hour in progress. This was the second *rushawa* of the day, the homeward-streaming one, and the familiar riot was in progress. He spent some minutes getting his bearings, and located the Lucky Strike. It looked no different from the other "business efficiencies" around the station, but it stood on a corner and had two entrances. This was its attraction, and he remembered it. They wouldn't remember him.

"How many nights?" the Lucky Strike clerk asked him.

"I'm not sure; say four."

"Say four, you pay up front four."

"Okay," Porter said, and gave him a credit card.

The man looked at it and turned it over.

"You American, Australian, what?" he said. He had been shouting in slow Japanese himself.

"Canadian."

"Ah. Sorry. Thought Korean," the clerk apologized.

Porter was pleased about that. "Give me some telephone tokens," he said. "Give me ten. I'll pay now."

"Sure. Canadian is all right," the man said. He gave the tokens and Porter waited while his card was checked out. It was very hot and steamy and he was sweating under the wig. His pigtail was fixed tight inside. "Isn't the air-conditioning working here?" he said.

"Sure, everything working. Only it gives me a cold so I turn it off.

And if you want room-cleaning service," the clerk said, "service is extra."

"I don't want service."

"Okay. Room 303. The elevator's around the corner."

"Where are the stairs?" Porter said.

"Past the elevator. Next to the coffee bar. Go around the corner, you'll see."

Porter went around the corner and found the stairs, also the coffee bar. Also the other entrance. It was as he remembered. It wasn't necessary to go through the lobby to get in or out of the place.

He skipped the stairs and rode up to 303. It was a neat small efficiency. Compact kitchen and shower room. European bed, not a futon for the floor. Normal furniture. Phone. He switched the air-conditioning on and used the phone. Then he unpacked and had a shower. He took the wig off in the shower.

He was resting in a towel, with his wig back on, when the doorbell went.

"Excuse me," murmured the individual outside. He was a neat Japanese with tortoiseshell glasses and a briefcase. "I don't know if this is the right place. I am looking for a Mr. Peterson."

"Okay, come in," Porter said. They were both speaking Japanese.

The man came cautiously in.

"You drink rye?" Porter asked. He was drinking some himself already.

The man did not disclose what he drank. He carefully looked the efficiency over, and then he looked Porter over. "Maybe you have something to show me?" he said.

Porter reached for his jacket and took the headed letter out. It introduced James B. Peterson of New Age Technology, Vancouver, to Makosha Microchip KK of Tokyo.

The man carefully examined the letter. "Some other details? Some details you yourself have to say to Makosha?"

"Oh, well, shit . . . ," Porter said, but he gave the details.

"Hey," the man said. He seemed nonplussed. "We were waiting with a car at the airport. What are you doing here?"

"I thought I'd come here," Porter said.

"This isn't good. We don't make changes."

"I'll remember," Porter said, and gave him his drink. "What's your name?"

"Just Yoshi. On the phone also you just say Yoshi. You don't say all the things you said."

"Okay," Porter said. "What have you brought me?"

Yoshi was looking round the room. "You can't stay here," he said.

"There's a place waiting for you. You have to wait in that place. I've brought the material but I can't leave it."

"Just show me what you've got," Porter said.

Yoshi opened his briefcase and took out a passport and a seaman's paybook. Both were South Korean and in the name of a Sung Won Choo. Porter had a look at them. They were well-thumbed and greasy. His photograph was slightly different in each but the same seaman stared out with the same piercing eyes, the same bushy mustache. His pigtail was over his shoulder in one and up in a bun in the other.

"And the ship blueprints," he said.

Yoshi took a transistor radio out of his case and turned it on. "You don't need them," he said, over the row. "There's better material. It's waiting for you. In the place where you have to be."

"Where's the ship?"

"At Nagasaki. It's still in drydock."

"What's the sailing date?"

"The thirty-first. You'll learn all this."

"That gives me only two days in between."

"It's a week before you're needed. You'll be briefed on it. We have to keep to plans."

"Okay," Porter said. He took a cigarette and offered Yoshi his pack.

"I shouldn't, it's not healthy," Yoshi said. But he accepted a cigarette, and blew out a stream of smoke.

"What's the stop-off schedule?" Porter asked.

"*You do not need this,*" Yoshi said, mouthing above the din. "Not here. It's not finalized, anyway."

"What have you got?"

Yoshi put down his cigarette and took out a map. A sheet of scrawled Japanese was attached to it. He opened the map out on his knee.

"The west coast—you know it?"

"No."

"No, it isn't used much by international lines. This is a cheap line. It does cheap business. Here, Nagasaki." Yoshi put a finger on it. "And here, Niigata—the first stop, about seven hundred miles up. In Niigata it discharges and loads."

"It loads what?"

Yoshi ground his teeth a little, but he checked the paper. "Forklifts, agricultural machinery, skates," he said. "The skates for Göteborg and Rotterdam, the rest Murmansk."

"Containerized?"

"Containerized."

"As deck cargo or what?"

Yoshi blinked. "The loading isn't finalized," he said.

Porter looked at him. Yoshi was the man he had to deal with, and he had been told he was a good man. But Yoshi didn't know this. There would be other things he didn't know. That was why Porter was at the Lucky Strike. "Okay," he said. "What's the discharge cargo?"

"Wool. The ship is coming now. It runs there and back from Australia. It drops the wool at Nagasaki, and feeder vessels move it on. This one will. First of all to Niigata."

"Wool is a baled cargo."

"Yes, baled," Yoshi said, checking.

"The ship handles break-bulk *and* container."

"It handles everything; it's a tramp. It goes to places the others don't," Yoshi said.

Porter thought about this. "Okay, Niigata. What then?"

"Then Otaru. Up here on the island of Hokkaido. The same thing, load and discharge. And final bunkering. It's the last stop in Japan. It drops the remainder of the wool, then off—up to the Bering Strait and the Arctic."

"What's the date for up there?"

"Nagasaki–Murmansk is twenty-eight days, their speed. They go a slow speed, it's cheaper. But they allow more for turnaround and delays. The one sure date, they'll be at Murmansk the first week of October. After that there's a good chance they'd be iced in."

"How about Green Cape?"

"I don't know about Green Cape. There's no consignment yet. There still could be. The Russians always leave it to the end. It wouldn't be the last word, anyway."

He explained. On rounding the strait the ship would radio its arrival in Russian waters, and the Russians would radio back if they wanted them to stop.

"Stop for what?"

"Fish. They have a small fish business with Murmansk." Murmansk was not on the map but Yoshi pointed out where it would be, somewhere near the door. "Way out there. That time of year nothing much goes that way. The traffic is all the other way, to the Pacific. Maybe this is the last ship of the season, so they'll want it."

"What if they don't?"

Two flutes of smoke came out of Yoshi's flat nose. "If they don't, there's a plan," he said. "And if they do, there's also a plan. You'll learn all this."

"Where do I join the ship?"

"At Otaru. It happens fast, before they have time to let anyone know. Actually, they won't *want* to let anyone know."

"Why?"

"No. Enough," Yoshi said. The minimal nose and the shell glasses gave him the appearance of a tough cat. "There's a lot for you to learn, but not here. In the place set up for you to learn. You stay out of sight there till it's time for you to move."

Porter nodded. "Yoshi," he said, "do you know what I have to do at Green Cape?"

"No. I don't have to know that," Yoshi said.

"It's not as healthy as smoking cigarettes."

"So?"

"I am the one that's going, not you."

"If you don't keep to the plan maybe you can't go."

"If I don't like the plan," Porter said, "I won't go."

Yoshi looked at him, blinking slowly.

"What's wrong with the plan?" he said.

"I don't know," Porter said. "I'll find out at Nagasaki."

"What are you talking about?" Yoshi said. His mouth had fallen open and his blinking had accelerated. "I told you—you join the ship at Otaru. You can't go to Nagasaki. You can't go anywhere. You have to stay out of sight. If there's anything you want to know, we'll find it out. What is it you want to know?"

"What equipment have they got on the ship?"

"What equipment? I've got a man who *knows* the equipment. He knows the ship. He'll explain it all to you. Everything is taken care of. I promise you!"

"Has the man been on the ship during refitting?"

"He doesn't have to go on the ship. He's a—a professional man. He knows these things. I can't tell you here—it's confidential!" Yoshi mouthed over the radio row.

"Yoshi, I've learned these ships have the worst accident record in the world, and a new man gets the shittiest jobs. Unless I arrive in one piece at the other end there's no point in going at all. I have to know about this ship. Do you *understand?*"

"I understand," Yoshi said. He was looking troubled. "But you can't get in the yard anyway. We also tried to get in, for information. We got it from the freight forwarders in the end. It's a private yard, very secure, they don't let anyone in."

"But they have to let workers out. Which yard is it?"

Yoshi checked with his paper. "Takeshuma. Around the bay, near Mitsubishi."

"I know Mitsubishi. You can look into it from the hill. How near there is it?"

"I don't know," Yoshi said. He took his glasses off, and put them on again. "Listen, come back with me," he said, "and you'll understand. Leave the cases here, if you want. They can be sent for. Just agree to that for now."

But Porter wouldn't agree to it. He said he planned to rest and look over the blueprints and his documentation. Yoshi wouldn't leave the documentation but he reluctantly agreed to leave the blueprints. He unfolded the sheets and carefully scissored off a strip along the bottom, which gave the date and the drafting details. Then he cut off another along the top.

This gave the name of the ship, which was the *Suzaku Maru*.

Rain was smashing down when he woke.

It was very dark, and the room was chill from the air conditioner. He took a warm shower and went down to the coffee bar. This place he found shut, so he crossed the street to the station. Plenty of small cafés were open there.

The rain had stopped but the night was damp and hot, alive now with neon. It glistened in the puddles, and cast a red glow over the enormous city. The station was still crowded, the streets clogged with hooting traffic. He found a sushi bar and picked at his plate, musing.

His Japanese would do. Over the years he had been running there and back; the last time, as it happened, to Hokkaido, where he now had to pick up the ship. On that occasion he had been picking up Ainu, from the remaining aboriginals there.

Japanese yes, but his Korean no. On the ship he was going to need Korean. He had brushed up a bit at the camp, and more had been arranged for him here. It was the ship that worried him more. As Yoshi had snipped off the details he had noticed the date. The blueprints were thirty-five years old.

He went back and studied them anyway.

He saw there was no provision for containerization. The ship hadn't carried containers thirty-five years ago, although evidently it did now. And what of the deck equipment: the derricks, cranes, capstans? Stinking old machinery, for certain, and by now dangerous. A ship that went to "places the others don't" made heavy use of its own lifting gear, soon worn out. A line like this would either get a cheap repair job or replace it with scrapyard junk. In any case the deck gear wouldn't be where it was on the blueprints—not if container shafts had been put in.

He pored over the sheets all the same, memorizing the equipment and its positioning. He did it until two in the morning when his eyes were closing, and then he phoned Yoshi's number again. It rang for a long time and then was abruptly answered by a female—very angry, almost in shock. He left a message for Yoshi, and went to bed.

15

The Theosophical Society of East Asia had a beautiful small courtyard, totally secluded, and approached by a long alley ending in a tunnel and solid wooden doors. The doors opened silently after Yoshi had beeped his remote control and received an answering beep.

A little old man with a rake was watching as the car entered and came to a halt. Yoshi nodded to him as they got out, and the old man nodded back. He was wearing a conical straw hat and scraping lines in a sand garden, and in addition to the rake he was holding the electronic gadget that had opened the doors.

The morning was very heavy and gray and they had driven for over an hour through back streets to get here. Away from the center the prosperous city was suddenly in the Third World: few pavements, puddled lanes. This area seemed more salubrious but was still a jumble of sheds, factories, small apartment blocks.

The Theosophical Society itself was wedged between a book depository and a tin-roofed works; but inside the gates was another world. A fountain played. Carp swam in a pool.

"You like this place?" Yoshi asked.

Porter looked around it, nodding.

A heavily eaved house, evidently ancient, covered with an elegant creeper, it enclosed all four sides of the courtyard, the tunnel and the gates merely set into it.

"You'll work well here, you'll concentrate," Yoshi told him. "You can rest in the garden. And this is Machiko," he said, as a young lady in glasses appeared in the doorway. She was wearing a track suit and an unsmiling countenance.

"We spoke," she said. "On the phone. At two o'clock this morning."

"Sure. Sorry about that," Porter said.

"It's okay. It's just that I like to get out and jog first thing. I didn't jog too much today." The appearance was little-girl Japanese, with black pudding-bowl haircut. But she was not a little girl. And the language was not Japanese but pure Canadian.

"She does all kinds of voices. She will do regional Korean," Yoshi told him. "Also your legend. You'll work with Machiko on the legend."

"What have you got for me here?" Porter said.

"You'll see it after breakfast."

"Maybe I'd better see it now," Porter said.

"Okay. We'll meet up later," Yoshi told the girl, and took Porter inside.

The house was a warren of corridors, with a faint smell of incense hanging about. "It's from the walls," Yoshi told him. "Religious people lived here a long time." The walls were of rough plaster, and brass oil lamps hung from them. Electric bulbs were in the oil lamps now. They turned a corner and then another, and went up a flight of stairs, to a room evidently over the entrance tunnel. Yoshi unlocked the door and switched the light on and relocked behind them.

The room was cell-like, with a single shuttered window. It had tatami matting on the floor and two chairs and a table. On the table was a model of the ship, a meter long and brightly painted.

"The man will come and explain it to you," Yoshi said. "He's a ship architect with the government." He took a side off the ship and exposed the interior. "You see what a good job it is? It's better than any blueprint."

"Yes," Porter said. The model was very good, immaculately finished, and in much better shape than the original was now likely to be.

He looked at the interior. Two shafts had been installed, he saw. For vertical container stacking. Little containers were stacked in them. He moved the containers up and down. "When was this put in?" he said.

"They did a big job ten, twelve years ago. The man will explain it all to you."

Ten, twelve years ago made sense. Then it was worth the expense. They wouldn't have spent much since. In particular they wouldn't have spent much on the deck gear. The deck gear was where it was on the blueprints—impossible in view of the shafts. Whoever had made the model was not interested in the deck but in the ship's interior. The interior was very precise and showed many changes; to holds, lockers, shuttering.

"Who built this?" he said.

"The man did it himself. He's an expert. He'll take you through it blindfold. He works for the narcotics bureau."

"What has the narcotics bureau to do with it?"

"We brought them into it. You're a narcotics agent, with the U.S. government. We supplied good papers. We've done a lot of work. And they keep excellent relations with the police, the transport ministries, all kinds of authorities. We're getting maximum help, and they know we'll be discreet. So you see why you can't go poking around and screwing things up. I'll tell you all about it. You can take your wig off now and we'll have breakfast."

The girl didn't appear at breakfast.

"She doesn't have to hear what I'm going to tell you," Yoshi said.

He began telling Porter as soon as the remains were cleared away. He produced two folders from a safe, and emptied one of them on the table. A number of photographs and papers spilled out, including the passport and the paybook.

"This is his wife. Parents. Children. The house they all live in, street plan. His service record—every ship he's been on, and where. Police record—some violence, as you'll see. Medical record. Letters from his wife. Examples of his own writing. You'll work through all this with Machiko."

"This is a real person?" Porter said.

"Of course. It's always the best."

"Where is he?"

"In Kobe. His throat was slit in a prison fight there three weeks ago. We're holding the ashes awhile. They'll have to go back, of course; he was a Buddhist. The family has not been informed yet— bureaucratic delay. We'll hold everything until you're on that ship, and off it."

"Had he served with this line?"

"Some time ago. You'll see it there."

"Won't any of the crew know him?"

"No. They're all signed, and we've checked every one out. Not one of them was ever in the same port with him, or even on home leave, at least not in the last six years. It's a very slight risk."

"Who else knows he's dead?"

"Outside the prison, a few officials. Inside it, maybe the hospital staff. Not even them, for certain. He was shifted out in an ambulance. A police surgeon was the only one with him when he died. The police know, of course. That is, it will be on a computer somewhere, if they have any reason to check you out. They won't have a reason. You'll be staying out of sight. I'll have one of your cigarettes now," Yoshi said.

Porter gave him one and lit it.

"Wasn't there an inquest?" he said.

"No. The narcotics department helped. *They* have asked that you stay out of sight. It's the only thing they've asked. They can't compromise the police."

"So how long am I supposed to stay here?"

"From now, six days. Perhaps seven. Your kit is all here. You pick it up at Otaru."

Porter thought about this.

"All right. What's the timing, from Nagasaki?"

"From Nagasaki," Yoshi said, "the ship undocks on the thirty-first, and loads. This is a fast operation, wool the only cargo. I'll have more information later, but provisionally she arrives at Niigata on the third of September."

He opened the second folder and took some sheets out.

"Niigata. A fully equipped port. It handles all loading and discharge—ship's own crew only partially required, so one watch goes ashore. Normal turnaround there is twelve to eighteen hours—again, I'll know more later. But trouble develops onshore among the crew, and it continues on the ship. A hundred miles or so out the captain suddenly has a casualty on his hands, quite serious."

He explained this, and Porter drew on his cigarette.

"This is already fixed?" he said.

"Oh, yes." Yoshi looked through his papers and turned one face around on the table. "Here's the deck crew."

Porter counted twelve names; four of them highlighted with red outliner.

"What are the red ones?" he said.

"One of them is the casualty."

"How do you know who'll be the casualty?"

"I don't," Yoshi said, "but the list is alphabetical, and they work the watches the same way. One of these men *has* to be the casualty. And three of them served together on a previous voyage, which will be useful. Anyway, I want to know what happens in Niigata before starting you off in Otaru."

Porter considered this.

"How long from there to Otaru?"

"Two days," Yoshi said.

"With this man in bad shape."

"Very bad shape."

"So what happens?"

Yoshi told him what he thought would happen.

"Won't there be questions about the casualty?"

"It will happen *fast*," Yoshi said. "And the captain will leave Otaru fast. After shipping another hand."

"Are we certain he absolutely *needs* another hand?"

"Yes. For a voyage through the Arctic, late in the season," Yoshi said, "he needs another hand. These ships already operate with minimum crews."

Porter smoked silently for a while.

"Okay. Green Cape," he said.

"There isn't anything for Green Cape. I told you, the Russian trade mission here is always late. They could still give instructions—even at sea. But whether they do or they don't," Yoshi said, "you get off there." And he explained this, too. "After which," he ended, "you know what to do. And I don't have to know. I've got you on the ship, and I've got you off it."

"Well. Okay." Porter said. "Maybe. If it works at Green Cape."

"I have no doubts about Green Cape. If you get *on* the ship, you'll get off it at Green Cape. And you *will* get on it, if you keep to the plan. You look good. You look how you're supposed to look," Yoshi said. Porter was now gnawing the end of his pigtail. "In seaman's rig you'll look even better."

Porter studied his image in the passport and the paybook.

"So here's the next thing," Yoshi said. "Why you stay out of sight. Koreans aren't liked here. Working people don't like them, the police. They regularly get stopped by the police. On no account are you meeting any police."

"I never had trouble before."

"It wasn't so bad before. And if it had been bad, you were a Canadian with good papers. Now you're a Canadian with funny papers. And a wig."

"Without the wig, with Sung's papers?"

"They run you in right away. One call from a police box, and they find you're not Sung."

"Why would they call?"

"They *do* call. I tell you, it's routine, Koreans have a bad time. They don't like them. Maybe there's been trouble recently, violence, theft, whatever. Then what? At Tokyo central, a man on the switchboard, he knows the arrangement with the narcotics bureau? Don't even think of it. This plan is nice because the timing is nice. Interfere with it in some way—get yourself locked up, an investigation—and there is no plan. This is why you don't go out," Yoshi said.

Porter continued gnawing his pigtail.

"Yoshi," he said, "I have to see the ship. They're probably patching it up for one last voyage, like the other ship, and using cannibalized parts. The man who made that model was interested in compartments where narcotics could be hidden—not deck gear where it wouldn't be. *I* am interested in deck gear. I'll be using it. I have to see it before the ship leaves dock. It's the only place I *can* see it before boarding. And if I don't see it I *won't* be boarding.''

Yoshi slowly blinked at him.

"If the ship can be seen," he worked out, "then it can be photographed. Why don't we photograph it for you?''

"All right. I'm still going to see it. I can't take a chance on this.''

Yoshi continued blinking.

"Today is too late anyway," he said. "It's a long trip. And you can't go on your own. If you go out at all, it's as a businessman in a suit, and we go together.''

"Okay," Porter said. "Keep me company.''

Nagasaki airport was at Omura, about twenty-five miles from the port. They landed there before noon, into almost subtropical heat, and Yoshi hired a car.

The waterfront came in sight presently, sparkling far below, and they followed it around. Houses clung to the hillsides, and narrow winding streets tottered down to the bay; the place was built on a series of terraces.

Yoshi had better information on the yard now and also a Port Authority map. On the map the dockyards were shown as a line of numbered blocks, and a key on the edge of the map gave the names. Porter kept his finger on Takeshuma's. As Yoshi had said, it wasn't far from Mitsubishi, and they slowed as they neared the area.

Just at two o'clock, they saw it.

The yard passed below, barely distinguishable; they drove on to the next pull-in and walked back. A steady stream of traffic was passing on the road, but on the hillside, above and below the road, people were picnicking and taking photographs. There was plenty to photograph. Far below, winking in the sun, was the Park Lane of the marine world—a glittering array of success—supertankers, giant container ships, prosperous monsters of all kinds, lined up row on row.

Mitsubishi was the most prominent of the yards, its activities not only visible but audible, even palpable. The thump of its heavy forges echoed between the hills of the bay, rhythmically shifting the air. Just about here Madame Butterfly had taken the air while awaiting the one fine day when a plume of smoke would herald Lieutenant Pinkerton. Yet it was not Pinkerton but another American who had occasioned the most momentous plume of all.

The B-29 with its atom bomb had flown directly overhead, with Mitsubishi as its target—the yard, the steelworks, and the munitions plant that had lain alongside. The bomb had landed almost half a mile away, demolishing the lot, and ultimately 73,000 citizens.

They climbed the hill, above the picnickers, and peered down through binoculars. Right away Porter saw why not much of Take-shuma had been distinguishable from the road. High shuttering screened it off from the road. From this height, not all of it was screened off. Two ships were in the yard. They were lodged side by side, on chocks, in separate drydocks. All the after parts were visible, maybe even three quarters of the ships' length.

"I don't know which one it is," Yoshi said.

"It's the nearer one," Porter told him. He couldn't see a name, but the gantry was clearly visible. It was a forty-tonner, right specifications. The other ship was a coaster, wrong shape.

"It's that one," he said.

He examined it for some time. Not only the gantry but the wheelhouse was in its blueprint position. He went over the ship section by section. Two of the derricks were in dismantled heaps on the deck. But he could see another, installed and standing. He couldn't make out the container-shaft openings. The sun was aslant now and casting heavy shadows. It was blazing fiercely down, however, and the workers below were swarming half-naked in the heat.

They were swarming everywhere—on the dock, on the ship, in cradles over the side. Propped high in the cement pit, the hull looked horrible; a bulbous shell, rusty, scabrous, salt-scarred. The men in the cradles were scraping at encrustations with long-handled implements, and being followed by others with power hoses and red lead. Floodlights were rigged round the dock and it was plain that work would be going on all night if the ship was to come out on time.

He heard a click and saw Yoshi at work with the camera.

"Let me take a look," he said.

Through the binoculars everything had quivered in the heat. He needed a clear view of the derrick.

The Nikon had a big telephoto lens and the reflex view was good. But the thing was hard to hold steady. Again the derrick swam in the air currents. A fraction of a second could make a difference.

"Is this thing motorized?" he said.

"Sure."

Yoshi set the motor and Porter held the camera and shot off half a roll. Then they moved position and he tried again. The view was no better here; the derrick was even obscured for some seconds by a group of men in hard hats gesticulating over it. But he kept the camera going and shot off the other half and they went back to the car.

It was after ten when they returned to Tokyo, and almost eleven as they rolled through the tunnel to the Theosophical Society. They had left it at seven in the morning, and thirteen hundred miles had been covered in between. Of the thirty-six photos four were good and one very good, and this one Machiko enlarged.

Midnight passed while she did this, and the thirty-first of August had arrived.

16

For the thirty-first of August the plan called for Porter to have his first session with the ship's architect, and also his try-on.

The architect came first, and he studied the photographs made the night before. Porter had also studied them, without being able to identify the derrick. The architect couldn't identify it either. He said the equipment was obviously old; he would have it looked up and get a copy of the works manual. But he was anxious to proceed with instruction on his model, and Porter moodily allowed himself to be instructed.

They spent the morning on it, but Porter barely listened. He had realized now what he had to do, and it worried him. In the afternoon he had his try-on.

The kit was all suitably shabby: shoes scuffed and well worn; darned woolens, oiled stockings, long johns, sweatshirts, jeans, sea boots, donkey jacket, headgear. They had had his measurements for weeks and little alteration was needed, but what there was Machiko attended to. Then she packed everything in a kit bag and a rope-bound case, all to go by hand next day to Hokkaido.

Afterwards they worked on his "legend." This girl seemed exceedingly responsible, acting as housemother in charge of the servants as well as of himself. Yet Yoshi instructed him to tell her nothing of his identity. The success of an operation, he said, depended on people knowing only what they had to—but attending to that with maximum efficiency.

This aspect he demonstrated himself by returning, after taking the ship's architect back, with the manual for the derrick. "He'd have forgotten about it in the morning," he said. "I stood over him while he searched. It was a long search."

Porter looked at the manual and saw gloomily why this was the case. It was dated 1948.

"Is there a working model of this around anywhere?"

"Only on these ships. It's been out of use a long time."

"Can we get hold of somebody who's used it?"

"No," Yoshi said. "We can't. But he'll study it himself and explain it to you in the morning."

"Yoshi, if this thing is out of use," Porter said, "it's because it's dangerous. I need somebody who's used it."

"We can't have anybody who's used it. We can't have anybody else at all. In any case, he doesn't know anybody."

"I know somebody," Porter said.

Yoshi listened to him, aghast, as he explained what he was going to do.

"Are you mad?" he said. "You can't do this. I've told you why. Don't you understand?"

"Yes, I understand," Porter said. But he knew he was going to do it anyway.

The bus was almost empty, and in the dark he couldn't see through the rain-smeared windows. But the driver was calling out the stops, and when he called out "Bund" Porter got off.

He could see the Bund Hotel twinkling to the left, and the Marine Tower to the right. He located himself then. This bit of Yokohama he knew. It was only half an hour's train ride from Tokyo, practically a suburb. The bus from the station had been grinding around the harbor, and in the open air now he could smell the diesel fumes off the water.

He was in jeans and a sweatshirt, his pigtail hanging. He had changed at the Lucky Strike. He had walked into the place as Peterson and walked out of it as Sung, by the side exit.

He crossed the road and cut through to the tinny music and the traffic of Chukagai. Away from the harbor the town was quite sedate, a commuter belt for the capital. But this area was not sedate. He passed the massage parlors and the pachinko parlors, the little steel balls rattling as the gamblers fed in coins. The topless places had now become NO PANTY, he saw. The gaudy glow of Chinatown hung in the air.

In a few minutes he was in the middle of it. The streets shone in the drizzle, narrow, crowded, crawling with cars. Restaurants lined both sides, the vertical Chinese signs flashing at each other. He looked for the laughing pig and the debonair donkey. The pig he couldn't see but the donkey was still there. He was flashing on and off in the air, legs crossed, leaning on his cane, asinine ears shooting up and down. Then he saw the pig, too. Its lights were off but the red-and-yellow snout still grinned its cheerful, cheeky grin.

The alley was a slit between the two buildings and emerged to the street behind. Shabbier bars and coffee shops. Ichiko's lane had had a barber's on the corner. Yes, still there. He went down the lane and found Ichiko's.

The same lantern over the door, the same curtain in the doorway and the smell of cooking coming out. Half a dozen men were supping up their noodles on stools at the counter. His pigtail attracted no attention here. He ordered grilled eel with his noodles, the specialty of the house; Ichiko, when on leave, used to catch them himself in the harbor. He supped his bowl with the rest and kept an eye open for Ichiko. He could hear pots rattling in the kitchen; evidently Hanita at work.

"Is Hanita around?" he asked the bar girl.

"Who?"

"Hanita. The boss."

The sleepy girl looked at him and went in the back room. A man came out with her, wiping his hands on a cloth. "Who did you want?" he said.

"Isn't this Hanita's place?"

"She died—two, three years ago."

"Oh." He absorbed this. "What happened to Ichiko?"

"The sailor? He moved out."

"Do you know where?"

"No. I let him have a room for a while. But he went. He's around somewhere still. Ask at the *koban*, they'll tell you. Just along the street at the crossroad, you'll see it."

"Okay," he said.

The *koban* was the police post.

He went out, brooding. He had attracted no attention so far. Yokohama was a seaman's place, and plenty of Korean seamen were in it. He wondered if he dared risk the police post. The *koban* would only be a neighborhood box, one of thousands. The streets were mainly unnamed, as everywhere else in the country. Each *koban* had its patch: the police there knew the streets and who lived in them, who moved in, out, who got drunk, who came home late.

The drizzle had eased a little, and now he could see the *koban*. The box was dimly lit. A policeman was sitting under the porch smoking a cigarette. He saw the man was looking at him. He took Sung's passport out of his jeans and held it in his hand, poised to snatch it back and run if it was inspected.

"Excuse me, I'm looking for a mate," he said. "Ichiko Nagoya. His wife ran a noodle bar up the street."

The policeman stared at the passport in his hand but didn't ask to see it.

"They said he'd moved away. They said you'd know."

The policeman looked back through the open door behind him. Another policeman was inside, writing. "Ichiko Nagoya—was he the one that went cuckoo?" he called.

The other man came out. He also stared at the passport. "Sure. They had him in the bin. He's out now. Along there," he said, pointing, "maybe ten minutes—the taxi office. It's the all-night one, lit up in red. He has a room at the back. He won't be there now," he said, as the "Korean" thanked him and began moving away. "He works as a night watchman, at the Kawakami works, farther along."

"Kawakami—is that far?"

"You can't go in there." The man stared at him. "What do you want with him? He owes you something?"

"No. Just to say I was sorry. About his wife," Porter said simply. "Maybe I'll leave a note, at the taxi office." He still kept the passport in his hand. They were watching him as he turned to thank them again. The drizzle had stopped now, but he was damp with sweat and didn't put the passport away till he was out of sight of the *koban*.

He saw the all-night taxi office presently, but didn't stop. Farther along, the policeman had said; the Kawakami works. There were few people about now and the street lamps were farther apart. There was the odd bar, a tenement, sheds. From some of the sheds he heard lowing: cows. There were few fields in the area, and milk for the town came from hundreds of sheds; Ichiko had owned a couple himself.

He walked fast for another ten minutes, and then wondered if he shouldn't go back to the taxi office after all. There was nobody in the street and nothing like a factory. He stopped and looked about him, and in the silence heard a distant clanking and screeching. The marshaling yard behind the station. He must have walked back parallel with the railway line. Except the screeching was not that of rolling stock. He walked on again, and as the sound became louder suddenly saw the factory.

Now that the rain had stopped the sky had cleared, and the ugly shape loomed against a slice of moon. It was a breeze-block structure, big, square, with hangar doors. Above the roof, iron letters were mounted on stilts, and he picked the Japanese characters out against the sky: K-A-W-A-K-A-M-I.

The screeching set his teeth on edge. It was coming from a gap in the hangar doors, open a few inches, perhaps to let air in. He peered through and saw nothing: total blackness. Then a kind of glimmering like the markings on a luminous watch. Denser shapes of blackness were shuddering along the markings. He tried to pull the doors wider but couldn't manage it, and felt with his hands in the gap and found a safety bar in position. He tugged it upward, and at once an alarm bell went off. He stepped back, but he had been seen; a flashlight was shining on him from inside. He stood away as the light approached, and then put his face into the gap.

"Ichiko! It's me—remember?" The light was blinding him. "It's Johnny. I came to see you."

The light swung about his face, then down to the safety bar, and the alarm bell stopped. The door slid open, and the flashlight waved him in. Inside, the noise was horrendous, the screeching and clanking grossly amplified and bouncing back off the walls. His arm was being tightly gripped, and the beam shone up to Ichiko's face. He had earmuffs on, and he touched his lips and shook his head. He put the safety bar back on and pointed the light at an end wall, and moved there. A little glass cabin, dimly lit, was up on the wall. An iron staircase led up to it and he followed Ichiko there.

In the cabin Ichiko took his muffs off and closed the door, and the noise abruptly decreased: The glass of the cabin was multiply glazed. A long desk and a console looked down on the factory. But it looked down on nothing—only the room lights shining back off the glass. Then, as he moved, Porter saw one panel greenly illuminated, like an aquarium, and a scene of weird activity taking place in it.

As if through night glasses, the whole factory was luminously in view there, and all of it crazily at work. Like a computer game, a hundred things were jerkily going on. Carts moved along aisles, moved, stopped, moved again. They moved along glowing lines in the floor. Skeletal arms reached out from bays at either side, and skeletal fingers weaved and bobbed in the air. They were picking up bolts, screws, drill heads; touching, feeling, coming back for more, occasionally letting off showers of sparks and filings.

"Ichiko, what is this?"

"The new world, no people. No people needed."

"They told me you were here. I went to Hanita's."

"She's gone. Not required anymore. Nobody needed."

"Ichiko, I'm sorry. I didn't know." It was only four years since he had seen him last, when Ichiko had just left the sea—always a cantankerous but a forthright and robust man, jovial in his way. Now he was like an automaton, withdrawn, as jerky in his movements as

the machines below. He had shown no curiosity whatever at seeing Porter. "So how do you like the night work?" he asked.

"It runs itself. I only watch. Nobody needed."

"What do they make here?"

"Robots. Robots make robots. You see? Who's needed?"

"Ichiko," Porter said. He had a lowering feeling he wasn't going to get far. "You used to give me advice." Ichiko didn't say anything, only looked at him with hollow eyes. "I need something, Ichiko," Porter said.

Ichiko came closer, and glanced absently through the panel in passing. "I'll give you something," he said. Through the panel Porter saw the carts had suddenly stopped and small bulbs on the console were flashing. "It's only coffee," Ichiko said. He was filling a mug from a flask. "No drink allowed."

"Ichiko, something has happened below. Are you supposed to do anything about it?"

"The robots do it. A drill broke and they're replacing it. They look after themselves, they doctor each other. They're cleverer than we are. Here," he said, and gave Porter the mug.

"Aren't there any workers here at all?"

"A small shift in the day. They sharpen parts, take away what's been done. At nights it's just the robots and me." He sneezed and blew his nose. "Johnny?" he said suddenly. He was blinking at him. "What do you want here?"

"I came to see you." Porter smiled at him, relieved at the abrupt return to sense. "I have to go to sea again, Ichiko. I need some advice."

"Leave it alone. That's my advice."

"It's just for a short while."

"You said you were going to the Ainu in Hokkaido."

"I went. This is something else."

"Another one of your projects?"

"Yes, another one."

"Ah." Ichiko looked through the panel and pressed buttons on the console. Below, the subdued row began again. "Where are you going?"

"North, the Arctic."

"Your Eskimos, eh? Well, best regards to them," Ichiko said. He screwed the top back on the flask.

"Ichiko," Porter said. He was glad to see the old robustness back, and he took the enlarged photograph out of his pocket. It was folded small and he opened it out. "It's one of the Yakamoto ships. Remember, you did some trips with them?"

"Stay away from the bastards. They're dangerous."

"One trip only. But I don't know the deck gear, Ichiko, the derricks. Take a look here. Maybe you can make it out."

Ichiko peered at the photo.

"Make it out? This is the bitch that took Kenji's arm. Kenji—that fine boy, you remember?"

"Kenji?" There were many Kenjis.

"The whistler, eighteen years old. He helped me catch eels. His first trip on the ship and they put him on this! They gave him nothing for the arm. I tell you—stay away, it's a killer."

Porter looked again at the photo. It was one of the last of the roll, among the shots he had thought obstructed by workmen, but it had come out the clearest.

"Ichiko, what's so bad about this derrick?"

"What's so bad? It cripples you! It belongs in a museum! See how it happened with Kenji," Ichiko said, and picked up a piece of pencil and began drawing on the back of the photo.

But he didn't draw for long and he didn't explain for long, his animation suddenly expiring. "No, I don't know. I forget. I don't know anything anymore. There isn't any more." He opened the door and the hellish uproar returned. "Just stay away from it, I tell you!"

"Ichiko, a single second!" He held the man's arm and tried to close the door, but Ichiko resisted. "About the greasing again—just once! You said with the greasing—"

"I don't know about greasing. I don't know anything anymore. Leave me alone now. Let me go," the old man said, and put his muffs on.

Porter followed him down the stairs and through the tumultuous blackness to the slit of sky in the wall.

"Ichiko, I'm sorry!" he shouted. But Ichiko couldn't hear him anymore; and at the hangar door, when Porter held his hand out, he didn't seem aware of that either, for he put the safety bar on and turned away.

It was still early, not yet eleven, when he got out of the train in Tokyo. He crossed the station forecourt and made for the side door of the Lucky Strike. No one inside, and he entered quickly. But the indicator showed the elevator descending, so he took the stairs, and let himself into room 303 with a sigh.

All as he had left it, his business suit on the bed, his wig in the wardrobe. From the wardrobe he took the bottle of rye and poured himself one, and drank it. Then he poured another, and sat and looked at the photograph and at the penciled markings on the back.

Yoshi wanted him to return tonight. He had promised to call when he got back from Yokohama. Well, he would call; but he wasn't going back tonight. Tonight he had to think. It suddenly struck him that this was the fourth of the four nights he had booked at the Lucky Strike. A figure produced at random, but the right one. This was somehow an omen.

He drank his whisky and called the house. Yoshi answered and he told him what he had to tell him. Then he hung up. It was a few minutes to midnight.

At just this moment, as it happened, the *Suzaku Maru,* under floodlights, was slipping out of the dry dock at Nagasaki.

17

For the first two days of September the *Suzaku Maru* steamed steadily through the Sea of Japan at her customary rate of nine knots. She had left behind the southern island of Kyushu and was hugging the mainland coast of Honshu. The weather was very fine and the bosun took advantage of it to turn the hands to painting ship. The hurried departure had left no time for this in harbor, and he knew her leprous appearance would produce rough treatment from the dockers at Niigata. She was in poor enough shape already.

Eight hours before Niigata the captain radioed his expected time of arrival, 1600 hours, and asked for his berth.

Would he require bunkering facilities?

No, he wouldn't; he would be refueling at Otaru.

He was given the berth and went off watch. He had stood the night watch himself for he intended to sleep the rest of the day. He knew he would be up all night: The loading at Niigata was the main one of the trip and he meant to keep an eye on it.

Also his stomach was out of order. There had been much nervous excitement before he had got out of Nagasaki, and several backhanders to various officials. He knew the ship was not in the pink of condition, but there was ample time ahead to rectify what was wrong and work in both ship and crew before they reached the Arctic.

He had taken breakfast on the bridge. Now he went below to the officers' head, the small convenience he shared with the mate, and eased himself before going through to his cabin. He looked over the loading plan before turning in, and also initialed the note left for him by the mate authorizing a six-hour shore leave for the off-duty watch.

At 1600 hours, exactly to timetable, the ship nosed into harbor, and an hour later, as unloading of wool commenced, the four off-duty men, in their best rig, trooped down the gangway and set off jovially for Taki's place. This was the first of a round of places, just outside the dock gates, and it was usual to sink a glass in each before finally tumbling into Yasu's. Yasu's was the ultimate place, an enormous cellar, the liveliest and most popular of all among the seamen. Madame Yasu was herself enormous, the widow of a sumo wrestler. In his retirement her late husband had given exhibitions to the clientele, and the establishment was still known for its entertainment. At Yasu's you could eat, drink, sing along, or accompany certain of the girls upstairs, where they served as efficiently as at table; there was always a steady turnover of talent at Yasu's.

By seven-thirty the jovial four had arrived there. The place wasn't yet crowded and a table was promptly found for them. It was found for them by the very latest talent, and they took an immediate interest in her. For one thing, she was a pert and pretty little thing, and for another she had taken an immediate interest in them, eagerly hurrying forward as they stood grinning and swaying on the entrance balcony. She efficiently took them in tow, shepherded them down the steps, and got them seated.

Madame Yasu watched the young woman's work with approval. She liked enthusiasm in a girl, and this one was very enthusiastic. Following house etiquette, she first of all gave her own name, which was Toyo, and then invited theirs as she whipped round the menus. And she was coquettish. She avoided the groping hands but still managed a playful pat for each of them as she took their drink orders. But in serving the drinks, as Madame Yasu noted with a frown, she was less than perfect, for in announcing the names and setting down the glasses she managed to upset one, leaving a disconsolate sailor without. She rectified the accident quickly enough, and gave him an extra big one, together with a contrite little peck on the cheek while he drank it, so everything passed well enough. All the girl needed was more experience.

From the off-duty four there were no complaints. Toyo was a little beauty—not, unfortunately, available for duties upstairs but very willing in all other departments. The place was famous for its seafood, and she swiftly served up helpings of sashimi, all fresh, raw and glistening, with seaweed and noodles, and rice amply drenched in soy sauce; together with several more drinks, not one of which the bright little girl spilled again.

By a quarter to eleven, in good heart and voice, the off-duty men were staggering back inside the dock gates and wending their way to the *Suzaku Maru*. She was bathed in floodlight and loading was in full progress. On the bridge the captain watched the containers swing aboard. On the deck the bosun watched his paintwork.

By ten o'clock next morning she was at sea again and settling to her stately nine knots. Not too much damage had been done to the deck works, so the bosun put the men over the side. His best chance of getting an Arctic sea coat on her lay between here and Otaru, two days away. It couldn't all be done in the time, but beyond Otaru the weather would worsen, so he kept them at it for long hours, ignoring all grumbles; except, in the late afternoon, from one of the hands who had to be pulled up in his cradle on the grounds of feeling dizzy and unwell.

The bosun looked at him as he came up. "Dizzy and unwell? Of course you're dizzy and unwell, you prick. You got pissed last night."

"I got pissed last night," the man allowed, "but it isn't that. I'm not right, bosun."

"What's up with you?"

"I'm just not right."

He wasn't right. And he didn't look right. He looked green. His teeth were chattering. The bosun told him to turn in for a spell. But over supper, with the engineer, the bosun was again called to the man. He had fallen out of his bunk and was shaking so much it was a job to hold him back in it.

The bosun went to see the mate.

"Who is he?" the mate asked.

"Ushiba. Seaman first class. He was ashore last night."

"What did he eat there?"

"Fish. Shellfish."

"Ah. Food poisoning."

"All the others ate the same."

"Yes, it's chancy, seafood. Give him castor oil."

The effect of the castor oil was to throw the man into convulsions, and at ten o'clock the captain was sent for. By then Ushiba was vomiting black, and his color had deepened. He was still shaking violently and in a high fever. The heat could be felt radiating off him from a distance.

The captain returned to his cabin and reached for his *Mariner's Medical Dictionary*. He went slowly down the list of fevers until he found the matching symptoms. At these his eyes bolted. But he read doggedly on through the rest of the fevers before returning to the fateful one. Then he reached for the voicepipe and asked the mate to step below.

"Where's this fellow been to?" he asked.

The mate failed to understand the question until he, too, read the symptoms. Then he got out the crew records. Ushiba had last been in Java waters—East Timor. Two other members of the *Suzaku Maru*'s crew had been there with him. All three of them had been drunk and disorderly, and Ushiba had fallen into the harbor. The ship's captain had paid a hefty fine for them all before being allowed to leave port the same night, July 28.

The mate looked at the calendar. It was now September 4, and he counted the days from July 28. He made it thirty-eight. Then he looked at the *Mariner's Medical Dictionary* again. Under "Yellow Fever (Jav) (rare)" the captain's finger still held the place: "Incubation period—14 to 42 days; highly infectious." At thirty-eight days the sick man was within the incubation period.

By midnight, Ushiba was locked up in the after head. This tiny toilet and shower, shared by the bosun and the engineer, had the advantage of being over the engines, so not much noise could be heard from it. None at all was now coming from Ushiba. He had been injected with a strong sedative. The mate and the bosun had waited for the crew to go to sleep before strapping him to a stretcher and carrying him through the fore ends.

There was not enough room for Ushiba to lie flat in the head, so the stretcher had been wedged at an angle, with his feet under the shower and his head over the toilet hole in the floor.

An anxious conference had taken place between the captain and the mate. Nothing seemed wrong with the other two men who had been to Java, but only Ushiba had actually fallen in the harbor. Obviously, he had to be put ashore in Otaru. But just as obviously, the ship must not come under suspicion there; the shortest delay could abort the entire voyage.

At a further meeting, joined by the bosun and the engineer, some other matters were agreed. The latter men would now of course have the use of the officers' head. There was no need to alarm the crew over a case of food poisoning. For Ushiba's comfort, and theirs, he had been removed to the convenience of his own head. If still unwell he could go ashore for medical treatment in Otaru.

94

For the same reason, there was no need to alert Otaru yet. After refueling had been completed, and if he was still indisposed, Ushiba could be put ashore just before sailing. Meanwhile it would be a good idea to have his bunk disinfected. The bosun should attend to this himself, preferably at a time when the crew would all be above deck painting. It would also be a good idea to have a replacement standing by in Otaru in the event that Ushiba did elect to go ashore there.

These matters took time to resolve, and it was the early hours before the captain at last climbed into his bunk. He took his *Mariner's Medical Dictionary* with him. There were details there that worried him and he wanted to read them again.

The disease was viral, he saw; "water-borne v." And unlike the constipation of normal yellow fever, the variant was "commonly accompanied by diarrhea, excessive perspn., dehydratn., & blood in vomit (black v.). Dvlpmnts: jaundice, convulsns." Yes, Ushiba had all those. "Patient shd be restrained, washed frequently, kept out of light. Treatment: saline solution, rice water, vitamins (inject. only); no solids. Duration of fever: 2 to 4 days, frequently fatal."

The captain got out of bed and looked in the medical chest. Vitamins, but no saline solution. Rice water was not a problem. And in the snugness of the after head, restraint was not one either. Nor were the requirements for washing and reduced light. There was a light switch there, and also a hose.

But the brief duration and frequent fatality of the disease worried him. Otaru still lay thirty-two hours away, and a further six would be spent in the port. Total thirty-eight hours. If Ushiba had been ill for twelve hours without knowing it—and the intensity of his symptoms suggested this—then his fever would have run fifty hours before they got out of Otaru. If he should prove one of the forty-eight-hour fatalities, he could be dead before they left port. In which case they wouldn't be leaving port. . . .

The captain stroked his chin. His present ETA at Otaru was 1000 hours. An increase of speed could get him there earlier. But this would give time for inquiries. It would be better to cut the time in port. Ideally he should cut it to two hours. That would allow him to leave at 1200. With Ushiba going ashore at, say, 1145. Still only forty-six hours into his fever. And in no position to give any details of it.

Yes, that was the best thing to do. He was not clear at the moment how to do it. But after a sleep his head would be clearer. He looked at the bulkhead clock as he switched the light off. Two A.M., September 5.

18

At two A.M. in Tokyo, Porter was also switching the light off. He had spent the last three hours alone on a final check of his notes. Since leaving the Lucky Strike he had slept every night at the Theosophical Society, the last two of them with Machiko; but this one he spent on his own. It was the last.

For most of the time he had been speaking Korean with the girl— the Pusan dialect of Korean, which was Sung Won Choo's. In this dialect he had repeated his legend, recited the parts of the derrick, and also the parts of the ship. She had used a pointer on the ship, and he had given all the alternative routes for getting from one place to another. Machiko was now satisfied with his accent and his knowledge of Sung Won Choo. And he was quite certain he knew the ship from one end to the other.

Their knowledge of the *Suzaku Maru*'s movements had become increasingly refined. Everything had gone as planned at Niigata, and they knew to the hour her timing in Otaru. She would dock there on the seventh, at 1000 hours, and leave six hours later: 1600. Apart from refueling, there was only a single cargo to load and the remainder of the wool to unload. He would present himself at the dock soon after 1500 and be away by 1600. There were no uncertainties anymore, and he didn't plan to study anymore.

He switched the light off and went to sleep.

Next morning, over a leisurely breakfast, Yoshi gave him a final briefing. There was no change in arrangements. The *Suzaku Maru* was keeping to her timetable, and Porter would keep to his. His kit was waiting in Otaru, his accommodation confirmed at a rooming house there, and his name and particulars lodged with the port office.

"So that's it," Yoshi said. "No problems?"

"No. No problems."

This leg, he had insisted, he would do by himself. He felt better by himself, and Yoshi had been forced to agree.

At 9:30 he said good-bye to Machiko. Then, with his single piece of luggage, an executive attaché case, he got into the car with Yoshi, and they took off to Haneda domestic airport. There Yoshi shook his hand and wished him luck, the car left, and he was on his own.

*   *   *

To Sapporo, the provincial capital of Hokkaido, it was six hundred miles, and the 11:30 plane landed him there just before one o'clock. He took a cab to the railway station and bought a ticket to Otaru. The port was only forty minutes away and he arrived there, his last planned destination in Japan, exactly on schedule, 2:55. An arrow pointed to the toilets, and he locked himself into one and changed his clothes.

Out of the executive case came the jeans, shirt, and rope-soled shoes kept back for this occasion, and also a folded canvas grip. Into the grip went his wig, and then every trace of the identity of James B. Peterson. He added the executive case itself, zipped up the grip, and went out to the left luggage office. There he deposited the grip, took a receipt, and in the station mailbox posted it off back to Tokyo in the prepared envelope he had brought with him. Somebody would be picking up the grip within forty-eight hours.

Now it was almost 3:30.

He had half an hour to wait.

He had a cup of coffee in the station cafeteria and kept an eye on the left luggage office. The two men there had been on duty since eight A.M. and were due for relief. At four the new shift would come on until midnight, when the office closed; they would have no knowledge of a man who had just deposited a grip. All this had been scouted out for him.

At four the new shift arrived, and five minutes later a Korean seaman presented a grubby receipt from his wallet. The attendant looked sourly at him, shuffled among the racks, and cursed as he hefted the heavy kit over the counter.

Porter shouldered the kit bag, lifted the bulging rope-bound case, and went out to the cab rank. In twenty minutes he was pulling up at the rooming house.

It was a shabby, run-down place, close by the docks. The proprietor was drowsing on a stool outside. He didn't bother getting up for the Korean seaman but confirmed that he was booked in and told him where to pick up his key in the lobby. Room 11, second floor.

Porter took his gear up and let himself into the decrepit room. Not a sound in the building. No one else seemed to be in it and he wondered if the phone worked. He had seen one, on the wall, in the passage below. He went down to find out.

"Phone? Help yourself," the proprietor said. "It takes tokens."

There was a push-button light in the dark passage. He read the number on his piece of paper, shoved a token in, and dialed the port office. The light went out twice before he had the right department, and he had to put another token in the phone. But they had his particulars and the man at the other end was irritable. They had been

97

given them that same morning, he said. Why inquire again? There was nothing new. No long-haul ship in. Maybe one would come, in a day or two. They had his number. He got them to repeat it, and found they had it wrong. He gave them the right one, and smiled grimly. Yoshi had told him just to wait. Keep to the plan and wait, he said. Well, it was on just such details—as with the derrick—that the best plan could come adrift. Check everything. He hung up and went back to his room. *Now* he could wait. Tomorrow; after three P.M.

A good sleep and a calm morning watch had cleared the captain's mind, and he now knew what to do. The load to be picked up at Otaru was a broken cargo of canned tuna—126 tons of it, salvage from a container ship, gone overboard and declared unfit for the Japanese market. The Russian Trade Mission had snapped up this bargain, for delivery in Murmansk. The crates had been reassembled on several hundred pallets, and were due to go in number one and number two holds.

This cargo, as a further reading of his orders confirmed, was "at captain's discretion." It was a late booking, and the Russians had squeezed a cheap rate. He decided he would exercise his discretion. A pity, but the fiddling job involved much crane work and would take hours; certainly three. Three hours gained. That left only an hour to dispose of. Not so bad. He would think of something.

He took what he needed from the medical chest, and went aft to inspect Ushiba. He unlocked the door of the head, switched on the light, and relocked behind him. The man's sweating face was going to and fro on the stretcher, and his eyes fluttered dazedly in the light. He was quite secure, however, firmly pinioned, couldn't hurt himself. It was hot in the tiny compartment and he was naked. The bosun had hosed him down a couple of times but the place still smelled very bad.

The captain held a handkerchief over his nose. "Ushiba, how do you feel, man?" he asked nasally above the rumble of the engines.

Ushiba's mouth opened and closed but only gurgling came out of it. He had been doing this for some hours. His lips had a white crust, probably from the rice water. It had stopped his vomiting, anyway. His color was the same.

"Ushiba, I'm going to give you another injection," the captain told him. "It's very good for you."

He tore open a new needle package and a vitamin ampule. Ushiba jerked a little as the plunger went home. The book had recommended buttocks but the captain was not anxious to pick about Ushiba's underparts; he chose a thigh.

"There we are." A little blood, not much. He stuck a dressing on it. "Keep your spirits up! Bosun will be seeing to you soon."

Bosun was at that minute seeing to Ushiba's mattress, over the stern rail. No seamen were working there. He had scrubbed out the bunk with antiseptic, and now peeled off his rubber gloves and sent them after the mattress, into the Sea of Japan.

Before turning in, which he did very late again, the captain discussed final plans with the mate.

Otaru was not a busy port and would not need much advance warning. They would need *some* warning, of course. For one thing, he wanted a fast turnaround, and for another they had to be told that he was not picking up the tuna. Since the cargo had been specially assembled, and was waiting for him, this could cause irritation in Otaru, and quite possibly requests for confirmation, from the freight forwarders or the ship's owners. This would not be a good idea.

A much better idea was to leave it to the last moment, a moment when Otaru would not be in a position to ask silly questions but would still have time to make the arrangements he wanted. The arrangements were only to dump his wool and take on oil. Two ship movements involved, it was true—for the refueling dock was not a cargo dock—but quite possible to do it within a turnaround of two hours. And also possible, since he was expected anyway, for them to arrange it at three hours' notice. This would mean radioing them at seven in the morning.

The mate agreed with the reasoning and the captain asked for a shake at 6:30, and at last got to his bunk. Two A.M. again.

But the anxious moments ahead robbed him of sleep, and his temper was not good when he spoke to the seven o'clock idiot at Otaru.

"*No* loading. Just *un*loading," he barked. "And oiling. I want to discharge, oil, and leave by 1200 hours. Have you got that?"

"Captain, you can't discharge and oil at the same time."

"I know that! I'll discharge *first*. I'll discharge and *then* oil. And there's one thing more. Are you there?"

"Yes."

"I want another deckhand."

"Yes."

"I want you to *get* another deckhand."

"Yes."

"Do you understand all that? I want to discharge, oil, and board another *deckhand*. Are you there?"

"Captain, I can't get you a deckhand at seven in the morning."

"I don't want one at seven in the morning. I want one when I get there!" the captain howled. "You've got my ETA. Have you got my ETA? Hello—Otaru? My ETA is 1000. Please confirm my ETA. Otaru, can you hear me?"

This taped conversation, greatly enjoyed by the next shift, was subsequently ordered to be kept under lock and key; but that was for a board of inquiry and some time later.

Meanwhile the *Suzaku Maru* plowed on, and at 0830 rounded the point and entered Ishikari Bay. Just a little later, peering through his glasses, the captain discerned the cranes of Otaru, and decided it was time to go below and have a look at Ushiba again. He invited the bosun to step below with him.

Ushiba, to the captain's eye, looked much the same. His head was going to and fro and he was gurgling. The bosun thought he was worse. He said he was no longer keeping down the rice water, and he hadn't slept. He had not been hosed much in the past few hours, but there was not much to hose. His strength was going, and without the rice water he probably needed more vitamins.

The captain made no comment, but he took a different view. It seemed to him (and he had it confirmed by the mate at the subsequent inquiry) that despite failing strength Ushiba was still too vocal. Better than a vitamin injection would be a sedative one. A sound sleep would do Ushiba more good than vitamins, particularly while being landed and stowed in an ambulance.

"It was my honest opinion," he said. And he acted on it as they entered harbor. But he was back up on the bridge as they tied up, which was at 1000 hours precisely.

A hammering on the door woke Porter at half past ten in the morning. The proprietor had insisted on his sharing a bottle of cheap *shochu* the night before and his head was thick.

"Phone for you—the port office," the man called hoarsely. He was cursing.

Porter scrambled down the stairs in his underpants. The phone was swinging in the passage.

"Sung Won Choo?"

"Yes."

"A ship needs a deckhand—long haul, through the Arctic, you interested?"

"I might be. When is she in?"

"She's *in*. Half an hour ago."

On time then. Bang on time. "What ship?" he said.

"*Suzaku Maru,* a tramp."

"A tramp. Well, I'll think about it."

"There's no time. If you want her, go right there—I'll let them know. She's sailing in ninety minutes."

Sailing in ninety minutes? He couldn't understand any of this but he went rapidly back upstairs. Give them less than an hour, was the plan. He'd barely *have* an hour. He took a shower, yelled for the proprietor to call a taxi, dressed, paid up, and departed with his breakfast in his hand.

For an extra 250 yen the driver took him onto the dock, inquired for the berth, and drove him right to it. The berth was vacant, and much confusion was going on in the wake of the ship's apparently rapid departure. In the confusion it took time to discover where she was now. She was now evidently at an oiling wharf. But for another 250 yen, the driver said, he would take him there, too.

The oiling wharf was also in a state of confusion. Hoses throbbed as fuel was pumped into the *Suzaku Maru.* Everywhere hands were busy clearing up tufts of wool scattered from bales broken open in the hurried discharge. In the wheelhouse the captain anxiously watched. Almost 11:30 and no new hand had shown up yet. On the dockside he could see the ambulance, its doors open. He could just make out the ambulance men themselves, on the deck. Ushiba was on a stretcher there, in a patch of shade. He had been inserted into a pair of pajamas and was now quite peaceful, eyes closed, a clean sheet tucked up under his chin. The ambulance men seemed unsatisfied about something. The captain drummed his fingers and looked at his watch.

On the deck the ambulance men were talking to the bosun.

"He's a funny color for food poisoning," one of them said.

"Isn't he? It's his liver. Masked by the booze, you see," the bosun explained. "Came back aboard pissed out of his mind and in the morning he was like this—shellfish."

"They don't usually go to sleep, though."

"No, you're right. He couldn't. Throwing himself about. Captain thought the best thing was, give him a sedative."

"Well, that wasn't the best thing. Hard to say *what's* up with him now. Still, they'll find out in the hospital."

"Sure," the bosun said, and watched them lift the stretcher. He was still watching, from the rail, when the taxi drew up below. A Korean got out. Pigtail. Sloppy kitbag and case. Always trouble, Koreans. Late, lazy, lippy. This one was going to need gingering up.

"Hoy! You!" he yelled, as the man had the nerve to stop and look at the patient, actually start chatting with the ambulance men. "Get up here!"

The man came up the gangplank.

"You the new hand? Sung?"

"Yes."

"You're late. Dump your kit here and go up and see the mate, on the bridge. Look lively, now."

The new hand went up to the bridge and saw the mate, who rapidly checked him out. Papers in order; had served with the line; knew the ships. He took him to the captain.

The captain had watched these proceedings with relief. The deck crew was back up to the needed twelve hands. He briefly catechized the new hand and got him to make his signature. A series of thumps had signaled the disconnection of the hoses. He signed for the oil, told the mate to cast off, heard the bawled orders to let go fore and aft, and took the ship out himself.

As the wharf slid away he reflected that in the confusion the ambulance men had not asked for Ushiba's belongings, not even his papers. Without his papers it was not possible to say where he had been. Well, it wouldn't interest them at the hospital where the man had been. They'd have their own procedures for finding out what was wrong with him.

In due course.

His stuff could be sent back from Murmansk; perhaps Sweden; even Rotterdam. The owners would have to be informed, of course. He would radio them after putting on a bit of seaway. Quite a bit of seaway. He decided to put it on fast.

"1315 hours. Cleared Ishikari Bay," reported the log. "Speed 12 knots. Heading 135. North." Later he would have to go northeast. Much later still, with the Bering Strait behind him and Cape Dezhnev to be rounded, another correction would be needed. North by northwest.

19

Five days and thirteen hundred miles out of Otaru, the bosun decided it was time to ginger up the new hand.

No definite signs of laziness had come out of him yet, and he hadn't been caught late for watchkeeping. But he was lippy. He seemed to turn things over in his mind before carrying out an order. He had commented on the new mattress in his bunk, had asked questions about Ushiba. And he showed too much interest in the ship's movements. All out of order for a new deckhand, and a Korean deckhand at that.

The bosun went briskly forward. He was a giant of a man, very thick in the neck and built like a tank. Despite his bulk, long years at sea had kept him nimble on his feet. He rattled down the steps now, and looked briefly into the fore ends.

"Sung! Topside now. Look alive!"

He said it once only, and was waiting in the lee of a container, out of the wind, as the man came up on deck, his eyes still puffy from sleep.

"Now then, Sung. Ever greased a Takanawa?"

"Not when I'm off watch," Sung said.

The bosun's lip tightened. "You're on again at night," he said, "when it's dark. I want to see you do it now. We'll be frosting up soon."

So they would. Sakhalin and the Kuriles were well behind them. The Kamchatka Peninsula had been passing for some hours on the port side.

"Tomorrow afternoon," Sung suggested, "I will be on again. Then it will be light."

"And maybe iced up. Get your gear."

The man gave his momentary stare, then shrugged and went below. But he was soon back, with his woolen hat and donkey jacket; also gauntlets, grease gun, and chipper from the locker.

He went through the drill properly enough, first switching on the eleven-ton derrick's electric motor. And standing back smartly as the dangerous thing kicked and the big arms shuddered around.

"All right. Now manual," the bosun said.

"Manual needs two men."

"Here I am," the bosun said, and winked. They could all work by the book. "Set her up for greasing."

He watched as the man unhoused the equipment, and located and fitted it: brake lever and distance piece, reduction gear and turning assembly, all properly fitted. He gave him little help. Whatever the book said, the job could easily be done by one man in calm seas. Two men were needed only with pitching and slippery decks—one to revolve the cogs in turn and clamp home the bar brake, the other to get in with the grease gun. That was when the accidents occurred to arms and legs, and invariably to the grease man.

No grease was needed yet, and both of them knew it. No seas had been shipped and the dockyard grease was still thick. But the man did the job without comment, then took down the equipment, rehoused it, and stood and looked at him, pigtail flapping in the wind. "Any more?" he said.

The bosun's big hands itched at the Korean's mulish stare.

"Not now. When we get into some weather will be time. You can get below now."

The man turned and went without a word, and the bosun's hands itched again. With surly crewmen he was used to ruling with his fists. Break them quickly; it was always best, and saved time in the end. With this one he knew the time would have to come soon.

Porter, returning to the fore ends, knew it, too. He saw the other men watching him from their card game.

"Bosun been riding you?"

"Tried to get me greasing a derrick."

"Why, the bastard—they don't need greasing yet."

"I know. Just got me at it."

"Watch yourself with Bosun. Show him respect. That's all he wants."

"Sure." He turned back into his bunk. There were no problems with the crew. He had soon established a reputation as a moody fellow, best left alone. Because of the two other Koreans aboard he had also established a prepared speech impediment. And because of his size nobody had mocked him for it. But his accent had passed with the Koreans anyway, and he was on reasonable terms with them all. He had dropped in bits of his background; had shown his photos, had looked at theirs. No; no problems with the crew.

But the bosun was something else.

The man didn't like him. Obeying orders wouldn't help. He would pile on the orders, give him every lousy job on the ship, until resentment showed, some spark of rebellion. Then Bosun would use his fists, beat him into submission. And get him greasing the derrick. He remembered what Ichiko had told him about the derrick. Greasing the derrick was the *most* dangerous job. The bar brake was hard to handle, couldn't be left for a second; and on icy decks, the operator slithering, it could slip—with the grease man in among the cogs. Someone else would have to grease, some more experienced hand. He wouldn't. So Bosun's first job would be to make him. Well, it had to be faced sooner or later, and sooner was better than later.

He turned over and drifted off to sleep. The dumb insolence had been designed to bring it sooner. Soon enough now the ice would come.

Two days later, five hundred miles north, the ice came.

Despite her economical rate, the ship had now chugged almost three thousand miles from warm Nagasaki into the approaching Arctic winter. From the Bering Strait, still some days off, a howling blast of wind and sleet had them pitching in heavy seas. Since early in the forenoon the hands had been securing the cargo, first down in the holds, then on deck, sliding about as they checked the container locks and cables.

They were warming themselves over mugs of coffee when the bulky figure peered down the companionway.

"Sung! Matsuda! On top now. Smartly."

The two men bundled up again and went on top. The bosun was waiting for them, hanging on by the gangway. "Derricks icing—get your gear. And start with number three. You'll need harness, she's pitching." He was already clutching a safety harness himself, and moved away at once.

Cursing, Matsuda led the way to the lockers. "The bastard derricks can be steamed off! Who needs them now?" He had fallen foul of the bosun the day before. He was a little wizened fellow with a wall eye. Right away Sung knew he was not having him on brake. They got the gear and the harnesses and staggered slowly through the uproar of wind to the bosun. He had secured himself to a bollard amidships; number three derrick was close by.

"Okay, hook up!" The bosun had to shout above the wind. "Matsuda, you're on brake!"

"Bosun," Sung said, "I haven't greased in these conditions."

"Good. Now you can learn."

"I'll be better on brake. I'm stronger than Matsuda."

"Ah, strong man! No—you grease, strong man."

Sung shook his head.

"It's an order," the bosun told him cheerfully.

Sung leaned over. "Fuck the order!" he said into the bosun's ear. "And fuck you."

The bosun looked pleasurably at him, and then around, scenting the freezing wind. The lights were on in the wheelhouse and the wipers were going there. Behind the wipers he could see the mate looking down, and beyond him the dim shape of the wheelman.

"Matsuda, go below for a while; I'll call you," the bosun said, and began unhooking himself. "Step aft, Sung."

Sung stepped aft, his heart beginning to thump. Aft, behind the wheelhouse, was where scores were settled, and he prepared himself to move fast. But they were still below the wheelhouse, and he was unprepared, as his head was jerked sharply back. The bosun had come swiftly on him, yanking his pigtail with one hand and smashing the other into his face. He went over backward, his feet sliding, but was not allowed to hit deck. His pigtail was still held, and his face still being smashed, two, three, four times. Then, still shocked, his feet still scrabbling the icy deck, he was being swung round and dragged by the pigtail farther aft, before the bosun let go and fell on him.

The bull of a man landed with his knees, knocking the breath out of Sung's body, the attack so sudden and so ferocious he was utterly stunned. He was still stunned as the bosun began pounding his head on the deck. His only thought was to get out from under, but with the bosun leaning his full weight forward he couldn't move. He brought his hands up and went for the man's eyes to get him to lean back, but the bosun evaded them easily and butted him for good measure. He felt the stunning blow on his nose, and knew his face was already running with blood, and through the shocked pain felt sudden raging anger as the bosun hawked and spat in his face. He had not been angry before. The fight had been coming, and he knew and accepted it. But now he was angry.

He clutched at the butting head as it came down again, and hugged it fiercely, using every atom of strength to draw it closer and closer until the bosun, straining, twisted his head to try and release it, and brought an ear within range, and Sung sank his teeth in it. He hung on tight and savaged the ear, shaking it from side to side, and heard the bosun swear; the man leaned sideways to ease the ear, and with the weight shifting on him, Sung came out from under.

He slithered fast on the icy deck and was on his knees, in a position now to go on top. But that was not his idea. The man had caught him—okay, he had relied on a sudden attack, and on his weight and toughness. What the bosun had to learn was that with all his weight, with all his toughness, on level terms, or any other terms, he could never win. Never! That he was simply entitling himself to a hard time, and that this time would come to him not by any fluke or momentary disadvantage, but always, every time, whenever he chose to have it.

Sung had to explain this to the bosun, but his head felt scalped from the dragging and was splitting from the battering, so he thought he had better disable the man first. He let him stumble to his feet and begin his rush, and even backed and got his hands up to defend himself and swung one back to strike, and when the bosun swung himself, he nimbly sidestepped and used his greater agility to kick the bosun in the crotch. He kicked him as hard as he could, and when the man grunted and held himself, he chopped him in the neck and kicked his feet away, sending him crashing to the deck again. Then he jumped on him with both boots. Then he knelt beside the bosun.

"Bosun," he said humbly. "Leave me alone. I'm a hard man. I fought many fights, very dirty, and I always win. Pick on me, and I'll cripple you for life. You'll never work again—I swear it. And I don't want that. I've got my own problems. They say I'm maybe crazy. Okay, I've done crazy things and I've done time, it's there in my papers. But it's only when people pick on me. I can't take that, Bosun. You understand me?"

The bosun didn't say if he understood him. He was crooning and gurgling in his throat as he held himself, his head down. This seemed to enrage Sung, who took both of the bosun's ears and shook them savagely, bringing the bull head up and staring into its eyes. "You no talk to me? Only spit in my face? Ah, you better fucking answer, man! I tell you, you better or I tear your fucking head off. You don't treat me like shit! Understand? Understand me?"

The bosun's head was shuttling so violently that his eyes were squinting. His mouth was still contracted in its painful crooning circle, but through it he grunted his understanding.

"Well, that's good. I've got things to say to you, Bosun. Look, give me orders, make me work. It's okay. I'll do what I should. But something I don't want to do, or I can't do, you figure it out, and I don't do that thing. Okay? Because you try to make me, I cripple you. I don't care, see. Just don't make me mad!"

The bosun was recovering slowly, and he shuffled himself into a sitting position. "Sung, you're a crazy bastard," he said, "and you don't know what you're doing. I'll break you."

"How you do that, Bosun?" He wasn't sure if he was coming on too strong with the broken Japanese, and his impediment had slipped. But the general craziness was working, he could see. "You want to put me in irons, you want to lock me up? And explain why. Go to the captain, say, 'Captain, this man too tough for me.' Or get help from the crew. What you need with that, Bosun? Look—you beat me up, you mark my face, anyone can see. I didn't mark *your* face. What I say? 'Hey, I beat up the bosun?' Everyone laugh at me. I no say that. I no say anything. I just want you off my back."

These arguments, he could see, were getting through to the bosun, who was slowly pulling himself together.

"Sung," he said, "you're going to be sorry for this. It's a long voyage, and you're going around the world. And you know what you'll get out of it? You'll get fuck-all. Not a yen. I'll have every bit of pay docked. I'll get you for one thing after another. See how you'll like it, big boy.''

Sung stared at him and his eyes glowed. "You think about that, Bosun. You think again, eh? You do that to me, I come wherever you are. I find you. I'm crazy? Okay, I put your eyes out. I break you up. I break your bones, your knees, your hands. You no step on a ship again. Say like now: I want to stamp on your balls, I do it. You walk bad for days. I don't do that. But I give you something, so you remember, eh? Give me your hand, bosun.''

The bosun wouldn't give him his hand so he jumped hard on the bosun's thighs and as the man jerked in agony chopped his bull neck so that the head crashed back again on the deck.

"Sit up, bosun. Give me a hand. Right hand.''

The bosun gave him his hand, and he carefully picked the little finger, and showed it to the bosun, and broke it. And then with the man gasping in agony he helped him to his feet.

"Don't ride me, bosun," he said simply. "I no hurt you anymore. See what a face you gave me. I go below and show that face and everybody see. You beat me up—all right? Just rest your hand and remember. You do something to me I don't like, I come and find you. Wherever you are, I come and find you!''

20

On the nineteenth of September the *Suzaku Maru* negotiated the Bering Strait, rounded Cape Dezhnev, and radioed her arrival in Russian waters. The captain had his notification acknowledged, and set himself to wait in patience.

He regretted the loss of the tuna cargo for Murmansk and was hopeful that something might turn up at Green Cape. He thought it very likely. From radio traffic he knew that fish in the area had been plentiful. His refrigeration capacity was limited, but if the stuff was boxed and ready-palleted he would lift it.

In the matter of instructions the Russians were not so much tardy as crafty. They waited till the last moment to catch you. They knew it would cost him nothing, except a few hours' loading, to carry the stuff along to Murmansk. On the other hand, *he* knew that nothing else was going his way. All the Russian vessels were now going the other way, to the ice-free ports of the Pacific; his, certainly, was the last foreign ship of the season. He could wait.

His charts showed him at roughly three and a half days' steaming from the mouth of the Kolyma River, which was where he suspected they would have the stuff sitting in barges. Foreign vessels were seldom allowed upriver to Green Cape itself; and crewmen were not allowed ashore at all. God alone knew what the Russians feared: that foreigners might seduce their citizens, tempt them to smuggle the gold and diamonds of the area. No. They were simply *Russian:* suspicious by nature, crafty.

That he had no cargo for Green Cape did not at all displease him. No trudging there and back up the Kolyma. He had been keeping close watch on the weather reports, and they were not good. The storms of the past few days had abated, but in the frigid calm the icepack was spreading rapidly from the north. He wanted to be away and out of it, Murmansk well behind him, before the whole sea froze. They would know this in Green Cape. They wouldn't delay long. They'd call him.

But by the next day, when he was again on watch, they still hadn't called, and the captain hummed to himself. Cat and mouse. *He* was evidently supposed to call. Any fish you want carried? Nice price. Well, he wouldn't. Let *them* call. It was growing colder and the wheelhouse windows were on permanent defrost. The new crewman, Sung, brought him up a flask.

"What's this?" he asked.

"Hot soup, Captain."

"M'hm." He hadn't asked for it but the man was showing himself willing, a welcome change from his surliness in the first few days. His face was badly marked, one eye black, the nose swollen, mouth cut about and puffy. The bosun had evidently taken him in hand. The captain had noticed the bosun sporting a bandaged finger himself and had tactfully refrained from inquiry; a too-enthusiastic collision with the Korean's face, he saw. The bosun had to keep order his own way, and a heavy hand was sometimes needed with the scum they had aboard. The captain kept himself above it, preferring to regard them as criminal children—simpleminded ones, very often. This one was now gaping all about him, the view here much better than from deck.

"First time north?" the captain asked him gruffly.

"First time, Captain, first. Is it Siberia?"

"Yes. Chukotka, this region."

"Near Murmansk?"

"Three thousand miles near."

He saw the fellow gaping again, but realized after a moment that he was doing it over his shoulder. "Look, Captain, look! They've got airplanes!"

The captain turned and saw a small one rising above the ice strip at Cape Schmidta, now going astern on his port beam. He studied it through his glasses for a moment and as he turned away noticed with astonishment that the Korean was bending over the chart table; that he actually had the impertinence to be tracing with his finger the penciled positions of their track. The captain had not long before added the last point reached: "Cape Schmidta: 1648 hours."

"All right. That's enough," he said curtly, and watched the man go. Simpleminded idiot! He watched the plane a little longer, and commenced humming to himself again. From Cape Schmidta it was under 420 miles to the Kolyma. They had less than forty-eight hours to call him now.

Sung, going below, knew that he himself had less than four hours now. He didn't know how much less. As well as Cape Schmidta he had seen Wrangel Island on the chart, directly north. When the cape and the island were in position, he had been told, there were 420 nautical miles to go to his destination. The time of arrival depended on their speed.

He sat down again to the letter he had been writing. He had left it open on the fore ends table, and saw from the grinning faces around that one of the Koreans must have read it out to them. The salutations and loving sentiments were exceedingly high-flown and imaginative. So was the account of his heroism in recent icy storms. He hadn't mentioned being beaten up by the bosun. Now the storms were over and they were sailing seas no one else dared sail and going fast as the wind. He paused a little over the last words.

"How fast we going?" he said.

The man opposite hid his smile and listened for a moment to the engines. "The normal. Nine knots," he said.

"Only nine?" Sung said, disappointed, and wrote on.

Nine knots into 420 nautical miles came to just under forty-seven. Forty-seven hours to go. Or rather forty-seven hours from the last marked timing, which was 1648. It was now after 1730. He had less than *three* hours. He had less than two and a half. It would have to be at 2000, eight o'clock.

* * *

At eight o'clock he went to the head and locked himself in. He un-zipped his jeans and produced his penknife. The small bulge was in the waist of his long johns and he carefully unpicked the stitches. The capsule was wrapped in a tiny polyethylene envelope and he removed the envelope. To ensure complete and rapid ingestion he had been told to bite it, in which case it would take twenty hours to work, as it had with Ushiba. Ushiba's dose had been much bigger, to secure a spectacular and unmistakable result. He wouldn't be as ill as Ushiba, but he would be very ill indeed.

He put the capsule in his mouth and bit it. There was the faintest taste, vaguely clinical, and then it was gone. Twenty hours to wait; until 1600 tomorrow.

He didn't relish the hours ahead. In particular he didn't relish being in the hands of the bosun.

Between 1600 and 2000 the watches were split into two-hour shifts, the first and second dog watches. Next day the captain took the second dog and came on at 1800, very fractious.

The ship was off Cape Shelagskiy and swinging wide, to stay well clear of Chaunskaya Bay. Some kind of military base was in there, at Pevek, and the Russians were suspicious—as ever—of anyone coming near it.

The mate handed over the ship and went below, and the captain stood at the chart table, humming. Still nothing from Green Cape. What the devil was up with them? He was barely twenty-two hours away. Either they *had* no fish, or they were playing games with him. Well, to hell with them! They could keep the fish. Or send it by air. Yes, very good, let them try that. *He* wouldn't call, anyway.

He brought the ship's head around after half an hour and kept dis-tance with Ayon Island, steadying his course. No more compass changes now till after the Kolyma. He would sail right past. He wouldn't stop now if they begged him.

The mate came hurriedly into the wheelhouse. "Captain," he said softly, and motioned him away from the helmsman, "there's some trouble below."

"What is it?"

"The new hand. Sung. He's in a bad way."

"The bosun been at him again?"

"No, no. He has a fever. He's vomiting badly. In Ushiba's bunk."

The two men stared at each other, and the mate slowly nodded. "I think you'd better take a look at him," he said.

The captain went below. He found Sung being held by two men as he hung out of his bunk and vomited into a bucket.

"Captain, sir!" The bosun anxiously drew him aside and explained.

It seemed that Sung had tried to turn out for his watch, the first dog, but had kept falling over. The bosun, recalling that the man had somehow banged his head on the deck a few days ago, had thought this might be a delayed reaction and had told him to take a spell off. But then he had started being sick. "And shaking. And turning green," the bosun said, peering into the captain's eyes.

"How long has it been going on?"

"Over two hours. First dog! At first I thought nothing of it. There didn't seem any need to—"

"Was it like this with—with—"

"The same. Teeth rattling."

The captain thought for a moment.

"You destroyed the mattress?"

"Mattress, cover, blanket, everything. All fresh, from the stores."

"And scrubbed out the bunk?"

"With my own hands. Antiseptic. A whole bucket of it."

"Captain, Captain!"

He was being called, hysterically. Sung was calling him.

"All right, what is it? I'm here." The captain went and leaned over the bunk. He saw with dismay the complexion, the glassy rolling eyes, the chattering jaw. The man was gesturing wildly. "Send them away, Captain! Only you! Only talk you. No one else—send them away!"

"All right," the captain said, and told the men to step back.

"And bosun! No bosun. Only you, Captain!"

"Very good. Leave us, Bosun. What is it?" the captain said. The man had gripped his arm, and with his other shaking hand was pointing to his face. His teeth were chattering so much, the captain had to bend closer. "Bosun marked me, Captain. See my face. No leave me with Bosun!"

"All right."

"No with bosun—like Ushiba in head! No like that, Captain. No with bosun. He mark me again—mark me bad!"

"All right. I'll see to it," the captain said, chilled by the man's extensive knowledge of Ushiba; evidently fore ends' tattle.

"Promise, Captain! Promise you no leave me!"

"I promise. I'll see to you myself. Rest quietly now. I have to look into some matters."

Which he certainly did. He went straight to his cabin and reached for the *Mariner's Medical Dictionary*. The ominous symptoms told him nothing new, but he read through them all again most hungrily. The man would be having convulsions soon, and diarrhea. He couldn't be left where he was. It was the bunk. Antiseptic was no use against a virus. It might even have activated the virus. "Water-borne v...." Whatever had activated it, Sung had now got it. It was the bunk; Ushiba's bunk. But with Ushiba there had been the convenient haven of Otaru to dump him in. Where in this godforsaken waste of the Arctic was he to dump Sung?

For a moment the golden idea of dumping Sung *in* the Arctic glowed in his mind, but died immediately. Fore ends' tattle . . . Somewhere in this waste there would be a medical station. He fumbled through his "Notices to Mariners" for the area. Longitude 170.

"Pevek: sick bay facilities." Well, not there—a military base. He continued west through the consecutive sheets, longitudes 169 to 163, and found nothing—nothing at all to find in this desolate area—and came on 162, and the ultimate irony.

"Tchersky: hosp. & isolation wing (call Green Cape)."

Call Green Cape! Which he had vowed not to call. Which he now would *have* to call. He looked at his watch—seven o'clock—and decided there was no point in calling them now. They would have closed down for the night. He was still twenty-one hours away. Morning would be time enough; before noon, anyway. That would still give *them* time to call him. And give him time to work a few things out.

21

At 2100 Sung was removed to the after head, in convulsions but not yet diarrheic. He became diarrheic shortly after, and the captain hosed him down himself. The mate spelled him on the bridge during the night, which was a restless one, for he looked in on Sung every hour. The man looked bad. His head threshed on the stretcher, his teeth rattled, and he gurgled continuously. Also his deepening pigment seemed to show up the bruises more, which worried the captain. The bosun had volunteered twice to take charge, but the captain kept the key himself.

At eleven in the morning, still sleepless, he called Green Cape and received a cheery response.

"*Suzaku Maru, Suzaku Maru,* hello! Good to hear you. Maybe we have something for you."

The captain smiled wryly. Playing games after all. For certain they had something for him. And now they'd got him. His Russian was rudimentary but serviceable.

"Green Cape, is good to hear you. I have something for you, too."

"For us? What for us, Captain?"

"I have a sick man aboard. I need assistance."

"What's the sickness, Captain?"

"I think jaundice; I'm not sure."

"It's not a problem. What's your ETA?"

"My ETA is 1600, repeat 1600."

"ETA 1600, good. Captain—you want a cargo?"

"What's the cargo?"

"Maybe fish. Boxed and palleted."

"Salt or frozen?"

"Maybe both. You want some?"

"How much is there?"

"Maybe not much. It depends."

Of course it did. It depended on the rate.

"Well, let's see," the captain said.

"For sure. We'll see! Okay, Captain."

"And my sick man?"

"We'll let you know."

They'd let him know. At the last minute they'd let him know. It was their way. They certainly wouldn't let him know before 1400.

At 1400 they let him know.

"*Suzaku Maru, Suzaku Maru!* Green Cape here."

"Hello, Green Cape. *Suzaku Maru.*"

"Captain, you are to stand off Ambarchik. A medical officer will board you there, okay?"

"Stand off Ambarchik, okay," the captain repeated. "Where off Ambarchik?"

"A boat will meet you at the point. You follow that boat, Captain. We made all the arrangements, okay?"

"Okay. Thank you, Green Cape."

He knew Ambarchik well enough. He hadn't made this passage for three or four years. Another one of the line's ships had been doing it, the one they'd broken up a few months back. Still, he remembered the place. It stood at the eastern mouth of the river. Several mouths led out of the big messy estuary, but he recalled that this was where they liked to keep the fish, waiting in barges. It was waiting for him there now, he didn't doubt it: they had "made the arrangements." . . .

He now had to make some himself. He went below and let himself into the after head.

By 1530, when a voice from the bridge reported they had the boat in sight, Sung was cleaned up and in the captain's cabin. Rice water had abated the diarrhea, but an arrangement involving towels and a rubber blanket was still necessary. The man was snugly wrapped in blankets and the stretcher was on the cabin floor, so the retaining straps were no longer required. He was lightly sedated, his head still moving restlessly, eyes open and glazed, some gurgling coming out of him. The captain had thought it unwise to put him out completely. In the case of Ushiba a fast exit from Japanese waters had been required. In this case the ship would be in Russian waters for days: time enough for them to stop him whenever they wanted. It was common sense to let them find out right away.

The boat led them around the point, and once they were in the estuary the captain changed places with the mate and took the ship in himself. He saw an old hand from Green Cape watching him through glasses in the boat, remembered him from years back, and returned his wave. And he nodded to himself as he saw where he had to pick up his buoy: half a mile offshore, near the first of the small islands. Four barges were strung together there, all laden. About a hundred tons, the captain estimated. The haggling would begin after they'd taken Sung off.

It was half an hour before the quarantine boat arrived, and he had the ladder out waiting. The medical officer, a bulky individual hugely wrapped in a dogskin coat and cap, came nimbly enough up the ladder, and the captain went down to meet him. To his surprise it was a woman and he led her down to his cabin, somewhat moody. He knew right away he had got a bad one here, haughty and officious, unlike the jovial rascals he knew from Green Cape. She looked down at Sung while divesting herself of her coat, irritably shaking off the captain's efforts to help her.

"How long has he been like this?"

The captain briefly outlined the duration and symptoms of Sung's illness, omitting all mention of Ushiba.

"Why is his face bruised?"

"Seamen fight." The captain shrugged.

She looked at him sharply, and bent to Sung.

"This is not jaundice," she said presently.

"I thought the yellow—"

"Jaundice is present, but this is not all. Have you kept specimens of his feces?"

The captain admitted that he hadn't, and by way of lightening the atmosphere remarked mildly that the process was continuous and that she might yet find some.

She looked sharply at him again.

"The man is very ill. I will need more details. Show me his quarters."

A purgatorial half hour began for the captain. The termagant examined not only Sung's bunk, now bare again, but every inch of the fore ends, the galley, and the head. Fortunately the captain was the only Russian-speaker and he saw to it that nothing compromising came out of the crew.

But he observed with gloom that the light was going. The haggling over the fish had still to be gone through, by which time it would be too dark to load. He would have to stay overnight.

"Very well," she said, back in the cabin. "I will take him to the isolation wing at Tchersky. I need his documents. Do you intend waiting for the results?"

"How long—the results?"

"Five days."

"No," the captain said.

"Then I will take his belongings, also. They will need treatment, in any case. What is your destination, Captain?"

"Murmansk."

"I'll contact them. Of course, if this is what I think, they won't let you in. You understand that?"

"Won't let me in?" the captain said.

"It's a highly infectious fever. You would be well advised to stay here until we can identify it."

"But the sea will freeze!"

"Then go on, if you want. I can't stop you. Or turn back."

"I have a ship full of cargo! I have to pick up more cargo here. *For* Murmansk."

"What cargo?"

"Fish. Tons of it, out there in the barges."

"That's quite impossible. I can't allow it. You have fever on this ship."

The captain felt himself unhinging. He couldn't pick up the fish. He couldn't stay here for five days; he'd never get out at the other end. He couldn't go back to Japan with a shipload of cargo for Murmansk. And they might not let him in to Murmansk.

"Well, decide for yourself, Captain. I have no power to prevent you, but I definitely prohibit the loading of any fish. Meanwhile, the first thing is to get this man off the ship."

KOLYMSKY REGION

EAST SIBERIAN SEA

● Ambarchik

Green Cape

● Tchersky

Tcherny Vodi

To Bilibino →

Little Ghost River

Kolyma River

● Novokolymsk

● Panarovka

To Provodnoye →

● Anyuysk

● Cave

| 0 | miles | 25 |
| 0 | kilometers | 40 |

And this was the first thing that happened. Sung was loaded into the quarantine boat and taken upriver to Tchersky. And the captain, after frantic cogitation, arrived at a decision, and took it, fast.

"1820. Ambarchik. Weighed & left. Speed 13 knots."
General direction, Murmansk.

22

Tchersky, four kilometers south of the river port of Green Cape, was the administrative capital for the Kolymsky district of northeast Siberia. Though small (population under 10,000) it had a sizable hospital, the only fully equipped one for an area the size of Holland and Denmark combined. The isolation wing was in use mainly during the brief mosquito-ridden summer, and it was empty when Porter was admitted on September 23.

The hospital's doctors were all specialists. General physicians, rare anywhere in the Russian Federation, were unknown in Siberia, and their function was supplied by a corps of *feldshers*—experienced paramedics. The senior ones, graded as medical officers, were each responsible for a particular area; and Medical Officer Komarova, who brought Porter to Tchersky, was responsible for the lower Kolyma including Ambarchik and the coastal strip.

At the hospital she registered her patient as a suspected case of yellow fever and he was assigned to Dr. P. M. Gavrilov, a young specialist from St. Petersburg. Dr. Gavrilov had not before encountered a case of yellow fever but was soon aware, from his observation of the symptoms, that this might be the rare Java variety. This excited him. Very little existed in the literature on this form and he instituted a series of careful tests, meticulously noting the results.

Porter knew nothing about any of this. As the only occupant of the wing he was left to be ill in peace. Drip-fed, bed-bathed, and sedated as necessary, he was aware of very little for the first two days. But waking from a sound sleep on the third he found a woman doctor examining him.

"Do you speak Russian?" she said.
Her face was vaguely familiar.
"Little Russian," he said. "Little."
"I have no Korean or Japanese."
"Little Russian."

"You are in hospital. I brought you. You understand?"

"Yes. Hospital," he said.

She looked him over for a while. A face mask was hanging loose around the neck of her white hospital coat. She felt his head, and he was aware that his pigtail was now up in a bun on top of it.

"How you feel?" she said, smiling suddenly.

It took him a moment to realize she had said it in English.

"Okay," he said, and closed his eyes at once.

He must have babbled. He had tried to train himself in advance not to do this. He wondered what he had babbled.

"You ill. Maybe you little better now." Again English.

He decided to keep his eyes shut and presently she went away. He thought about the English, but soon drifted off.

A male doctor came to see him. This man he didn't recollect at all. The man also spoke to him in English, quite fluently.

"I am Dr. Gavrilov. How do you feel now?"

"I don't know how I feel. What happen here?"

"You were brought in with a fever. This is Tchersky hospital. You don't remember anything?"

"Just—sick. How long I'm here?"

"Three days now. I think you have been ill maybe four days, perhaps a little more. We can talk of it later. Is it hard for you, speaking English?"

"When I speak English?"

"A few words, in delirium. I couldn't understand the Korean," Dr. Gavrilov said, smiling.

"Where my ship?"

"Don't worry about it. You're very weak. Rest now."

Next day he was off the drips and on light food, and the woman doctor came again.

"Good. You're much better," she told him in Russian.

"What fever I have, doctor?"

"We thought yellow fever, but it isn't. Some other kind of virus."

"I can go?"

"When you're stronger. You've been very ill."

"But they wait for me on ship!"

"The ship went."

"It went? All my things there!"

"No, they're here. We have them."

"Well—what happen to me?"

* * *

It was a good question, and it was to exercise the hospital authorities all that day and the next. The seaman was the first foreigner ever to be admitted as an inpatient to a hospital in the Kolymsky district. Normal patients, upon recovery, went home. This one's home was in Korea, some thousands of miles away. The Kolymsky district, which was anyway a restricted district, had no procedure for dealing with such a case. Presumably he could be flown to Vladivostok, or more likely Nakhodka, which had a shipping service to Japan. Nakhodka would then have the problem of getting him home. But even getting him to Nakhodka was a problem.

Tchersky could not deal directly with Nakhodka, which was in another autonomous region. The matter would have to go through Yakutsk, the capital of Yakutia, which was Tchersky's autonomous republic. Dealing with Yakutsk was a major headache at any time, but after a preliminary talk with the hospital's director the medical officer was given to understand that an even bigger one was looming. In whisking the seaman off his ship, she had omitted to get a guarantee for his upkeep and future transportation. The matter had never arisen before. But Polar Aviation would want payment for taking him to Yakutsk, and Aeroflot for taking him to Nakhodka. At Nakhodka, they would want to know who was picking up the bill to Japan.

Obviously, the man's employers were liable for all bills. But between liability and payment there was a hiatus, which Yakutsk would want closing before doing anything. This could take weeks. And meanwhile the man was causing the hospital grave problems. Although recovered he could not be moved out of the isolation wing. The area was banned to foreigners and it was impermissible for him to be placed in a general ward with other patients. He couldn't be allowed the run of the hospital, and he couldn't be allowed outside it.

In his frustration he was also creating considerable uproar himself. While he was ill his pigtail had been unpicked and disinfected. He wanted it regreased and replaited. He also wanted his mustache groomed. Above all he wanted to get out. And since, in his fury, he had lost what meager command he had of Russian and English, he had taken to bawling loudly at the staff in Korean; and when they didn't answer, even more loudly in Japanese. The hospital director tried to explain that everything possible was being done to get him out; but it still took time to make him understand that they were trying to get him out to Japan. At this he almost went out of his mind.

"No Japan! Ship! Ship!"

"The ship has gone."

"*Job* on ship! Money. No Japan. Ship!"

"But it isn't here. The ship went."

"My job ship. Ship wait me."

"The ship didn't wait for you. It went."

"Yes, went. Where he went?"

"To Murmansk. It's gone."

"Murmansk no gone! Wait. My job ship."

Amid the gibberish the hospital director at last discerned the drift. The man seemed to think the ship would wait for him in Murmansk. But the ship had now been gone five days and would have left Murmansk. He didn't bother explaining this. The medical officer, whose patient he was, seemed to have a better time with him, so he thought she could explain it. But before informing her he checked on the ship himself. A call to Green Cape revealed that the Korean might not after all be out of his mind. The ship was a slow tramp whose upper speed would not have got it to Murmansk yet. A few minutes later the port called him back to say that the ship was still three days out of Murmansk.

He hung up with considerable elation. This put a new complexion on things. If the ship's captain signed the bills, there was no need to worry about Yakutsk, Polar Aviation, Aeroflot, or Nakhodka. And the captain would have to sign the bills, or he wouldn't get out of Murmansk. A single call to the militia or the security service would fix everything. Then Komarova, who had signed the seaman in, could sign him out, the isolation wing could be closed down, the Korean would stop shouting at everyone in Korean, and they would be rid of him.

And this the following day all came about. Komarova handed her patient and his belongings over to the militia. The militia put him on Polar Aviation's flight for Yakutsk. At Yakutsk he was escorted to the Aeroflot flight for Irkutsk and Murmansk. And at Murmansk, late at night, he was conveyed to the International Seamen's Hostel and signed in as a transit visitor awaiting ship. Here he was given a locker and a bed, and after the long day slept most soundly.

Transit visitors at the hostel were not allowed "shore rights" but as most of them were foreigners with hard currency this was never a problem. Five dollars was the recognized contribution for taking a breath of air, and taxis were always available at the end of the street. Since all passports were retained by the hostel, and there could be no question of absconding anywhere, the system worked well enough. It was usual for discreet taxi-loads of three to take the air together, and the taxis took them to the red-light district.

Porter made up a threesome at eight the following evening. His

Norwegian companions couldn't understand him, so at the first place they amicably agreed to split. There was no shortage of taxis in the red-light area either, and he took one to the airport, again using dollars and taking his change in rubles and kopeks. With the kopeks he made three telephone calls, at precisely twelve-minute intervals. He allowed each one to ring twice, and then cut off. Then he made a fourth, and let it ring twelve times, when it was answered.

He said in Russian, "I am here."

Murmansk was a major naval base, and the airport was thronged with uniformed sailors. He watched quietly from a seat in the concourse and saw the man arrive thirty minutes later. The man had a seafaring look himself: a solid, chunky individual dressed, like Porter, in donkey jacket, muffler, and woolly hat. He carried a hefty grip. The plan, if no seat was available next to Porter, was to move elsewhere. But a seat was available, and the two men were soon in warm conversation. Then the new arrival asked Porter to watch his bag while he made a call and suggested that they meet in the Automat. Porter agreed and off the man went; and so presently did Porter, with the bag, following the arrow marked TOILETS.

Familiar with the routine, since Otaru, he locked himself in and went swiftly to work. In the grip was a set of clothing, new documentation, a wallet, and a toilet bag. He started with the toilet bag, taking out the towel and wrapping it around his neck, and then the scissors and the hand mirror. He cut off the pigtail at the roots, and dropped it in the bag, and then scissored away all over his head until it was down to the shortest fuzz he could manage. This too went from the towel into the bag. Then he lathered his scalp and his mustache with the liquid soap and started work with the razor.

He had been clean-shaven before but never totally bald, and the effect was startling. He wasted no time examining it but right away changed into his new clothing. This was handsome: winter-weight velvet corduroys, fine white woolen turtleneck, a stylish fur-lined leather jacket, two-tone ankle boots, and a splendid bushy mink for his shaven head. Kolya (Nikolai) Khodyan was a snappy dresser. Dark snow glasses were in the top pocket of the jacket. He briefly tried the effect, and took them off again. Then he packed everything of Sung Won Choo's in the bag, and went back with it to the concourse.

The seaman was in the Automat, by the samovars, at the busiest corner, as planned. Porter jostled his way through and got himself a glass, and they amicably exchanged a few words. Then the man picked up the bag, they nodded to each other in the crowd, and he was gone.

Porter remained a while, finishing his tea, and made his way to the left luggage office, fishing the receipt out of his new wallet. The two pieces awaiting him were every bit as opulent as the rest of Khodyan's effects: a fine large Scandinavian case and a soft antelope grip. He took them over to the check-in desk.

In his breast pocket he had the sheaf of open-flight tickets. It took almost thirty minutes to get the stages of the journey booked, a computer being out of action at one of them. Then he handed in the case, and went and bought himself another glass of tea. The place was still swarming, flights still being called to take the fleet sailors to distant parts of the country.

But he was smoking in the lounge when, at midnight, the first of his own flights was called. This was to Irkutsk. At Irkutsk he changed for Yakutsk. At Yakutsk, in a blizzard, he made Polar Aviation again for Tchersky.

Three days after leaving it he was back. This was the second of October, just over a month after his arrival at Narita airport in Japan, and ten weeks since he had first heard of inaccessible and forbidden Green Cape. He now took a taxi there, and fifteen minutes later let himself into the apartment.

Four

The
Pale
Women
of Siberia

23

He switched the light on, closed the door behind him, and stood quite still, looking and listening.

He was in a living room, a warm and fetid one. A faint smell of rotting fruit. The place had been empty for four months, its last occupant hurrying out to catch a plane in June. He had left a mess behind—newspapers on the floor, a discarded grip, scattered work boots, half-open drawers. A toy panda sat on the sofa, cutely watching. It had lipstick on. He could see all the flat at once, all its doors open, bedroom, kitchen, bathroom. A subdued noise of music and voices came from surrounding apartments.

He waited some moments longer, then moved to the window and closed the curtains. He saw that the port was not visible from here, or even the street. He was at the back of the building, third floor—a big block, 165 apartments. Directly opposite was its twin, five stories of lighted windows. At the end of the stamped-snow courtyard the two blocks were joined by a glassed-in walkway. Through the panes of the walkway he could see, beyond, a supermarket, part of the same complex. A few lights glimmered in it, but the place was shut. It was late. He sighed and took his mink hat off.

Apart from the night's sleep at Murmansk he had barely stopped moving for three days. He took Khodyan's jacket off too, and prowled the flat, sniffing, touching. The furniture looked new, Finnish, good quality. Bed left unmade; a huge king-size; fine pillows, plump duvet: "Swansdown," the label said in English. The slob who owned all this was a bachelor who liked his comforts. Wardrobe stuffed with winter clothing, all good.

The bathroom too—towels of fine quality, fluffy foreign ones; the tub and shower also far from standard, all extra, all paid for by this high earner. There was a lingering smell of used clothing. He looked around and saw heavy winter socks and underwear spilling out of a laundry basket. A bra and panties were mixed in with them.

In the kitchen further signs of hurried departure: rinsed breakfast things upside down on the drainer and, in a sink-tidy alongside, the source of the fruit smell, orange peel and pear cores. Not much food in the cupboards: tea, coffee, a few cans. He had a look in the fridge. Sausage, eggs, fuzzy cheese, all due for dispatch. But not tonight.

Tonight sleep. But the sheet, on closer inspection, showed signs of use, so he changed it first. Piping hot from the linen cupboard, the new one was beautifully silky, the elasticated edges slipping neatly and smoothly under the mattress. He marveled at it. He'd never had such stuff himself. They lived high, in the Arctic. Alexei Mikhailovich Ponomarenko had lived high.

"Alexei! Are you back, Alexei?"

In his sleep he'd heard the ringing and thought himself again in the hospital. But now an accompanying rapping at the door brought him to, and he turned out. He turned out in Ponomarenkos's fine woolen dressing gown. It was eight o'clock in the morning.

"One minute, I'm coming!" he called, as the rapping continued.

"Alexei! It's good to hear you again. Welcome back, Alyosha!"

"Yes, but it's not Alyosha," he said. He was smiling as he opened the door. Kolya Khodyan was a smiler; sometimes taciturn, always temperamental, mainly a smiler. He smiled at difficulties. All this had been worked out.

"Oh." A little old lady in carpet slippers was gazing at him. Her face was lined and like a tabby's, and it was now gazing up in astonishment at the startling Siberian native with his shaven head. "Isn't Alexei here?"

"No, he's still at the Black Sea. He lent me the place for a while. He can't come just yet."

"Is he in trouble there?"

"No trouble! He's enjoying himself."

"Ah. A girl, is it?"

"A beauty. Don't worry about *him*."

"Again—that bad boy! But you—excuse me—you're—?"

"Khodyan. Nikolai Dmitrievich—call me Kolya," Porter said, and warmly shook her hand. He hadn't stopped smiling. "You don't know me, but I know you, Anna Antonovna. I know everything about you! He never stopped speaking about you down there."

"He did? At Batumi he spoke of me?" The old lady was delighted.

"All the time. He said you kept him like a prince here. He said you'd do the same for me. So here I am!"

The old lady did not have many teeth, but all of them were now radiantly on display in her smile.

"Well, well," she said, and nudged his arm. "But he could have dropped me a line at least. If only to say you were coming. I've got his mail here. I've been emptying his box, he left me the key." Over her arm he now saw she had a string bag stuffed with papers—magazines mainly, by the wrappers. "He didn't have an address when he left. Does he want it sent on now?"

"No, no. He knows it's only his magazines. Keep them for him," Porter said. "And meanwhile keep *me* like a prince."

The old lady was peering past him into the room. "Well, the usual mess, I see. I thought it was him banging about—I'm just next door. You want me to start now?"

"No, I'll take a shower first," Porter said. He hadn't investigated Khodyan's cases yet and wanted to do so without the old babushka's scrutiny. There was a sharp look on the catlike face. He hadn't been banging about. He had made no noise at all. She must have spotted the light come on before he'd drawn the curtains last night.

She asked, "Have you anything to eat here?"

"I brought something with me, enough for now. I won't waste time. I want to run down to the port office."

"Ah, you're on boats, too?"

"Boats?" Porter said. Some of the sunshine faded from his smile. Ponomarenko was supposed to be a truck driver.

"The trucks. You're not a driver?"

"Ah, you know our slang!" It was as well that he did himself now. The first example of the casual dangers. "Sure. On the boats. How are things shaping here this season?"

"The usual mess at the beginning—they're running in all directions. But the ice is nearly right. They'll be glad of you. You're not from these parts, then—Kolya, is it?"

"Kolya. No—from Chukotka, the Magadan circuit. But I go anywhere—a boat's a boat."

"Of course—you boys! Well, give me a knock, Kolya. You want the same arrangements to carry on: wash, clean, get in the shopping?"

"Everything. Whatever you did before, old lady, do it again. You'll tell me what you need and I'll leave the money."

"And if I find anything?" Her eyes were still roaming the little apartment. "Return it? Or?"

"Let me take a shower, a mouthful of coffee," he pleaded, "and I'll come and see you."

But he was thoughtful as he closed the door behind her. It wasn't till he was in the bathroom and his eyes fell again on the bra and the panties that it occurred to him what the ''or'' meant. There would be a claimant for these goods.

That was another thing they hadn't told him.

24

The Tchersky Transport Company, at this season, had the running of Green Cape. The river had frozen, not solidly as yet, but solidly enough for all the shipping to have vanished. The half-mile length of dock showed no trace of a gangplank, and would not show any for eight months. Now it was crammed with freight, the last frantic unloading of ships that had dashed for open water before the ice trapped them.

Not only the dock but the sheds that lined the dock were crammed; and the huge warehouses on the hill above the dock, acre upon acre of them, all crammed. Through this one small Arctic opening all northeast Siberia was supplied: its gold and diamond mines, its processing plants and power stations, and all the industrial settlements that had developed around them.

In the short summer, when the Kolyma flowed, barges carried the supplies south, for distribution through the river's tributary system to east and west. But that was in summer, and in the south. Up here no long-distance tributaries ran to east or west. To east and west the area was impassable in summer, and had to wait for winter.

In winter the Tchersky Transport Company took over.

On the steep hill above the dock, Porter watched them doing it. From here he could see the spread of warehouses on top as well as the frenetic activity below. Below, some dozens of teams were at work freeing the crates jamming the dock. The crates towered crazily, dumped one on top of the other as the ships had hurried to leave. Snow had fallen and an icecap had formed, freezing the stacks together. The bulky figures, earflaps down in the bitter wind, were chipping them apart, while cranes and forklifts shifted them onto trucks. A steady stream of trucks was grinding uphill and churning into the storage area. Here the loads were being stowed under the last of the cover—a roofed and pillared overhang extending the length of the warehouses.

He watched for some time, and then turned and trudged through the rutted snow to the administrative block. He had identified it immediately, a squat two-story building on short piles at the beginning of the warehouse row.

In the dismal morning all the lights were on inside, and the drafty foyer bustled with activity. Clusters of men were going from one wall roster to another; others gathered round the samovars, talking and smoking. He stood for a while, jostled on all sides, and presently made his way to a double set of glass doors at the end. He peered through to a large room filled with desks. Men and women were writing, phoning, passing papers to each other over glasses of tea. He couldn't make out anyone noticeably managerial, and turned away to get himself some tea at a samovar. There were no glasses here, just paper cups and a drum of somewhat grubby lumps of sugar. He reached for a couple of lumps, and as he turned jostled another man, spilling his tea.

He apologized.

"It's nothing." The man wiped his leather jacket.

"Some crush here!"

"Start of the season. Nothing's rolling. You new here?"

"Just got in. Is Bukarovsky still here?"

"The road manager? Sure. Upstairs."

"I suppose he's the one to see."

The man was looking at him curiously. "For driving, or?"

Porter noted again the "or," evidently local style. It hadn't appeared on the tapes.

"For driving, sure."

"Then it's him. End of the corridor up there. You'll tell by the noise."

Porter sipped his tea, looked around, and shouldered his way to the rosters. There were several of them, listing the teams and what they would be driving. The lists showed three drivers to a truck, two on, one off. He saw that Ponomarenko's name wasn't there. There was a large variety of trucks, different models of Tatra, Kama, Ural. He knew about this. They had some hundreds of heavy trucks, almost fifteen hundred drivers and mechanics, close on a million tons of freight to be hauled.

He finished his tea, threw the cup in the bin, and walked upstairs. Even at the stairhead he heard the uproar, and as he neared it, a name-plate on the end door confirmed the source: P. G. BUKAROVSKY, ROAD MANAGER. He paused there, uncertain whether to knock or enter, until a girl emerged in a hurry and left the door for him, and he went in.

A sunken-chested man with a haggard face was shouting into a phone, his feet on a desk. He was doing several things at once: drinking tea, furiously smoking, coughing, pointing out something to a girl hanging over him with a clipboard, and offering advice to an older woman who sat talking on another phone at the other side of the desk. "Tell them to rot at Bilibino!" he told her. "With my compliments. Not you," he said into the phone. "I *promised* you! Two–three days. When I see fifteen centimeters. Not a minute before! What do *you* want?"

The last was to Porter, who was standing before him, flashing a smile. He'd hesitated whether or not to take his fur cap off and had decided against; the men below had kept their caps on.

He carried on smiling, waving the manager on with his conversation, and looked around the room as it proceeded. The walls here were also covered with rosters, and with large maps. A phalanx of colored flag pins was stuck neatly at the bottom of each map. No flags were yet distributed on the maps. He turned as the phone smashed down.

"What's your problem?" the man said.

"You want a driver?"

"Where are you from?"

"Chukotka."

"What are you doing here?"

"A favor to Ponomarenko. We met at Batumi. He can't come for a few weeks."

"That bastard will stretch his holiday once too often! What can you drive?"

Porter offered his papers. "Whatever you've got."

The phone rang again, and the man picked it up and laid it on the desk, where it angrily chattered. He glanced through the papers.

"You're square with the union?"

"All square."

"What trouble are you in at Chukotka?"

"No trouble. . . . Look," Porter said amiably. He hadn't stopped smiling. "I'm doing Ponomarenko a *favor*. You also. You want me, it's okay. You don't—also okay. I'll go."

"Bukarovsky!" Bukarovsky said into the phone. He continued glaring at Porter. "Leave your songsheet here," he told him. "And go around to the sheds. Not you," he said into the phone, between spasms of coughing. "Tell Yura to try you on a Kama 50, and to call me back. The *50*, right? Hello—Pevek, what the hell is it now? . . . Here, *you*—take a *bobik*," he said to Porter.

"A *bobik?*" Porter said. A *bobik* was a terrier.

"So now *I'm* telling *you!* I'm sick of your problems. I've got my own problems," the man told the phone. "And I'm sick of talking about *them!*" He was groping in a tray of keys. He tossed one to Porter. "Give him the book," he said to the woman across the desk.

Porter looked at the key on its leather tab, and at the book the woman shoved across to him. She pointed where he had to sign. It was against one of a row of numbers. He signed "N. D. Khodyan" and left as the roaring continued behind him.

Below he threaded his way through the foyer, and at the door asked a man, "Where do I get a bobik?"

"Back of the building, right behind here."

The number he'd signed was the number on the key, a car key. He went around the building and found the cars, in an open shed. There were four or five pickups and a number of jeeps. There was nobody there. He walked around examining the registration numbers and found his bobik. It was one of the jeeps, a solid enclosed job, very square and ugly like a little tank. The tires looked half flat. He walked around, kicking them, and saw that all the tires in the shed were half flat; evidently it was intended.

He got in the car, found the ignition, and turned the key. It sparked immediately, a rough throaty snarl. It was dark in the shed and he couldn't see the display on the dash. He fumbled the gears and got the thing moving, out of cover and into the light. In the light he saw there was no display on the dash, and hardly any dash: a speedo, a switch for the wipers, and that was all. There had to be a switch for the lights but he couldn't find it. But the thing was powerfully heated, and had a motor that surged at a touch with a satisfying grating bark— evidently accounting for the name. He took to the terrier at once, and got it moving again, to the front of the building. Someone was coming out, and he hailed him out of the window.

"Hey! Where do I find Yura?"

"Which Yura?"

"For a Kama. A Kama 50."

"Straight on, half a kilometer, turn up the ramp, you'll find him."

He kept on along the line of warehouses, dodging in and out of the path of spinning forklifts, and found the ramp. The whole massive hangar was up on short piles, evidently as air insulation from the permafrost below. Inside, as far as he could see, was an amazing army of trucks, row upon row of them, all lined up, waiting, and bearing the logo of the Kamaz Auto Works: Kama 30s, 40s, 50s. The front line, he saw, had laden trailers already attached, but farther back were just the tall cabs.

He parked the bobik and emerged into a rush of warm air from big blowers spread out over the area. Around the walls work was going on at long benches, and nearby the spit and flash of welding gear. He walked over to the man there.

"Where's Yura?" he yelled in his ear.

The man put his visor up. Who?"

"Yura."

"The boss? In the office—the glass booth at the end."

He found the booth, and a white-overalled Yura, on the phone,

133

busily scribbling on an inventory pad. He was a little brawny pug of a man with a shock of gray hair. Porter waited till he'd finished, and flashed his smile.

"I'm Khodyan—Kolya. Bukarovsky wants me to try a 50."

The man looked him up and down.

"Ever driven one before?"

"Sure."

At the camp all they'd had was a 40, but he'd been assured it was the same. Sixteen gears, almost identical to a Mack.

"Where have you driven?"

"Chukotka, Magadan—that circuit."

"Roads." The man grunted. "None of that here. Here we run soft, low pressure. Better traction, but a heavy wheel. All right, then." He opened a tall cupboard. It was neatly laid out with several lines of hooks, keys hanging from them. His scarred hand flitted about the keys and selected one. "Let's see what you're made of," he said. He put a fur cap and leather jacket on and led the way.

An experienced ex-driver, evidently, and an injured one, Porter saw: one leg was shorter than the other. The man limped down a row of cabs, their umbilicals hooked up at the rear, and stopped at one. He went rapidly up an iron ladder, and Porter took the other side. He climbed the six or seven feet and swung himself behind the wheel.

Yura, settling himself, slammed the door and handed over the keys. "You're sure you can handle her?"

"No problem," Porter said. His smile was dazzling. Right away he saw the bastard didn't have sixteen gears. It had twenty. Reverse in the normal position, though.

"She's warmed up, take her right out. Hard on the wheel, remember, she's heavy."

Porter started up, slotted into first, and pulled slowly out of line and along the aisle.

"Down the ramp and to the right."

The cow *was* heavy. And the brake was heavy, and snatched when he stood on it.

"Easy, easy, you're pulling nothing," Yura said. "Keep rolling now. To the trial ground, at the end."

The trial ground was beyond the warehouses, and lay under unmarked snow, already iced. He took her around the perimeter at varying speeds, slow, fast, slow, working up and down through the gears. He'd done all this at the camp, as also the emergency stops and the figure eights that Yura now put him through. But the extra gears flustered him and he fumbled the positions, though he was certain it didn't show.

"All right, now back and park where you found her," Yura said.

This one had him sweating as he maneuvered and reversed in the hangar to get tight back in line.

Yura switched off for him and took the key.

"You're sure you drove a 50 before?" he said.

Porter decided his smile had better go.

"What are you calling me?" he said.

"You drove a 40 before," Yura told him, "with sixteen gears."

"I drive anything! I drive sixteen gears, twenty. Any boat you got I drive! You're saying I'm a liar?"

"Easy now," Yura said. His little pug's face had suddenly opened up in a great smile of its own. "Easy, Kolya. You a Chukchi?"

"Never mind what I am! No business of yours what I am. I drive. You don't want me, I go home."

"Easy, Kolya," Yura said, still smiling. "You're okay. You're fine. I'm passing you, Kolya. Give me your songsheet."

"Bukarovsky's got my songsheet," Porter said sulkily.

"So I'll call him. Don't get so hot, Kolya. I like you. I never had a Chukchi before. You just need a little more time on the 50, you'll take the righthand seat a few trips, it's nothing. Come on, smile now."

Porter sheepishly gave him a smile.

"That's better. You're *on,* Kolya. You're with friends here, we want you. Go back there and sign now." The little man was chuckling as he scrambled down the ladder. "Hey, you got transport?"

"Sure. A bobik," Porter said.

"Good. I don't like my drivers walking. Never had one of you before," Yura said. He was still chuckling as he limped away.

Porter got in the bobik and drove back. He felt dizzy. A lot had happened in just over twelve hours. He had arrived in Green Cape and installed himself in an apartment. He had taken on a housekeeper. He'd got himself on the strength of the Tchersky Transport Company. And he had taken in some new lore. Songsheets, bobiks, soft tires, twenty-gear trucks, "or". . .

He'd also learned a few things about Ponomarenko they hadn't told him. Before leaving that morning he had removed a plinth under the kitchen unit and found a hidey-hole there. Under two floor tiles, grouted in with a slightly newer-looking mastic (and finding a tube of the stuff in a cupboard had set him off on the hunt), was a taped-up plastic bag. Other bags were inside it. He had found a few grams of what looked to be cocaine, together with a sniffing reed. An ounce, maybe an ounce and a half, of gold dust; and, oddly, twelve South African Krugerrands. There was also a photo of Ponomarenko, slightly younger than in the ones he'd seen but not much. He and a woman were sitting smiling stiffly at the camera, each holding a young child, each child the image of Ponomarenko. The raised lettering on the bottom of the photo gave a studio address in Kiev. Porter parked the bobik back in the shed and thought about this. He was a funny fellow, Ponomarenko. He had a wife and kids somewhere. Was he the one who'd drawn the lipstick on the panda?

Or?

25

As the last man to sign on, Kolya Khodyan joined the reserve list. He had seen the short block of names at the bottom of the wall rosters—men who were sick or for some other reason not assigned to a team. Now he saw his own name added there, as available for general duties. At the beginning of a season, with nothing yet rolling, this was not important, but from the other drivers he heard that to stay with general duties was bad news.

Under union agreements the men were paid whether the "boats" ran or not. But once they were running, the teams were eligible for bonuses. With the distances involved here, the bonuses were huge, easily outstripping the already high basic pay. The trucks ran through storms, through blizzards, through every kind of hazard the country could offer, and they ran twenty-four hours a day. Any hour over the week's norm was an overtime hour and paid double. Long hauls were obviously much in demand, and general-duty men rarely got them. They got short hops and road maintenance jobs, seldom running into overtime.

The new Chukchi driver accepted his listing with good grace, and this together with his cheerfulness soon made him popular. He was very cheerful; he smiled all the time. He took on any job without argument—and in fact volunteered for one the same day, when a call was put out. He could stand on his dignity (and it was understood he wasn't to be addressed as a Chukchi), but in general he was a good comrade and, as a Chukchi, almost a mascot.

The job he volunteered for was to haul freight up from the dock. This was, strictly speaking, the work of the Green Cape port authority, and the men doing it were dockers. But when further snow made the task urgent, he took a Tatra flatbed down and joined the shuttle. He had seen right away that many of the workers below were Siberian natives and he wanted a closer look at them. He saw that several were Evenks or Yukagirs; this was the end of their seasonal work and soon none would remain in town. Ponomarenko had given some information on this.

He jockeyed his truck into line and saw he'd won a team of Yukagirs. He climbed out in the swirling snow and stood by, beating his gloved hands as they loaded the truck in front. It didn't take long to identify the likeliest man; a cackling bundled-up little fellow, robustly swearing, the wit of the gang.

"Warm work, brother!" he called to him.

The man glanced around in surprise. He had called in Yukagir.

"You got the tongue?" the man said, looking him over.

"A few words. Glad to see the end here, eh?"

"You're right. Except for the money. And the booze. Here the bastards keep it to themselves. We don't smell it where we go to."

"Where do you go—traplines or the herds?"

"Traps. But first the collective. The maniacs here work you till you drop. We need a rest."

"There's a collective here?"

"Sure. Ours. Novokolymsk. You don't know the area?"

"Not so well. A few friends who work up at the station, in the hills. You know that place?"

"With the scientists?"

"That one."

"See, it isn't any use now," the Yukagir told him. "They don't allow traps there anymore, not for years. It's useless."

"You could make it up there on foot?"

"Sure—a few kilometers, no distance. But it's useless now. Your friends are Evenks?"

"Evenks."

"Yes. It suits them. They do a few weeks with the herds and a few weeks there, turn and turn about. They fly them in, they don't want whites, and not bad money. But it isn't for us. This is good fox country, and ermine—the best ermine. Not prime for a couple of months yet, but the best when they come on. You speak the tongue nice," the Yukagir told him.

The line moved then, so he got back in the Tatra, and no further opportunity offered. But he'd heard enough. . . .

In summer, in the camp, he had watched week by week as the research station had been repaired. He had watched it from satellite photographs, a world away. Now he was there—a few kilometers, no distance . . . and now the planning was his; and now he was on his own.

* * *

He learned something about the bobik that week.

He had been sent out with spares and some instruments to a road gang fifty kilometers out. The road stretched seven hundred kilometers to Bilibino and it had been out of use all summer, a bog. Now it was hardening, and this was the first section to come into condition. When fifteen centimeters of new frost showed, treatment could begin. The heavy equipment for it was kept at road stations a hundred kilometers apart; the stations served also as rest centers for the drivers and as bases for the rescue and recovery service, tracked vehicles that patrolled the route all winter.

Porter ran out to the gang, dropped his supplies and headed back, and was halfway into the journey when the bobik stopped.

He got out and had a look at the engine. Nothing wrong with the supply or the plugs. Or the points. No shortage of fuel. He turned the engine by hand—the little brute also packed a handle. Nothing. The weather was not yet tremendously cold, maybe fifteen degrees below, but his fingers were freezing up without gloves. He swore. He tried everything again. Fuel okay and getting through. Distributor okay. Spark. What the hell!

On all sides the dreary taiga stretched for miles, snow-covered, iced. He must be twenty, thirty kilometers along the way, and nothing whatever would be coming past. Not for several hours at least, until it occurred to somebody at Green Cape to come and look for him. He had no communications set. He couldn't walk to Green Cape. He couldn't walk back to the road gang. The road was like a rink. He'd had to use a gentle hand just to keep the thing moving.

You bastard, he told the bobik, and took a swig at his hip flask; and while doing it thought of something. In midwinter, he'd heard, they often had to start the engines with White Dynamite, high-proof vodka. He had no White Dynamite in his flask but plain vodka might help. Maybe the fuel was contaminated or the carburetor faulty; a drop of the volatile spirit might fire and clear it. He warmed his hands in his gloves first and beat them together before fumbling with the carb. Then he gave himself a small swig and the carb one, and got a kick and a cough, and the thing rumbled hesitantly into life. He kept it running, revving cautiously by hand till he was sure of it, and then closed the hood and got back in and started off again.

It happened twice more on the way, and he knew it was the carburetor. The trick worked with petrol, too. He'd sucked a bit out of the tank with a plastic tube, and he dripped it in and got the kick and the cough. The fuel was okay. The carb was dodgy.

He drove back to the Light Vehicles Depot where he had picked up the loaded bobik in the morning, and looked around for Liova.

Faults had to be reported to the chief mechanic. But Liova and all the mechanics were at lunch and only Vassili, the old Yakut storeman, was there, eating out of a pot on a kerosene stove. He told Vassili the problem.

"This isn't a problem," the Yakut said. "I'll give you another carburetor and you'll fit it. It takes two minutes."

"I'm reporting a fault. I don't need a carburetor," Porter told him.

"You do. You have another load, a rush job. There's no spare bobik, and they have no time to repair it. Here, I'll give you it now."

And the old man left his meal, wiping his mouth, and took the Chukchi into the storeroom and gave him a carburetor; and Porter's eyes popped. A whole bay, neatly arranged, was stuffed with bobik spares. Gearboxes, shafts, clutches, doors—engines, even. The old man looked at him and shrugged. "It's a toy," he said. He hunted around and found a greasy manual. "A child can do it."

And Porter did do it while the old Yakut, picking his teeth, pointed out the details on the exploded diagram. It took a single wrench. The carb worked right away.

"I told you, it's nothing," Vassili said. "Did you eat yet?" They had been talking Yakut, which had intrigued and pleased the old man.

"Not yet. What have you got there?"

"Proper food. My old woman's. Not that garbage in the canteen. Join me."

Porter joined him, grunted favorably over the food, and presently signed for the carburetor; the Yakut helped him load up. He was gone before Liova and the mechanics returned. He drove down into Tchersky, listening to the engine. Not a thing wrong with it. A workhorse, robust, primitive, and all of it put together the same way, with a wrench. He thought about this. A number of plans had been prepared for getting him out. They were neat enough plans, but obviously someone else must know of them. It might be an idea to have other plans. He thought about this all the way there and all the way back.

That same night the doorbell rang and a young woman stood there; of considerable development, he saw, and had already gathered so from her underwear.

"Nikolai Dmitrievich," she said, "you don't know me. But I have a request to make."

"Is it Lydia Yakovlevna?"

"Ah, you know!" Both hands had gone up to her mouth, but whether with embarrassment or amazement at his shaven head he could not as yet tell. "You have a small parcel of mine, I think."

"The linen you lent Alexei—yes, indeed. Anna Antonovna said you might call. Please come in."

The old lady had cooked up the story herself. She had laundered the goods and asked if she should return them; the girl only worked in the supermarket below. No, he had said, if she wanted her pants and bra she could come and get them. But Kolya, Kolya, Anna Antonovna had said, cackling and nudging him, only think of her feelings! I'll put them in a parcel as if it's handkerchieves or something she lent Alyosha—it will spare her blushes.

And indeed the girl did seem to be blushing a bit. A big girl, big all over, somewhat puffy, and pale—anemically pale, as all the white women of Siberia seemed to be, winter for nine months of the year and the summer tan soon gone. But an easy mover, and with a co-quettish look. He knew Anna Antonovna had told her he didn't know the contents of the parcel, but he saw from the girl's knowledgeable eyes that she knew that he did know. It intrigued him. Was she so short of knickers and a bra? Surely she could have waited for Ponomarenko's return. Why the hurry for collection?

"Coffee? A drink?" he said.

"Oh no, Nikolai Dmitrievich. I didn't mean to—"

"Kolya. Please," he said.

"Kolya. I didn't mean to disturb you. Just in passing I thought I'd see if maybe you were in. You men spend so much time in the clubs—"

"I know few people yet, Lydia Yakovlevna."

"Lydia—please."

"A lovely name. *Have* a drink, Lydia!"

"Well, a small one, perhaps."

Just in passing she had jumped into her party boots: stiletto heels. Her outdoor ones must be in the large shopper she was carrying, hurriedly changed in the hall outside. A huge plunging neckline appeared once she was out of her fur coat. And hair piled ornately high as her head scarf came off, together with a seductive odor not long applied. Her eyelashes flickered about the room.

"Ah, that *kotek!* Still here."

Kotek: pussycat. She had picked up the panda.

"Yes. And still wearing his lipstick. Now, I wonder," he said gravely, "who gave him that?"

She laughed. "A crazy night. Friends . . . "

"Ah." From Anna Antonovna he had already learned that the only friends in the apartment that night had been Ponomarenko and this girl; it had been the first of their friendly nights.

"I think," he said, "we are both good friends of Alexei."

"Ah, Alyosha, that crazy boy . . . Thank you." He had given her a cherry brandy, and noted her approval of his good manners. A lady's drink; although he had also heard from Anna Antonovna that this girl had no trouble with a vodka.

In no time they were chatting easily, and he saw that his startling head in no way fazed her. Quite the reverse; she seemed fascinated by it and was coming on fast.

"Your Russian—so beautiful," she softly told him.

"Thank you." Her own was far from high-class, and he was fracturing his in the manner he had adopted here from the start. But he saw the remark as less a tribute to beautiful Russian than as a hint that ethnicity was no problem here. At the drop of a hat this girl could be tumbling in the Finnish bed. But the blatancy of it puzzled him. It also alerted him. Did she know that Ponomarenko would be absent a long time? And if so, how?

"So what do you hear," he asked, handing her a third shot of cherry brandy, "from our friend?"

"Alyosha? . . . What, another drink? I shouldn't. But I also get lonely sometimes. . . . Oh, *Alyosha* doesn't write. Too busy with those Georgian girls, I expect."

"After you? Water after wine? Of course not."

"Liar," she said delightedly, and showed him more leg. "I'm sure you're just as bad. Didn't you go for those gorgeous Batumi girls?"

"In Batumi I just relax."

"And have parties? *He* loved parties. I'll bet you had parties."

"Parties, yes. There were parties."

"*Loved* them. And now he'll miss one here. He'd be back if he knew that! Oh yes, like a shot. Pavel Grigorovich's."

"Pavel Grigorovich?"

"Bukarovsky. His sixtieth. Everybody's going. You didn't know?"

"Oh. Yes," he said. And now he saw. Everybody *wasn't* going. The mayor was going, and the top brass of Tchersky and Green Cape were going. Many of Bukarovsky's drivers were also going. But supermarket assistants weren't going.

"He'd be showing me off there, all right. He loved to see me dressed up. I mean, what I've got on now isn't anything. I've got some lovely clothes—and nowhere to go in them."

"I'm sure you look lovely in anything. Isn't that cherry brandy a little sweet for you?"

"It is a little sweet, yes."

"Try a sip of vodka."

"Oh, no. I must be going."

"From mine," he said, and displaced the panda to sit beside her and give her a sip; which the girl refused so playfully that she managed to spill it down her dress front. He helped her mop up with a handkerchief.

"Quite dry now?"

"I *think* so."

"It didn't go down further?"

"I don't know," she said.

He tried further, without the handkerchief, and left his hand there.

"Naughty Kolya," she said, looking at him.

"Naughty Lydia."

He kissed her and received a mouthful of cherry tongue.

"We're only human, aren't we?" she said in his ear.

She said it again, next door, some time later, when he had begun to doubt it. The girl was a tiger. Presently she propped herself on an elbow and gazed down at him. "You know I haven't been with a man since Alyosha. You know that, don't you?"

"I'm sure," he said honestly. A minimum of four months' energy had gone into her activities, and he didn't think much could have gone spare.

Later, lying more comfortably, she said reflectively, "Yes . . . that will certainly be a party, all right."

"Would you like to go to it?"

"Who could I go with?"

"Why not me?"

"I don't know. I don't know if Alyosha would like that." Her eyelashes flickered at the ceiling. "I haven't thought of it really," she said.

26

Pavel Grigorovich Bukarovsky, the road manager of the Tchersky Transport Company, had been given his job by Leonid Shevelyev, the founding father of the company and the man credited with opening up northeast Siberia. Shevelyev, arrested in 1947 for "unsound political beliefs," had served his time in a local labor camp, and Bukarovsky had served time in the same camp. Most of the senior staff of the company had done time in the camps.

The camps of the Kolyma, strung out all along the river, had been the most infamous in the Soviet Union, and yet when they were closed in the 1950s many of the inmates had chosen to remain in the area. Their reasons were simple. The land of restraint had suddenly become the land of the free—freer, at least, than anywhere else in the Soviet Union. It had fewer police, fewer party officials, fewer bureaucrats. It also, of course, had fewer amenities.

But even that changed; for after the great gold and diamond finds of the 1960s, it suddenly had *more* amenities than elsewhere. It had more food, more housing, more pay. And by another reversal, what had once been the worst had become the best. By common consent Tchersky had been the worst. Under its former name of Nizhniye Kresty it had been a byword for horror even in the days of the czars; the remotest outpost of the Russian empire, the least accessible, a final hell for the most desperate prisoners. Now, as capital of the Kolymsky region, it had become the center of all good things.

Pavel Grigorovich Bukarovsky in his own life had witnessed these changes, and on his sixtieth birthday, forty years after arriving in the Arctic, he planned to celebrate them. Although he lived and worked at Green Cape, he had to celebrate at Tchersky, which had the largest premises: Barbara's.

Barbara's was a labyrinth of rooms running one into another; it had been converted from a double row of log houses. Deloused, debugged, completely sanitized, it all the same still retained the atmosphere of another Siberia and was the most popular venue in all the Kolymsky region. With the assistance of the mayor, who served as head of the planning committee, walls had been removed and temporary plinths inserted to open up the area for the largest party Tchersky had ever seen.

Several hundred people were already there when Porter arrived with the girl, and Lydia Yakovlevna was both excited and nervous.

"Oh God, it's huge. Oh God, everybody's here! How do I look?"

She looked like an overdressed tart, but was not out of the ordinary. And not everybody was here. The winter roads were now laid and hundreds of the drivers were away. But the upper echelons of the two towns were here, and their women were here, and all of them were in their best and overdressed. Stiletto boots were everywhere, and ornate hairdos and plunging necklines and eye shadow and makeup.

There were thirty tables for ten clustered around a space left open for dancing, and guests were now packed tight in this space, greeting each other and taking early refreshment from laden trays pushed through the throng. Music was playing—accordions, balalaikas, brass—and people had to shout to be heard. The girl was soon flushed and dewed, her mascara smudging. "Oh God, it's wonderful, it's marvelous. Everybody's here! Just look at the tables!"

The tables were indeed a sight: a mass of crisp napery and sparkling silverware, of glass, flowers, fruit piled high. And bottles, battalions of bottles.

"Kolya!" The limping Kama chief, Yura, was shouting in his ear. "You're at my table! And your lovely lady, eh? You're with me! Wonderful, very good! Never had one of you before."

"Was that Uri Sergeivich?" the girl asked, her eyes brightened still more at being named a lovely lady.

"Yura, yes." He hadn't heard Yura's patronymic.

"Oh, God, he's important! He's really important—an old comrade of Pavel Grigorovich! We must be at a good table. You don't think we can be at Pavel Grigorovich's table?"

"I don't know."

They were not at Bukarovsky's table, but at one close by. Liova, the Light Vehicles head, was also at this table, and some other departmental chiefs and their ladies. And a great hubbub rose from all the tables as the guests settled and saw what was before them, and what was still to come. Before each one of them was a bottle of champagne and of red wine, and for each couple a bottle of vodka and of cognac. And what was to come—on the elaborate commemorative menus—was the most extravagant meal Porter had ever seen. It was served on the trot by a small army of waitresses, Russian and Yakut, course after course of it.

Three kinds of soup and sour cream; caviar, smoked salmon, Kamchatka crab; roast chicken and beef with venison and tongue; salamis, sausages, stuffed piroshkis; salads, vegetables, pickled everything in profusion; with sugared cranberries and macaroons and ice cream. And a box of chocolates with the coffee for every lady.

Bukarovsky, his haggard face relaxed and grinning, had appointed himself master of ceremonies and gave the first toast. And the toasts went on throughout the meal: toasts to the guests, and the ladies, to Shevelyev and the company he had founded, to comrades now absent with the boats and those left forever absent in the camps, to Tchersky and Green Cape, to the Kolymsky region and Yakutia, to peace and prosperity.

They had grown somewhat slurred before a crash of cymbals announced a surprise event: a huge cake wheeled in as a present from Tchersky. The cake, iced to represent the original log premises of the Tchersky Transport Company, was set all around with models of the company's first primitive trucks.

Bukarovsky, highly emotional, had to reply to this, and he said that proud as he was of the company's development it could never have happened without the willing help of the Tchersky municipality; this suggested further toasts from those who had not yet given any.

Liova was on his feet, to toast the Tchersky Road Services Committee and its ambulance section whose vehicles he had the honor to service. Then Yura was on his, to praise not only the ambulance section but all the health services, and in particular Tchersky's magnificent hospital! And gazing around to where all the grinning faces had turned, Porter saw Medical Officer Komarova staring at him.

His heart gave a single great thump.

She was at a table beyond Bukarovsky's, and now, through the cigarette smoke, he saw all the senior staff of the hospital. The director of the hospital was there, and Dr. Gavrilov, and the isolation wing sister he had abused so loudly in Korean and Japanese. They were all looking and smiling quite amiably. But Medical Officer Komarova was not smiling. She was simply staring.

But was she staring at him? Perhaps she was staring at Yura. He looked quickly away, and was grateful that Yura then sat down and the impatient band struck up and people began taking the floor. Lydia Yakovlevna wanted to take the floor. The girl was now quite drunk and nibbling his ear.

"I want to dance. I want to make love. First I want to dance," she said.

"Yes, we'll dance."

"Lovely lady, why hurry from me?" Yura was now quite drunk himself and dribbling at her.

"Oh, Uri Sergeivich, I don't hurry from *you*—"

"Ah, you know my name!"

"Uri Sergeivich! Who doesn't know your name?"

"Uri Sergeivich," said a voice from the rear, "I would like, on behalf of the Medical Services Committee, to thank you for your kind words." Komarova was in the rear. She was bending over to shake hands. She was bending over Porter to do so.

He dropped his napkin at once and got his head under the table to pick it up.

"My privilege and my honor," Yura told her, drunkenly kissing the hand he was shaking. "But what's this—not in your dancing clothes, not dancing with us tonight?"

"Tonight it's not possible. I am on call. But I felt I had to—"

Porter ducked out, dragged by Lydia Yakovlevna, and glimpsed the arm of a severely tailored suit before he was on the floor and lurching with the mob.

"Oh God! Oh, pussycat! Isn't it wonderful? I feel wonderful," Lydia Yakovlevna said. She was nibbling his ear again. "I love you. I want to do things. We'll do things, won't we?"

"Yes, we'll do things," Porter said.

Komarova had certainly seen him. She had come over to see him better. Why else would she have come over to give thanks for kind words?

The hospital director could have come and given them. But the hospital director didn't seem to have recognized him, and nor had any of the others. All of them had examined him in the hospital; conscious and unconscious, clothed and naked: a sullen Korean seaman, bruised, with a pigtail and a mustache. Now he was a smiling Chukchi with a shaven head and a smooth face, a guest of Pavel Grigorovich's. What connection could there be between the chance foreign seaman and this driver from Green Cape? But she had seen a connection.

Or had she?

He went frantically over every encounter he had had with her. She had seen him on the ship. She had brought him to the hospital. She had examined him every day. The others had examined him more—this was true—yet he was her patient, and her responsibility. She had had to make the arrangements to get him to Murmansk. Perhaps she had now heard from Murmansk. . . .

Or there could be another reason entirely.

She was the *district* medical officer; perhaps in her district she had not before seen any Chukchis. He hadn't seen any himself. He had certainly been a novelty to Yura, to Liova, even to the old Yakut Vassili. Bukarovsky had been puzzled as to what he was doing here from Chukotka. She could be asking just such questions about him now.

Yes, it was that. It had to be that.

"Pussycat, one more dance and then let's go," Lydia Yakovlevna said. She was rubbing herself against him. "Oh, God, I want to do things. I want to do everything. We'll do everything, won't we?"

"Yes, we'll do everything," Porter said.

He had signed for a bobik to get down to Tchersky, and now they went back to Green Cape in it, and up to the second floor and did everything. But his mind was not on his partner, now strenuously enjoying herself in the Finnish bed, but on the stern figure in the tailored suit.

This was at the end of October.

27

At the end of October, General Liu Shih-Yu, commander of the military region of Sinkiang in west China, flew from his headquarters at Urumchi to the desert station of Lop Nor.

At Urumchi, a town of half a million people, he maintained an infantry division. At Lop Nor, with almost no people, he had two armored divisions.

Lop Nor was a nuclear test base, his country's oldest.

General Liu was not today on nuclear business, however. He was here to observe the impact of a test missile. It was coming from Manchuria in east China and it would cross the intervening 3,200 kilometers in nine minutes. A new guidance system had been designed to land it within a target area (CEP: circular error probable) of 250 meters.

At Lop Nor he inspected the target area. Instruments had been set to record the impact from the air, from the ground, and from below the ground. Then he went to his observation bunker. Here contact was already established with Manchuria, and he greeted his opposite number, the commander of the Shen-yang military region.

Was all in position at Lop Nor? he was asked.

Yes, all was in position at Lop Nor.

Then launch procedures could commence immediately.

Liu and his staff listened to the launch procedures on the loudspeakers, and then to the blastoff, and themselves joined Shen-yang in a small cheer as the missile departed Manchuria on its nine-minute journey.

After ten minutes—and then twelve, fifteen—confusion developed between Shen-yang and Lop Nor. No missile had appeared.

The first explanation was that its final stage had failed to ignite.

A few minutes later, a correction. It *had* ignited, but after transiting Inner Mongolia the small flight-correcting rockets had evidently misfired, for the missile had swung south. Its descent had been observed, however, and a true burnout velocity logged at 24,000 kph.

The vehicle carried no payload, but this velocity had produced a large crater. It had produced it in the region of Lan-chou, which was outside General Liu's area.

Cursing, he led the way to his aircraft. He knew nothing of the research station at Tcherny Vodi—a frozen world away, far, far to the north. But at Tcherny Vodi much was known of General Liu.

At Urumchi he learned that soon he would be back at Lop Nor. A retest had been ordered—extremest urgency. It had been ordered for November.

28

By November, with the weather hard and the roads good, Kolya Khod-yan had won golden opinions from his comrades at the Tchersky Transport Company. This was due to his cheerfulness, his modesty, and his generosity. His generosity was exceptional.

Already sickness and injury among the crews had moved his name high up the reserve list, and already he had twice declined lucrative long-distance hauls. Family men needed the money more, he said; he was a bachelor, just filling in for a friend. He didn't mind pottering about the area.

By now he had pottered widely and knew every route in and out, short hops that had him frequently back in the dispatch depot. At the depot, too, he was very popular—no moans, no arguments from Kol-ya. Anything to go, he took it, wherever, whatever. And always smil-ing, a lovely fellow. He'd even help with the loading—no way his job!—to give the fellows a break.

He was familiar now with every aspect of the depot, knew the stacks, the destinations, was never in the way. A really bright Chukchi, true gold.

He'd seen the four one-ton crates stenciled TCH. VOD., in Local Delivery: radius fifty kilometers. Tcherny Vodi! He hungrily haunted this bay, fearful somebody else would get it; and as the bay emptied, tried to precipitate the action.

"No, Kolya, no. That's not to go yet."

"What is it?"

"Turbines. For a place up in the hills. They had some kind of blowout a few months ago. There you don't just deliver. They have to call through and say when. They have the stinking heads there."

"Ah, stinking heads." Stinking heads were high-ups, usually se-curity services, usually Moscow, but here sometimes Irkutsk or No-vosibirsk. "What do they want with stinking heads there?" he asked in surprise.

"God knows. We don't ship them much. They fly in what they need, they have a strip. It's just sometimes heavy gear—this has been here weeks, from Archangel, maybe they don't need it yet."

"Is funny that. Stinking heads! I have friends in that place, I think—Evenks."

"Right. They have Evenks there, you're right, Kolya."

"I like to see my friends there. I take this stuff, eh?"

"Sure you will. Sure, Kolya. You'll take the job—just, when we get the call."

And they got the call, and he took the job. He took the four crates on a Ural and helped load and strap them right way up. The Ural had a hoist and a hydraulic tailgate. He headed out of town and followed his map and picked up the creek, going east. The creek was flagged at entry to show the weight it could take, and he drove fifteen kilometers along it to be sure he had it to himself, though there wasn't much doubt. Apart from the road gang who had checked it, nobody had used the creek this season. Then he got out and climbed in the back.

He undid the straps on the tarpaulin, picked out a crate, and got to work with a screwdriver and a pot of paint. He scored out parts of the stenciling and overpainted fresh marks. Then he smudged the result with a grease rag until it was hard to tell which was the correct marking. It was now very cold. The exterior thermometer of the Ural showed forty below, but the air was dead still, no wind. The oily mess hardened immediately and he refastened the tarpaulin.

Twenty kilometers farther along the creek he saw the red flag and the turnoff he had to take out of it. The riverbank was steep, but a ramp had been lowered and strewn with grit. He saw the bundled-up figures waiting on top, and they waved him on as he crunched slowly up. There were two men, their breath standing in the air, quite jovial, ear flaps down, automatic weapons slung, beating themselves in the cold. They had come out of a wooden guard hut in a small leveled area. A military jeep stood next to the hut.

"Found it okay?"

"No problem."

They were gazing at him curiously, not expecting a native; quite friendly, though.

"You unload all this on your own?"

"Sure. Only there's a problem with the manifest."

"Bring it inside."

It was snug inside, two oil stoves going; and it became snugger still when he produced his flask. He heard, what he knew already, that they had run down here an hour ago, to open up the post, flag his turnoff, and lay the ramp. They would wait until the tracked vehicle came down to pick up the load, and then take up the ramp and return; the post wasn't manned normally.

"What's the problem with the manifest?"

"See, is some kind of cockup," he said. "The marks don't tally— we couldn't understand it there."

He took them out and showed them the marks and they puzzled over them.

"Well, the crates are all the same."

"Sure, we got a hundred crates like that. Is Archangel crates."

"Just dump them anyway, and they'll sort it out."

"Is fine with me. You sign for it, you got it. But you don't sign, I can't leave it. Maybe you sign and it's wrong."

The two men looked at each other.

"Well, what's to be done about it?"

"I don't know. Either I run it up there and they check it or someone comes down and checks it here."

They went back in the hut and made a call on a communications set. The call established that someone would come down and check it.

They finished off the flask while waiting for the tracked vehicle to come down. Two Evenks and an officer came down with it. The officer was irritable and he paced impatiently while the Evenks prized open the suspect crate. Then he mounted the Ural and perched on the cab top while consulting a piece of paper and peering down into the crate.

"It's all right. Of course it's all right. Bloody nonsense! Seal it."

Then he paced again while the crate was sealed and Kolya and the Evenks transferred the load. They chatted merrily while they did this—the Evenks, like the other Siberian natives, intrigued that he "had the tongue."

"How is it up there, brothers?"

"Fine. Good conditions, good pay. A job."

"It's as well you came down. I thought I was going to have to run up there with this."

The Evenks laughed. "Not in a million years. They'd never let you."

"Oh, the stinking heads—I forgot. What goes on up there? What kind of problem with stinking heads?"

"They're no problem. Not if you have a pass. We don't mix with anybody. It's just scientists there—who knows what they do?"

But he learned more. The Evenks' reindeer herds were far away, at the other side of a mountain. From there they helicoptered you in. You rotated the jobs at the hill station, a month at a time. They didn't let you stay any longer. But anybody could do it. A stinking head came down and made out the passes; he dealt with Innokenty, the headman.

Then they finished the loading and took off, and his manifests were signed and he took off too, and drove back along the creek, thinking.

The Evenks were the way in, obviously. They were the only way in. Herdsmen, nomads. With a headman, Innokenty. He would have to meet this Innokenty. He would have to get out to the herds. But there were no deliveries to the herds. . . .

He turned the matter over in his mind. Somehow there would *have* to be a way of getting there.

And in the days that followed he found it; and before it, something else.

The load was for a big Kama to Provodnoye, 260 kilometers each way and nobody wanted it, not while the huge backlog for Bilibino and Pevek still remained, real mileage and proper money. Good Kolya took it, in a Ural, two journeys. They broke up the load, window frames and central heating for a new apartment block, and he took off, single-handed. A jewel, a piece of gold dust!

The Provodnoye route was a new one to him, and it looked interesting: You could lose yourself here if you needed to. He ran south on the river, and turned off for the section of made track to Anyuysk. This part he knew. Then he left the made track and picked up the winding tributary to Provodnoye. The tributary ran between steep banks, and in season it evidently ran fast: In the narrow bends coves were gouged out of the banks.

He kept a steady sixty kilometers an hour, slowing to thirty and twenty on the bends, and was changing up as he pulled out of one when a flock of ptarmigan exploded out of a piece of bush. A beautiful sight! White rockets in a lead sky. He watched them in his rearview mirror as they returned to the bush but they did not return to the bush. He could not make out where they returned.

He stopped the truck and got out and walked back on the river. The cluster of bush grew out of the bank; stunted willow, white with ice but mottled where the birds had nibbled the twigs. He padded softly but still they knew and rocketed up again; fox also padded softly.

They had rocketed not from the bush but from behind the bush. The clumps overhung a hole in the bank. Quite a large hole, torn out by fast spring floods. He pulled the frozen vegetation aside. All dark inside, but high, broad, deep. He felt cautiously with his hands. Ice on the walls, a crackling underfoot; twigs the birds had brought in. He could see nothing, but it was deep, deeper than the span of both arms. A cave. He had left his flashlight in the truck, and did not venture any farther. He had started a little late. Provodnoye was still a couple of hours away.

He slept the night at Provodnoye, was held up in the morning by faulty goods for return, and made Green Cape in the afternoon, too late for another journey. He did it the day after.

The bend, the ptarmigan rocketing up again. He stopped the truck alongside, unshipped the ladder and went in.

It was even deeper than he thought. Some obstruction, centuries past, had sent the river thundering in and out of here. He shone his flashlight around. Only a skin of ice on the walls, and under it rock. The same with the roof. Rock, not permafrost. He tried it, all the same; set the ladder, climbed it, bored with the battery drill into the roof. Granite. After an inch he didn't bother anymore. He could go as deep as he needed. It could hold what it had to hold.

Soon after this he had his chat with Vassili, the old Yakut who presided over the parts depot. In between he had made a trip to Ambarchik on the coast and from there had brought back a fish, an Arctic char. Vassili's old woman had been bemoaning the lack of char, and this was a present for her. Very often now he had been sharing the old Yakut's food.

He produced the fish in a sack; quite fresh but stiff as a board, and Vassili's eyes popped.

"This is a *fish*," he said. He examined it all over. "This fish goes a meter."

"Yes, it's a good fish."

"She'll go mad with it." He stood the fish on its nose and with his knife pared off a sliver and ate. "By God, an excellent fish. Full of oil." He pared a sliver for the Chukchi and gave it to him. Kolya ate the sliver and nodded. A nutty flavor; not fishy, not bad, slight oily aftertaste.

"Good," he said.

"The best. With a half of this fish she'll make a fantastic stroganina. You'll come and eat it."

"With pleasure."

"Did you eat lunch yet?"

"Not yet."

They shared the Yakut's pot.

"Vassili," he said, chewing, "I need a bobik."

"Take one."

"To keep. For myself."

"What for?"

"I want one."

The Yakut nodded, cutting a piece of meat between his teeth. They were eating boiled foal and blood sausage stewed in mare's milk.

"Do you know any Evenks?" Kolya asked him.

"There are no Evenks here now."

"Where would you find them?"

"You said you knew some at the station in the hills."

"They're not there. I ran a load for that station."

"Then either they're with the herds or at the collective."

"Which collective?"

"Novokolymsk. What other?"

Kolya pondered this. Evidently the collective was not only for the Yukagir. For Evenks also. And they rotated not just from the herds to the station. They rotated from the collective as well.

"I don't know," he said.

Vassili cut off more meat in his mouth. "I hear the Evenk women are good," he said.

"I hear that."

"I never tried one myself. Where is she?"

"Who?"

The Yakut's face split, but whether with a smile or from tugging at the meat he couldn't tell.

"I think you are a young bastard," he said. "You have an Evenk girl and don't know where she is—the collective or with the herds. Right?"

Kolya grunted and got on with his meat.

Vassili wiped his mouth. "All right," he said, sucking his teeth, "you need a bobik. I'll think about it."

Next day he told Kolya, "She wants you to come and eat stroganina. You can come tonight."

"Good. Thank you."

He went and ate stroganina. The two elderly Yakuts lived in a tiny apartment in one of the earliest blocks; the Europeans had moved out to better blocks. A table came with the apartment but they ate on the floor, on cushions. Vassili's wife gave him a bowl of his own but the two old people ate out of the pot. The stroganina was a rich oily fish stew, highly seasoned, and on a wooden board alongside it was a mound of the raw fish flaked like coconut.

The old woman had put on a Yakut party dress, brightly embroidered; her center parting and brilliant dark eyes were directed intently on him as he ate. She was silent as a mouse but very busy, refilling his bowl until the pot was finished, and piling on the flaked fish.

"A man needs oil," she said to him significantly. "A young man has to have it."

It was all she said to him, but in the morning Vassili told him, "She says you have a nice face."

"Well, it's younger than yours," Kolya said.

"She also says you are a young bastard. She says you should stop fucking Lydia Yakovlevna."

"Who says I am fucking Lydia Yakovlevna?"

"Our granddaughter cleans in the supermarket. Lydia Yakovlevna says you fuck her every night and give her presents, also take her to the best parties. Is that the way a young man like you should get it?"

"Or?"

"It's better to fuck this Evenk. She says they don't want presents and it's healthier for you."

"Well, it's true."

"Of course it's true. Where would you keep the bobik?"

"I know a place."

"You can't just steal one—they're all registered. You know that, don't you?"

"Of course I know it."

"So how would you get one?"

"I could put it together, if I had a friend with the parts."

The Yakut smiled. "You think you could do it on your own?"

"With a manual, why not? It's a toy, you said."

"One man can't fit an engine on his own. It's too heavy."

"With a block and tackle?"

Vassili mused. "The block and tackle would be for borrowing only? I can't make a deficit out of a block and tackle. I only have two."

"Of course for borrowing only. What do I want with a block and tackle?"

"It's a strong heavy engine. The block would need a strong roof to support it."

"I have a strong roof."

"Well, I'll see. Don't bother me with it now."

Kolya began taking parts for the bobik the same week. Vassili gave him a printed specification of the car and they ticked off the parts as he took them. The first parts he took were the wheels. He had been angling now for regular deliveries to the area.

To Anyuysk was no problem. Scattered developments there meant frequent trips by light truck. The problem was the further leg to Provodnoye. Factories and apartment blocks were going up there—top-class ones, an inducement for European Russians to stay in the wilderness: good heating, big boilers, triple glazing. Heavy loads, and for a big Kama. As the season went on, and the drivers could pick and choose less, big Kamas would regularly do this journey. Two-man crews. No good. He had to be on his own.

He saw he was going to have to do it at night. He could always get a bobik for the night. But there were difficulties here, too. He could get a bobik, but how about the parts? The Light Vehicles Depot wasn't open at night. He would have to take the parts during the day and keep them somewhere. Where? Not in the apartment. How could he run an engine up there, gearbox, transmission?

He thought about it while taking the wheels, and a load, down to Anyuysk. He dumped the load quickly, and took off with the wheels toward Provodnoye.

Off the made road and onto the tributary; around and around the tight bends. It took him sixty-five minutes from Anyuysk to the cave. With a bobik he could cut that to maybe forty-five. And from Green Cape to Anyuysk itself—another hour and a quarter. Total, two hours. Four hours there and back. If he started at nine at night when nobody was about, he could be back soon after one in the morning. Nothing.

It would take time to build up the parts before anything could usefully be put together. The heavy engine would be a problem. He would need help getting it in the bobik. Vassili would help him get it in. Then he would have to take off immediately with it, in the lunch hour—whatever other jobs were scheduled for him. He couldn't leave an engine dumped in a bobik. He would have to take it right to the cave. And then? How to get it out of the bobik and into the cave? A block and tackle could raise and lower it. It couldn't get it *in*.

The ptarmigan had shot up again as he approached.

He left the engine running and walked over to the cave and parted the frozen branches. The entrance was wide, far wider than it looked. He tried to find a way of keeping the shrubbery held back but couldn't. He got back in the truck and, with his headlights on, drove slowly through the screen of branches, careful not to break any off; the screen effectively hid the cave.

He got the nose of the truck in and climbed out and looked about him. The headlights brilliantly lit up the place, a hoary icebox: roof, walls, floor, all glittering like diamonds. A spacious icebox, too. Plenty of room to build a bobik, and also to drive one right in. He looked up at the roof, and the hole he had drilled. In the wrong place, but yes! Of course. A piece of cake! He could fit the block to the roof at the rear of the cave. Then *back* the bobik in and *hoist* the engine out. No problem.

He wasted no more time, got the wheels out and stacked against the end wall, reversed the truck onto the river, and drove back to Green Cape.

He'd build up the supplies fast, on as many days as he could. And night after night if possible. Yes, he'd start seriously now.

And this he did, by day and also by night.

29

The dispatch depot: "Kolya—Yura wants you. Run down and see him now."

"But I've got a load here, ready to go."

"Leave it. He's in a temper, very excited. Take the bobik there—the key's in."

He drove down to the Kama hangar, puzzled and cautious.

The place had greatly changed, he saw. No longer the vast array of vehicles lined up row on row. Only a dozen or so of the giant trucks were scattered about now, most being worked on by mechanics.

Yura was in his glass booth and on the phone again. He frowned at the Chukchi and motioned him in.

"Kolya, what's this?" he said, putting the phone down. "Piddling about all the time to Anyuysk—and with little Tatras and Urals. What *is* it?"

"It's trips. It's okay. They give me the jobs."

"They're taking advantage of you. This is no good, Kolya."

"I don't complain, it's fine."

"You don't complain, but it bloody isn't fine! You're picking up no money! And getting no time on a 50! What experience are you getting?"

"I didn't come for experience. I'm filling in."

"You're mine! My driver! I told you so. There's a good distance man in you—young, stamina, plenty of go. You need time on a 50. Piddling about locally is no good. It's no good, Kolya!"

"They want me, what can I do?"

"You can go to Bilibino. Tomorrow. I've cleared it with Bukarovsky. You're down on the sheet. No arguments. It's done!"

Well, if it was done, on the sheet. He couldn't make a fuss about getting off it. To Bilibino and back was fourteen hundred kilometers—a plum three-day job for the drivers, and soon to be scarce as the backlog cleared. . . .

He cursed as he drove back. Three days away, and what shape would he be in for his night work afterward? To hell with Bilibino!

But to Bilibino he went, southeast.

* * *

They left at eight in a snowstorm, and day didn't dawn till almost eleven. They drew a twenty-ton trailer, with another one hitched on behind, and were in a convoy of four, all big Kamas. The two in front could not be seen through the wall of snow in the headlights, but as the day slowly came and the dim shapes emerged lumbering ahead, Vanya relaxed. He was a grizzled elderly fellow, specially selected as a mentor for the Chukchi.

"You'll take over after the first stop," he said. "There's a straight stretch coming, but plenty of uphill shifts. Mustn't lose your footing— it's a long slide down for these bastards." His yellow teeth showed in a grin.

The first stop came soon after eleven, number one of the road stations. The two trucks in front had pulled in, together with another couple going the other way; and behind them, as they parked in a clutter of bobiks, came the fourth of their convoy.

A radio was going and it was very warm and smoky in the log hut. Cooking smells drifted from the kitchen, and cigarette smoke hung over the tables where the drivers sat, so that in the fog it was some minutes before he saw that one of them was a woman. She was also smoking, and in conversation, and his eyes were drawn in that direction because he heard his name mentioned. The drivers were grinning as he looked over.

"Sure, that's him, our Chukchi. . . . Kolya, come over here. She wants to meet you. Medical Officer Komarova."

Her eyes gazed at him coolly as they shook hands. She wore an open parka and a cap like the others, and was sitting with a cigarette over a cup of coffee.

"You're new here, I understand."

"Yes, not long. A few weeks." They had made room for him on the bench opposite, and his smile flashed brilliantly at her. He decided to take his fur cap off.

"Tea or coffee?" the old waitress said. She had slapped his plate of kasha and gravy down, and was also staring at his shaven head.

"Coffee."

"From Chukotka?" Medical Officer Komarova said.

"Chukotka. I'm filling in for a friend."

"They haven't sent your papers in yet. Have you had all your shots?"

"Sure."

"Tetanus, polio, yellow fever?"

"Sure, sure." He forked in the kasha, smile still flashing.

"Don't worry about his shots. He's getting all his shots in," one of the drivers said.

"The condoms come from her place. She calls the shots," another said, as the laughter continued.

Medical Officer Komarova smiled thinly herself. Under the cap her face looked paler, longer, slight anemic; but the eyes were as uncompromising as he remembered.

"Check into the office, anyway," she said. "I'll see they have your papers. Are you outward bound now or coming back?"

"Outward. Bilibino."

"That's three days." She held the cigarette in her mouth and with her eyes screwed up opened a zipper bag and took out a notebook and a pen. "Today's Tuesday? . . . Make it Friday. That afternoon, four P.M. You'll need a lie-in in the morning." She wrote in the book and on a card and gave him it. "It's the administrative building in Tchersky. Anyone will tell you."

"You want to check me over or what?"

"I won't be there. They need to update your papers and get you on our records."

She went soon afterward and he finished his breakfast, still in doubt. *Had* she recognized him? Would she so specifically have mentioned the yellow fever if so? Surely not. It was the Chukchi interest: He *looked* different from the others. And totally different from the Korean seaman. No. He was a new face in town, a new driver. A matter of papers.

He finished his coffee and in twenty minutes was out with the convoy again. The snow had stopped. He took the wheel and steered the big rig into place in line.

"We keep two hundred meters," Vanya told him. "Give him plenty of room to get off in front. And practice the gears. You'll be running up and down them soon."

"Okay. She seems a decent sort, that medical officer."

"You think so? Don't bet on it. The slightest thing wrong with you, she has you off the long runs."

"Does she check all the drivers?"

"See, the company sick bay is hers—the nurses, the supplies, all from Tchersky. They keep the medical histories there. She's a strict manager, Komarova."

"To me, she was like one of the boys."

"Try getting a dose of clap, and you'll find out. All this is her district and she knows what goes on in it. Change down now. Watch him in front—he's climbing."

They were climbing, and they continued climbing, the ice road running through a series of passes, first between hills and then mountain peaks. From Green Cape they had ascended 2,800 feet, and now went much higher, on all sides the icy crests smoking in clouds. More snow was waiting in the clouds, and Vanya silently observed it through his window. But the road was straight and continued straight, even in the switchbacks that now came. After the climb, a sharp drop, and then up again, and down again, and up and down, a glassy and treacherous ribbon of ice.

"Not your brakes! Only the gears!" Vanya yelled. "And leave him room—two hundred meters."

The convoy pulled on, stopping every hundred kilometers at the road stations. At each one they replenished the flasks of tea and coffee, and the day slowly went. The straight also went, and with night came the snow, and Vanya took over; and sharp bends now began to zigzag through the mountains.

Between stations the men were supposed to alternate in sleep. But with the bends and the snow, Vanya now drove from every station. And there was no sleeping through the constant roar of oaths that came from him as they swung and lurched behind their headlights in the white dazzle of snow; only a few meters of track visible ahead. He drove through the night, and he drove the first turn of the day as well, until the road straightened out. At one o'clock Kolya took over, sleepless himself, and he drove into Bilibino, Vanya snoring beside him.

Bilibino, named for Bilibin the geologist who first assayed the reefs, was the center for the most northerly goldfields of Siberia, and the big trucks and the ice road were the only means of getting heavy equipment there; this was what they carried. Scores of thousands of tons of it had built up, shipped from St. Petersburg and Archangel in the summer. Only in summer could it be shipped, and only in winter could it be hauled. And now it was here, Bilibino.

They reached it at four in the afternoon, left the trucks for unloading and reloading, and went to bed at a hostel. Eight hours later, after a meal, they left again on the return journey; midnight; the night black, road white in their headlights.

A hard country, an exhausting routine, and he took the first leg. Over thirty hours of driving still ahead—thirty-two, in fact, the time-keeping good through all difficulties—and nonstop except for brief rests at the road stations. Which would get them in—what?—late tomorrow. No, not tomorrow; the time confusing. All tomorrow they would be driving. The next day. Friday, early.

Well, after a good rest he'd organize a bobik for that night, see Vassili in the afternoon. But in the afternoon, Jesus, the medical center at Tchersky! Well, he'd do it, wouldn't make waves, an administrative matter. Nothing wrong with Khodyan's papers; they just hadn't received them. He'd handed them in himself when Bukarovsky had signed him on. In the early confusion, the start of the season, they hadn't been sent on. An administrative matter.

He would sleep all morning. Get up and see Vassili. Arrange a bobik. With the bobik run into Tchersky and get his papers settled at the medical center. Then the time was his. Yes.

He finished his stint at the first road station and Vanya took over. And now he tried to sleep, and managed it, no curses coming, just slow steady driving through the zigzags.

The next turn, still in the mountain labyrinth, still not snowing, Vanya put him on the wheel again but remained awake himself to watch. And the night went, and the day went, and the following night; and at eight on Friday morning, seventy-two-hours after leaving it, they pulled back into Green Cape.

30

At half-past two, as arranged, Anna Antonovna woke him and gave him his dinner. He was stiff, creaky, aching all over. But after a shower he felt he could make it. He went to see Vassili.

"What do you want to take?" Vassili said.

"The frame members."

"All *four?* The sides won't go in a bobik. You'd need a roof rack. Take something else."

"The axle assemblies?"

"Yes, they'd go."

They ticked off the pair of axle assemblies on the specification, and Vassili made a careful note in his deficit book. These goods had never arrived at the depot—either hadn't been sent or had gone missing on the way.

"What time are you coming for them?" he said.

"I don't know. Say five."

"Remember, we shut at six."

"It will be before."

"And the back door *here.*" They were in the storeroom. "Don't go through the garage. People will be working there. Bring the bobik around to the back."

"Okay. First I have to get it."

By a quarter to four he had the bobik and was running down to Tchersky in it. He knew the administrative building and parked outside. He found the medical center and presented himself at the enquiry window.

"Khodyan," he said to the woman clerk who answered the buzzer. "I was told to be here at four."

"For what?"

"I'm a new driver with the transport company." He handed in the card he had been given. "You were getting my papers."

She had a look at the card. "Oh yes. Khodyan. We have to update you. Just a minute, I'll get them."

He looked at the two other clerks at work in the room while she went out, and presently she was back and letting him in. "Yes. Come through," she said, and he followed her through the room and into a corridor, and into another room. "Khodyan," she said, and left him.

Medical Officer Komarova was in the room, writing at a desk. She was in her white hospital coat. She glanced up briefly. "Please sit down," she said.

He did so, after a small jolt.

"I thought you wouldn't be here," he said.

"I thought so, too. Work." She continued writing for a few moments and then screwed the top back on an old-fashioned fountain pen. She drew a dossier toward her.

"You had rheumatic fever at age twelve," she said.

"Very slight. If I even had it at all." He flashed his smile.

"Diagnosed at Anadyr. Streptococcal infection."

"But at Novosibirsk, not. There everything fine. All checked out. Nothing wrong with me."

She read further. "Yes. What were you doing at Novosibirsk?"

"My father was a teacher, without a degree. Nothing doing for our people then at Anadyr. We went to Novosibirsk and he got one."

"I see. And then the family went back?"

"No. They like Novosibirsk."

"And you?"

"I don't. I just knock about—no student. For me is better up here."

"Where did you learn your—Russian?"

"Everywhere. Is not very good, I know."

"Better than my Chukchi," she said. She said it in Chukchi and his smile flashed wider.

This tough and knowing babe knew something. What? The faint smile was there again, elusive, slightly mocking. If she had Chukchi, she had mixed with Chukchis. Did she know he wasn't one? He couldn't make her out. She looked different every time he saw her. In the hospital, the cool doctor; at Bukarovsky's banquet the stern, suited specter; at the road station the gamine in the cap; here, calmly managerial. Yet the same face—pale, thin-nosed, vaguely anemic. No lipstick or makeup. The hair blondish, severely drawn back, not remarkable. Nothing about her was remarkable, except the air of pale competence. Was she forty, thirty? Impossible to say. The gray eyes were looking him over.

"Are you pure Chukchi?"

"I don't know how pure I am. I'm Chukchi." He allowed a spurt of temper to show as he said this, and she looked down at his dossier again.

"There's nothing further we should know about, here?"

"Nothing."

"All right. Let's have a look at you. Strip off over there. There's a bench."

His mouth opened, but she had risen immediately and was washing her hands at a basin. The bench was behind a plastic curtain. He took his boots off, then closed the curtain and took everything off down to his socks and shorts.

"I'll need to see your feet," she said, briskly parting the curtain.

"My feet? My feet are fine."

"Have you had frostbite ever?"

"No, never."

"Show me."

He took his socks off, and she closely inspected the feet. "Yes. Good. A fine instep—all you northern people have it. Now the shorts."

"My shorts? What—"

"I will examine your testicles."

He silently removed the shorts and she examined the testicles.

"Cough." He coughed.

"Again." Again.

"Yes." She examined further in the area, and then his abdomen, ribs, arms, armpits, mouth, ears, eyes, head.

"The head. Have you had alopecia?"

"I had delayed shock, after an accident. All the hair fell out."

"This has been shaved recently."

"I shave it. You don't like it this way?"

She made no comment, adjusting her stethoscope. She listened to his chest. She listened to his back. She listened to his chest again.

"Well, I think Anadyr was right," she said, "and Novosibirsk wrong. You have a murmur."

"A murmur?" He had no murmur. Khodyan might have one, but he didn't. "What murmur?"

"The streptococcal infection had an effect on the heart. Very slight, but it's there. You can get dressed now."

He got dressed, thinking this over. What was going on here? He absolutely had no murmur. He had been checked out thoroughly at the camp. He went out of the cubicle, very wary.

"I can't recommend that you drive long distances," she said. She was writing again, and nodded to him to sit. "It's dangerous, for you and for others."

"But I'm a driver!"

"You are entitled to a cardiological examination. I will arrange it for you at the hospital if you wish. But for the present, no long journeys."

"Then what will I do?"

"Are they so important to you, long journeys?" She had glanced up quickly as she said this.

"Well." He had seen the advantages at once: a word from her and no more of Yura's Kamas. But what was *her* game? "It's my work," he said.

"You can do other work, short journeys. That I will allow. After a rest. You are quite tired. I am authorizing a week off work for you. Hand this in to the office there."

He stared blankly at the form she gave him.

"A few days' rest isn't a punishment," she said, the faint smile appearing again. "You have friends here, I believe."

"Yes, friends."

"But not Chukchi—is that it?"

"No. No Chukchis here," he said with more confidence.

"Oh, but there are. At Novokolymsk, the collective. You haven't been there yet?"

"No." Chukchis there, too? It must be a collective for all the native peoples.

"And even nearer at hand—at Panarovka, this side of the river. I go there tomorrow. It should have been today. If you want I'll take you. Then you can talk Chukchi." There was now—was he wrong?—something taunting in her expression.

His smile easily outshone hers. "I would like that! Thank you."

"All right. I have a few things to do at Green Cape. Be outside your building at eleven and I can pick you up. I have to stay overnight, but there's accommodation for you, too. Bring what you need—pajamas, toothbrush. A razor," she said, looking at his head.

He went out in a daze.

In the bobik, he saw it was a quarter past six. He'd missed Vassili; the Light Vehicles Depot would be shut. But there was more urgent and serious business here. She knew something. The inch-by-inch examination of him. She had examined him before. . . . *She knew.*

But had she told anyone else? So far as he could tell, he hadn't been watched. Perhaps she hadn't been sure until now, perhaps was still not sure. But tomorrow she would be sure. The Yukagir had not thought him a Yukagir, or the Evenks an Evenk. Was he any more likely to fool the Chukchis? . . . Perhaps with Khodyan's screwed-up background—Anadyr, Novosibirsk, here, there—he might just swing it.

But *she* had swung it, against him. A clever as well as a tough operator. With Khodyan's suspected murmur she had effectively stopped him from leaving her district. She wanted to keep an eye on him. And tomorrow she would have ample opportunity. With Chukchis to confirm her suspicions.

What, then? Should he get out of it? And afterward be stuck here, a week off work, not knowing what she was doing? No, not that. But was it any better staying close to her?

He couldn't think

"Pussycat, where have you been?" Lydia Yakovlevna was huddled in the doorway. "I haven't seen you for days!"

In the same confusion of mind, he had driven back, parked the car, walked into the building, quite unaware of any of it. He looked at her.

"I've been to Bilibino," he said.

"To Bilibino! Oh, what a lot of money. But poor lamb, you'll be tired. Come in, have a drink and we'll do things. Tonight I'll really relax you."

And that night she almost wore him out. But relax him she did, and as the big girl worked away he knew what he would do. He would go with the medical officer the next day, but if anything untoward happened, it would have to be her last day on earth.

31

The broad Kolyma, shining white, a blinding white. At eleven-thirty the day had not long dawned, but already they needed their snow glasses. She was in her cap and parka, and she handled the bobik efficiently—a white one striped with red which he recalled having seen at the road station.

"You drive everywhere yourself?" he said. This he said for something to say; she had said almost nothing, buzzing quite fast on the river.

"I fly if I have to. It means arrangements. Driving is easier."

"Yes. On a fine day."

Today was very fine, the sky clear, faintly blue. Smoke stood straight in the air from occasional houses on the bank; from the opposite bank also, three or four miles away across the white expanse, the air crystal clear.

"But not in bad weather," he said, "or for long distances. The road station we met at—a long distance."

"Yes. The limit of my district."

"You treat people there?"

"Settlements. They send a tractor over for me."

"And take them food also?" She had picked up a couple of crates at Green Cape, evidently from stores: fruit and vegetables, canned goods.

"No."

She had seen him glance behind at the stuff, but made no other comment.

All right, tough baby. No questions from her about Chukotka, or even his driving experiences, which would have been normal. Well, he could wait too. Until tomorrow, anyway. He needed information from her first, to find out how far the thing had gone. He had decided, whatever happened, that she must not get back to Green Cape. The matter of Murmansk would always remain in the air. All he needed was a place for the accident.

"It's up a creek, this settlement?" he said.

"A small river. Panarovka."

"That's the name of the river?"

"Of the village. The river is the Little Ghost."

"A strange name. Why Little Ghost?"

"A camp used to be there—an old one, from Czarist times. It was used since, of course. Many people died there. Their ghosts remain."

"You believe that?" he said incredulously.

She smiled.

"The Chukchis believe it." And now she became suddenly talkative. "You'll know a good many of the old beliefs, I expect?"

"Well, some. A broken childhood," he said cautiously. "And my father a teacher—he didn't believe."

"These are old-fashioned people here. *They* believe. They've been here for generations. And they know many things. Maybe they even know you."

"I don't think so," he said regretfully. "I never was here."

"But they go there—to Chukotka. They fly out, they keep up their contacts."

"They do?"

"Oh, yes. Regularly. They know everything that goes on there—a wonderful knowledge of family networks. It's good to keep such things alive. Don't you agree?''

"Yes, it's good. It's nice," he said.

"They'll certainly know of your family—parents, aunts, cousins. You will have a lot in common. It will be interesting even apart from the language.''

"Yes, interesting," he said.

"I thought so. I have a good relationship with them. They tell me everything. Now here,'' she said, "we're just coming to the Little Ghost. Over there, the opposite bank, is Novokolymsk, a few kilometers farther, you can't see it from here. It isn't far in a bobik. They are more up-to-date at the collective. As a modern person perhaps you'll have more in common. If you want to visit, I can arrange it for you.''

"Yes. I'd like it," he said. "Maybe while I'm off work I can run an errand for you there?''

"Maybe. I'll try and think of something.''

"You could write me a letter here. I could take it later.''

She smiled behind her snow glasses. "You prefer more up-to-date people," she said.

"Well. While I have nothing else to do—I could meet them.''

"All right, I'll write a few lines. Remind me.''

"I will. Good," he said. And everything now was good. The Little Ghost River was good. The bank of the Kolyma had fallen away and they were in the tributary. A wonderful little tributary, like the one to Provodnoye; winding, sharp bends. The banks were not so high, and not so vertical; but high enough and vertical enough. And quite narrow, no more than four meters, in places only three. Yes, easily done here.

He sized it up carefully as she wound around the bends, but in twenty minutes—rather too soon—Panarovka came into view. The river widened suddenly into a small curving bay, and the bank fell to form a beach. The village was set back on a snow-covered slope, perhaps three hundred meters away; at first glance it was a huddle of small blobs with a taller one behind. A track had been made, climbing from the river, and she turned up it.

Closer to, the small blobs became recognizable as three rows of houses. The taller one was no less recognizable.

"A church," she said, as he peered. "The place is old.''

"Do they use it anymore?''

"Yes, they use it.''

Both the church and the houses were of wood, the houses detached and with a fence of palings around each. Smoke came from the houses but no one was about, and she drove along the upper row and parked outside the last house on the corner.

"Your clinic?" he said.

"Yes. Bring the other crate." She had gotten one out of the back and was walking up the stamped snow path.

So that was it. The bearer of gifts used one of the Chukchi houses as her clinic. She could have explained, if she'd wanted. What she wanted was evidently to confront him right away with some Chukchis. Okay; he braced himself.

A Chukchi woman, elderly and shapeless, opened the door as they reached it. "I heard the car," she said in Russian.

"Yes. I'm sorry I'm late. There's fruit here, Viktoria." To his surprise she kissed the Chukchi. "And some tinned stuff. Bring it in," she said to Kolya.

The woman barely glanced at him as she took the crate of fruit and looked into it, and he followed with the other crate through a little hall, curtained to keep out the drafts, into a large room. It was very warm, a big porcelain stove set againt the far wall. The walls were of wood and the room dark, the windows small. Another woman was sitting in a big armchair, knitting, and Komarova bent and kissed her too.

"Tanya!" the woman said. She was a little bag of bones with a shawl; a walking stick leaned against the chair. "We expected you yesterday."

"I know, I'm sorry. Wait—she'll come and take it from you," she said to him. "Mother, I've brought a visitor—Nikolai Dmitrievich Khodyan. He's from Chukotka. Alexandra Ivanovna," she introduced her mother. "He can't shake hands with you now, he's holding a crate." But the Chukchi woman returned just then and took the crate, glancing at him as she did so.

"Nikolai Dmitrievich?" the old lady said, holding out her hand.

"Kolya," he said, shaking the hand.

"You are visiting us from Chukotka?"

"Bend down, she can't see you," Komarova ordered.

He bent and the old lady felt his face, and his head. "Ah, an old person?"

"Not as young as I should be, but not that old."

"His hair fell out. He's my age," Komarova said.

Was he now? Khodyan was thirty-six.

"*Khodyan?*" the Chukchi woman said, returning to the room. "One of the Khodyans from Anadyr?"

"Yes, I am. You are Viktoria—"

"Eremevina." The Chukchi woman shook his hand. "And if I am not mistaken—did you say Nikolai Dmitrievich?"

"Yes, I did."

"The son of the schoolteacher?"

"That's me." They were talking now in Chukchi.

"Then I was present at your birth! Heaven save us all!" She gave him a resounding kiss on the lips. "But your family moved to Novosibirsk! And your elder sister, the one who was so ill—what was her name?"

"She died," Kolya said promptly. "It hurts me to talk of it."

"Oh, I'm sorry!"

"What are they babbling at? Why babble?" the old lady said. "I am also here."

"Viktoria is telling him she was present at his birth. His father was a schoolteacher in Anadyr. He had a sister who died."

"Well, I'm sorry to hear it. But they can speak a Christian language. While I am still here! Nobody has come to talk to me for half a year!"

"I was here six weeks ago," Komarova said resignedly. "And this is a busy time. Is my consulting room ready?" she asked the Chukchi.

"Of course. And ten people were sitting here waiting yesterday!"

"Well, tell them I'm here now. And prepare a room for Nikolai Dmitrievich, he will be staying the night. I expect you'll find something to talk about," she told him.

She was looking at him curiously, and he returned the look.

She had understood every word of the Chukchi. Well, what of it? His story had held up—indeed had been miraculously confirmed. If Khodyan did not have too many other siblings to dispose of, he could hold his own. She would question this Viktoria, he had no doubt of it, and the other Chukchis; ten patients. . . . A very comprehensive checking out of him. A thorough bitch, and cold; brusque with her mother, and this old retainer. All of a piece, at any rate. He could handle her as long as he had to. Not so long now.

He brought in their two bags, and was shown to his room; all wood, dark, smelling of camphor.

She had gone to her consulting room when he returned, and he sat and took a glass of tea with the old lady. But presently, as patients arrived and, after introductions, began talking loudly to him in Chukchi, the old woman struggled wrathfully to her feet, and was helped by Viktoria to her room.

But so far, so good. His story was sound, reasonable. A schoolmaster a little above himself had taken his family to a big town, and preferred it there. The daughter had died and the boy, detached from his background—even speaking his own tongue with an accent!—had gone on the loose. But he had hankered for the far north, had healthy instincts himself, a good young fellow.

He heard Khodyan's antecedents discussed, flashed his smile of rueful ignorance, listened to their own stories, told of his driving experiences, of the money to be made. A levelheaded young fellow, as well as charming.

So many invitations came his way that he was able to skip the late lunch at the house and take it elsewhere: a snack here, a drink there, mainly among women and old men; and he learned the reason for this.

In summer the villagers fished and farmed. Because the river had no bank here, when the ice broke the first flood came up and washed the top meter of ground almost all the way to the village. In the good soil they grew everything: potatoes, cucumbers, tomatoes, onions, beans—flowers, even. Yes, in the gardens, sunflowers, this high!

But in winter the men went to the traplines, came home maybe only once in ten days. They sold the pelts through the collective at Novokolymsk. All sorts were there, Yakuts, Evenks, Yukagir, Chukchi—yes, Chukchi, too. Not *quite* our sort, but decent people. If he was interested someone would always take him there, easily arranged.

He began to see he wouldn't need Komarova for this. But he needed her for something else, of course, and he took dinner at the house. An endless meal, in which the daughter's impatience with her mother grew.

The old lady talked. And talked. The villagers had told him, no doubt, of her late husband, Dr. Komarov? An angel to them. When he had come out of the camp he had been eagerly awaited in Leningrad, where his reputation stood so high. But no, he had set up his surgery here. An angel. They kissed his feet. *Wouldn't* leave them, had selflessly ministered to all here. And now lay in his final place here. Which she would never leave, no never. Had he seen the graveyard?

No, he had not yet had that opportunity; he would like the opportunity.

Just beyond the church, on the high ground. Was he a churchgoer?

Sometimes he was a churchgoer; in his job it was not always easy. And there were not that many churches!

Well, tomorrow he could go to church, Sunday. They would all go to church. This one had a beautiful, a holy history—

"We will go out now," Komarova said.

"Out? Out where?" her mother said.

"To the graveyard. He wants to see it."

"Tatiana, are you mad? It will be pitch dark."

"There's a moon."

"If you can see it, it will be freezing hard. He'll see it in the morning, of course. We'll all go."

"There might be no time in the morning."

"No time—what are you thinking of? I've arranged flowers for you to lay there!"

"And tell Viktoria we'll need fresh tea. We'll have it when we return. It won't be long."

"But you'll freeze! It's iron hard out there. Put everything on that you have!"

They put everything on, but he still gasped as they stepped outside. The cold was so intense it seemed to burn the backs of his eyeballs. The night was dead still, glaring white. Below her cap Komarova had wrapped her head and mouth in a woolen scarf; he held gloved hands to his mouth and smelled the leather.

They mounted the path to the church. It stood squat in the moonlight, its wooden steeple sheathed in ice. Beyond, the graveyard was set out like a camp on the white slope, neat rows of small knobs, the tops of iced crosses. They crunched between the rows. On the mounds wisps of dried flowers poked through the snow like bits of tinsel. She paused between a couple of mounds and bent to brush the snow off one, peering.

"Your father?"

"Piotr Petrovich . . . yes. More flowers here. Five bunches. Remember that, she'll ask."

Her mouth was muffled through the scarf, but her eyes when she straightened up were looking at him very levelly.

"But we didn't come out here to look at graveyards, Nikolai Dmitrievich," she said. "There is something I have to say to you."

32

The church was not locked and he followed her inside. In the blackness a tiny point of red wavered above the altar. She led the way there, groping along the aisle. "There are candles somewhere."

He heard a rattling. "Here. And they make a charge. Put a few coins in the box. I have no money."

He lit the candle with his lighter and searched his pockets. "All I have"—he peered—"is a bill."

"They won't complain," she said dryly, and took the note off him. "Incense," she said, sniffing. "That's what they spend money on? Well now, Nikolai Dmitrievich, I have an apology to make to you."

"An apology? For what?"

"An attitude you might have found—incorrect. Perhaps unfriendly, even racist. Do not mistake my mother's attitude for my own. There is no trace of racism in me. Quite the contrary. I have profound respect for all the peoples of the north. The fact is, I was not sure who you were—even if you were a Chukchi at all."

He stared at her.

"What else could I be?"

"Well, you could have been something else. You know we have few strangers here, a security area. But a few weeks ago we did have one, in Green Cape. A Korean seaman, very ill; I took him off his ship to Tchersky hospital. I thought you resembled him."

He shook his head. "I don't understand," he said. "You have a seaman in hospital, and think I—"

"He isn't. He recovered and went away, to Murmansk, to rejoin his ship. But there were certain things about you—your accent, for instance. It didn't sound to me Chukchi. . . . In short, it's why I brought you here. These people would know, of course, and I trust them."

He flashed his smile. "Well, I hope Viktoria Eremevina's guarantee is good enough. I don't remember my birth personally, but she was there!"

"Yes, I know. But understand my grounds. Even now the people here say you have some other accent—maybe a little like Evenk. It's what I thought myself, and it puzzled me."

"Well, my friends are Evenk, it's true. And my own language—I mainly lost it in Novosibirsk. Without even speaking Russian properly. I'm a mess, I know."

"Don't worry," she said, a little more warmly. "But I wanted this opportunity to apologize, and to tell you not to be alarmed if the police question you."

"The police?"

"As the medical officer for the district I must report any stranger I cannot vouch for absolutely. But there's nothing to worry about. They will simply check over your background—" She frowned at his expression. "Is there something you have not told me?"

He was silent, staring into the candle.

"Nikolai Dmitrievich," she said, "speak in confidence. I know there are people here who don't want their affairs looked at too closely. Particularly drivers. Matters to do with women, things of that nature . . . It's why they're here. I don't report such things. *Is* there something?"

"Well, in confidence . . . There is. A woman, yes."

"Then have no fear. The police won't tell her—they don't bother with that."

He was silent some moments longer.

"Can I trust you further?" he said softly.

"If it's not of a criminal nature, of course."

"It's not criminal," he said. "But I'm not Khodyan. All that I've said of my life—the broken background, Novosibirsk—all that is true. Yet I'm not Khodyan. In Novosibirsk I knew Khodyan. *His* father was the schoolteacher. We were friends, and we became drivers together. But he was unsettled and went back north, to Magadan. Then this year—this summer, just a few months ago—we met again, at Batumi on the Black Sea. He wanted to stay there and lose his identity. An affair of the heart, a girl he wished to marry. And he already had a wife and children! So we exchanged papers. It was crazy, I know— although at the time it seemed a joke! But that's it, and I can't have the police searching through papers."

She stared at him. "But this is a lunatic thing," she said. "If they had to investigate you for any reason—a driving accident, anything— they would soon discover the truth."

"How?"

"I'm not a policeman. But fingerprints?"

"What fingerprints? I have done nothing wrong, ever."

"And Khodyan?"

"The same. I would swear to it."

"Then what have you to fear from an investigation, either as Khodyan or—whoever you are?"

He lowered his eyes.

"Well. There is still something else, something very upsetting. Khodyan drowned. He drowned there at Batumi, a tragic accident. And he is buried there. Under my name! It upset me deeply. The authorities informed my parents—that I was dead. And also—also this other woman I mentioned to you. What was I to do? I couldn't go back to Novosibirsk. I was dead! Or to Magadan—where Khodyan was known. Also I couldn't stay at Batumi. He was known there too, Khodyan. And I had his papers. So in the end . . . Ponomarenko, who knew all this—the three of us had teamed up together—Ponomarenko said I should come up here for a bit, take his apartment, his job, until I'd sorted myself out. And that is the whole truth, I swear to you!"

She looked at him a long time in the candlelight.

"Well, you made a good impression on your comrades, at any rate. As well as here. But this is an insane thing you did!"

"Yes. I'm a fool. I think I have always been a fool," he said sadly. "But not bad! If I could convince you of that, Tatiana Petrovna!"

She pursed her lips and moved down the aisle with the candle.

"You will not submit me for police investigation?"

She blew the candle out and set it on a bench and opened the door. "I must think about this."

"You know I am not a bad man!"

"Look, Nikolai Dmit— What do I call you now, anyway?"

"Kolya?" he said, smiling anxiously.

"All right. Kolya. I have a responsible function here, a trusted one. People trust me."

"Then trust *me*. You know me now. You have examined me— every part of me," he said, smiling more widely. "Tell me . . . do I have a murmur?"

"No." Her own faint smile came on. They crunched down the path together. "I had to restrict your movements, in order to— Well, never mind. But it's true you are very tired and need a few days off. Hand that form in on Monday. And we'll leave early tomorrow. No church!"

"Thank you. I know I can do with a rest."

"And while having it—your eagerness for the collective. It was the Evenks you wanted there, wasn't it?"

"They have always been my friends."

"A secretive man." Her smile remained. "And I can understand why now. But I was right to have my suspicions."

"I hope you didn't mention them to anyone else?"

"Of course not. I rely on my own judgment."

"Yes. I see why it is so respected. May I mention how much I admire you, Tatiana Petrovna—your thoroughness, your observation . . . among other things?"

She glanced at him swiftly. "Just remember the five bunches of flowers. But thank you, anyway . . . Kolya."

They went into the house, and he was asked, and mentioned the flowers, and they took tea with the old lady and went to bed.

And then all that was over, and only the events of tomorrow remained.

It had to be done. There was no escaping it. In the past hour she had become, suddenly, warmer, more human—even, in her perplexity, likable. Yet it had to be done. She couldn't remain. But he had gentled her, he had disarmed her; she would give no trouble. And she had told nobody.

He undressed and got into bed. There was still the question of Murmansk, whether inquiries had come from there. He would ask her. Also whether she had written into his record the ban on long-distance driving. She had been writing something, not only the sick note. He would ask that, too.

And the letter to the collective. Had she written it? Not that he any longer needed a letter. They knew him now in this place, Panarovka. He would come up for her funeral, perhaps. . . . They would take him to the collective; he would meet the Evenks, go out with them to the herds, see this headman, Innokenty.

Yes, it was shaping up.

He blew the light out and lay back. He had better do the driving himself tomorrow. He could stop where he wanted then, and do what he had to do. . . .

He had a sudden image of the Little Ghost River winding in the moonlight. He would need a spot to overturn the car afterward; a broken neck had to be explained. He thought it over for some minutes and then stopped and eased himself down in the featherbed. There were plenty of spots, and there would be no problems. Yet he slept badly.

They were out at nine, still in the dark, despite ructions from the mother. "I am too busy this time," Komarova said, patting her hand and bestowing perfunctory kisses. He received one himself from Viktoria, and shook hands with the old lady.

"Let me drive," he said, at the car. "I am quite relaxed today."

"No, I don't like to be driven. And get in quickly. She will send Viktoria out on some nonsense. Anything to delay me!"

He got in, and the reliable little bastard started immediately. Well, some other way.

She took off down to the river, and drove carefully onto it. "It's even more slippery this morning—last night's low temperature."

This was true. In the headlights the river ice had a greasy sheen. He knew he had only about twenty minutes on it, twenty-five at the most, if she drove slowly.

"Drive slowly," he said. "There were many sharp bends I noticed on the way in."

"I know them. And I trust myself more at the wheel than you. Your hands are shaking."

"Perhaps I am tireder than I thought."

"You are. You need your rest."

"Well, sometimes the patient isn't the best judge."

"He never is. The drivers try to fool me—particularly after sick bay, when they want the long-distance jobs."

"Yes. Did you write it in my record—that I can't drive long distances anymore?"

"I did. But I can change my mind," she said, the slight smile appearing.

Yes, but you won't, he said silently. They had gone a kilometer. He decided to give it another eight, perhaps nine; halfway between the village and the Kolyma. He kept his eye on the clock.

"Are you watching my speed?"

"No. I didn't know I was doing it. A habit of the job."

"Of the 'boats'?" She smiled again.

"Yes. The boats . . . This seaman you mentioned, the Korean. You thought I looked like a *Korean?*"

"Just a look. He had more hair than you." She glanced at him, still smiling. "A head of hair. With a pigtail, and a mustache. A very angry man."

"What was the matter with him?"

"We thought yellow fever. But it wasn't."

"Why was he angry?"

"Frustration, mainly. He had almost no Russian. He kept shouting in Korean, bits of Japanese. We thought he wanted to go to Japan—he'd come from there. But it was Murmansk he wanted, and his ship."

"So he went there and sailed away?"

"Yes, I suppose so. He went, anyway."

"And you heard nothing more?"

"No." She steered carefully around a bend. "Not yet. They'll acknowledge receipt in time. I discharge a patient from my district, they accept him in theirs. You can't board a ship after a fever without a proper discharge, which they have first to accept. We get it with Russian sailors sometimes. They're always slow with the paperwork, Murmansk."

So something would come. Well, somebody else would deal with it. Two kilometers to go, he saw.

"Can I smoke?" he said.

"You know I don't permit smoking while I drive."

"Then stop for a minute. We'll both have one."

"Don't be silly, Kolya. You can wait."

"It's true my hands are shaking. Look. A cigarette will pull me together. It confused me, that village. I was quite confused."

"So many Chukchis?"

"Yes. And perhaps—your attitude." She had a scarf around her neck. It wouldn't be in the way. An elbow crooked around the head, a hand at the base of the neck. "Stop awhile and we'll talk about it."

"I'll drive, you talk," she said dryly.

He took his cigarettes out and opened the packet.

She glanced at him swiftly. "Put them away, Kolya. I told you!"

"Stop the car," he said.

"Don't talk to me in that way!" she said angrily.

"Stop the car."

"What do you—"

He got a foot up and kicked both hers off the pedals, at the same time wrenching the wheel. The car slewed and hit the bank and he pulled on the hand brake, still fighting her for the wheel, and managed to steer it around, and again, two complete circles, before it bounced again off the bank, and slowed to a long slithering halt, aslant the track.

Her mouth was open, her face chalky in the reflected light of the headlamps.

"What are you—"

"I'm sorry," he said.

"No don't! *Don't!*"

He had an arm around her neck, could feel her breath.

"It's me! Understand! Kolya—it's me you want! You've come here for me. For Rogachev—don't you understand? *Rogachev!*"

Her head was crooked in his elbow, and he relaxed it slightly, staring at her. "What are you saying?"

"I *know* who you are! I landed you from the ship. I waited for you! Idiot—fool! Let me go!"

He let her go and they stared at each other. Her mouth, her whole jaw was shaking, eyes still glassy with fright. "Were you going to kill me?"

"Yes."

They still stared at each other.

"Where are the cigarettes?" she said.

He found them under his feet, the packet crumpled. He found two whole ones, and lit them, one for him and one for her.

Five

The House of Dr. Komarov

33

Her ankle was bruised and swollen where he had kicked it—kicked much harder than he'd realized. They sat in the dark room and he watched as she bound a compress on the swelling. They had barely spoken since reaching the house.

He poured himself another vodka. "For you?" he said.

"No. It's too early. One is enough."

It still was early. It wasn't yet eleven.

The house was a wooden one, like her mother's, on the outskirts of Tchersky. It was crazily lopsided, a veteran of many thaws; but it stood alone, no neighbors within eyeshot. There was a large shed alongside. The bobik was now in the shed. He had noted all this and was now turning it over in his mind, together with all the other matters revolving there.

She finished binding the ankle and sat back with her own drink. The eyes were still somewhat glassy, but now from the vodka, perhaps. She was palely controlled, watching him.

"Why did you wait so long?" he asked at last.

"To see how you managed here. If you were capable."

"Did I manage?"

"Yes. I had to be very sure."

"Then why Panarovka, the inquisition?"

She took a sip of vodka. "To see what story you'd produce if it came to a police investigation. Also how you'd be with genuine Chukchis . . . You were very lucky."

"You also."

She nodded, looking into her glass.

"You planned to kill me before we left here, didn't you?"

"Yes."

"Your story in the church, about Khodyan, Ponomarenko—were you given all that or did you make it up?"

"I made it up."

"Glib. As well as lucky. All right, put a drop more in here. . . . So where is Khodyan?"

"I don't know." He poured into her glass and into his own. "I don't know where his papers came from, either. But the background came from Ponomarenko."

"Ponomarenko *is* in Batumi?"

"Maybe. He's somewhere. They have evidence against him of drug dealing—a capital offense, a long term at the least. He's under control."

"Why Ponomarenko?"

"It happened to be Ponomarenko. Many drivers go to the Black Sea for the summer. Ponomarenko was *not* lucky."

"What did he have to do—provide his apartment, all the details of his life here?"

"That, yes."

"Including his relations with Lydia Yakovlevna?"

"No. Those I found out for myself."

"Did you also find out she had gonorrhea?"

He drank, poker-faced.

"Eighteen months ago," she said, "I had to send that girl to Tchersky hospital. She had concealed her condition, and it had become serious. I couldn't have *you* going into hospital again. Every mark on your body is detailed there. Which is why I examined you. Stay away from the girl. She's promiscuous."

The vodka had brought faint color to her cheeks, and the eyes gleamed more brightly now.

Again he made no comment.

"So what plans have you for getting to Tcherny Vodi?"

"Obviously, the Evenks—first a visit to the collective, and then the herds. They have a headman there, Innokenty. He chooses the people to go to Tcherny Vodi. A stinking head comes down and makes out the passes for them."

She stared at him. "Passes, stinking heads, Innokenty . . . Did you know all this before you came?"

"No. I discovered it here."

"And this is why you wanted a letter to the collective?"

He smiled faintly. "I also discovered," he said, "that I didn't need it. They take their pelts there from Panarovka. I would have gone with them."

"You were going again to Panarovka?"

"For your funeral."

Her mouth dropped open, and something flickered momentarily behind her eyes.

She drank some vodka.

"Well," she said presently. "You don't need that plan. *I* go out to the herds, every six or eight weeks. In a helicopter. You'll come with me."

"Is this Rogachev's idea?"

"No. Mine. It's true you'll need the cooperation of the Evenks. Which I see from your performance you have a good chance of getting." She finished her drink quickly. "He hasn't told me any detailed plan yet."

"Does he know I'm here now?"

"Yes. He knows."

"When did you see him?"

Her thin smile showed for a moment.

"The last time? I should think—thirty years ago."

Thirty years ago, she said, Rogachev had stayed in this house. He had been a fellow prisoner with her father years before in the camp at Panarovka. When it had closed down he had gone back to Moscow, while her father had remained here. Panarovka couldn't be lived in at that time—the Chukchis were still dismantling the camp and turning it into houses—and her father had made this place his surgery. Her mother had come up from Leningrad, and here she herself had been born.

At the time Nizhniye Kresty (Tchersky's old name) had been very rough, very primitive; detested, abominated, by her mother. Many released prisoners were still roaming; a proper medical service was not yet established; there was nowhere for visitors to stay. And Rogachev had traveled up on a visit, in connection with some scientific mission, and had stayed with his old friend Dr. Komarov.

"And soon became *my* adored friend! There I was, a little girl of six, without any friends, and this delightful man—I remember he insisted they take me along when they paid a visit once to Panarovka, to have a look at it again, see how it was getting on. It was very old, much older than the bigger camps along the Kolyma. Old from Czarist days—old, old, with its church. Is this too complicated for you?" she said, at his thoughtful expression.

He was pouring himself more vodka, and the thoughtfulness arose from his growing awareness that Medical Officer Komarova was getting drunk.

"No. I'm following," he said.

"Then pour me one, too."

"Tatiana Petrovna, there are important—"

"Tanya will do."

"—important matters here. Is it wise for you to drink so early?"

"It isn't wise. But is it every day one faces one's murderer? And discusses the subsequent funeral. My God—in cold blood!"

"You aren't facing your murderer. There was no murder."

"Through my presence of mind! And your Russian has improved. Who *are* you?"

"Tatiana—Tanya. Questions will be asked about me later. Isn't it better that you don't have the answers?"

"All right." She drank a little, watching him. Her eyes were now very bright, the flush in her cheeks accentuating the pallor. She lit herself a cigarette and sat back with it in her mouth. She looked different again—longer, lankier, the injured foot stretched out on a stool, the drawn-back hair no longer unremarkable but now severely elegant.

He looked away from her, around the dark room.

"You think this a strange place for me to live?"

"Perhaps I would have expected a modern apartment."

"I married into a modern apartment."

"It didn't suit you?" he said, after a pause.

"Neither the apartment nor the little brute I married. A cardiologist, from the hospital. Now making his fortune in Moscow. Private clinics, rich crooks. His specialty was the heart, but he had no heart. Far less a soul," she added, nodding. "No children, thank God. Do you have children?"

"No . . . You were speaking of your own childhood."

"Correct. Well then, Rogachev stayed here three months, to my great delight—a playful man, good with children—and I was desolate when he left."

"Did he come in connection with the research station?"

She shook her head. "He couldn't have known anything about it then. Nobody did. It was thought to be some kind of weather place. No, he had some low-temperature experiments going on, he went out with the trappers. Then he'd come back and we would play. He was full of little games. I was Tanya-Panya, and he Misha-Bisha—our secret names."

"Misha-Bisha?" Rogachev's name was *Efraim*—Efraim Moisevich.

"Misha the *bear*. He was a burly man. Just funny names. He gave people names."

"Yes." He remembered them. "Then what?" he said.

"Then he went away. And later so did we, to Panarovka. My father retained this house; he was helping them set up the medical service here. . . . Anyway, there I was at Panarovka, apart from school and medical studies. And later I became a paramedic—all leading us to the point." She took a sip of vodka. "Which was when I became medical officer of this district a couple of years ago, and he asked me to help him—Rogachev did."

"You said you'd never seen him again."

"I haven't. A note, unsigned. Just greetings from Misha-Bisha to Tanya-Panya."

"He sent it to you?"

"Through an Evenk. In an envelope."

"Where?"

"There. At Tcherny Vodi. They have a surgery. I provide the medical supplies. It's in my district."

"You go *into* the place?"

"To deliver the supplies. And to treat patients—the Evenks and the security staff. The scientists have their own doctor, also on the staff. I've never seen him. I receive a list of what he wants and I supply it."

"Wait a minute," Porter said, slowly working this out. "If an Evenk gave you the message—*they* see Rogachev?"

"*An* Evenk does. Rogachev's body servant. The job's hereditary. That is, his father had it before him, and so on with all the previous heads."

"The manservant gave you the message?"

"No, I've never seen him, either. But he's allowed to meet the other Evenks, to discuss family affairs. He's totally trusted. He wouldn't discuss anything else—even if he knew anything. He just does what he's told."

"And he was told to get this message to you."

"Yes. It seems Rogachev had heard there was a new medical officer—the daughter of Dr. Komarov. That first note was just to check it was truly me. Later he told me what he wanted."

He got up and walked about the room. In a recess beside the stove, an icon was on the wall. The stove was cold, the house now electrically heated, very stuffy, very warm. Books were everywhere, on shelves, tables. He couldn't make out the titles in the dark.

"What did he want?" he said.

"He said he had discovered something of great value, which they were preventing him from publishing."

"Did he say what it was?"

"No."

"Or what they're doing up there?"

"Not that either. Except I know now that it involves dangerous substances. They had an accident a few months ago, and the results of it contaminated the lake. Their filtration plant was out of action for some days and we had to send them drinking water. A few scientists flew in and made a great fuss checking out the area. But the wind was the other way and there were no effects here."

"Were the Evenks affected?"

She shook her head. "It was at night and they were in their dormitory. They were locked in all next day, too. There'd been a fire, and fumes were still in the air outside. It was some kind of explosion. . . . You know about it, of course," she said.

He made no comment on this.

"How did he think you could help him?"

"Stepan Maximovich—that's the servant—had to get some cigarettes to me. You know all this, too."

"And what did you have to do with them?"

"A Japanese ship had been coming here for the past couple of years. Some of the Evenks work as dockers during the summer, and they'd told Stepan Maximovich that one of the sailors had been asking for drugs. It was a joke—the Evenks had no access to drugs. But he passed it on to Rogachev, a piece of gossip. This was the first Misha-Bisha heard of the ship, and it gave him his idea."

"Which was what?"

She sighed. "For me to board the ship, of course, when it came. And contact the drug taker."

"The Evenks pointed him out to you?"

"Of course not. They know nothing of this. I saw it in the man's eyes. I was taking the crew one at a time in a cabin set aside for me. The man was on heroin. I offered him a derivative, rather less dangerous, if he would do something for me. I explained what it was and told him I would give him more when he came around again. The ship was coming twice in a season—in early June and in September."

"In Japanese you were explaining all this?"

"In my bit of English. Enough for a hungry addict . . . Is this some kind of interrogation?"

He shrugged.

"What reason did you give for examining the crew?"

"That I was tightening up health requirements. The ship had come from tropical parts; it was due to take on fish after unloading. And

you are now making me very tired. And also hungry. In the kitchen you will find salt fish, and some bread and sour cream. Also a tray.''

She hobbled on a stick when she had to and for the rest of the day sat with her leg up. The day was very overcast, and the windows of the old house small, but by three o'clock it was night anyway, and he had gone around switching on lamps and drawing curtains. She watched him doing it.

''You're a long fellow,'' she said, ''for a Chukchi. But you're not a Chukchi. Or an Evenk. Or anything I know. You're *of* the north, of course?''

''You identified my instep,'' he said.

She smiled coldly. ''Also very careful. Well, how far have your automotive works gone?''

He had told her some details of the bobik—having decided he needed her shed—and now he told her a few more.

''You plan to leave here in this machine?''

''If necessary. An alternative exit,'' he said.

''Some more formal exit is planned for you, of course.''

''Yes, it is.''

''Do you want to tell me it?''

''No.''

''All right.'' But she remained staring at him. ''So where are you building this vehicle?''

''You don't need to know that either.''

She lit herself a cigarette. ''Too much smoking. But this is hardly normal. I'll have another drink, too.''

She had it on the sofa, her leg more comfortable there, and she gave him more information on the herds. They discussed the matter until supper, which he also assembled and brought from the kitchen; together with a coffee jug and two mugs.

''Well, quite the housekeeper,'' she said.

''Practice. Do you have help here?''

''Yes. A Yakut woman comes in twice a week.''

''Does she go into the shed?''

''No.'' She stared at him. ''You're the most cunning man, I think, that I've ever met. That's where you'll keep the motor parts, is it?''

''A few things, yes.'' He got on with his meal, and she got on with hers, glancing curiously at him.

She told him the layout of the research station and he listened closely.

''So where's your consulting room?''

"In the guards' quarters. The Evenks come there."

"Is that the only place you have contact with them?"

"Well, they have to unload the car and load it again."

"What with?"

"Various supplies. Big distilled-water jars. They use a lot of it there, laboratory work. It's not worth flying in, and we produce it in Tchersky anyway. Various other drums and containers. I take the empties back."

"Where do they keep this stuff?"

"In a storage shed, near the airstrip."

"Is that where you park?"

"No, I'm not allowed there. I go to the commandant's office. And they bring along a sled, or a tractor. It depends how much there is."

"Do you supervise this operation?"

"The security people do. They have to check everything that goes in or out. Were you thinking I might smuggle *you* out?"

"Well . . . What if somebody's ill?"

"They'd be flown out. And not to Tchersky. No contact is allowed with Tchersky. And nobody goes in or out without an escort anyway."

He drank his coffee, musing.

"So how do *I* get out?" he said.

"The same way you get in?"

"And stay there a month?"

"That would complicate matters in Green Cape, wouldn't it?" She nodded. "Well, you're not thinking so badly. Go and bring the cognac. Maybe you'll do better."

He went and got the cognac, puzzled. She had drunk a lot today, but it had not noticeably affected her judgment or the authority of her manner. Evidently he was being subjected to some other test, a probe of his reactions. She had done it before, in the church. She was taking risks, of course, for herself, for Rogachev.

He turned with the cognac, and saw she had shifted position on the sofa.

"Come and sit here," she said. "I'm tired of shouting."

He sat slowly, and carefully poured.

"Your hands are long," she said. "Also your femur." She examined the femur. She examined it all the way up, and unzipped him and slipped a hand in.

He gazed at her.

"What's this?" he said.

"Are you surprised?"

"You have examined me once already."

"Now you can examine me."

With her other arm she pulled his head down and kissed him. It was quite an affectionate kiss, and she was smiling as she drew back and looked into his face. "Long fellow," she said, "today you tried to kill me, and I could be dead. But I am not dead, and nor are you, and this is my house. You attract me. I am accustomed to getting what I want. And it's something to celebrate, after all—being alive."

She was not as buxom as Lydia Yakovlevna; lankier, less cushioned. But she was lithe, controlled, and very much more genuine, arching without histrionics when her moment came. He arched at the same time, and afterward she kissed his face and stroked it. They lay comfortably together, at peace with one another.

"Yes, worth celebrating," she said at last. "And altogether satisfactory. But now there's work to do."

They got up and did it for some hours, planning how he could get into and also out of the place he had come around the world to reach. Before midnight they had agreed the first steps, and these were detailed steps.

34

On Monday he took his sick note to the administration block, and immediately afterward went to see Vassili in his storeroom.

"You didn't come Friday," Vassili said.

"They gave me a medical. I'll take the stuff at lunchtime, Vassili. And, listen, I need a bobik for a week."

"A *week?*"

"They laid me off, at the medical. They say I'm tired and need a week's rest."

Vassili looked him over. "Well, you're looking shagged," he said. "That's your Evenk girl, is it? What use are you going to be to her if you're worn out?"

"Never mind—I need a bobik."

"So go and ask Liova."

"If I'm off work I'm not entitled. . . . Vassili, put in a word for me."

The old Yakut chuckled silently. "All right. But let him take a look at you himself. He'll see what a wreck you are. You don't need to mention anything."

He grunted and went to find the Light Vehicles chief.

"Well," Liova said, staring at him, "you need a rest, it's obvious. You've been working hard."

"I don't. But it's what they said. I'm sorry."

"Kolya, take it easy, now. You're a good lad."

At lunchtime he went back to the depot and found Vassili alone, eating from his pot.

"You got your bobik," the Yakut told him, chewing. "And Liova said shove one into her for him, too. I never saw him laugh so much. You want to take the axles now?"

He took the axles and he also took the manual, to see how to put the thing together. And in an hour and a quarter was at Anyuysk.

He took the made track fast and was soon off it and onto the tributary. The days were now shorter, barely two hours; this one gray, clear, very cold: a still life, set in ice. It was a week now since he'd been here. He found the overhanging bushes and got out and inspected the cave with a flashlight. All as he had left it. He drove the bobik in with the lights on, kept the engine running, and unloaded the axle assemblies. Then he stood back and looked around. Spacious enough, but no room for two bobiks. When he started assembly, the other one would have to stand outside.

He became aware of another problem. For the assembly he was going to need light. Not light from the delivery bobik—that was out of the question; even from the air it might be seen. And not just torchlight. Proper lighting. He needed a generator, and some wiring rigged, and a tarpaulin or sheet for the entrance. Well, it could be done.

The icebox was chilling him to the bone and he got back in the bobik and sat with the heat on, leafing through the greasy manual. The first job: Bolt the chassis together. And get it on wheels. Then what? He studied the drawings and the exploded diagrams. Steering assembly, brakes, transmission, clutch. Hours of fiddling in the deep freeze. He would need a heater, too.

It was dark outside now, and he reversed out and drove back along the tributary. He drove slowly with only sidelights until he came to the made track and Anyuysk, and then put on speed. The plan called for him to go home now.

Anna Antonovna heard him enter the apartment, and shortly afterward was tapping on the door herself. He had given the old lady her own key but she was discreet in using it.

"Well, I tidied you in here," she said. "But what happened this weekend? You said you wouldn't be working."

"No, I was with friends."

"Here, or in Tchersky?"

"Neither. At Novokolymsk." This was the story they had agreed. "I've got a week off so I thought I'd pay them a visit—with a bobik I borrowed. I'll be running out there again," he told her, grinning.

"Ah, you found the natives at the collective, did you?"

"Sure. And they can sleep me. I only looked in to pick up a few clothes."

"What, you're going back now?"

"For a few days."

"Well, I know who won't be pleased at that," Anna Antonovna said; but the old cat face was smiling as she left.

She would be passing on this interesting item to the young lady in the supermarket. All as planned. Everybody had to know. He took a shower and sat in one of Ponomarenko's bathrobes, with a vodka.

There was no phone in the apartment, and he didn't want to use the public one below. He waited until he could hear no traffic and then dressed and packed a bag and left. At Tchersky the lights were on behind her curtains, and he turned into the driveway. She had given him a set of keys and he parked the bobik with hers in the shed and locked again. Then he let himself into the house.

35

The house of Dr. Komarov had stood a hundred years—a long time for a simple one of wood, but the wood was good. It had seen out Czar Alexander III and Czar Nicholas II, and also the entire Communist régime. Though tilted sharply in two directions, it still looked good for many years to come, for now it was rooted firmly in the permafrost.

Now but not always. In 1893, when the cellar had held prisoners of Alexander III, they had lit a fire in it to try to stay alive. This had thawed the permafrost and occasioned the first tilt. The second was Dr. Komarov's. In an onslaught on the bugs and lice that infested the place he had treated every centimeter of it with a chemical solution, and to make sure of remaining larvae had boiled them with a steam hose. He had steamed out the cellar too, and in the summer of 1959 the house had lurched slowly forward.

The timbers had stood up well to this, and the house would not now lurch anymore. His daughter, Tatiana, had seen to that. Her first act had been to drive piles into the permafrost, pinning the structure in its present position, and then to isolate the cellar with half a meter of insulating material—floor, walls, and roof. A trapdoor enabled it still to be used as a storeroom, and it provided quite a capacious one. Here Porter found the kerosene stove and the generator—the latter a neat job from Japan, not much needed in the past few years as Tchersky's power supply had improved.

He tried them both. The stove needed a new wick but was otherwise quite serviceable, and the generator started at once.

For the time being he left them there.

In the next three days he ran parts down to the cave. With Vassili's agreement he picked them up at eight in the morning, using the back door of the storeroom to avoid going through the garage, and returned at lunchtime for the second load. He went back to the house right away then, for Komarova had told him not to absent himself for long. The plan for getting him to the herds depended on the weather, and for this he had to be ready at short notice.

Now he knew far more about her.

She had been divorced six years and had not looked for other relationships. Had there been any? Of course—brief ones, she was human, what did he think? But just hospital people: doctors who came on two- or three-year contracts and then left, for Moscow, Petersburg, God knew where. *She* couldn't leave, at least not yet. Her mother was a trial, but still her mother. Later maybe. But where else would she find such wide responsibilities and such work?

She loved the work, and she loved the country—the native people better than the Europeans. So she kept her distance, and was considered aloof; yes, she knew it. But better that than join a white élite and patronize the natives. Her father had never patronized them, and neither had Rogachev, and she had loved them for it. They were not treated equally—he must have seen it for himself. Plenty of extras for Europeans in these northern parts, but natives excluded, even in such matters as drink. She got them drink, and why not? It was a hard country. Yes, she was in some ways detached here, in some ways out of place. But she would be out of place in a town.

So what *would* do for her?

She didn't know what would do. Her work would do!

She had scrupulously avoided asking him anything further about himself; so on the second night, trusting her suddenly, he told her.

She sat up in bed and looked at him.

"An American Indian!"

"Canadian."

"Not *the* Porter—Dr. Johnny Porter?"

"Well, that's my name."

She stared at him. Then she got out of bed and ran into the next room and returned with a book. It was his *Comparisons,* the study of tribal legends, in a Russian translation—a standard reader in universities of the north, he knew, but a surprise to see here.

"This is yours?" she said.

"Yes."

"You mean, you're not a—not just an agent? So what are you doing here?"

"Well." He hesitated. But then he told her—the background at least. The meeting with Rogachev in Oxford. The strangeness of his own life at the time—a widower, at twenty-three.

She'd only been nineteen herself—a little thing, very pretty: long black hair, ponytail down to here.

"An Indian girl?"

"Oh, sure. Minnehaha, Laughing Water—doe-eyed Bride of Hiawatha. Name was Trisha, actually. She didn't have doe eyes."

"What happened to her?"

"She skipped out to catch a bus at lunchtime. The bus caught her. Somebody said she probably hadn't heard it."

"She hadn't *seen* it?"

"Being blind, no."

"Oh."

"She could hear a *pin* drop—in the next room!"

"You mean—"

"Ah, hell, who knows what I meant? I was seeing plots everywhere. Politics. All a long time ago . . . I guess she missed the curb and slipped. Anyway, Rogachev told me to quit brooding. An amazing man—I'd never met anyone like him. A polymath, interested in everything. In blindness too—especially in blindness, actually . . . We were discussing congenital things—turned out *his* wife was going blind, degeneration of both eyes. He was depressed as hell, under all the cheerfulness. But he said brooding was no good for me. There was something for me to do in this world, and he'd help me any way he could. Which he did, actually."

He was silent a moment.

"See, earlier on I'd been trying to get to Chukotka, a security part you couldn't get to. It was to research the Inuit there, Eskimos. And he got me permission, and I went. I didn't use the stuff at the time, and I heard nothing from him directly. And later on I discovered why. His wife had been killed in an accident, he was in all sorts of trouble himself. Yet he'd done that for me—he'd meant what he said. So when they showed up with these messages . . . "

"But to take on such dangers! To disrupt your whole life in this way—"

"I've disrupted it before. And lived rough before—he knew that. He knew I *could* do it, that I was the only one with a *chance*. And that I'd take it if only I saw what he'd—"

He decided to skip what Rogachev had written.

No more sit in darkness nor like the blind stumble at . . .

"Anyway," he said, "I did."

"Good God!" She was still clutching the book. "Well, *you'd* do," she said. She lay on top of him. "My God, you'd do!"

On the Thursday he took the engine.

There were now only three days left of his week off. It meant taking the block and tackle, too, and also the lighting.

"Lighting wire? What do you want with lighting wire?" Vassili asked.

"I might need some. Give me twenty meters. Also eight sockets and light bulbs."

"This is a lot of favors," Vassili said. He measured off the flex. "When are you going to do some for me?"

"What do you want?"

"She is talking stroganina again."

"Okay. I'll get a run to Ambarchik next week."

Vassili took a careful look out of the back door of the storeroom, and together they manhandled the engine in its harness out to the bobik. "You're coming back lunchtime?"

"No. This is a lot of engine," he said, rubbing his back; he had carried the greater part of it.

"I told you. See the block is secure before you lift it. Don't skip any screws. There'll be no other engine."

"I'll be careful."

He went back to the house and picked up the generator and set off on the river to Anyuysk. By half past ten he was at the cave and he drove straight in, with his headlights on. He had already had a trial on the roof of the bobik and the position gave him enough room. Now he knelt on it and got to work.

There were eight holes in the securing bracket. He held it against the roof and lightly bored the eight placer marks with the battery drill. Then he laid the bracket aside and drilled the full depth. He went seven centimeters into the granite, and got through three drills and two sets of batteries. Then he plugged the holes and screwed the bracket home and swung hard on the tackle. All secure.

He took a rest then, and had some coffee, while figuring out the lighting. This was a finicky job, but child's play after the heavy overhead boring. Only shallow holes needed, and short plugs for the hooks. He spaced out two on the roof and two along each of the three walls. Then he paid out the wire and draped it loosely from the hooks. The twenty meters didn't give anything to spare, and he still had to cut it to connect the light sockets.

His fingers were numb and he fiddled with this job in the bobik with the heater on. He spliced in the sockets, attached the terminal plugs for the generator, and got out and hung the circuit. Then he went around screwing in the bulbs, got back in the bobik, and gave himself a vodka. It was after two o'clock and he was very tired. He was tiring too easily, too much running about. He lit a cigarette and read through the scrappy leaflet that came with the generator. It had worked in the house but here, only twelve volts needed, he could blow the whole damn array.

He got out and checked the controls again. Then he made sure the output switch was off, and started up. The thing coughed into life and chugged solidly away. He let it run for a minute, then switched the output on. The bulbs lit up like a Christmas tree, and stayed lit. Okay. The engine now.

He switched the bobik's lights off, reversed out, turned on the frozen river, and backed in again. The light was well spread. He opened the rear of the car and hooked up the engine. They had bedded it on a felt pad in its lifting harness, and he hauled on the tackle chains and saw the pad begin to shift as the engine moved. The pad slid out and fell to the ground and the engine swung loose. He kept it hanging and guided it clear of the car and lowered it slowly to the ground.

Done.

He took the bobik outside and went back in for a final look. There was a lot of stuff now; almost everything. Tomorrow he'd pick up the remainder, take it to the house, sleep all day. At night back to the cave and start the assembly. He would work the whole night through.

He switched the generator off and drove back. He felt unsure of himself suddenly.

Something had changed. He didn't know what. But all his life he had respected these feelings. He went over in his mind what it might be. Nothing. Yet something had changed.

He drove slowly, and it was six o'clock before he reached the house. There he learned that something had changed. Tomorrow there would be no cave, but the herds. For now the time had come. Tomorrow *night,* if everything worked, he would be with Innokenty, the man who sent people to the research station.

He was unsure about this, too. The story they had concocted seemed now utterly childish. Earlier it had not seemed childish. Now it seemed childish. It was too late to think of another, though, so they worked over it, far into the night; all the time his lowering feeling persisting.

He had no idea, still, why he was here; what was expected of him at Tcherny Vodi; what activities went on there.

In China at this time they had no idea even of Tcherny Vodi's existence. But they were aware of some activities. A very strange one had come to light.

36

The military commission met in Beijing, before them the reports on the test missiles—the missiles of October and of November.

The October missile had gone off course six minutes into its flight, so that the new guidance system had not operated. This system switched on only in the last kilometers of flight. A visual device then compared what it read below with a prestored computer image, correcting course and trajectory until the two images matched exactly. But *so* far off course, nothing had matched. A fault of the missile, not its terminal vision.

The second vehicle was of an older type, but with a totally reliable flight record. And it had been reliable. It had flown to Lop Nor, anyway, and hit it, but so wide of the mark that, again, the visual system had obviously not switched on.

However, it *had* switched on. It had reported itself switched on. And then it had switched off.

Between these two missiles, there was an important difference. The one arriving at Lop Nor had been conventionally wired, all its networks connected by electrical cable. The other was optically wired, with fiber. The commission knew the reason for this, so their experts wasted no time, going immediately to the main problem.

Both missiles had been interfered with in flight.

The first had suffered interference after six minutes, when its signals had ceased. It had then been executing a fractional turn to the west; and it had stuck in this turn, which by burnout had taken it due south to Lan-chou.

The second missile had reported an unidentifiable buzz, but it had reached Lop Nor. It had reached it with its video switched off. Shortly before, it had reported the video switched on.

The missile diverted from its course was optically wired.

The missile not diverted was *not* optically wired, but its optical system had switched off.

The experts pointed to an obvious conclusion: The interference was optical.

On this they offered two further comments.

The first was that they knew of no scientific explanation for such interference; and the second that it could only have come from an altitude much higher than the missiles.

At an altitude a quarter of the way to the moon, two satellites were at present in stationary orbit over China. They were electronic intelligence (ELINT) stations, one of them American and the other Russian. The American had been launched from Vandenberg Air Force Base in California, and the Russian from Tyuratam in central Asia.

The experts' recommendation was that Vandenberg and Tyuratam be targeted, urgently, for anything that could shed light on this development. This was possible, for agents were available at both centers, and already much was known of events in these important vicinities.

Of events in the unimportant vicinity of Tchersky nothing was known.

37

Tchersky airport, so late in the season, had extended itself on to the river ice. A dozen or so fixed-wing planes of Polar Aviation were parked there, and also a huddle of helicopters, large and small.

Medical Officer Komarova and her Chukchi assistant boarded a small one, already warming up for them, and took off at once, heading southeast. The day was dark and gray, ominous with gusts and waiting snow. A blizzard was expected within hours.

The pilot chided Komarova on the fact as they rose above the town. "Couldn't you have made it earlier? I still have to get you back."

"A rush of work all morning. I won't stay long."

"You say that, but always you stay hours. What is it with those natives there? . . . Who's this one?"

"An employee of the transport company." They had taken care to let the pilot see the Chukchi driving the bobik and carrying the two heavy bags from it to the helicopter; Komarova herself was hobbling on a stick. "Pay attention to your own duties," she added coldly. "Just fly."

The pilot grunted and flew, and Porter marveled at the sternness of this creature who had last night so riotously straddled and caressed him.

They didn't have to fly long, barely fifty minutes. But darkness was gathering fast as they spotted the weird cloud on the ground. The spectral shape rolled and tumbled there, shot through with silver—the breath of reindeer, an immense herd, crystallized in the air. They came down low over it, the pilot peering in all directions before he found the group of tents that housed the Evenk herders. He had to hover almost on top of them before deerskin-clad figures came peering out, running and waving. Then he put the helicopter down, and kept the rotors turning.

"Aren't you coming out?" Komarova called, at the door.

"No, I'll keep her running. It's cold out there and the wind is high—they couldn't hear me." He was having to shout, listening to a weather report on his radio. "Remember—I don't spend nights with a tribe of Evenks!"

"I'll be as quick as I can."

Outside several women were among the huddle of Evenks, and they bear-hugged the medical officer, gazing curiously at her Chukchi assistant. The wind was indeed high and howling, all the ground below knee level shifting with flying snow and ice. They were hustled into a tent—a leather one, Porter saw, and double-skinned. Its entrance flaps opened into a heat-lock vestibule, and beyond it more flaps led to the circular living space, a big room, six or seven meters across, entirely carpeted with bushy reindeer robes. A sheet-metal stove roared in the middle of it, standing in a large tray piled with logs and cooking pots.

The heavy canvas bags were speedily taken off him and their contents greeted with approval. The bottles had been wrapped in cloth to prevent clinking, and one of vodka was opened immediately.

"No—no time for that!" Komarova said. "The pilot has to get off. What complaints are here? How's everybody?"

The complaints were the normal ones: sprains, sores, inflamed eyes. But one of the women was pregnant, and Komarova took time examining her behind a screen. She examined others there too, and he kept careful check of the time, calling it out to her. It was after three o'clock, now totally dark and less than two hours before the predicted blizzard. The plan needed the pilot to be able to take off, and his radio could still ground him.

"All right, I'm coming," she called back, and presently was hurrying out. "But Evdokia, you're coming with me. I want you checked in hospital. And Igor, too. That back looks a disc problem. And more vitamins are needed here—too many sores. I'll send supplies tomorrow. And the instructions with them. There's no time now, no time!" And out they went, struggling against the wind to the helicopter: the pregnant woman, the man with the back, Medical Officer Komarova, and her assistant from the transport company.

"What's this?" the pilot shouted, as they clambered aboard. "How many of you?"

"Just two patients and us."

"What, two patients and you? Two patients and you two make four. With me, five. The machine carries four!"

"You've carried five before."

"In high winds, with a blizzard coming? No way. One of them stays."

"These patients have to be in hospital!"

"Then let *him* stay!"

Which he did, after some angry words.

So far, so good. The childish story, still to come, was another matter.

Innokenty he had spotted immediately. The headman had sat smoking his pipe on the carpet while the medical examinations were carried out.

"I never heard anyone speak the Evenk tongue so," the old man said, "not any stranger. How does it come about?"

Porter told him, and he told them all, over a venison dinner and ample drink, how it came about. He told of his childhood in Chukotka, of the schoolteacher father, of Novosibirsk and the Evenk friends he had met. How in the big town he had almost forgotten his own tongue, but his Evenk friends, true souls, had not forgotten theirs, and of how it had almost become his. Of his hankering for the north, and his driving experiences ever since. They were charmed by him, and charmed also at his interest in their own lives. Every aspect interested him, and they gladly answered all questions.

No, they didn't remain in the one place; that was plainly impossible with such a large herd, over two thousand beasts. The reindeer grazed the moss under the ice. They grazed it and were moved on every few days. No problems. A small party dismantled the tents and carried them ahead and re-erected them. The same with firewood: every week or so a party would go south to a great wood stack nearer the timberline and collect it. Sure, on sleds, you harnessed up a couple of reindeer; wonderful beasts. They carried you, clothed you, fed you. Better than beef. And cheaper to produce than beef, and fetching better prices! Yes, everywhere, all over Russia, and Japan too, and God knew where else. The collective did all that.

He didn't know the collective? Novokolymsk. All that work was done there, the carcass-handling, packing, dispatch, accounts. They went back there themselves regularly. A big helicopter came and transferred them. One party went back, another party came out. The schoolchildren stayed at the collective, of course; only came out to the herds for holidays. No, not everybody returned regularly; Innokenty didn't, and many of the older folk also. They preferred the wandering life, didn't feel the need for television, videos, parties. All that was for the younger ones. But a good life for everybody, a natural one, full of variety.

Indeed, he said, indeed it was. And he'd heard they also found time to fit in work at the docks in the summer. How did they fit all that in?

How did they fit it in? They could fit anything in. They were free. They did what they wanted. And it wasn't the only thing they fitted in. They also worked regularly at a science station up in the hills.

Ah yes! He knew about that. Had actually met a couple of them when he'd freighted a load to the guard post there a few weeks ago. He explained the situation, to their very great interest. Which Evenks were they? Well, he hadn't caught their names, but from his description it was generally agreed who they must be—and what a pity they weren't here to greet him. They wouldn't be down for a week yet. Yes, the same system, one party came back and another went up to replace them.

Truly an interesting life, he said admiringly. And he regretted not having picked up any science himself. They'd had a scientific training, had they, the people who went up there?

This occasioned a great deal of laughter, and also another round of drinks.

You wouldn't call it science, old Innokenty said, smiling. Just honest work—cleaning, laundry, cooking, maintenance. And the heating, and such things. Scores of people had to be looked after up there, a big government station, scientists, guards—yes, stinking heads. You didn't have much to do with them. And they had nothing to do with Tchersky or Green Cape. All their supplies came from far away, thousands of kilometers. Which the Evenks offloaded and shifted, too. But not to the people below, of course. All the science happened *below,* and nobody was ever allowed there.

"Only my Stepanka!" exclaimed a very old lady, smoking her pipe and nodding.

"Of course Stepanka. But nobody else."

"Who's Stepanka?" asked the Chukchi.

"Her son. Stepan Maximovich. He looks after the boss of the place—took over his father's job when he died. It's in their family. He lives there. And he has a wife—not old, but beyond childbearing age, so they let him take her. For his natural needs," Innokenty said, winking.

"Ah. Aren't there any other women there?"

"No, none."

"So what do the rest of them do for—you know?"

More laughter. Well, with the guards there was no problem. They were shifted regularly—in fact, a new crew would be on next week. As for the scientists, a party of them went out, every couple of months, to opera houses, concert halls, things of that kind. They got private boxes, and various stinking heads had to go with them. But Stepanka thought they were given a ration of the other as well, it was only right.

Oh, they got to see Stepanka, did they?

Of course they got to see him. Stepanka had to know how his family was getting on—and all his people! And they were *trusted*. They were the only outsiders trusted. They wouldn't trust any white workers in there. Or Yukagirs or Chukchis, for that matter. No offence to Chukchis, it was just a different way of life in these parts. And the Yukagirs could never keep to timetables. They were out scouting their traplines all winter. Go and find them! No, the Evenks with their regular herds were the only ones the authorities took. And they took them *from* the herds, not the collective. Took them and brought them back to the herds, so they shouldn't contact anybody in between. That was the way of it with stinking heads.

Well, a fascinating life, he said. But where was the opera house in Tchersky they'd mentioned, or the concert hall? He hadn't found these places yet.

More laughter—hilarious laughter, everyone rolling on the carpet— and also more drinks.

Tchersky! An opera house in Tchersky! Oh no! Not that, Kolya! No opera houses in Tchersky! At Novosibirsk! A cargo plane came with scientific supplies from there, and it took the scientists back. They stayed a few days—some place run by the stinking heads—and then they flew back. In Novosibirsk they had opera houses now, and theaters, everything. Well, they must have had them when he was there last.

Ah, when he was there last, he said, and grew solemn. (The moment had come now and he braced himself.) The vodka had flowed very freely all evening and a tear now stood in his eye. When he was in Novosibirsk last!

What, Kolya? What? Unhappy memories?

Yes, unhappy. A person had to keep them to himself.

Why to himself? It *helped* a person to speak.

No. He wouldn't burden them with unhappy stories.

What burden? With friends? Take a drink, Kolya. Speak.

He took a drink. Well then, he said, and wiped his eyes. Well . . . In Novosibirsk he had left a most tragic case. A white girl. Dying. He had met the family in his early tearabout days there. The father had worked at an institute outside the town; Akademgorodok—Science City. He had done odd jobs for the family, a fine family, just the three of them, father, mother, daughter.

And then evil things had happened. The mother, still a young woman, had taken ill and died. And a grandmother had come to look after the girl—just eight or nine years old at the time. This was twenty years ago. Until one day, out of nowhere, another disaster. The father too had gone—not dead, just gone, disappeared. A letter saying urgent government business and he would be in touch. But he had not been in touch. Not from that day to this, not a single word—nothing.

What nothing? Innokenty said. How could they live on nothing?

Money wasn't a problem, Kolya said. Money came, regularly, from the ministry that had employed him. It was just—no word from him, no idea what had happened.

The ministry couldn't tell them what had happened?

The grandmother tried. She tried everybody: the ministry, the place where he'd worked, his colleagues. Nothing.

So then what?

So then time passed, he went back to Chukotka, got a driving job. And the girl wrote from time to time. Told him the grandmother had died. Until suddenly, this year, a few months ago, she wrote again, very urgently. Could he come and see her at once? Which as it happened he could. The driving season had just ended, it was June, he was going to the Black Sea. So he went to Novosibirsk first, and saw her. And was shocked by what he saw. The girl was desperately ill, wasting away—the same disease as her mother, and the same age, twenty-nine. And the doctors said nothing could be done for her.

Well he couldn't accept that, wouldn't believe it. On the Black Sea they had *other* doctors, different cures. So he had taken her there, gone to top specialists, paid them privately. But the same story: nothing to be done. And the Black Sea was too hot for her, so he had taken her back to Novosibirsk. And there they had stayed, and had wept together . . .

Until, he said, wiping his eyes again, one day she had asked him to do something for her, one last thing.

When she first knew of her illness, she had gone herself to Akademgorodok—the place her father had worked. Had pleaded with them, pestered them, gone from office to office. And in a certain room, where records were kept, had overheard officials whispering together about a place in the Kolymsky region. And dimly from her childhood she remembered her father had also spoken of this place. A mysterious kind of place, a weather station, from which he had received reports, also spoken of in whispers. And from this she had got it into her head that it was the explanation of his disappearance. He was *in* this mysterious place. He was not allowed to write!

And this was what she wanted of him—to take a letter to her father, begging one last word and his blessing before she died. She knew Kolya drove about in the north. To her, Chukotka, the Kolymsky region, were all the same. They knew nothing of the north down there, none of them. So, for a dying girl, what else could he do? He had come up to Tchersky and taken a job with the transport company and looked for this weather station. Of course he knew now there wasn't such a place. . . . But yes, that was the reason Novosibirsk had sad memories for him.

Wait a minute! Innokenty said. He had been staring hard at him. Twenty years ago you say this man disappeared?

Twenty years ago.

But twenty years ago there *was* a weather station here—our science place up in the hills!

You don't say so! Kolya said.

I do say so, Innokenty said. That's what *they* said then. And there has never been any other weather station in the region.

God above—you mean I've actually found it? Kolya said.

God has found it! Stepanka's old mother said. She had thrown her pipe down and was weeping. He has led you to it! My Stepanka will take this letter for you. He'll see her father gets it.

It's a miracle! Kolya said. I can't believe it! Only tell me when it can be done!

In just a week, Innokenty told him. When the helicopter brings the others down, the new party will take the letter *up*.

And the reply—when would I get it?

Four weeks later, when they come down again.

Ah God! Too late! Kolya said, bitterly. She'll never last that time. In *two* weeks I have to leave. To be at her deathbed.

Then what's to be done?

They had another drink while thinking what was to be done.

Nobody could think what was to be done.

Was it possible, Kolya said at last, his face creased up as he puzzled the matter out, was it possible for them to get him up there somehow?

Well, Innokenty said. Possible, yes. He could go up as a member of a party. The stinking heads didn't know one from another. But what was to be gained? He would still have to stay there four weeks. They didn't bring them *down* again for four weeks.

And if he was switched?

Switched?

Kolya tried working this one out, too, his face again very creased. He worked it out once, and he worked it out twice, and by the second time tears had turned to laughter and even the old lady was rolling on the floor with her pipe.

Oh God, yes! Oh God, why not—if it could be done? Comfort for a dying girl—and in such a way, from people who were free and did what they wanted!

All night the blizzard raged and he drowsed by the stove, disturbed occasionally as men stumbled out to re-tether the leaders keeping the herd together. But in the morning the weather was clear and the helicopter came with the vitamins, and he went back with it, the Evenks waving boisterously up at him as he rose in the sky. "We'll meet again," they had told him, winking. Oh yes! Yes, indeed they would!

So that part too was over.

Now there remained only the last.

38

After his week's rest Kolya Khodyan signed on for work again at the Tchersky Transport Company. And he returned the bobik.

The story of his supposed Evenk girl had passed around, he saw, for he was greeted everywhere with hilarity.

"Had your rest cure, Kolya? Found something nice and comfortable to rest on?"

He smiled sheepishly, and took all this.

From Yura, the Kama truck chief, there was no hilarity. The plan called for him to go and see the little man anyway, but that same morning he was sent for.

He decided to walk the half kilometer to the hangar.

"What's this, Kolya?" Yura furiously demanded. "What? I put you down for a long haul. And this note comes back: 'No long distances—struck off.' What the hell! What's happening here? What?"

He assumed his sullen expression.

"My skin is what! They no like it. Say bad heart."

"Who says bad heart?"

"At the medical. They make me do medical. Look at my papers, say no good—bad heart. Is all lies, those papers! Nothing wrong with my heart. Is my skin!"

"Wait a minute. What trouble with your heart?"

"I have a fever as a kid—is nothing! Some doctor in Anadyr says later maybe I get bad heart. I don't get a bad heart. Nobody says so, nobody in Chukotka! *Here* they say it! Not my heart. My skin, eh—Chukchi skin. No good!"

The heavy-truck chief breathed loudly through his nostrils.

"We'll soon see about that!" he said.

He picked up the phone and called Bukarovsky.

Kolya lit himself a cigarette and waited. Nothing would be coming out of Bukarovsky. All the road manager could ask for was an urgent hospital check. Which Komarova would hold up for two weeks. In two weeks he would no longer be here.

He listened to the shouting match, and the phone slammed down. "Okay, all fixed! He's getting you a hospital check—urgent. Komarova will arrange it herself. You'll have the long hauls, I promise!"

"Did I ask for them? Did I ask anything? Is my skin!"

"Kolya, come on! It's a fuck-up with your papers. Everywhere there are fuck-ups! You're *wanted* here. Everybody wants you!" He came and put his arm round the Chukchi and squeezed him. "And didn't I hear you've got a little bit somewhere who also wants you? Somewhere out at a collective? Eh? Eh?"

"Is my business," the Chukchi said, sullenly.

"Sure it is, Kolya. Sure. Shagging your ears off, you dog. What? Tearing down there every night in a bobik!"

"Yes, one thing more," he said. "*No* bobik. I come in, give up bobik. No-good driver, no bobik. I have to walk here now."

"*What!*" Yura reached for the phone again. "*Liova?* Liova, what's this—"

More minutes of shouting before the phone slammed down.

"You've got a bobik. He said you never even asked him."

"Why ask? If I'm no good? No favors."

"Kolya, Kolya." The little man squeezed him again. "Nobody *says* that. You're the best! Don't get so hot. Okay, for a few days you do short runs, until your checkup. After that, I promise you—Bilibino,

Baranikha, Pevek, everywhere! Go on, off now. And someone will run you back. My drivers don't walk!''

So that was settled: his medical condition established, hospital checkup in motion, a bobik once more at his disposal, and short runs a certainty.

He started on them at once.

He managed a trip to Ambarchik in the week and brought back a fish for Vassili, and also one run each to Provodnoye and Anyuysk. He carried the rest of the car on them.

The same week he started the night assembly.

''She is making stroganina,'' Vassili told him on Friday. ''You want to come tomorrow?''

''Vassili, what I am getting is better than stroganina.''

''Sure. I told her. Your eyes are hanging out.''

''It's not the only thing.''

''I believe you. You're overdoing it. She says you need oil and if you can't come she'll send you stroganina.''

''I'll be very glad. Also for the oil.''

''So what work did you manage with the bobik?''

''A bit, not much.''

''You'll find the underside can be a bastard. Unless you have a pit. Everything fits from below.''

''I expect I'll find it.''

He found the underside a tremendous bastard. He took sacking and a bit of carpet with him, but still his back froze as he lay under the chassis.

As Vassili had said, the thing was a toy, but an unbelievably heavy toy, clumsy, rugged, all of it unexpectedly difficult. He had brought the block and tackle just for the engine. He found he was using it for everything.

To fit the front suspension, the completed frame, immediately fast-frozen to the ground, had to be lifted. The block and tackle lifted it. To fit the other end he had to attach wheels to the front, drag the thing out like a wheelbarrow, and turn and back in again, to get the rear in position. The block and tackle lifted that, too. He was improvising all the time, and swearing all the time; yet everything fitted— laboriously, painfully; but locking together like a meccano set.

He slept all day Saturday and Sunday and worked through both nights, muffled to the eyebrows, the kerosene stove pushing out feeble warmth. But when he drove back Monday morning the chassis was on wheels, the steering in, the transmission ready, even the exhaust loosely attached.

"Look, you can't continue like this," she told him. It was five in the morning. She was in a dressing gown, having heard him come in. "You can't finish it before you go up, anyway. In two or three *days* you will be going up. Even today I could be given a date. And you need to be thoroughly rested for it."

"Yes," he said, dully. He was truly desperately tired.

"Today you *won't* accept all jobs. They'll understand—your medical coming up . . . this Evenk girl. And stay near the depot. My office could phone in at any time."

He fell into bed and slept like a log for two hours, until she woke him with coffee. Then they left together, still in the dark, Komarova scouting the street before signaling him out in his bobik.

The call did not come that day, but the next. It came when he was out on a local run, and he returned to find Liova signaling him over.

"Kolya, you want a light number with the medical center?"

"What is it?"

"They need somebody tomorrow morning—a three-day job. Komarova has a sprained ankle and can't drive out of town. She has a few trips, maybe including the collective. And since you know the place," he said, grinning, "it's yours if you want it."

"Okay, I don't mind," he said.

He went to his own apartment after work, to pick up his ID and some clothing out of the wardrobe. He had worn very little of it, had been in the apartment very little the past few days.

He was taking a shower when Anna Antonovna looked in, and when he came out she was still waiting, ready for a chat. And within ten minutes of her departure Lydia Yakovlevna also looked in, alerted by the old lady, he had no doubt. The girl was furiously resentful.

He had someone at the collective, didn't he? Everyone was saying he had a girl there. It was very insulting for her. People knew *she* was his girl now; she was braving Alexei's future wrath, risking her reputation. And for what—for him to go with a filthy little Evenk whore? Come on, the truth now. He had an Evenk girl, didn't he?

Not an Evenk *girl,* he said. Just Evenk friends. They were good people. He had always had Evenk friends.

Oh, yes? And Chukchi ones, too? He had been *seen!* Going off with high and mighty Komarova, to that Chukchi place. And what had that haughty bitch said about her? Had she been spreading any lies?

What lies? Nothing. Why should she? Everyone knew what a lovely person Lydia Yakovlevna was. Everyone spoke well of her, her charm, her warmth—as he did himself.

Oh, did he? Well, let him prove it. He was a different person since he'd come back from Bilibino with all that money. Go on, let him spend some of it, a good meal, she'd dress up for the occasion, and they'd share a full night together.

Ah, that he couldn't; he was tired, had to start early in the morning. He was *driving* for Komarova the next three days. His knowledge of native languages was useful to her. She mustn't see anything wrong in that. Green Cape was full of gossip, she knew it. After the three days, *then* they'd get together again.

The girl reluctantly went, and he mused over what she had said. It was true the place was full of gossip. Anna Antonovna had told him plenty of it. But nothing about Komarova had come up. Would she have told him if it had? Maybe he had been seen near the house. . . . He decided not to go back tonight. He went below and made a guarded call from the public phone in the hall. Then he fixed himself a couple of drinks and some food from the fridge, and watched television.

There was a talk show on television and he saw again the jolly little man in reindeer boots—the deputy mayor of the town, he now knew, a token Yakut—and remembered where he had seen him first. The flickering tapes, rainy Prince George . . .

Suddenly he could not eat the food. The events of tomorrow rose up in his throat.

At Prince George he should have backed out. At any time since he could have backed out: at the camp, in Japan, on the ship, even here with the Evenks. But *tomorrow* he couldn't back out. Once started then, he had to continue. And it would end—he knew it suddenly, could recollect a distant voice warning—it would end in tears.

One call now, then, and cancel?

He poured himself another drink.

No. To hell! To come so far, and give up? Something for him to do in the world—Rogachev had told him long ago. See it through to the end. He tossed back the drink and went to bed.

39

He was up early in the morning, and was early at the medical center, in one of Ponomarenko's jazzy lumber jackets.

There he helped load up, in the packing bay at the rear.

The distilled-water jars were jammed tightly into heavy crates, and the packers normally loaded them last to hold the lighter materials in position: the crates went fifty kilos apiece.

As the driver, he had other views on this. It would make them tail-heavy, he said, and the route was very slippery this season. The track up to the guard post was bad enough—he had hauled a load there not long before—and the stinking heads had said the farther slope was even worse. For that final leg stability up front was needed; the big crates ought to go in first.

The packers bowed to his superior knowledge, and they were amicably completing the job when Medical Officer Komarova showed up, leaning on her stick.

"Ah. A driver for me today. Good."

The bobik's doors were closed and they were off, and soon on the river. It was still dark.

"What problems last night?" she said.

Her face was very pale, he saw, and stiff.

"Nothing serious." He explained them.

"That little tart. Still, you were right not to come. You've brought your papers?"

"Everything." His particulars had been telexed to the research station and would be waiting at the guard post.

They left the river and entered the creek, and he drove a few kilometers along it and stopped.

She wound a scarf around her head and chin and put her fur cap back on, while he shrugged into Khodyan's balaclava. It was a Finnish one, decorated with ski figures; he topped it with the opulent mink hat.

"All right?" he said.

"Yes. Very becoming." But her voice was dry and tight.

He drove on again, and presently the red flag for the turnoff ramp came into view in the headlights.

"Switch on the circuit radio," he said.

She switched it on and got the familiar crackling voices.

"I'm not sure I can go through with this," she said.

He wasn't sure himself. He didn't answer, turning up the ramp.

The logs had been gritted again, he saw, and on top the two men were waiting again. Not the same two, for, as the Evenks had said, the security staff had changed over; but a pair almost identical. Bundled-up figures, ear flaps down, breath standing in the air, automatic weapons slung. A military jeep stood by the guard post.

The men saluted the medical officer, and one of them, a sergeant, bent into the window.

"A hard morning, Doctor. No trouble getting here?"

"No." She licked her lips. "Do you want me out?"

"No, stay where you are. You've got a bad leg, I hear. Just your papers. He can come out. What's the name—Khodyan?" He was checking his own sheet, but spared a look at the fancy headgear and the lumber jacket.

"Khodyan." He managed to crack his face into a smile. He got out; produced his papers; had them checked; waited while Komarova's papers were also checked.

"How's the track up there today?" she said, her voice forced.

"Not so bad. There's four-wheel drive on this?" the man asked the Chukchi.

"Sure, four-wheel."

"Follow me. In first gear. Open the back now, I'll check it out."

The rear doors were opened and the sergeant checked off the goods crammed inside. "Okay, close her," he said, and walked off to the military jeep.

"How long you staying there, Doctor?" The remaining man was beating gloved hands in the frigid air. He had just opened the gates barring the upward track. A harsh wind was sweeping from the mountain.

"No time. There's been—an emergency call." The radio was still crackling out. "I'll be down almost at once."

"Thank God for that!"

"Stay in the hut—this wind isn't good for you."

"I don't need telling!"

"Okay, let's go!" The sergeant had backed the jeep and was signaling them, and the small convoy set off.

They exchanged a quick glance, but he said nothing. The path up was a sunken road, plowed into the slope and zigzagged to keep the gradient manageable. It was still very steep, and they ground slowly up in first gear.

In just over a kilometer the top of the dome came suddenly into view, pinkish floodlight reflecting off it. He recognized it at once from the photographs. And after the dome, the whole camp, laid out on the plateau: two, three hundred meters of low buildings, spread out, enclosed by tall chain-link fencing, all floodlit.

Just as they reached the gates he identified the storage sheds too, and the generator housings, and the landing strip. The jeep halted at the gates, which opened, admitting them to a pen and another guard post, where they were stopped again.

Here papers were once more checked; both sets of gates, those behind them and those in front, kept shut. Then they were motioned on, the jeep leading the way. It stopped at a squat concrete building, until a couple of uniformed men emerged; and then left, the sergeant waving them to remain.

"This is it," she said. Her voice was barely a croak. "Open the door for me."

"Remember your words. And that you're in a hurry."

He ran around to the door; and she emerged stiffly, poking with her stick.

"What's this, Medical Officer?" The first uniformed figure was a major, very smart in his fur hat and shoulder boards. "They say you've hurt yourself."

"A sprain, nothing. It doesn't interfere with my work. Apart from this wretched driving," she said irritably. "I can't stay, I'm afraid—an urgent case on my radio. A wasted journey, except for these stores. Have them unloaded at once, if you please. Open the back," she ordered the Chukchi.

He ran around to do so, and the officer looked in.

"Yes. I heard it was a fair load. The tractor's called for—here, it's coming. You'll step inside for refreshment?"

"Not—just for the moment. I'll see them started first. I don't want any dawdling here. Be so good as to bring me the requisition order, Major. I'll look at it on the way down. And I'll join you inside very shortly. Come on, now, hurry it along!" she called to the approaching tractor.

An Evenk was driving the tractor, and another one was in the small flat car that it was pulling. Porter recognized them both—they had been with the herds; the changeover had taken place.

As the major withdrew inside, his subordinate took over and supervised the unloading.

"Now, men, make fast work!" he urged the Evenks. "The medical officer has to get off on a case."

"You won't be seeing us today, Doctor?" one of the Evenks asked. Maddeningly, both Evenks were grinning at her broadly.

"Not today. I'll have to come back. Careful with those cartons," she said severely. "There are bottles inside."

"What case you on, Doctor, what's the urgency?"

"Never mind the case! Just look what you're doing. And don't throw, now—carry them!"

The driver was pulling the light goods out of the back and tossing them to his mate for stacking on the flatcar.

"Only two pair of hands, Doctor," the man complained. "And if we're to hurry it up—"

"Shall I get a few extra hands?" the guard asked her.

"No, no, they can manage perfectly well. Just see they do it properly. Look, they're stacking too high, everything will tumble. See it's redone"—she looked at her watch—"and the crates have still to go on!"

The guard hurried to supervise the restacking, and the Evenk at the bobik hurried to haul out the crates. The crates, having been stowed well up front in the van, required him to jump inside to get them; and to assist him the Chukchi jumped in with him. Once inside he swiftly removed his mink hat, balaclava, and lumber jacket; and just as swiftly the Evenk removed his own upper gear. The Evenks were clad in deerskin jackets, fur side in, their crude caps worn flaps down. In no time they had swapped over.

"Quick, take my papers!" Porter said. "You'll need them to get out."

"Papers? Where the devil should I put—"

The man had still found no place to put the papers when the guard, at the flatcar, noticed the Chukchi in the bobik.

"Hey! You there—come out!"

The two men looked around at him.

"You, in the fur hat, come out at once! You're not allowed!"

The man now in the fur hat came slowly out, shaking his head at the medical officer, and the guard walked suspiciously over.

"Now, officer," Komarova said, swallowing. She had observed the shake. "Those crates are very heavy. One man can't handle them on his own."

"Well, *he* can't handle them. You know that, Doctor. No outsider handles anything here."

"Yes, you're right," she said, but remained staring at him. "This— it's your first trip here? I don't remember examining you before."

"No, first time, Doctor."

"Put your tongue out."

"My tongue?" The man bemusedly extended it.

"Yes. Slight soreness. And some nausea, too, I expect." All the guards had slight soreness and some nausea the first few days. "Let me see your eyes." She helped herself to them, pulling down a lower lid and getting him to gaze skyward while she did so; at the same time noting that papers had changed hands behind him and were now secreted. "It's the altitude. Not so good for your heart, I'm afraid. I'll take a look at you later. For now, carry on. And get the men moving."

This the man did, at speed, but still in a state of abstraction over his heart.

"You're coming back *when,* Doctor?" he anxiously asked.

"Not today. And tomorrow's out of the question. It will be the day after. Ah—and I have a message for you!" she called to the Evenks. "Tell Stepan Maximovich his grandchild will be premature, perhaps with complications. Let him choose names without delay, for a boy or a girl."

"Wonderful! We'll celebrate. But they keep us dry as a bone here, Doctor! Can't you bring us up a drop?"

"No, I can't. Tell him to write the names down, and I'll take them when I come. You *shouldn't* be drinking up here," she told them sternly.

"Doctor," the guard said. He was earnestly staring at her. "Is there anything *I* shouldn't be doing here?"

"Yes. Try not to sleep on your back. Or the left side. Use the right."

"The right," he said.

"And call the jeep for me now. I won't be long with the major." She glanced at her watch again. "A sick woman is waiting down there! See the sergeant is here in the jeep. And I'll be out in two minutes."

And in two minutes she was, with the medical sheets and a flurried major. The sergeant was there in the jeep. The Chukchi was there in the bobik. And the small convoy was off once more, through two sets of opened gates and down the icy path to the guard post. There the two certified visitors—checked down below, checked on top, and now checked out—were saluted off the premises; security one hundred percent. The guards saw them safely down the ramp and removed it. And the medical officer was back in the creek again, with her driver. It was the first time the man had seen it.

Up on top, his replacement was also seeing things for the first time. He had accompanied the tractor back to the storage sheds, receiving many winks from the Evenks working there while the guards slowly patrolled. Now he was helping transport another load, to the supply bay.

The supply bay was at the rear of the complex, and as they neared the boundary fence he suddenly saw what he'd come for. Beyond the perimeter, a lake. A great basin of it, now iced, but with machinery of some kind mounted, evidently at work to keep a section of the floodlit water open. The water that it kept open was black, inky black. Reached at last. It was here: Dark waters. *Tcherny Vodi.*

40

Major Militsky, the camp commandant of Tcherny Vodi, was a rosy young man, not quite thirty years old, but risen fast in his profession. His present job he greatly disliked. Twice before he had been rotated to it, and each time he had disliked it. But this time he disliked it the most. It was his first time here in winter; and for an ambitious security man in winter Tcherny Vodi was an insult. The place was impregnably secure.

In summer some problems could arise. All supplies had to come by air then, and strict routines were needed to prevent contacts between the Evenks and the aircrews—vetted crews, naturally, but given to stretching their limbs and loitering in the fine mountain air.

In winter there wasn't even that. The crews that arrived went right to the heated crewroom and stayed there. And not so many did arrive. For in winter, deliveries could also come by land; and they did, to the lower guard post, for later collection by the camp's own vehicles. An excellent system—no contact possible between the truck drivers and the camp.

With the *Facility,* of course, no contact was possible at any time. It was perched twelve hundred meters up a mountain. It was built actually into the mountain, with the camp securely on top of it.

The camp occupied Levels One and Two of the plateau: Level One for the guards' barracks, the major's suite, and all other visible structures. And Level Two for services: the kitchen, bakery, laundry, boilers, workshop, and Evenk quarters. Underneath all *that,* on Levels Three and Four, was the Facility, but about this the major knew nothing. The Facility ran itself, through a body called the Buro.

Major Militsky had never visited the Buro, and was not permitted to do so, but three channels of communication existed with it. These were the internal postal system, a telephone, and a teleprinter. The printer was the most regularly in use, and messages chattered to and fro on it several times a day. The post, in the form of a deed box that went up and down in a lift, was for papers requiring signature (the administrator's or, more rarely, the director's hieroglyph) and was also quite regular.

The telephone was not regular at all.

The telephone was a hotline, for emergency use only.

No emergencies had so far arisen in the major's tours of duty and he had not had to use it. He greatly hoped he wouldn't have to do so now, though an emergency showed signs of developing. To nip it in the bud, without any panic on the hotline, would need fast action from him on the teleprinter. And some of the clearest explanations in the world to the swine at the other end.

The swine at the other end was a colonel of security, the administrator of the Buro, who had proved a great pain to the major. On more than one occasion he had reported adversely on the major's competence. Aspects of the present situation could easily provoke him again, but there was no help for it.

The matter was so ridiculous he didn't even know how to explain it. He jotted down a few notes for himself. But even with the notes it was difficult.

It concerned the naming of a baby. The baby, not yet born, was about to be born, prematurely. When born it would be the grandchild of Stepan Maximovich, the director's manservant. Tribal custom among the Evenks required the grandfather to choose a name for the baby.

The visiting schedule for Stepan Maximovich entitled him to one visit per rotation of Evenks. And he had already had it, two days ago. Because of the baby the Evenks were now demanding a further visit; in fact, two. This was because he would need to consult his wife in between. It might even be necessary for him to have a third visit, in case he changed his mind. Grandfathers often changed their minds. If this one changed *his* it could easily take them into tomorrow. It couldn't be *after* tomorrow, because the day after tomorrow Medical Officer Komarova . . .

The major tugged at his collar. Rough going.

. . . because the day after tomorrow, Medical Officer Komarova, who had *herself* informed them of the imminent baby (brief details of visit), would be coming to the camp again. The Evenks were insistent that by then the baby's name had to be known. Evenk belief was that a dead baby, even more than a live one, had to have a name in order that God . . .

Well, skip God. The colonel would have views on God. But how then to . . .

What they had to understand down there was that Evenks were free workers, not conscripts. Could withhold their labor. They were asking that matters be brought to personal attention of *Director*. Great importance of avoiding Situations. Camp commandant was holding a guard escort available. Speedy approval requested for immediate visit by Stepan Maximovich.

Well, it was untidy. But it was all there.

The major tapped out the message and waited, in some trepidation, for the reply.

In twenty minutes the teleprinter started chattering back.

He read it, amazed.

"Best wishes to Evenks and best hopes for the safe arrival of their newborn. Camp commandant to be congratulated on his tactful handling. Visit of Stepan Maximovich approved. Guard escort to be posted immediately at entrance to Level Three."

"To be congratulated on his tactful . . ." He read it again, goggle-eyed, very far from expecting that.

The Evenks, in their dormitory, had expected nothing less. They had stopped work and assembled there, having informed the major that they would remain until Stepan Maximovich arrived; which he did within minutes of the major conveying best wishes.

Down the corridor came two guards, Stepan Maximovich between them, and halted at the dormitory.

"Stepanka!" They jumped about him and wrung his hand and slapped his back and continued doing so until the two guards, grinning, left the natives to it and departed outside the door.

The Evenks carefully closed the door.

"By God!" Stepanka said. He was a merry little fellow, one eye half closed in a permanent wink. "I've started believing it myself. Is that girl of mine so premature?"

"A little premature—Komarova confirmed it today. But Kolya here says there's nothing to worry about."

"Worry? Why would I worry? All six of my grandchildren were premature. Forward children!" Stepanka said proudly.

"And not one named by you, you old bastard! Did you bring up something to drink, at least?"

"Not now . . . But Kolya! I'm glad to know you, Kolya." The old Evenk shook hands most warmly. "They told me about you, and this poor girl. And I told the chief the whole story. He knows the father—has him working down there. I don't know these people myself, you understand. But the chief's spoken to him, and he expects the letter. You've got it with you?''

"It's here," Kolya said, and took it reverently out of his waistband. It was in a lavender envelope, folded in two, and he smelled it first and put it to his lips before handing it over.

The old Evenk was greatly touched by the gesture. "Kolya, I see right away," he said, "you're a good fellow. And you'll certainly get your reward—in this world or the next. I'll bring you the reply and you'll take it to the girl. But tell me—how did the switchover go?"

They told him how the switchover had gone, and soon all of them were slapping backs again in another burst of hilarity.

It went on so long that the guards, thumping on the door, called out that they were on escort duty only until lunchtime, and to hurry it up. And Stepanka announced he was ready, and left; this time winking with both eyes.

He was back before time, at four; for they had expected him at night. And this time he was not cheerful, but serious, even mystified.

He had brought an envelope with him, concealed in his felt boots, and when the guards had left he produced it. It was not from the father, he said. It was for Kolya's eyes alone. He was to see that only Kolya read it.

The Chukchi separated himself and opened the envelope.

A single short note was inside, and he read it twice. Then he looked at Stepanka with his mouth open.

"You know what's here?" he said.

"The father wants to see you himself."

"But how is it possible for—"

"I don't know how. It tells you how. The chief wrote it. You are to read it until you understand it, and then tell me either yes or no, and burn it. This is all he told me."

The Chukchi muttered to himself, "What should I do?"

He saw that all the Evenks were staring at him.

"Kolya, is it a dangerous thing?" one of them asked.

"I don't know. . . . Maybe."

"Then listen, you've done enough. You came to bring a letter and to get one. Why does the father want to see you?"

Kolya looked at the note again.

" 'He does nothing but weep,' " he read out. There was nothing about weeping in the note. "I don't know. . . . I've come so far," he said.

"Well, whatever you decide," Stepanka told him, "decide now, and burn it." He was looking around at the door. Two of the Evenks were standing against the spy hole of the door.

"Well." He licked his lips. "Say yes. Tell him yes," he said, and flicked his lighter and burned the note, and then he burned the envelope too.

The main corridor of Level Two was under constant patrol during the day, and all doors had to be kept open; this was to prevent smoking in the service rooms, and also drinking, for illicit drink had been known to turn up in the stores. At night the patrols were reduced to two an hour, and although all doors were now bolted each one was methodically checked. An ingenious Evenk had once hidden in a workshop and had managed to introduce industrial alcohol into the dormitory.

At 10:55 Kolya Khodyan slipped out of his bunk in the locked dormitory. He was fully dressed, even to his deerskin hat. The room was faintly aglow with the blue lighting that burned all night—a convenience for the guards checking the spy hole. He quickly pulled on the felt boots worn in the dormitory, and padded softly to the washroom; and before closing the door looked around once to the watching Evenks and raised a hand.

The washroom had an exterior door to the corridor, for the use of the Evenks during the day. The guards had already passed—they had heard them try the door—but he did nothing, waiting as instructed, listening for the scrape of the bolt. He counted out the full five minutes on his watch, but there was no sound from the bolt. Had the job already been done? He tried the handle and gently pulled the door. It opened easily.

He took a look out, up and down the long length of the corridor, brightly lit, totally empty. The ceiling was studded with smoke alarms, and the walls with bulkhead lighting. At the far end he could see the barrier with an illuminated sign of some kind over it. Just around the corner there, at the locked entrance to Level Three, was a guard post, and he could hear a faint rumble of laughter from the sentry detail. The shorter length of corridor, to the right, contained only the laundry and ended in a blank wall with a bulkhead light in it.

He waited a few seconds more, watching the guards' end. Nothing: no movement, not even a shadow. He stepped out into the corridor, closed the door behind him, quietly bolted it top and bottom, and turned to the right. This was what the note had told him to do. It was all it had told him. Obviously it had to be the laundry, there was nothing else there. The laundry had big double doors but no bolts, only a keyhole. Locked. He ran his hands over both doors, and lightly tapped, not knowing what else to do, before noticing that the end wall of the corridor had suddenly opened. The thing had swung inward, about a foot, and he hurried swiftly to it and slid himself inside.

As soon as he was in, in darkness, the wall closed again and a flashlight came on. Stepanka was standing there. Stepanka wasn't looking at him, but at a periscope. The periscope was looking along the corridor, evidently through the bulkhead lamp on the other side of the wall. Kolya looked himself, and saw the whole well-lighted length of it, deserted, everything securely locked. Stepanka was looking frightened when he turned to him, and he had a hand to his lips. He fiddled with the knob of a combination lock, checking it with a piece of paper in his hand, and then beckoned him to follow, waving the torch.

They were in a small room, a cement room—walls, floor, ceiling, all of cement; bare, windowless.

Stepanka opened a door and they stepped onto a landing—also cement, unfinished, very stark and cold, with a descending flight of stairs ahead; and he closed the door behind them and let out a breath.

"By God!" he said. "I never was here before! I never saw this." He was holding his heart. "Come, Kolya."

He kept the light pointing downward at the stairs, two steep flights of them, and they came to the bottom and a short corridor ending in a blank wall. A rail was set in the wall, and Stepanka pressed it and pushed the wall in, and a slant of light came out. He hurried Kolya inside, immediately pushing the wall to. The combination knob inside was hidden in a decorative grille, and he hastily reset it, studying the paper.

Kolya was studying the room.

It was a most spectacular room.

It was at least seventy feet long, at least twenty high; chandeliered, galleried, and with a library set all around the gallery. It was full of works of art. There were paintings on the walls—magnificent paintings, of all periods: Gauguin, Picasso, Rembrandt, Mondrian. The room was full of color. And sculptures. And flowering shrubs and trees—trees in great tubs on casters, evidently for moving in and out. The chandeliers were not lit, but they sparkled softly in the light of lamps spaced out on small tables along the walls. There was a long coffee table—a great slab of black basalt—with comfortable couches around it, and club chairs.

Stepanka saw him staring all about and at the ceiling.

"It's two levels high here," he said. "Level Three and Four, both. This is his library, he sleeps the night sometimes. . . . I find him here. Now, Kolya!" He was holding his heart again. "You stay here. I have to go and tell him. He will get the father for you. I can't do it myself."

He went through a door, leaving it very slightly ajar. And presently there was the sound of tapping on another door and Stepanka's voice speaking softly in Russian. And then silence; and Kolya waited in it, looking about the room.

At each end was a spiral staircase to the gallery; and in a shadowy corner a huge television set and a globe and a drink trolley. Also a cage. Something moved in the cage, and he walked slowly toward it; but the cage was only an elevator, and it was his own image moving there in the mirror that backed it, and he turned sharply around to the door again, listening.

Another door had closed somewhere and he heard a click as it was locked. And then an odd whining sound, and the door nudged open and a wheelchair drove smoothly in.

"Well!" Rogachev said. His hand was outstretched, a great smile on his face. "I have waited for you, my friend. I have waited so eagerly."

Six

The Ring and the Book

41

And now what am I to say to you? It was a lifetime ago we met. And now I am an old man, and will not get much older. I will show you what I have to show, and you will take back what I have to give. It's all done now, everything complete.

That you are here, I know, and you will tell me how it happened. That you would come I never doubted. It was not lighthearted, that discussion of ours those years ago. My own part I kept immediately and I know you took advantage of it—although I saw no result. As you see, I have followed your career. . . .

As to my own . . .

My own is so bound up with the events of this land, it cannot be separated. Over seventy years the Soviet Union lasted—a mighty structure, solid as rock. Now, like an optical illusion, all gone. Only two things of value, I believe, ever came out of it, and of these one would have happened elsewhere. The other could only have happened here.

"I will have two things to show you," Rogachev said.

They had spoken for a few minutes but Porter still stared at him, trying to recollect the man. The red hair had gone. *All* the hair had gone. Much skin had gone, too—great blotches left on scalp, face, hands. And the big body, once so robust, was shrunken away, wrapped in a shawl.

"What the hell happened to you—the explosion?" he said.

"The satellite saw the ruins, did it?"

Porter told him what it had seen, what both satellites had seen, and the scarred forehead wrinkled.

"The roll call, eh? And the bandages. Not bad. Still, it's nothing,

nothing at all, the earliest subjects. But now we have to move. There's a lot to do."

He was steering toward the gallery.

"My electric chair," he said, "once my predecessor's, who gave a name to the device. You won't know of him."

"Zhelikov? Sure, I know of him," Porter said.

"You do?" Rogachev glanced at him. "Well, you're going to learn more," he said.

He was opening a door under the gallery. A small cloakroom led off it, all its surfaces insulated with padding. Fur coats hung from the hooks. Rogachev carefully bolted the door behind them.

"Help me up," he said. "We are going somewhere cold, and must clothe ourselves."

Porter helped the old man into a coat, also a fur hat and gloves, and did the same for himself.

"You'll find goggles in a pocket. Maybe you don't need them—I can't stand the cold anymore." He strapped a pair around his own head and opened a door in the far wall. A blast of icy air emerged. Beyond the door a line of strip lights had come on, revealing a long ramp descending into a tunnel.

The wheelchair hummed softly down the ramp and Porter held on to the back. Frost glittered everywhere; abnormal frost, huge multi-colored wafers, delicate and glassy, that clung trembling to the walls and fell in tinkling showers as they passed.

"I accustom in a minute or two," Rogachev said, his voice muffled. He was holding a glove over his mouth and nose. "But I can't stay below more than ten minutes, anyway."

They were going evidently into permafrost, unchanging, unthawing, so that the frost had vitrified. At the bottom, the tunnel leveled out into a wide chamber. Here the lighting was not only on the roof but also set into the tubelike walls, the whole place brilliantly illuminated, sparkling with crystal.

A block of ice stood in the middle, and Rogachev steered toward it.

Except that it wasn't ice, Porter saw. Some kind of plastic, its upper section hollow. A coating of frost wafers had fallen on it, and Rogachev took a little spatula from his coat and carefully removed them. A transparent case was beneath, embedded with a network of fine hairlines.

"A temperature control," he said, "to prevent shriveling."

Porter couldn't at first be sure, but it looked to him as if a girl was in the case.

"It opens quite easily—a silicon seal. Just give me a hand to hold it," Rogachev said, and raised the lid.

A girl was in the case.

She was on her back, eyes closed, very pale. A white sheet covered her from abdomen to knees but she was otherwise naked. Blond braids of hair were draped at either side of her breasts, and her closed eyes, slightly slanted, were set above high cheekbones, the lips a little open as if breathing. Her wrists were crossed on the sheet, right over left. She was tall, shapely, very handsome.

Porter looked from her to Rogachev's goggles.

"What's this?" he said.

"A young woman, perhaps seventeen. We had to carry out some operations on her, as far as possible from the back. But also a Caesarean section: She was eight months pregnant. Hold the lid."

He leaned over and very carefully drew down the sheet, exposing a row of sutures above fair pubic hair; there was no reddening of the skin, and the neat stitching looked new. "The scar couldn't heal, of course. But the baby was there, perfectly formed. As you see, the girl is fair. Her eyes are gray. In life her color would be better, but that's how we found her so we kept her the same shade." He drew the sheet back in position.

"Who is she?" Porter said.

"We call her Sibir, after the country. It's a Tartar word, you know, not Russian; something like 'sleeping,' 'still.' This is how I found her. She had died instantly and was preserved instantly—quick-frozen. Don't be afraid, you can touch her. She's well embalmed now."

He reached forward himself and raised the upper wrist. The hand came up quite flexibly. It was a broad hand, the fingers long but square, the nails short and ragged.

"The arm underneath is broken, the left one. She fell on it—she was a left-hander. The finger pads and the palm are quite deeply scored there. Leave that alone, but touch her, make contact. You won't get another chance."

Porter drew off a glove and gingerly felt the girl's face. It was smooth, full, by no means cold—indeed, to his own chilled hand, it felt warm. He stroked the skin, the nose, felt the earlobes beneath the braids.

"I can't stay much longer—it needs heated suits, from the labs," Rogachev told him. "That door at the back leads up there. This is my own entrance. I come often. Take a good look—walk around her. She's tall, isn't she? Distinctive. A good face—Slav, would you say?"

Porter walked around the case. The slant of the eyes didn't look

Slav to him. "I don't know," he said. The legs were scratched, but the nails on her toes better than on her fingers: She had worn footwear. "What's the story?" he said.

"A unique one. You'll never see anything like her. She's been in that state for forty thousand years. Before Slavs, before any of the present races of the world. I found her in a block of ice. She's one of the two types we all spring from, perhaps the matriarch of millions—she had given birth before. I don't know what became of her earlier offspring, but the child she was carrying I know a *lot* about. Oh yes!"

He closed the lid and turned his chair and set off immediately, and Porter followed him.

A few steps up the ramp Porter stopped and looked back. He could still see her in her case, alone in the brilliant tunnel; could see her lips a little open, and for a moment had the illusion that they were moving. But it was only the crystals, again fluttering down.

Rogachev had braked the chair and turned, his goggled eyes also looking down. His mouth was twisted slightly in a smile.

"Do you know the story of King Saul?" he said. "His father sent him out to find lost donkeys, and he found a kingdom. Zhelikov sent me to find a mammoth and I found a lost world. As a matter of fact I found something more—something quite . . . incalculable. It's the reason you're here. But where to start?"

42

Where does it start? At Pitsunda, with the accident that led to my appointment? Or a little before, the chance meeting at Oxford? Or long before, the first meeting with Zhelikov? Well, say that one: 1952.

In 1952, suddenly, inexplicably, I found myself under arrest. I had done nothing wrong—nothing at all. The director of my institute had perhaps done something, although I doubted it. But the whole research team was rounded up, and sentenced, and scattered to the four winds, myself to the Kolyma and the little camp at Panarovka.

At that camp, met Zhelikov for the first time.

Zhelikov, already most eminent, was also by then a most seasoned prisoner with many terms and many camps behind him. At Panarovka just then he was preparing a series of lectures, and on my arrival—a young low-temperature specialist—he obtained permission for me to assist him.

Those lectures were a great success, with camp officials and prisoners alike, but afterward he told me he had given them only to get off onerous camp duties. He also confided how he had come by this useful trick, and of the events surrounding it.

At another camp, during the war, Zhelikov had found a most interesting pair among the prisoners, Korolyov and Tupolev. Both were "enemies of the people," Korolyov's particular crime being sabotage: the misuse of munitions for making fireworks. This pair had got up a seminar, on the subject of aerodynamics, which had relieved them of hard labor for a considerable time—the source of Zhelikov's later inspiration.

Which was only the beginning of the story. For when Tupolev one day was unexpectedly released, he immediately pulled strings to get his friend Korolyov released also. Tupolev then went on to make the bombers bearing his name that helped win the war, and Korolyov returned to his fireworks: the model staged rockets that preceded his ballistic missiles and enabled him, some years later, to put the first man in space.

Even that isn't the end of it. For Korolyov had planned to put not a man but a monkey first in space, and for this purpose he later secured Zhelikov's release. Zhelikov's work on the conditioning of monkeys was of course well known, and he sped off right away to start conditioning *this* monkey.

Of that particular development nothing came. For one reason or another, not a monkey but a dog was ultimately chosen (the celebrated Laika), and Zhelikov's public protests at the decision won him another sentence. This time to Panarovka . . . and the course of lectures.

From Panarovka, not long after the lectures, Zhelikov was suddenly plucked one night, for reasons I did not know, but which I learned years later, at Tcherny Vodi.

There were three reasons—the first a freakish idea of Stalin's.

In his late-night reading, the restless insomniac had come upon a little book of Zhelikov's on the subject of hibernation. He had become interested in hibernation. This was partly for the purpose of preserving the lives of cosmonauts in future space voyages, but mainly with a view to preserving his own. The body of his predecessor Lenin he had had embalmed as a lasting icon for the people. His own he thought of having "hibernated" so that at some future time it would be of greater benefit to them.

With his security chief, Beria, he had discussed this idea.

A corps of the most faithful guardians would be required to maintain his body, as he himself had maintained Lenin's. But even more urgently work had to begin, by the leading experts and in the greatest secrecy, on *how* he should be hibernated.

The leading expert on hibernation was Zhelikov, and the most secret place in the Soviet Union was Tcherny Vodi.

This was the craziest of the reasons.

The other reasons were not crazy, and the second concerned Tcherny Vodi itself.

In 1952 the research station was engaged solely with work on chemical and bacteriological warfare, its activities covered by a weather station that had stood on the site for many years. The work required large numbers of test animals, and the severe climate combined with a shortage of air transport had seriously reduced the stock, hampering the military program. A project for breeding hardier test animals had begun, but the methods were primitive and not successful.

On examination (by Minister Beria and his assistants) it was found that the prisoner at Panarovka could be the man for this, too. As well as being a world expert on hibernation he was also one on the conditioning of animals: As early as the 1920s he had worked in this field with his great mentor Pavlov.

But the third reason—Zhelikov's own—was one he had already raised in his lectures. It concerned Siberia.

Some little while before, a large-scale geological survey had shown the land to be, without question, the richest on earth. It had more oil than Arabia, more gold and diamonds than Africa, more mineral value than anywhere else on the planet; the vast bulk of this treasure being locked in permafrost, dormant. The attempts to exploit it, always with forced labor, had been inefficient and in any case had barely scraped the surface. It seemed unlikely that people would ever come in useful numbers to work in this hostile territory. Zhelikov's idea was to enhance the intelligence of animals to do it.

His own last work had been with the *most* intelligent animals. At his station in the Caucasus he had got chimpanzees solving problems on an abacus, having first conditioned them to that place from their habitat in the tropics.

This idea he suddenly found himself discussing in the most bizarre circumstances, and at the highest level. The night he was plucked from the camp he was taken by helicopter to an airfield. In an airplane he was given a decent suit—for he had left camp in his prison footcloths and tunic—and presently found himself, dazed, being driven through the streets of Moscow to the Kremlin, and the dictator's lair.

Stalin watched him eat a meal, and then talked with him throughout the night. The dictator was in his field jacket with pockets and he walked slowly round the room smoking his pipe. "Well—enough," he said at last, waving his pipe. "Now give your opinion on the proposal for hibernation."

The proposal for hibernation is horseshit, Zhelikov said, but he did not say this aloud.

"Yosef Vissarionovich," he said aloud, "I must tell you frankly that this is a very good proposal. It needs much work. I would first have to hibernate many other subjects, and be assured of their complete resuscitation before beginning to think—this goes without saying—of hibernating *you.*"

He had worked himself up to such an extent over the other proposals that it only then dawned on him (so he told me) that this was the one to buy all the rest.

"First-class laboratories, proper conditioning chambers, the highest degree of security, and the whole work under my own direction! Enemies are always about, prying for information—which on any subject concerning you should on no account be given. On that my stand would have to be inflexible. Whichever place is chosen, I need to have charge of it."

Stalin had emitted puffs of smoke and a series of grunts at these remarks, and he now took a long squint at Zhelikov.

"Well, we'll see," he said. "But what of this place they talk about, Tcherny Vodi? Is it a suitable place?"

"I don't know this place," Zhelikov said. "When the plans and a map become available I could give an opinion."

Stalin picked up the phone and called Beria, in bed.

At a quarter to six in the morning Minister Beria arrived with the plans and a map, having roused his ministry for them.

Zhelikov scanned the map and whistled.

"So near Panarovka—and I knew nothing of it!" he said. "Well, the place is good. But the station . . . " He was turning over sheets and decided he could now expand himself. "The station is horseshit."

"How horseshit?" Beria said.

"All on top. Where would I put my conditioning chambers?"

"Where do you have to put conditioning chambers?"

"Below. It would mean excavating the mountain."

"Excavate the mountain," Stalin said.

"And shifting the present station to do it. Shift a whole station?

And have engineers sink laboratories in a mountain?''

"Shift the station, sink engineers in a mountain," Stalin said, and laid down his pipe. "I will take a nap now." He patted Zhelikov on the shoulder. "You will stay some days, Lev Viktorovich. We will talk more of this," he said.

Zhelikov stayed a week in the Kremlin, and during the following one he took over at Tcherny Vodi.

In the summer and autumn of 1952 engineers leveled and removed the top of the mountain, and began mining inside it. Zhelikov supervised these operations.

At this time the research station had been a *sharashka*—a special camp for scientists. Some scores of these establishments were scattered about the Soviet Union, together with fifty reserved cities for less secret work. All of them came under the administration of the Ministry for State Security. The cities were normal cities, containing shops, apartment blocks, schools, and they were for free employees, the only restrictions being that permits were needed to get in or out.

The *sharashkas,* on the other hand, were for prisoners serving sentences. Some of the sentences were quite short—eight, ten years—although in the special case of Tcherny Vodi it was understood that nobody would ever get out. A man coming to the end of a ten would merely get another ten for accumulated infringements; or in exceptional circumstances he might get off and become a free worker with privileges. But he would never get out. This was because certain advances in bacteriology could also not be allowed to get out.

Zhelikov made this the first of his changes. All the workers became free workers, although still unable to leave; and he had inquiries made by the security service to attract other specialists, people whose particular situations made them suitable for a life that, while cloistered, offered the highest scientific freedom together with unparalleled living conditions.

The living conditions he set about making.

And he had his chimpanzees flown in from the Caucasus.

In this period Stalin died (of a heart attack, March 1953) and Minister Beria was shot. Their successors had no interest in hibernation but a large amount in Zhelikov's other developments for the exploitation of Siberia. And these by now had cost billions.

* * *

The original military installation he had had shifted back into position, although now underground. This interested him not at all, but he had its laboratories attached to his own on Level Three. On Level Four he had installed the living quarters—the studio apartments, library, gymnasium, tennis courts, swimming pool, and gardens—with special solar lamps, to his own design, roofed in the "outdoor areas" and controlled to give night and day inside the mountain. He also made the first hybrid apes.

"Is this real?" Porter said.

"Of course." Rogachev watched him pouring a drink and nodding up at a Rembrandt. They were back in the library.

"I choose the pictures from old state catalogues. If they're available I get them on loan for a few months. We get anything we want—films, music, books, papers. The staff join me here for social evenings occasionally. Or I look into their club. They have their own library of course; this one is Zhelikov's, built up over his twenty-five years here."

Porter glanced around the room.

"You didn't bring me here for this," he said.

"You know I didn't. Still, he was a truly great man, as history will one day acknowledge. His fellow jailbird—Korolyov, you know—they acknowledged only at his state funeral. Then the world knew who had made the satellites. The man himself was kept secret before. His *space* station they kept secret even for years after his death. But he began the exploration of space. That's one of the things that came out of the Soviet Union."

"Zhelikov's ape being the other?"

Rogachev smiled.

"No, no. What *I* have found is the other. I could certainly not have found it without his work—which was in every way remarkable. Yes, he made apes. But he also made problems."

Zhelikov's apes, by the early 1960s, were far ahead of anything in the world. This he knew for certain, for he was receiving all research papers, and he also knew the reason for it.

Although still in its infancy, genetic manipulation was causing concern abroad. The scientists engaged in it were finding difficulty in raising funds, were uncertain where the work would lead, and were worried at possible damage to their future careers.

Zhelikov was unconcerned about his future career, had no budget worries, and knew exactly where his work would lead. It would lead to a hardy animal that could live in Siberia and perform intelligent tasks. He had no ethical doubts at all.

He had a further advantage. The foreign workers, almost to a man, had no special training in physiology. In his own extraordinary life he had trained with the greatest physiologist of his age. Pavlov was noted not only for the "Pavlovian reflexes" of dogs but for his brilliant studies on all mammalian structure.

At Tcherny Vodi Zhelikov had sent for dozens of the late Pavlov's unpublished papers, on which they had worked together, with careful sketches of embryonic development. Pavlov had urged him always to study the embryo for an understanding of limbs, organs, and other structures, and had passed on his own exceedingly dexterous methods of doing so.

By the mid-1960s Zhelikov had not only a hardy chimpanzee but one that walked upright, that could drive home a nail with a hammer, select and use a nut for a bolt, dress itself in warm clothing, go and find a chosen package in a cold conditioning chamber, and return to unpack and then correctly repack the package.

He bred from the animals, and encountered his problem.

Although his apes reproduced they did so divergently. The intelligent ones proved to be not hardy, the hardy ones not intelligent. This problem occupied him into the next decade, and his advances—all in intelligence—became increasingly self-defeating. An intelligent ape was of use in the Arctic only if it was hardy; there was no present need for one elsewhere. The problem was to combine intelligence *with* hardiness, and reliably reproduce it, generation after generation.

He began a fundamental review of hardiness, of cell behavior at low temperature—and also, again, of hibernation, as an aspect of it. He examined a hibernating bear, and the fetus of a bear. He examined what was known of mammoths, close relatives of elephants, adapted to ice ages. A whole mammoth was not obtainable but he obtained the best-preserved museum specimen, and found it useless. Without the required soft tissue it was not possible to learn anything from a skeleton. (Not at that time. Only a few years and it would be possible; although not for him.)

For him some more dramatic events intervened. In 1976 he developed a virulent cancer, and some months later urgently asked to see his chosen successor, a specialist in low-temperature work. (He had been following my career, had heard of my misfortune.) And in the week that I was due, in February 1977, he heard something else. A fresh mammoth had been discovered. A very fresh one, entombed in ice, quick-frozen.

"He never saw the result, of course—what you have seen. Or could even have *dreamed* what I produced from it. But now"—Rogachev was looking at his watch—"it's almost three in the morning. Stepanka still has to get you back."

"You said you had two things to show me."

"Yes. The other is . . . not quite ready. Tonight you had the prehistory, in both senses. . . . What the satellite saw was mainly Zhelikov's work, a few modifications by me. What *I* have done, you will see for yourself. The subject will demonstrate it to you."

Porter looked at him.

"The subject is an ape?" he said.

"You'll tell *me*. I'm not sure that I know. You will chat together. Soon enough you'll know why you are here." He was smiling. "Anyway, you'll have to come down again. And I have thought how this is to be managed."

He explained how it was to be managed.

"Now I'll get Stepanka. Remember, you have not met *me*."

His chair whined out of the room, and presently Porter heard the sound of a key turning. Then silence for several minutes, and a shuffling sound, and Stepanka came in, very rumpled. He had a big watch in his hand.

"By God! Almost three o'clock." He was dazed. "You were with him half the night. You've got the letter?"

"No." Kolya was very serious. "He's rewriting the letter. He says I have to come again."

"What!"

"Stepanka—this man isn't normal! He wanted every detail, all the years between. Every kind of thing that happened to the girl. Then he would break down and question me again. He doesn't seem able to accept it—which doctors, which tests, have we done this, that." He shook his head. "He says he will bring me a ring—the mother's wedding ring. I am to take it back, it's to go to the grave. Tell me, is he mad?"

Stepanka's mouth had fallen open.

"I don't know. I've never met him," he said. He licked his lips. "The chief will have to arrange it again, then. And he isn't well himself. He said nothing about the chief?"

"Nothing. Only about the girl."

"Well. I don't know." He looked at his watch again. "But come—we'll just catch the guards. Or we can stand and freeze there for half an hour."

He produced the flashlight and the piece of paper from his pocket and attended to the lock in the grille. Then they were out in the cement passage again and going up the stairs. "It's a part of the building they never used. I knew nothing of it."

In the tiny room above, Stepanka looked through the periscope, and he motioned Kolya to look.

Through the periscope the brightly lit corridor was quite empty. "In one minute they'll come," Stepanka whispered. "Don't make a sound. You can hear through the wall. The moment they've gone is the safest. It's what I did before."

Kolya remained looking through the periscope, and in a minute the two figures appeared. They materialized suddenly, from the far end of the corridor, one behind the other, a few paces apart. The leading guard peered through each spy hole, and then checked each bolt; and the second made a mark on a clipboard. As they approached he could hear their footsteps and their voices repeating the name of each room checked.

They checked the dormitory, and they checked the washroom. Then they tried the laundry, and that was the last. Now they were only a few feet away, and through the periscope Kolya watched them; and as their backs retreated he gave place to Stepanka at the periscope.

Stepanka remained peering intently through it, and then he nodded and manipulated the lock, and switched the flashlight off and opened the wall.

Like a mouse he scurried to the washroom and drew the bolts, and Porter swiftly entered and closed the door, and heard the faintest scrape as the bolts went home again. He stood for some minutes with his ear to the door but heard nothing more; neither the shuffle of footsteps nor any other sound.

He went quietly into the dormitory.

A little snoring there, the Evenks all asleep. In the blue lighting he undressed and returned to his bunk, and for some moments, drifting off, thought of the girl in the tunnel, and of a night with Stalin, and prison camps and the exploration of space. Then he thought how he could chat with an ape and what it was that the ape had to demonstrate to him.

43

"Ludmilla—Ludmilla, my dear, how are you?"

"Thank you, I am well."

"I have brought a visitor. You don't mind seeing a visitor, Ludmilla?"

"No, I don't mind," the ape said, and put her glasses on.

She smiled at them from the bed. She had a sweet face, although her eyes were bandaged. She was wearing a nightie; and also, Porter saw, a number of other bandages. She seemed to have lost much hair and skin. It took him a moment to realize that the glasses had gone on over the bandaged eyes and that she was now shielding them slightly with her hand.

"Is the light too strong for you?"

"Only for a moment, when it came on."

"They don't hurt—your eyes?"

"No, they don't hurt, Uncle."

"She has no eyes," Rogachev said, in English. "A result of the explosion. We could have restored them but I wouldn't put her through the operation. She hasn't long to live. You are seeing well, my dear?" he asked in Russian.

"Yes, I am seeing well, Uncle."

"This visitor is Raven. Are you pleased to meet him?"

"I am pleased to meet you," Ludmilla said, and extended her hand.

"Ludmilla. I am very pleased to meet you," Porter said, and shook the hand. The palm was brown, the back of it a blotchy pink, tufted with down. The face was similarly blotched and tufted. It was finely boned and there was a sweet docility about it, a thoughtful docility as she gazed through her spectacles. But she was certainly an ape.

"You were hurt, I hear," he said.

"Yes, I was hurt."

"How did it happen?"

"In the fire. Uncle made me better."

"Was it a long time ago, the fire?"

"She hasn't much idea of time," Rogachev said in English. "It was a *long* time, Ludmilla—days and days. But it didn't hurt for long. Tell Raven how nicely you see now."

233

"I see nicely now," Ludmilla said, smiling.

"Take your glasses off, my pet."

Ludmilla took them off, and Rogachev shone a flashlight at the bandages. "Now we'll play a game again," he said. "Have I put the light on?"

"No, of course you haven't." Ludmilla was smiling.

"All right. Now," Rogachev said, and switched the flashlight off. "Now what have I done?"

"Silly! You haven't done anything," Ludmilla said, giggling. She felt for his hand, and he moved it, and she groped in the air until he gave her it. She squeezed the hand and kissed it, and he bent and kissed hers and then her blue lips.

"My little sweetheart—you're so clever! Stay in the dark a moment. I want Raven to examine you. It won't hurt." He parted the sparse hair behind Ludmilla's ears. "The glasses are her eyes," he said in English. "And these are the terminals."

A small metallic strip was set behind each ear.

"It's a very small implant, smaller than a pacemaker. The trick is to make the right junction. She has practically 20-20 vision now—the lenses self-focus, like the quite cheap video cameras. These are set in a plasma. Take a look at them."

Porter picked up the glasses. There was a vague flutter of movement in the lenses as he raised them, and at the end of each arm he saw the metal connecting strip.

"Of course with the same principle you can fabricate an eye in its natural socket—much more complex. Put the glasses on again, my dear," Rogachev said, and put them in her hand, and Ludmilla slipped the glasses on, smiling at him.

"Will you show Raven how well you read?"

"Yes, I will show him," Ludmilla said, slowly.

"Ah, my little sweetheart, you're tired. Is it this room? Don't you like this room?"

"It's . . . a nice room," Ludmilla said, gently.

"It's only for tonight, so that Raven can see you. We won't read, then. She reads," he told Porter. "Just simple sentences. We won't read. We'll look at pictures. You like pictures. Raven hasn't seen this book. Show him the pictures."

He handed Porter a book from the bedside table.

"Well, this looks a nice book," Porter said.

"Oh, it's a nice book," Ludmilla said.

"I wonder—what's this?" He had stopped at a page. There was a big picture on every page.

"This is a sledge," Ludmilla told him.

"Oh, of course! Is it—a blue sledge?" he said, peering.

"No! A red sledge," Ludmilla said.

"I was only playing games."

"I know you were," Ludmilla said, and laughed at him.

"Well, *this* one I know. A water tap! I can wash myself."

"No—silly!" Ludmilla said and giggled again, covering her mouth. "It's a samovar! With a samovar you make tea."

"She's so clever. You're so clever, my pretty," Rogachev said. "But now you must sleep. Raven wanted to see you so much, so I brought him. Do you like Raven?"

"Yes, I like him," Ludmilla said.

"I like you," Porter told her.

"You can kiss her. She likes being kissed," Rogachev said in English. "But no pressure on her body, she is very fragile."

Porter kissed Ludmilla's hand and then her face, and Ludmilla smiled and kissed him back.

"Now it's l ite for you, my precious. I'm sorry it's so late. Raven couldn't come any earlier. Tomorrow you can go back to your room. Say good night to him now."

"Good night, Raven," Ludmilla said.

"Good night, Ludmilla."

"And take your glasses off. It's time for sleep. Good night, my little sweetheart."

"Good night, Uncle."

"Well, then," Rogachev said, as they left the room, "so now tell me what I have made. And this is only the half of it."

But Porter remained silent, watching him relock the door.

He had had a long day. A bitter wind had blown on the mountain-top, the snow flurries whirling like devils over the compound. But the Evenks had remained cheerful and understanding of his lost sleep, seeing to it that he was allotted only indoor tasks in the morning.

He had told his news—of the distraught father, the letter to be rewritten, the ring that had to go to the grave—and they were certain that Stepanka would soon be up with new instructions.

But by afternoon Stepanka had still not come, and at two o'clock all of them had been ordered outside. A freighter plane was coming in, and immediate unloading had been requested before the weather worsened. For this the storage sheds had to be reorganized.

By three o'clock the plane had come and gone; and by four, though not all the cargo was yet inside, a cheery Major Militsky had called the men in from the wind and the snow.

A name had been chosen for the baby! Stepan Maximovich had an announcement to make.

"Ten o'clock," was Stepanka's whispered announcement to him. "One hour earlier than before." He didn't know why. But by 9:55 Kolya was to be in position.

And by 9:55 Kolya was, in the washroom. And by ten was going through the wall again.

"And this is only the half of it," Rogachev said. They were now in his study. The study adjoined the library and was part of a suite that included an apartment for Stepanka and his wife and also two bedrooms. The second bedroom was for a security official who visited regularly; Ludmilla was now in it.

"It's not even a half of it. There's more—far more. And yet we had set out to do something totally different. . . ."

44

We had set out to copy parts of a fetus: Sibir's fetus.

The father of the fetus had been a Neanderthaloid—not *Neanderthal* of Europe, which was in many ways a regression, but the earlier type, with a larger-domed skull. Of this there was no doubt. Sibir was typically "Cro-Magnon"; her child, broadly Neanderthaloid. And the differences between them were very remarkable.

Sibir was 1.89 meters in height, and her brain capacity 1,300 cubic centimeters. Her child would have grown much shorter, but with a brain much larger—1,500 cubic centimeters, our calculations showed. Since a modern brain is roughly 1,350 cubic centimeters, Neanderthaloid had 11 percent more. This curious fact, already speculated on from skull finds, was in itself exciting. But here we had an *actual* brain—unborn but whole, easily projectible from standard scales.

From hundreds of computer studies, we observed many differences in this brain. Zhelikov in his work had accumulated a large stock of brains (the heads of executed criminals), and these we used for comparison.

An immediate difference was in the visual-receptor areas—here very large. This was expected, for the fetus's eye sockets were also large. Neanderthaloid was a nocturnal creature: He came out in the dark and had to see in the dark. For us this had important implications. Half the year *we* are in the dark here, and Zhelikov had sought with his "worker" apes to improve their night vision, but without success.

So an extraordinary opportunity had opened up: to copy what we could of this new/old visual system.

Our own system is barely understood to this day. We know that the brain receives its signals in symbolic form, the eyes transmitting thousands of digits of information that the receptors in the brain can decode and assemble. But the method of transmission, the network of transmission, even the receptor areas themselves, were by no means clear.

These receptor areas (set beside our criminals') were altogether clearer, as was all the visual network, making the functioning as a whole more comprehensible.

With our fetus we found so well-defined a network (and of a night-sighted primate!) that we were almost beside ourselves. The aim was to increase, by cloning, the visual networks of our apes and to enlarge the receptor areas in their brains.

We set about it in this way.

(All our genetic work is this way.)

First, trial operations were conducted on the lower animals: rats, mice, etc. Portions of the network were excised and later replaced, to establish the method of surgery. Excising parts of a visual system of course results in blindness, and many rats were blinded before we learned (with cloned material) the technique of reinsertion. Then we moved on to the brain, to try to do the same with the receptor cells.

It took us seven years, until 1985, to get a result. But in that year, with extra material we had managed to clone, we got a good one: a 20 percent visual improvement with test rats. Then we moved to the apes.

This was an altogether more critical undertaking.

The trained animals were valuable, their whole visual apparatus much more complex. Also they were semihuman, able to express themselves. Even for the first stage—the trial removals and reinsertions—two full-scale operations were necessary, with recuperation after each one, and eyes kept bandaged until after the boost to restore vision.

The technique of boosting we had learned with the rats; vision will not resume without it. The visual network is in fact a complex chemical chain; the section we excise is therefore a chemical section. This section (or a cloned version) will not on reinsertion resume function by itself.

It needs a boost, a "jump start," from an electrical source. (We use a high-frequency signal, crystal-regulated—like quartz in a watch or silicon in a computer.) Light will not do the job and can produce permanent blindness, for the network must be intact and operational before the eyes are allowed to work.

This boost we pass directly via a cable to electrodes in the skull—just a brief burst, the eyes remaining sealed. And by means of a scanner we observe the effects on a screen.

The frequency we use is a "harmonic" (the so-called doppelgänger or ghost echo of a frequency); and to get this echo two crystals have to be set vibrating simultaneously.

With rats, the screen view of the boosting procedure had always been the same. The newly replaced network between eye and brain was dormant—not dead, but dormant, and we conjectured that the rat was "seeing" a shadowy gray. With the boost we could see the network activating—carrying current, as it were. Within fifteen minutes, though the animal's eyes were still covered, we knew the new material had been accepted and the system was up, and running.

With our first ape, a very different story—in fact, a disaster.

After the boost, an instant flash, like lightning through the network. Followed by blackout, and from the animal a cry of pain. The pain was momentary, and he told us so. But the network was now blank, the whole outline gone.

This was catastrophic. We had no idea what to do. The boost was a safe one—a harmonic specially selected from a range of ten. This range we had used on the rats.

We watched the screen for one hour, two. We tested the crystals, remeasured the harmonic, checked all the instruments. Nothing was wrong. But *something* was wrong. We returned to our records, and there found what was wrong.

The selected *range* had been used on the rats, but not this harmonic. (The harmonics that we generate, I should explain, do not exist in nature. They are modulations, calculated mathematically.)

As a precaution, with the first ape, our specialist had chosen the weakest harmonic of the range—the lowest, the faintest, the most remote from its original frequency. With the rats we had used the strongest; it had been unnecessary to try so far down the scale.

Needless to say we tried then. We tried ten rats—normal rats, with normal vision—not operating, just delivering the boost, with this same harmonic. Each one was blinded. Then we tried other rats, with other harmonics in the range. And no ill effects. Just *this* harmonic, the weakest, a freak, we had used on the ape, and had blinded it.

Blinded rats are destroyed. But we could not destroy an ape; the trained animals are still of use. In this case, after a few days we simply removed the bandages and put the animal (his name was Anton) on an instructional course. He was in no discomfort but needed eye patches, for the muscles controlling blinking had also been damaged.

And now a very strange incident occurred.

At that time the animals were engaged in a simulated postnuclear exercise. They were required to enter a maze, perform a number of actions, find their way out again, and report what they had done. Anton was participating in this (for even blinded apes may be useful after nuclear accidents), and he emerged from the maze and reported. It took his trainer some moments to observe that he had taken off his eye patches. He asked why he had done this and Anton said it was because he wanted to see.

"But, Anton, you *cannot* see."

"Yes. Can see. Can see," Anton said.

It seemed that he took off the patches to shower in the morning, and that morning he had found that he could see. He had put the patches back on again because he had been instructed to keep them on. But in the maze he had taken them off.

I was told at once, and rushed to test him. Through instruments I saw that every part of his visual system had reactivated. This happened ten days after the boost.

To understand what happened now I must explain something of our organization here. We come under the aegis of a Moscow body called the Scientific Directorate. This directorate I keep informed of our work, and I had informed them of the accident with Anton.

Every few weeks a member of the directorate visits me: a security official, but a well-informed scientist, a friendly fellow. This man now called up and asked me to repeat the experiment with the freak harmonic on another ape. He wished to see for himself how the network reactivated.

I did as he asked, used the same harmonic, and got the same result. Complete blanking of the newly installed network. After some days my friend arrived. In good time I started a machine to record the events; and presently we watched them. On the screen, a faint graying. An emerging outline. And within minutes, a full one—the same ten-day timing as with Anton.

My friend, greatly interested, took a copy of this recording and left with me something infinitely more interesting. Papers—research papers I had urgently requested: the latest studies in another field of optics. For in the days when Anton was blinded, I had brooded on other possibilities.

The network we had blasted out was a *chemical* network—enormously complex, but one we had been able to follow (at least to clone in part). I wondered now if we could back it up in some way, as a safeguard against other accidents.

Science had long backed up hearts, kidneys, many other systems, by copying the action of the systems. With the visual system our only sure knowledge was how it started—optically. Could it perhaps be backed up optically, with fiber optics?

Our experts studied the papers on fiber optics. Novel types of fiber would be required, some means of grafting them discovered, all this work quite new. I drove them on, however, standardized a procedure, and presently was able to move from theory to practice on rats.

Here the first job was to get a signal through the fiber. In the laboratory we had got one—nothing "visual," but a measured change in a bit of brain material. With a real rat, a functioning brain, this would be very different. We removed the rat's visual network, grafted our fiber in its place, allowed it to bond, and delivered the boost.

What followed was a moment of history.

It was something, I should say, almost beyond belief.

On the screen the newly connected fiber, a shadowy outline. Which within minutes began to firm up and then embolden. In *fifteen* minutes—full strong outline! The brain understood the fiber, had accepted it.

This stunning success—we had looked only for an instrumental blip—held us at the screen for hours. A whole day passed before we dared expose the rat's eyes and allow it to see. But there was no doubt it *did* see. It saw not well, for we had been unable to tune fiber to a real eye. But it saw! For the first time a blind creature saw—through fiber!

From Moscow, my friend made two watchful visits.

His first was to see us repeat the work—from fiber insertion, through boost, to final sighting.

And two weeks later—again. The directorate required another trial, this time with the rogue harmonic. (The bureaucrats still had our old harmonics program on their agenda, needed further information for their records!) We did the job, and got the same result. The rogue harmonic "blinded" optical fiber too—although again, as with Anton, only temporarily, as a retest some days later showed.

But with this distraction out of the way, our serious work commenced. I had found an answer to blindness! A synthetic channel had connected to a brain. To complete the circuit we needed only a synthetic eye, and a framework in which to use it.

The framework was obvious, for it already existed: the familiar spectacle frame. And the eye, too, was no problem now.

At that time rapid advance was going on with superfast self-focusing lenses, both commercially and militarily (they are used in the nose cones of missiles). We asked for and got whatever we needed. And very soon had made extraordinary progress. For a start, it proved unnecessary to remove a whole network. Only a tiny section of fiber needed splicing in: The smallest "patch" can serve as a connection for our lenses.

We moved rapidly to apes. (All this information you will be taking with you; here I give the sequence.) To locate the right junction behind an eye we make an incision above an ear. The small patches, two of them for stereo vision, are then inserted and grafted in place—all this by endoscopy, microsurgery, and no more difficult than fitting a pacemaker!

The patches go in with extension fiber attached; this exits through the incision, where a terminal is fixed to make contact with a spectacle arm. Inside the arm, matching filaments lead to the regulator chip for each lens—and that is it!

We now had something of a problem. A scientific advance of great magnitude had been made and the question of publication arose. Nobody doubted that it had to be published, or that a Nobel and other prizes must follow. Just as obviously, *I* could not be the one to take them. But who then could? No respected academic could take credit for work he had not done—which his colleagues knew he had not done!

To this, after a time, my friend thought up an answer.

For years we had been receiving help from various research bodies. (Unknown to them, of course: Their papers came to us through the directorate.) The suggestion was for these bodies to be fed bits of our work and steered to the same conclusions. An idea acceptable to me, although obviously it would take time.

As indeed it did. Two years passed; no papers, and my impatience grew. I understood the problem. People on major work will not rush to publish until sure of their results. And not everything could be fed to them at once! All the same my friend agreed to steer more strongly; and in another year was able to advise that a promising paper was on the way from the Voronsky Institute (of Electrochemistry; they had done the early work on the visual chain I have mentioned).

This paper I saw, and it was a good one, although still a long way from the necessary breakthrough into optics. Patience! advised my friend. He had several lines out. Very soon now we would have news of optical developments.

And so we did. But not, I think, in the way intended.

It happened just then that a specialist in optics, whose work I had been following, became unexpectedly available. I asked for him to be approached, he accepted, and joined us. This man was greatly surprised at our advanced work, and especially with the boosting techniques.

In the week of his arrival he asked for a private tête-à-tête and told me the following story.

Some time before, while touring facilities, his plane had been forced to land in a remote area where the only accommodation was a certain rocketry center. He had stayed the night and one of the staff, hearing of his specialty had asked his opinion on some recent work. This staff member was a designer of circuits and the question he was interested in concerned optical fiber.

In the designer's laboratory, miniature rockets, bench-mounted, were used for the testing of firing programs—rather precise and exacting work. Missiles must constantly correct themselves in flight, and their terminal homing devices depend for accuracy on very brief rocket bursts. This requires exceedingly rapid startup and shutdown procedures, the man's particular field.

Some weeks before a party of officials had arrived with a new device to test. The device was an electronic circuit, boxed with two quartz crystals. The device was placed in the laboratory, the man instructed to demonstrate a program for one of the bench rockets; and they all retired to an adjacent observation room.

From here the rocket was activated—a normal ten-minute program, allowing for many timed and recorded bursts—and after some minutes the electronic device was also remotely activated. The firing program instantly changed. The device had been activated while a short burst was actually going on, and the burst continued, not following its program—a single prolonged flare until burnout.

When it was safe to strip down the rocket, nothing was found wrong with it. The circuits were intact, contacts and breakers all as they should be, the heat-protected wiring (of optical fiber) perfectly cool. The designer was asked to pass a signal through the fiber. He could get no signal through it. In some way it had been rendered inactive. All the same he was asked to leave it in position for a certain number of days, and then repeat the program. This he did. And everything worked, the optical fiber again quite operational.

The designer then asked the optical specialist, with much curiosity, what theory of optics could explain such a thing. . . .

This was the story the specialist told me, and he said that having now heard of the incident with Anton he wondered if there could be some connection.

I asked if he had told anyone else this story, and he said he had not. Optical fiber was not his field; he had almost at once forgotten it. His stay at the rocketry center had been a mere overnight accident. A chance event.

I asked him to let me think over this event.

I thought it over, and I thought most soberly. Three years had now passed, with publication of our discovery no nearer. And far more, of course, since the work with the rogue harmonic—all that well behind us.

But evidently not finished with.

The officials' device with quartz crystals, the remote boost, the "certain number of days" of waiting . . . all this had surely to do with the rogue harmonic. The use of harmonics is not original. But *this* harmonic was original; it was not a thing come by accidentally. Somebody was using it.

I asked the specialist to remain silent a little longer and waited for my directorate friend to visit.

When he did, I asked if work was going on with harmonics.

Yes it was going on, he said.

When was it intended to publish this work?

In time, Efraim, in time.

Had a use been found, perhaps, for the *rogue* harmonic?

He gazed at me. "Why do you ask?"

I told him why, and he sighed. "I am very sorry, Efraim. You should not have been embarrassed in this way."

But he explained everything to me—and very frankly.

We had come on a principle of extraordinary military value. And to explain it he had to outline, first of all, the phenomenon of EMP, electromagnetic pulse. This pulse, a side effect of nuclear explosions, halts all electrical current in its vicinity—all current flowing in *wires*. Power stations stop, cars stop—and telephones, radios, elevators, lights; everything depending on electricity stops. Including, significantly, military command and control centers; no counteraction could be ordered.

The answer to this paralysis was found in optical fiber, a material not susceptible to EMP but very efficient in conveying signals. Because missiles in flight could also be affected—the firing circuits and fuses immobilized by nuclear blasts in nearby orbit—they, too, had been reequipped. Now every nuclear power's armory was invulnerable to EMP.

To EMP but not—now—to everything. For our chance discovery had opened a new window of vulnerability; and several security establishments were now at work on it. It had been found that the harmonic could be transmitted in a variety of ways—by narrow-beam radio for instance, where tracking devices could lock it on to moving targets.

At the simplest level (as a scatter weapon) it could physically blind ground forces—on foot, in tanks, or in bunkers, for the frequency penetrated all structures. Against missiles, its potential was incalculably greater.

At present the tests were at laboratory level, but it was hoped later to conduct them on a missile in flight. Under current agreements the flight-testing of missiles had to be internationally supervised. Plainly we could not have *this* test supervised. But as it happened, China was not a party to these agreements, and a new guidance system was under development there. It would be flight-tested to their base at Lop Nor; indeed the regional commander there, a General Liu, had already received advance instructions. Means were now being considered for a *directorate* establishment to track this test, by satellite.

And how, I asked him after a moment, would this affect our discoveries for sighting the blind?

"Efraim," he said gently, "you *know* what is needed to sight the blind, and how that operation is completed. To produce a paper showing your harmonics would lead to an investigation of all that range of harmonics. And then?"

He went on much longer—in fact, with good arguments.

(Our country was in a state of great instability. There were nuclear adventurists on all sides. The people might yet be exposed to horrors. The directorate had a duty to protect the people. Sighting the blind was a magnificent thing. But for the moment *this* must have priority. People lived with blindness, but could they live after events that this was designed to prevent?)

"Come—think it over! You'll agree!" he said.

I did agree—why not?

But all I thought was, *They aren't going to publish.*

Not now, perhaps not ever. It was slowly sinking in.

"Efraim," he urged me, on leaving next day, "forget this military application! Your own achievement is very great and no resources will be spared for you to develop it—and the world one day to have it! Each one of us at the directorate, I assure you, is absolutely aware of what you are doing. Press on with it!''

They were by no means aware of what I was doing. (For that same night I thought, *To hell with them all!* For everything they had an argument, and everything could be used for good or evil. Now the good must have a chance; and I embarked on the course that you know.) But we certainly pressed on!

Our lenses at the time were bulky, heavy, quite awkward in use. This our optical specialist (the man who told me of rocketry!) soon changed, for he was a leader in the field of thin-film layers. Now, although cased in glass, the lenses consist of superfine membranes, almost weightless, which maintain constant focus by a new principle. And soon, too, we were engaged on improvements to the insertion procedures, trying them out on a batch basis (the operation is quite reversible), and were still doing it at the time of the explosion.

Of our military work here I will not speak. I have never taken part in it, though I am nominally responsible for all activities here. So I say nothing of the explosion, except that safety procedures regarding certain gases were not observed, and that the result was calamitous. We lost the genetics lab. We lost the apes' quarters, also their adjoining sick bay. Several apes were then recovering from operations, their eyes bandaged, and those who survived the blast we got outside as soon as possible, for a roll call—although they were very few in number.

The situation, in fact, grew worse. Those apes still alive were badly contaminated. In a few weeks, only one of them was left—as it happened, the least representative one, a testimony to my own hubris and of a line that must not be crossed.

This creature I had made myself, in a Petri dish: a nonhardy female. By then we could identify early the nonhardy and should simply have washed her away. But I was then working with the fetus and investigating what else we could draw from it.

Since the contents of the dish would be nonhardy, they would be "intelligent." I decided to discover how *humanly* intelligent I could make this cell cluster, by copying cerebral material from Sibir's fetus and trying to incorporate it. And this experiment was a success—but a frivolous one, an unforgivable one, and one that must not be repeated! For this creature that I made (now fifteen years old and called Ludmilla) is neither ape nor human. In fact she is part Sibir, part Neanderthaloid, and part ape: an animal of a kind, but with a mind that seems human. The apes did not accept her and she lived apart, attached only to me. I gave her lessons which, alas, she found tiresome. On these occasions she had to sleep the night in a room kept for my directorate friend; which room by association she also disliked!

This she was doing in the night of the explosion—in safety. I rushed out myself, ordering her to *stay* in safety. And an ape would have done so, for they obey instructions. But she was concerned only for *my* safety and ran crying after me—into the secondary blast. This happened as I picked my way through the genetics lab. I had put on the mask and goggles we always wear in this lab, but the poor child was without them. . . .

But see how things turn out.

She was contaminated, of course, and also horribly blinded—her eyes requiring removal, for they were destroyed and infected—and thus became our first real patient. The others, remember, were *experiments,* still with their own eyes. Ludmilla had none, and so became the first true case of blindness ever to be sighted by our operation.

Well . . . It's standardized now, the operation—simple, brief, and all the parts of it I explain here: the junction, the incisions, the graft, the fiber, the regulator chip, the lenses. *And* the harmonic—to be used for good or evil, you see. They're here.

"All here."

Porter thought at first he was being offered a chocolate. The old man sat looking at it in his open palm: a gilt-wrapped dinner mint. Then he took another one out of the drawer, silver-wrapped.

"On disk. Four-centimeter disks. The silver one is by way of a history. A personal one, for you. The other has the technical information, a few hundred pages. It's compressed—they'll know what to do with it, the people you give it to."

Porter looked at the fancy coins.

"What do *I* do with it?" he said.

Rogachev poked again in the drawer and withdrew two slim pouches, themselves not much wider than dinner mints.

"They go in here. And the pouches in a belt." He found the belt, too, a canvas one. "And the belt next to your skin. The disks won't deform or break. They're encased, but don't try to open the cases. It needs laboratory conditions to open them—below minus 240 centigrade anyway, or they'll be erased. There's a temperature lock. That's the most important thing to remember. Now—it's late. Do you want a last drink?"

It was indeed very late. It was almost three, and again they had talked the night away.

Porter went and got himself a drink, and when he came back found the old man sitting with his eyes closed, deathly tired. But the disks were in the pouches, and the pouches in the belt, and on the desk under his hand was an envelope.

"Here's the letter. You'll need it to show the Evenks. It's just blank paper—a few sheets."

"How about the ring—I tell them it couldn't be found?"

"No. It's here." He opened his hand. "My wife's, actually . . . There's no one to send it to, and they'll cremate me in a few weeks. You have it. You may find the inscription a little sentimental."

He turned it over and over in his hand for a few moments, smiling rather crookedly, and offered it with a magnifying glass.

Through the glass Porter examined the gold band. The engraving was on the inside, its Russian words very worn: "Like our love the circle has no end."

He read them silently.

"Her death is why I'm here," Rogachev said simply. "This is how it happened. A funny circle, life, eh? Well, that's the ring. And here's the book. Put the belt on."

Porter put it on, under his clothing.

"You've remembered the temperature?"

"240 degrees."

"*Minus* 240. Even below that. Say liquid hydrogen, it's easier. That's to allow it to be opened. Once safely opened, no special conditions are needed. They'll figure out how to read it. Remember, the gold one has the technical information. Now. . . ." He gazed warmly at Porter. "I knew you would come. And I hope you think it was worth coming for?"

Porter looked steadily at him in return. "If I can get it out. Then it will have been worth coming for."

"Yes," Rogachev replied. "There's that." His chair turned to one side. "Do I thank you again, or is it just good-bye?"

It was just good-bye, without words. And it was in the library; two pairs of hands clasped for long seconds. Then the chair was whining out of the room, and Porter's last view was of a single arm raised. *Vale!*

In ten minutes, farewell to Stepanka too, and he was back in the washroom. And soon after that, back in his bunk.

All done now. Everything accomplished.

That the people shall no more sit in darkness, nor like the blind stumble at noonday.

Under the covers he felt the belt.

Just a few hours to go. And in two or three days he'd be gone for

247

good. He thought over what had to be done, but the day had been long. Up most of the last night, little rest after it, and none at all since they'd been called in from the wind and the snow. He closed his eyes, drifting into sleep.

45

At the time that Kolya Khodyan and the Evenks had been summoned from the wind and the snow to learn that a name had been chosen for the baby, another man was learning some news, far away.

It was eight time zones away, and eight o'clock in the morning. And it was a very curious piece of news.

He knew he must have read it wrong.

He read it again. The print was so poor, it was hard to read anyway. His eyes were bad today. He looked up from the newspaper and blinked at the sea. It was at the other end of the short side street and he could see just a bit of it, beyond the promenade, the water a surly lead color. A palm tree was lashing about there.

He had drunk a lot last night, for his cold. It hadn't done anything for his cold but it had given him a bad head. God, how he hated the Black Sea!

Alexei "Alyosha" Ponomarenko sat under the flapping awning outside the café and longed for the north. He'd never had a cold in the north. Wonderful Green Cape. Wonderful Kolymsky. Pure, pure snow; good comrades, plenty of money. New frost outside every morning. Good dry heat inside. Not drafty, not damp. He longed for the princely apartment he had left behind in June. Here he lived like a pauper. Above this shitty café! Him! Even apart from the civil war now messily spluttering on here, his money was running out and he'd had to move from his decent place on the front to this back street.

He lit a cigarette but left it smoldering in the ashtray, and went in to get another cup of coffee. A kerosene stove was stinking away inside, which was why he was sitting outside. Nowhere in the place was there central heating.

"Put a shot of brandy in it," he said.

"Cash," the surly proprietor said.

Ponomarenko slammed the cash on the counter. The coffee he'd poured himself; it came with the breakfast.

"And who gave you exclusive rights to the newspaper? Others are waiting for it."

"Buy another paper," Ponomarenko told him. He hung onto the paper.

"There's no hurry," one of the other guests said. A few disconsolate individuals were sitting about eating their lousy breakfasts. Ghosts, wrecks, pensioners. "It's all lies, anyway. They tell you what they want to tell you. Who's winning today?"

"Everybody's winning," Ponomarenko said, and took the newspaper and his coffee out with him.

The paper was full of tanks going here, there. Sod the tanks. He swallowed the improved coffee and felt his eyes improve. He concentrated on what interested him. The two panels were side by side, one in Georgian, one Russian. He read the Russian one again. "Edict of the Government: Ministry of Justice."

He read it twice more. Very tricky, the bastards here. Very. There was bound to be a catch in it somewhere.

He lit another cigarette and thoughtfully smoked it, blinking in the distance at the thrashing palm tree. Then he folded over a few pages so they wouldn't figure out what interested him and took the paper inside.

"Tell me," he said to the fellow behind the counter, "is there a respectable lawyer anywhere in this town?"

The lawyer was a small man with a very large mustache, and he was an Armenian, which made Ponomarenko anxious; he had wanted a Georgian, one who knew all the shifts and changes of Georgian law anyway. He was also not impressed with the premises. To enter the lawyer's office he had had to walk through a room with a dentist's chair in it. The man reassured him on both points. He had practiced for twenty years, he said, both in Batumi and Tbilisi; this was his week in Batumi. The dentist's chair was his brother-in-law's, who was this week in Tbilisi.

The lawyer first of all had a point of his own to make. He understood his visitor had come to consult him on behalf of a friend. Did the friend understand that such consultations were on a cash basis, and the cash was U.S. dollars?

Ponomarenko put twenty down and when the man merely looked at it explained that his friend wanted only one simple question answered before deciding whether to go further. The lawyer remained looking at the money, but he nodded, and Ponomarenko told him the question.

There had been a government announcement in the paper that an amnesty was being offered to drug offenders who disclosed the source of their supply; what was the meaning of this announcement and what was the catch in it?

The lawyer nodded again.

The meaning of the announcement was that the government had recognized that an enemy of good government was organized crime. For the maintenance of law and order in the present turbulence it had identified it as a principal enemy. Organized crime was based in this region upon powerful drug rings. To isolate the rings it had been decided to pardon lesser offenders. That was the meaning of it. There was no catch.

Ponomarenko remained silent for some moments.

"Your friend is known to the police?" the lawyer quietly suggested.

"No."

"Is being blackmailed, perhaps, forced to continue with . . . certain activities?"

"Not exactly . . . "

"It's a well-known squeeze. Speak freely."

"Well—what if certain things came to light—after he'd gone and said everything—things that aren't really, sort of, to *do* with it?"

The lawyer looked at Ponomarenko and then he looked quite hard at the twenty dollars.

"That's not the same simple question," he said.

Ponomarenko put another twenty on the table.

"If I understand you," the lawyer said, leaning back more comfortably, "your friend is worried that the police might start investigating other misdemeanors, once they've got him. Forget it. They're interested in *drugs*. They want to eliminate the small offenders. A fault of the previous system was the harsh sentencing—capital punishment, life terms. They want to wipe the slate. Once the facts are given, that's the end of it. Finish. Nothing on the record. Have no fear—for your friend. Unless it appears, when they look into it," he said jovially, "that he committed a couple of murders. Has he?"

"Christ, no!" Ponomarenko said indignantly. "Not that. But supposing, if they look into it, they find out he has a wife and various things. That maybe he hasn't kept up with . . . payments, things like that."

The lawyer laughed heartily. "My dear friend," he said, "they are interested in powerful forces challenging the *state*. Once your friend has reported the facts regarding *drugs,* he will be pardoned. It's guaranteed. Take my word for it."

"Well, *I* would," Ponomarenko said. "But there's my friend. How do I get him to believe this guarantee?"

The lawyer leaned back and hoisted a telephone directory from a shelf. He leafed through the pages. "You read Georgian?"

"A bit."

"What does it say here?"

"Ministry of Justice."

"Call them." The lawyer pushed the phone across. "Ask for the chief prosecutor's office. When you've got somebody—I'll talk."

Ponomarenko dubiously dialed the number and followed instructions. He got the deputy prosecutor and handed over the phone.

The lawyer identified himself and spoke affably to the deputy prosecutor. He said that on behalf of a client he would like today's amnesty announcement for drug offenders explained in simple terms, and listened, nodding for a few minutes.

"Quite so . . . Well, I have here, Deputy Prosecutor, a friend of the client. He would like it confirmed that no action whatever would be taken against his friend once the full facts have been given. And that a pardon would be automatic—nothing on the record, and no other areas investigated. Exactly. And the same with revenge evidence? . . . Oh, I expect the usual—photographs, tape recordings. Yes. Yes. Destroyed and no copy taken—very good. Well then, Deputy Prosecutor, if you would not mind repeating that to my visitor I think I can deliver the first success in your campaign. Eh? Very good, ha-ha. Yes. Here he is."

He handed the phone to Ponomarenko, who asked a few husky questions, and listened intently.

"Satisfied?" asked the lawyer, when he had hung up.

Ponomarenko lit a cigarette. He was not so much satisfied as stunned with relief. The slimy little bastard blackmailing him had been met barely two weeks after his first joyous arrival in Batumi. Six nightmarish months ago—in June!

He let out a great lungful of smoke.

"Actually," he said, slowly, "there isn't any friend. It's for me. I'm the client."

"No!" the lawyer said, opening his eyes very wide. "You surprise me!"

But what Ponomarenko had to tell him soon surprised him much more.

The lunch hour was twelve to two in Batumi, but half a chicken each was sent up to the prosecutor's office and they talked right through it. By then the discussion was exclusively on the agent who had trapped Ponomarenko, and on making arrangements to meet him again. In this matter, too, Ponomarenko had been given immunity, and was gladly cooperating.

His earlier statement—on handing over the keys to his apartment in Green Cape, on the detailed information he had given of conditions there, on the strange interest the man had shown in a chance Asian companion—had already gone off to Tbilisi.

With regard to the chance Asian, Ponomarenko could remember very little. He had met him in a bar. His name was Kolya, also a driver from the north. The agent had seen them drinking together; had been very interested; had wanted every detail about him. God knew why; Ponomarenko didn't. But Kolya had been glad to talk about himself and he had let him talk and had later given the details.

Kolya what? Couldn't remember. What details? Couldn't remember those, either. Something about Chukotka and his background, he vaguely thought, and various places the guy had been. He was a native, a Chukchi. Only stayed a few days, anyway. Hadn't seen him again.

But at two o'clock a fax arrived from Tbilisi that threw more light on this chance-met Chukchi. It also threw Ponomarenko into something like a stupor. The name of the Chukchi was Khodyan—Nikolai Dmitrievich Khodyan—and he was presently occupying Ponomarenko's apartment in Green Cape.

The fax, transmitted via Yakutsk and Irkutsk, had originated in Tchersky.

Tchersky was in the same time zone as Tcherny Vodi.

There it was now ten P.M., and Kolya Khodyan was just going through the wall.

46

The Evenks were especially jovial with Kolya Khodyan on this, his last morning at Tcherny Vodi.

One of them, cleaning Major Militsky's suite, had heard that the lower guard post was being opened up at eleven. Medical Officer Komarova would be at the camp before noon. And surgery would be held as usual in the *guards' barracks,* which had occasioned so much winking and chuckling that Kolya was apprehensive that even the thickest of the staff must notice it.

Major Militsky noticed it.

"They're cheerful today, Sergeant," he said, on his rounds.

"They are, Major. No accounting for these fellows."

"This baby's name, is it—making them so happy?"

"Ah. That. Never thought of that, Major. I think you've got it. Childish people."

"Yes. They *are* childish," the major confirmed, with a nod. "Respect their traditions, though, and you get good work out of them. Makes for order."

"Well, that's certain. I've known 'em turn very awkward, otherwise. Oh yes, that's certain."

"Yes," the major said. He was never more certain of anything in his life. *To be congratulated on his tactful handling.* He felt tactful. He felt well braced. His face was rosy as an apple this morning. "Good morning all," he said in the storage sheds. "Everything in order here?"

"All in order, Major." The corporal of the stores detail saluted him. "Empties stacked. Got them ready for a quick hitch in case the medical officer has to take off fast again."

"Ah well, she won't be in such a hurry today," the major said, smiling. "That was a special situation before." Although said with a smile there was nothing particularly humorous in the remark, so that he was surprised at the great explosion of mirth it drew from the Evenks. He continued nodding kindly at them. "Very good news— that the baby now has a name. Excellent!"

"Yes. Excellent, Major!" agreed the Evenks, grinning.

"My congratulations again," the major said, and took his leave; but somewhat puzzled. There was something anticipatory in all the grins, as though they expected him to say something even funnier. Well, they just felt good, and it made them smile. He felt good and it made *him* smile.

It had not, however, made Kolya Khodyan smile. There was a childish delight in guile among tribal people that he knew too well. He hoped the guards didn't know it so well. Just a few hours more to get through. He felt very tense. He had a sense of premonition. Something wasn't right today. He scented the freezing air. Something not right.

He had shown them the sealed letter, and the ring. They knew, and very joyfully, what they had helped him do; and what still had to be done. And an unexpected problem had arisen. In the guards' barracks, where the surgery would be held, the rule was "hats off." The Evenks in the general business of the camp remained always covered but here, as a courtesy in the guards' quarters, they did uncover. Obviously he couldn't uncover. The matter had been debated. Since the present squad of guards had only seen them covered they couldn't tell whether or not one of them had a shaven head. But it would draw attention to him, at the last moment, and he could do without that.

Then what?

Then they would all keep their hats on.

And say what?

"We'll see," they said.

This happy-go-lucky attitude filled him with foreboding. He wondered if it was responsible for his feeling. He didn't understand the feeling. He was very tense.

But he continued at work. Yesterday's plane had again filled the storage sheds, and the tractors were kept on the go to the delivery bay at the rear. A good deal more snow had fallen and he wondered if she could even make it today, whether the thing wouldn't be canceled at the last moment. But at a quarter to twelve, returning to the sheds, he saw the small convoy appear at the perimeter gates, and his heart leaped.

He carried on working. The guards would be attended to first at the surgery; and the dinner hour was being staggered so that everybody would see the doctor in turn. Already it had been agreed he would be among the last.

He had his dinner. He had trouble eating it, but he ate it; and while doing so was joined by the first returning Evenk patient, grinning.

"It's okay with the hats."

He looked up inquiringly.

"For the baby!"

He didn't inquire any further, wiped his mouth, and went out to take his place. A guard stood in the porch outside the barracks keeping the few Evenks in line. As one came out he sent another in. Kolya evaded the grinning eyes and looked around him. It was dark, but under the floodlights he could see the bobik. It stood outside Major Militsky's office and a guard was standing by it, beating his hands together. The motor was running and the driver was sitting inside out of the cold.

"Okay, next."

An Evenk had come out, and the first in line went in.

She was taking them very briskly. Within three or four minutes another man was going in; and Kolya had been joined in the rear by two more. One further man was still to come; this had been arranged. The further man arrived at just the moment when Kolya was at the head of the line.

"Next man inside."

He went inside.

The guards' dormitory was exceedingly tidy; iron beds, not bunks, and all made up with military precision. There was also a long table and a few comfortable chairs, but these had been moved to the far end of the room, beyond reach of contaminating Evenks. The only piece of furniture for the Evenks was a bare bench, and three of them sat on it, with their hats on. A guard stood beside them, his uniform fur hat held ostentatiously under his arm. They moved up, winking, and made room for the new man, and Kolya sat.

There was a small sauna off the dormitory. It had running water, and here the surgery had been set up. Another guard, hat under his arm, stood sternly outside it. The door was a little ajar and he could hear her voice. She dealt just as briskly with the new patient, and soon another man had come in and he was moving along the bench. In no time he was at the head of the bench—the last three Evenks shuffling along with him and grinning so broadly that even the guards began to stare. He couldn't tell what they made of it. No sense was expected of the Evenks; what sense was there, after all, in keeping hats on because a baby had been named? But it kept him on tenterhooks, until it was his turn to go in.

He saw at once that something was wrong.

Her face was tight, stiff, paler than ever.

She sat at a table with a pile of papers, her medical case open. A sheet had been spread on another table and a pillow placed on it. She was writing.

"Well? Any medical problems?"

"I've pulled a muscle, Doctor. Here, in my back."

"All right. Let's see. Take your top clothing off."

He did so, and she shook her head at him as he opened his mouth. "Yes. I can feel it. I'll give you an injection, and a preparation to be rubbed in. Guard!"

The guard outside the door looked in.

"Send my driver in."

The guard looked at her, and shook his head.

"Can't do that, Doctor. If there's something you want, I'll send for it."

"Yes, very well. It's the diethylamine salicylate solution, camphorated, and quickly, please."

"The—what was that?"

"The diethylamine sal— Just a minute." She irritably shook her head and wrote swiftly on a slip of paper. "It's in the fixed brown compartment, left upper quadrant. And I want a spare 100-milliliter bottle. And funnel. Lift your arm," she said to her patient.

"Fixed brown compartment, hundred milliliters, upper quadrant, and a funnel," the guard said and went bemusedly out of the room with the slip of paper. This he gave to the guard outside the barrack door, who went with the instructions to the bobik. He returned presently and conferred with the surgery guard, who tapped on the door and put his face in again.

"He doesn't know what you mean," he said.

"Doesn't know what— How many patients are out there?"

The guard had a look.

"Three," he said.

"*Still* three? Send that driver *in!*" she said, with fury.

"Doctor, I— Well, for a moment," he said, seeing her mouth open again; and in a minute or two the driver was lounging in, with his fancy balaclava and his fine hat, chewing gum. "Sorry, Doctor, I couldn't make out—"

"God above! . . . Just a minute—*you!* Leave the room!" she said abruptly, noticing that the guard had come in with the man.

"Doctor, he can't come in here unaccompanied."

"And *you* can't come in when I have a patient!" The patient was now bent over the sheeted table with his shirt up, and she was bent over him. "Get out at once!"

The guard hastily vacated the room, and the medical officer slammed the door on him, and stood against it, while the two remaining occupants swiftly changed places, and clothes. Papers, too, passed.

"A bottle, a funnel, and solution from the brown case!" her voice rang out. "Here, written in the largest letters. Does it take so long to understand a simple—"

It didn't take so long, and the driver was soon out again with the paper, ruefully shaking his head. He was not allowed to remain unaccompanied for long. The surgery guard accompanied him outside. The barrack guard accompanied him to the bobik. And the bobik guard watched closely as he unlocked the rear of the vehicle. The rear was now stacked with cases of empty jars and drums, but the fixed compartment was accessible and it took him no time to pick out the large jar of liniment, with an empty medicine bottle and a funnel.

These he was not allowed to take back in himself, so he returned to the driving seat; from which, less than ten minutes later, he hopped out to open the passenger door for Medical Officer Komarova. She was leaning on her stick and carrying the file of medical papers, one guard holding her medical case and another the liniment jar and the funnel.

Major Militsky, forewarned, hurried out of his office.

"I can't tempt you to stay for a bite, Medical Officer?"

"No, thank you, Major. I must get on—the weather is very threatening." She handed over the file. "And thank you for facilitating the matter of the baby's name. The Evenks are happy about it. It means a great deal to them."

"We must respect their traditions. It was a pleasure."

"Very good. Is everything ready here?"

Everything was ready. The funnel and the liniment were back in the fixed compartment; the rear shut; the escorting jeep waiting.

"Good-bye, Medical Officer." Major Militsky handed her gallantly into the bobik, and snapped off a most happy salute.

"Good-bye, Major."

"Until next time . . . Off you go, Sergeant."

And off they went, through the two sets of gates and down the icy path.

"Something's wrong," he said.

"Yes. I'll tell you later. I feel sick."

He slowly followed the jeep down. They halted at the lower checkpost to be signed out, were saluted off the premises, and entered the creek.

"What is it?" he said.

She had heard the news this morning at a settlement where she and the driver had spent the night—both nights had been spent at European settlements, the man unknown at either. Her secretary had telephoned to say that Tchersky militia wanted the Chukchi driver, Khodyan. Why? The secretary didn't know, but the militia had asked for the medical officer to call them.

This she had done immediately.

The militia chief was an old patient, and he had told her that a small matter had cropped up: an inquiry late last night from Batumi on the Black Sea. A man called Ponomarenko was being held there, and Tchersky had been asked to find out who was at present occupying his apartment. He had told them it was Khodyan and they'd asked for him to be held and his papers checked. From the transport company he had learned that Komarova had him for a few days. Was she coming back now?

Yes, sometime today. Was this man a *criminal?*

Not as far as the police chief knew—probably just needed to confirm some aspect of Ponomarenko's story. They'd be sending him more information on it. Anyway, get him to look into the station with his papers when they returned.

They drove for some minutes in silence.

"You can't go back to Green Cape," she said.

"No."

He kept silent and she looked at him.

He was like an animal, scenting.

"If they're inquiring who's in his apartment," he said at last, "that's a funny inquiry. Why should anybody be in it? Why should they want to know? He's told them. He's told them how he was fixed. I'm blown."

He stopped the car suddenly.

"You spoke to this policeman soon after nine? Now it's two. Call your office. See if he's been in touch again."

She switched on, got the crackling, and called in.

No. Nothing. No messages.

"You may be delayed," he told her, softly. "You want to know if the militia call."

"Irina, I may be delayed a little. Let me know if there's anything— or if the militia call again, right?"

"Right, Medical Officer."

He lit a cigarette.

"Soon they'll have photographs," he mused. "Of Khodyan. They won't match mine."

"Things don't happen so fast here."

"Faxes happen fast. They'll transmit them. . . . Why didn't they get in touch with Tcherny Vodi? They knew you were going."

"They can't get in touch with Tcherny Vodi. Only the medical office can do that, and on medical business. It's a sealed line, tele-printer. The commandant can make calls *out;* the militia certainly can't call *in.*"

He nodded, thinking.

"The inquiry came late last night, from the Black Sea?"

"That's what the chief said."

"Then, there it must have been earlier. They're some hours back, surely—four, five?"

"Eight, I think."

"Eight. Then the inquiry was made during the day. And now it will be—what, six in the morning there? Maybe nothing happened in the night. After all, they'd have to get hold of photos, probably from other regions. We could still have a couple of hours."

"For you to catch a plane?"

"A plane to where? No, no. If Ponomarenko told them who fixed him, maybe they have the agent. I don't know how much he knew, but I can't risk . . . I have to think this out. We'll run into Tchersky—to the outskirts, and you'll call again. I'll think it out as we go."

He started the car again and they proceeded in blackness along the creek. He stopped before the end and took the pouches out of the body belt and gave them to her.

"What are they?"

"I'll tell you later. If I don't get the chance, hide them. Don't try to open them, they will be destroyed. They aren't any danger to you. But keep them safely," he said.

She handled the tiny pouches uncertainly. "What do I do with them?"

"For now, put them in your bra. They're no danger to you," he repeated, and got the car moving again.

Outside Tchersky she called in once more. It was now after three o'clock.

Nothing. And also no concern expressed. He listened carefully to the voice on the radio.

"You're calling because you want the car unloaded right away," he told her, quietly. "You'll be in soon."

This message she passed; and now he told her what they would do.

Lights were on in all windows of the administrative building in Tchersky, and he drove once around the square looking for any sign of unusual activity.

There was none, so he drove through the gates at the rear to the packing bay of the medical center. His own bobik was still standing there, and a rubbish truck, and that was all, the dimly lit yard with its stamped snow quite deserted. He helped her out and went in through the swing doors of the packing room. The two packers there expected him and came cheerfully out to unload the van.

"Kolya, remember the militia," she said, as they did so. "And don't forget your papers."

"I'll do it when I'm through."

"You don't have to unload—they can do it themselves."

"It's all pretty light now. I'll just help finish."

And this he did, carrying in the very last drums.

"That's the lot. See you again, boys."

"Sure. And thanks, Kolya."

He went out and found her in the dim light fiddling with the car keys at the open rear doors. He swiftly entered the back of the bobik, and she locked the doors and went into the building.

It was almost four o'clock, and she didn't stay long.

The expected headache, she said, after a three-day trip . . . She glanced over the new paperwork, inquired into a few cases, saw that everything was under control, and left.

Back in the bobik she drove the short journey home. She parked in the shed and let him out of the back, and he waited there until she had unlocked the front door. She didn't switch the light on but returned to close the shed, and in the dark he went ahead of her into the house.

47

The militia telephoned at six o'clock, and fifteen minutes later were ringing at the doorbell. The lieutenant and a sergeant found her in her dressing gown.

"I'm sorry, Medical Officer. A few things the chief couldn't go into on the phone. There's something funny about this fellow who was driving you."

"Good God, Lieutenant, you haven't woken me for that? I've been traveling three hard days—I need some sleep!"

"We can't find him. He didn't go home."

"Maybe he went to a friend's."

"Not to any we know about. And his bobik is still at the medical center. He left it there."

"Well—he knew he had to go and report with his papers. I think I even reminded him."

"You did. The packers at the medical center remembered it."

"Then—probably he found a bottle, and is sitting over it somewhere. You know how it is with them."

"Yes, it's what I think myself," the lieutenant said. "And he'll turn up with a sore head in the morning. The thing is, they're worrying us at Irkutsk for a report. They don't understand how things are here. Can we sit down?"

"Of course. I'm sorry. Help yourself to a drink." She got a couple of glasses. "Irkutsk?" she said, puzzled.

"Counterintelligence," the sergeant contributed. "They run about looking for spies there. It keeps them happy. Your good health, Doctor. The leg's improving?"

"Yes. It's nothing. A *Chukchi spy*?" she asked in surprise.

"I know, it's crazy," the lieutenant agreed, raising his glass. "But this fellow isn't who he says he is. They sent in some pictures, from Magadan, where he was supposed to have worked. It's a different man. The chances are, this one stole Khodyan's papers. It's how he got in here. The *papers* are okay—the transport company checked them in with us, of course, when he started—but he'd changed the photo. No way we could tell that. A Chukchi's a Chukchi.''

''Why would he want to do that?''

''Who knows? Trouble with a wife, a paternity suit? He must have met Khodyan on the Black Sea. What he's doing with Ponomarenko's apartment is a puzzle. They've told us nothing yet. To them it's espionage, of course, so they're giving nothing away. What these people can think up—a spy from Chukotka!'' he said, drinking, and wiped his mouth. ''Anyway, if you'll just give a statement, the sergeant will take it down.''

''What else is there I can tell you?''

She watched as the sergeant took his book out.

''Maybe his reaction when he heard we wanted him.''

''Well—he was irritated. He thought people were picking on him because he was a Chukchi. I'd had to take him off long-distance journeys, you know; his medical record showed he had a heart murmur.''

''Yes. He was due for hospital tests next week, I understand.''

''Cardiological. For the murmur. That annoyed him too.''

''He didn't want it?''

''Well, he wasn't too happy about it.''

''Aha. Did he talk about that?''

''A little. He understood I had no choice—from his record. I couldn't risk allowing him on long journeys, whatever they'd allowed in Chukotka. They asked me to arrange a hospital test for him, and I did. He accepted that.''

''He did, eh? Well, they think a bit slow, you know, these natives, but they're very crafty. I guess he'd have skipped, even without this inquiry. Still, it must have worried him, being called in. You say he was just irritated?''

''Well. He cursed.''

''He cursed,'' the lieutenant told the sergeant. ''And what then? He asked questions?''

''He asked what I thought it was about. I said it was a routine check of his papers.''

''Did he want you to find out more?''

''Well, I called the office for any messages.''

''Did he ask you to do that?''

She thought. ''Maybe. I'd have done it, anyway.''

''How many times did he ask?''

''Oh, now, Lieutenant, I don't know how many times.''

The lieutenant had leaned over and was turning back a page of the sergeant's book.

"You called in at two o'clock," he said. "And again at five past three. Did he ask you both those times?"

"Lieutenant, I've got a splitting headache, and I can't remember what he asked me or how many times."

"I'm sorry, Medical Officer. But with these natives—if a problem isn't so serious, they'll wait for it to happen. I'm wondering how serious *he* thought it was. . . . This last time, now, you must have been pretty near Tchersky, and he's driving you in. He knows he's on false papers and will have to produce them. . . . Didn't he seem nervous at all?"

"Well . . . not that I could tell. He just drove into the yard and went in to get the packers, and helped unload the van. Then he came out and asked if there was anything else I wanted, and I said no, and he went."

"Where?"

"Out of the yard, I suppose."

"And left his bobik standing there?"

"What would he want with the bobik? The militia station is almost next door."

"He didn't go to it. Where the devil *could* he have gone on foot?"

"Look, Lieutenant, I'm tired. Probably he's drinking somewhere now, wondering what to do."

The lieutenant nodded. "He'll be in Tchersky, anyway. He won't have walked four kilometers to Green Cape. He could have hitched a lift, of course. . . . Still, thanks for your help. If he calls in—which he might, when he's had a few—find out where he is and calm him down. Let us know."

"All right."

She waited till the noise of the car had receded and went and opened the cellar door.

This was Friday night.

They left at nine o'clock when traffic had ceased and it was silent outside. The two disks he now had back in his body belt. He was certain that a house-to-house search would begin and knew he had to be off immediately.

She had three ten-liter jerricans of petrol in the shed. These he put in the back of the bobik, with a small extra one of kerosene for the stove. He packed some clothing in a grip, took a sleeping bag and food and the remainder of a bottle of vodka.

The route to Anyuysk she knew, and he stayed under a blanket in the back while she drove. But once they were off the river and onto the made track he took over the wheel.

The dark was intense and in the featureless country the headlights showed no sign of the turnoff to Provodnoye. He had clocked it at nine kilometers, and at the eighth he slowed so that she would see. Next time she would be doing it on her own.

They made the tributary, and he took the bends slowly so that she would know them. From the entry, fifty-five kilometers to the cave; this too he had clocked, and she had to remember.

The overhanging willow came on a sharp bend—the bend where spring floods had eroded the cave in the first place—and if not spotted at once it could be missed while negotiating the bend.

At fifty-four kilometers he slowed again, and she made it out for herself.

He turned the nose of the bobik into the cave. The tarpaulin had been left hanging, and it draped over the windshield. They got out and in the headlights she saw the place for the first time: all as he had left it, last weekend, when he had turned up at the house at five in the morning.

His own spirits sank as he took in the skeleton of the car. It was more of a mess than he remembered. He started the generator and backed the bobik and parked it and switched the lights off. They began unloading in the dark and he took the jerricans.

In the naked lights the cave was exceedingly dismal, the walls gleaming with ice, the bare chassis strewn with half-fitted parts. She came in with the food and bedding, and looked around.

"Oh, my darling—you'll freeze here!"

"I'll survive." He lit the stove and examined the tarpaulin at the entrance, frowning.

Then he went outside, and came in again.

"The light shows. There's a glow," he said. "Anything changing down at the bend would see it. . . . With the generator going I'd never hear what's coming."

"What should be coming here?"

"Trucks could be running regularly to Provodnoye now. I'll have to put the blanket up as well."

"All right, I'll bring another. I'll put it on the list."

The list was growing. He already had four jerricans of petrol stacked in the cave. Her three made it seven; and he now calculated he needed at least three more. He also needed a map and a compass and extra batteries for the flashlight, and more provisions.

"Okay, don't wait now," he said. It would take her at least two and a half hours getting back, and it was now almost midnight. Tomorrow she had to let her Yakut cleaning woman in; she would put in only an hour or two at the medical center, and then go out to the stores. "Have you remembered the turnoffs?"

She had remembered them: nine kilometers off the Anyuysk road for the tributary, fifty-five more to the cave.

"Okay. Tomorrow night. Be very careful," he said.

"Oh, Johnny!"

"Kolya! Only that!" he said, removing her arms. "And no goodbyes, just go, Tanya-Panya."

He waited outside while she turned the bobik, and watched the rear lights recede, and went back in. Now, on his own, it looked starker than ever. To turn this mess into a car! But he would have to turn it into one, and by the time she returned. Whatever state it was in, he'd start the engine when she appeared, anyway; it would give them both a boost. But then he realized he couldn't start the engine. The last item taken from Vassili was still in the shed at the house. The car battery was there, charging. He had hidden it under a sack, and it was not on the list, and his stomach turned to lead.

48

With the December solstice so close there was now no daylight at all.

A little after one in the afternoon the sky grayed faintly for an hour as the sun rose and set below the horizon, but this was only when there was no overcast. For some days before and after the blizzard there had been heavy overcast, perpetual night. Despite this, normal hours were kept in the region, and he took account of this in figuring when trucks could pass.

He was midway between Green Cape and Provodnoye.

From either point it would take the heavy vehicles three hours to the cave. From Green Cape they would leave at eight in the morning, so around eleven they could be outside. By then his lights had to be off. Even with the blanket a faint glow was noticeable in the dark. He couldn't tell when they would return from Provodnoye, but it was unlikely to be the same day. He himself had stayed overnight and returned in the morning.

Eleven in the morning was the time, both coming and going. The generator had to be off then.

He would grab three hours' rest, from ten o'clock to one, all lights out.

He worked through the night, worked solidly; but at ten in the morning he hung the bobik's floor panels, took a good swig of vodka, spread the sleeping bag, and got in.

In the biting cold he got all of himself in, including his fur hat, and slowly warmed up and dozed. And was glad of the precaution when after an hour he heard the distant sound of a truck. He listened carefully.

From Green Cape.

He could plot the bends as it slowed and picked up.

It ground slowly past; a few meters from him. A big Kama. They were using them now. In the blackness he went off to sleep, and slept soundly, and woke abruptly. One o'clock, he saw on his watch by flashlight: one in the afternoon. As planned.

He got out and started the generator, and topped up the little tank of the kerosene stove. It had been going all night. Then he gave himself something to eat: bread, cheese, a cup of coffee from the flask. He hesitated over pouring a drop of vodka into the coffee, and decided against. There was not much left and it was going to be a long day. She was leaving later, and he didn't expect her till one in the morning, another twelve hours.

He relieved himself outside, and shifted his production, immediately frozen, to a crevice in the opposite bank with the bobik's little snow shovel; it came with the kit.

Then he got to work again.

The short sleep had done him good and he felt considerably more cheerful. He had passed some gloomy hours considering his prospects. Ponomarenko would have led them to the agent, and the agent, however little he knew, must have received instructions from somebody. He himself had a number to call at Tbilisi—perhaps the agent's own number.

Tbilisi, nearly bordering on Turkey, was one of two exit routes planned for him. Both exits involved a trip first to Yakutsk, where new papers awaited him. Now Tbilisi was out. But Yakutsk was still good. The Tbilisi agent (so he had been told) knew nothing of Yakutsk. All he had to do was get himself there. But not from Tchersky airport. That too was out now.

Perversely, this cheered him. The idea of the bobik had occurred as a means of avoiding Tchersky. Too much security at that airport, the gateway to the Kolymsky region. It had seemed best, if he had to leave in a hurry, to find some other airport, a more relaxed one. And he had found it, at Zirianka, a few hours along the river.

Zirianka was the distribution center for the summer barges sailing south: a sleepy small place, with a sleepy small airport. This sleepy small airport, as he had discovered when running a load to it, had regular service to Yakutsk.

That had been the idea—wheels to take him fast out of Tchersky's control. But Zirianka too was not on now. For though away from Tchersky, it was still on the Kolyma, within the region; and soon the hue and cry for him would be regionwide. He needed an airport outside the region. And the reasoning still held good—a bobik could get him to one.

A bobik with a battery could get him to one.

The battery, obviously, was going to hold him up. She would have to make an extra journey out.

But after some hours he saw it wouldn't be the only holdup. Assembling the parts was one thing. One after the other, he found he had been assembling them in the wrong order. The book showed the exploded parts; it showed how to take them down for repair and how to put them back. It didn't show how they had to go in in the first place. He leafed there and back. Each section covered a different one of the bobik's systems. At the back there was a two-page plan of the whole thing complete. There was no plan showing how you got the thing complete.

He struggled and cursed, dragging the chassis out and dragging it in again, to get at one part or another with the block and tackle. The transmission came in and out, and the differential. The engine was twice hoisted out. But slowly, by trial and error, the logic of the thing became clearer. The rugged little beast, apparently so simple, was in fact highly complex.

At a quarter to seven in the evening, with the best part of another six hours' work behind him, he stopped again. If the Kama had decided to return after just a couple of hours at Provodnoye—unlikely, but possible—it would have left at four, and would pass here again at seven.

He hung the floor panels back, laid his sleeping bag out, had a snack, still left the vodka alone. Then he turned the generator off and got back in the bag.

Seven o'clock. No Kama. He listened for an hour, decided to sleep anyway.

He woke at ten o'clock, as he had planned—no novelty, but it still pleased him for he had been very exhausted. He got out, started the generator, and lit up. And now he had the vodka. He drained the bottle, a good whole measure, and felt it lighting up his whole body. Wonderful.

The bobik didn't look so bad now. Still only at chassis level and with a mountain of work to do, but it was beginning to look real. She would be here in three hours. He decided to make it look more real.

He sorted through the body panels and saw how to put them on—a couple of hours' work. The whole thing could be taken down again in no time. But it would look a real bobik and cheer them both up. He drank the last of the coffee and got moving.

Again, the little bastard was perverse, no section fitting as expected. There was a lower frame bar that obviously had to go in first. The book showed the parts attaching to this bar. But *how?*

He swore, kicked the thing, crawled underneath. Found the little holes presently, at regular intervals in the steel pockets of the frame—well concealed, wisely concealed, against the snow and the weather. Located the right bolts for them in the pack. Fitted the frame bars, and started with a side.

Half an hour's work showed you couldn't start with a side.

The rear had to go in first.

The framework for the rear *doors* had to go in first.

The constant problems, one after the other, exhausted him again, and by half past midnight he still hadn't finished. He put a spurt on. He had the back and the sides loosely in position by one—no point in tightening anything, since it all had to come down again—but she had not turned up, so he hung the hood, too. The windshield had to go in with mastic so he didn't bother with it, or with any of the glasswork, or the lighting array, or even the catches and handles. But the thing looked real.

He lit a cigarette and walked around it.

He could do with a vodka. Well, soon. It was nearly half past one, she was taking it slowly. He finished the cigarette and decided to fit the catches and handles.

By a quarter past two she had still not arrived, and worry began to gnaw at him. Had she missed the turnoffs? But she knew the way to Anyuysk. After a few kilometers she'd realize the mistake and turn back.

Or had she got onto the tributary and *passed* the cave? With the generator going, he wouldn't have heard. Well, it was possible. She'd done it only once. But how far would she go? Not more than twenty, thirty kilometers. Half an hour, three *quarters.* And back again. Well.

He smoked another cigarette, fiddled some more with the catches. He couldn't concentrate. At half past two he went outside. It was pitch black, unbelievably cold—at least sixty below. In the cave, the kerosene stove going for over twenty-four hours had had some effect. Here a thick mat of frost was growing by the minute, dragging at his boots. He looked both ways for some hint, some glancing reflection, of a car's lights. Nothing.

Had they stopped her, maybe, on the main river? Perhaps stopping cars there now . . . And she'd dreamed up some excuse and gone back. Or an accident. Or a breakdown. She was stuck somewhere. But she had her radio phone. Except she couldn't use the radio phone. How would she explain? . . .

He began walking along the track to Provodnoye. He didn't know why he was doing it and he only walked as far as the next bend. Nothing. Blackness. His face froze; eyelashes stuck with frost. He walked back again. A faint glow from the cave, and he could hear the generator chugging away. He got to the cave and passed it and walked to the farther bend. Still nothing. Not a hint of light. If she was coming, there'd be some faint flicker down from the overcast.

She wasn't coming.

He went back to the cave.

He didn't know what to do. A quarter to three in the morning. Even if she came now, it would be six before she got back.

She wouldn't be coming.

The stove needed replenishing, and the generator. He attended to these things, brooding over the situation.

If she couldn't come now she would come tomorrow. She wouldn't leave him like this. He had nothing to eat or drink. He was trapped here, stuck, couldn't leave the place. Had there been an accident? She couldn't have gotten lost. Not for this amount of time. Something had held her up. It would be another whole day and night.

There was no point in doing anything now—all the bodywork to come down first. The truck would be back from Provodnoye at eleven; eight hours to go. He had better sleep a while, and start again.

He laid the sleeping bag back in the bobik, switched the generator off, and got into the little van. The loose structure swayed and creaked with his weight, and he had barely settled himself when he heard the sound of a motor. He lay for a moment listening, and raised himself, and grasped a heavy wrench and got slowly out.

A bobik engine. And from the direction of Green Cape. He went to the entrance, raised the layers of curtain, and peered through the branches. He saw the flicker in the sky and suddenly the headlights, swinging blindingly around the bend. The car came on, very slowly. He couldn't see who was in it, how many were in it. Then it slowed further, and he saw the shape of her head, peering, and he switched the flashlight on.

"God!" She got out and hugged and kissed him. "I'm sorry—I'm

so sorry, my darling! I couldn't leave before. They were searching.''
She had hungered for him, he could see. As he had for her. But in
the present hazard the hunger couldn't be indulged. He took her inside, and got the lights working, unloaded what she had brought, and
right away took a long pull at the vodka while listening to her hurried
story.

The militia had started in the afternoon. She thought they were now
at Green Cape, searching the transport company. Her own house had
been the last in Tchersky and they had not started till 10:30. They
thought he had broken in somewhere and was lying low. They had
gone through every nook and cranny—the shed, the cellar. It was
midnight before they'd left and they were still poking about the
area, so that it was another half hour before she had dared take the
bobik out.

She had got everything: full jerricans from the pump at the ambulance depot. Sausage, cheese, black bread, two bottles of vodka, more
coffee. From the little general counter at the post office, flashlight
batteries and a child's compass, it was all they had; from the same
place a school atlas of Siberia—there was no public map of this reserved area. If he could delay a little she might lay hands on one in
the ambulance section or her own administrative office: it had been
locked when she had realized the lack. And a blanket.

"But you've finished it!" She was tired and dazed from the journey, and had only now noted the transformation in the bobik.

"No. I haven't." He explained about the bobik.

"To encourage *me*, you put the doors on?" She enfolded him again,
stroking his face, breathing his breath.

He breathed hers. Still breathing it, he told her about the battery.

She pulled back, staring at him. "Oh, God! I didn't even know it
was there. I didn't see it. . . . They didn't, either. . . . Maybe people
keep spare batteries. . . . Well—I'll bring it, then."

He saw she was swaying, deathly pale, and he held her. He opened
the rear of the bobik and sat her there, and poured a little vodka into
the vacuum flask cap. But she took only a sip.

"I've still got to get back. . . . Well, maybe I'll be able to get you
a proper map now. . . . But no, I *can't*—how?" She shook her head,
still dazed. "The office won't be open today."

"What day is it?"

"It's Sunday."

"Sunday?" He had lost a day somehow, both of them dazed.
"Okay, you'd better go. You'll make it before anything's moving in
Tchersky. But take it easy. You're very tired."

"Yes. I'll come earlier tomorrow—that is, tonight." She dragged herself up. "I'll try to get here by midnight. And I'll find out what I can."

He turned the bobik for her on the river and saw her into it, and she smiled wanly as he kissed her. "With all these mechanical activities—the disks are safe?"

"Yes. They're safe," he said.

She stroked his face and he kissed her again.

"Go safely, Tanya-Panya."

"Yes."

He watched the lights recede and went back in the cave. On his own again.

He ate a little and took another swig of vodka and turned the generator off and got back in the bag. As he dozed off to sleep he felt the body belt. Through all the activities, safe.

49

By noon on Sunday an embarrassing situation had arisen in Tchersky. The native driver posing as Khodyan had driven into town at four P.M. on Friday, had helped to unload a van in the yard of a building next to the militia headquarters, and had then vanished into thin air.

Almost forty-eight hours ago.

There was nowhere that he could have gone. The militia had searched every building where he could have gone; they had even searched buildings where he couldn't have gone. They had searched the *jail*, the schools, the old women's baths, the militia chief's own home, apart from all other private dwellings.

He wasn't in Tchersky.

But if he wasn't in Tchersky, how had he gotten out of it? He hadn't taken his own vehicle, and he hadn't taken anybody else's. No vehicles were missing. Apart from Green Cape, four kilometers away, there was nowhere else to go.

He could have *walked* to Green Cape, or taken a lift. Nobody had knowingly given him a lift, although he could have grabbed one, hidden in the back of something. But once arrived there, then what? He wasn't in any private dwelling, or in the basements or boiler rooms of any apartment blocks. He wasn't in the supermarket or its warehouse; or in any of the premises of the port authority.

That left the sprawling sheds and stores of the transport company above; and the militia chief thought they were the most likely. By some means or other he had got himself there. Plenty of booze crated in the place, and food. He was familiar with it and he was resting up there, deciding what to do. He couldn't escape, and there was nowhere to go if he did. But you could look a long time before finding him there; and this was a problem for the chief, who did not have a long time. He was being driven mad by urgent calls and faxes from Irkutsk.

Irkutsk was 3,400 kilometers away and it was a big town; they didn't understand there how it was possible to lose someone in a little settlement of ten thousand people stuck out in the taiga. In particular, they didn't understand the nature of the people here. Oddballs, many of them, running away from something, but not *bad*. There was no crime here, no theft or fraud. Everybody knew each other. The jail was for drunks, fighting mad at night but best of friends in the morning.

This particular individual had been the best of friends with everybody. No one had a bad word to say of him, only that he could be touchy, if picked on as a Chukchi. Well, here he'd been picked on, for having funny papers. Knew someone had told on him. Plenty of people here had funny papers; the militia chief knew that. But this one had gone broody. A broody native hid himself. With a bottle. Obvious. He was holed up, would come out when it suited him. Explain that to Irkutsk!

He had tried to explain it, on the telephone, and had been asked to put the details more concisely in a fax.

This he had done, setting the matter out with clarity and authority. It annoyed him that his competence seemed somehow to be under question at Irkutsk.

The person concerned, he dictated, had almost certainly smuggled himself in a vehicle into the premises of the Tchersky Transport Company. The premises covered a vast area, stacked with hundreds of thousands of crates, many containing alcohol and canned food. The person was a native person, brooding on a slight. To find him in this maze was a matter of time. But in his own good time he would come out anyway. This was the way of natives. There was nowhere for him to go, and the situation was under control.

The chief signed his memo and faxed it off, and ten minutes later got one back. He got a series of questions back.

If the wanted person had smuggled himself *in,* Irkutsk said, why couldn't he have smuggled himself out? Of the premises of the Tchersky *Transport* Company? What routes were taken by vehicles of the company? How many of them had left since four P.M. on Friday? What communications were there with these vehicles?

The militia chief looked up at his lieutenant. Both of them had been staring down at the fax as it rolled out.

That was the embarrassment at noon on Sunday.

By one P.M. it was established that seventy-three vehicles of the Tchersky Transport Company had left its premises in the relevant period. Communication with the ones on long-distance journeys was by means of the road stations. The road stations were spaced one hundred kilometers apart—roughly three-hour intervals for the big trucks.

Within three hours all those still traveling were being searched and their cabin crews questioned.

The short-haul trucks presented a different problem. On the shorter distances there were no road stations. But there had been far more journeys. The purely local ones could be ruled out, but many had not been purely local. Ambarchik, Anyuysk, Provodnoye, were not local, yet trucks had visited all of them. The police posts there were contacted and inquiries started.

By five P.M. all the road stations had reported negative, and so had most of the police posts; a few half-constructed buildings had still to be checked in outlying parts. But within an hour all this was tied up, too, to the militia chief's great relief. There was nothing in it, and he told Irkutsk so.

Since they liked faxes he gave them a fax.

He added that the drivers had been quite astonished. The man had not been up front in any of the cabs, and behind he would have frozen to death; any driver in these parts knew this, and this experienced driver certainly knew it. A knowledge of local conditions was necessary. The warehouse search was continuing.

His message was curt, and he was pleased with it.

The fax went off soon after six and he waited for a reply.

From Irkutsk replies were very prompt, if not immediate. This one took two hours and the message, when it finally came, was even curter than his own. Control of the operation was being assumed, with immediate effect, by Irkutsk. A major general of the security service was flying in. All vehicles of Tchersky Transport Company were to be halted. Details and locations of all other vehicles within fifty kilometers were to be prepared. Acknowledgment of these orders required immediately.

In shock, Tchersky's chief of militia acknowledged the orders, and then he set about halting all the vehicles of the Tchersky Transport Company.

Such a thing had never happened before. The economy of northeast Siberia had not been so disrupted before. And a major general of the security service! Obviously he had underrated what he had been told so far. But he had been told very little so far. He was totally dazed.

"What is it with all other vehicles in the area—not *everything* to be halted surely?" he asked his lieutenant.

"No. No," the lieutenant said, looking at the message again. "Details and locations only. Just the company's vehicles to be halted."

This was as well, for it was now nine P.M. and Medical Officer Komarova was just setting off in her own. She had the battery aboard.

While the commotion had waxed and proliferated all Sunday in Tchersky, the lost man spent a productive day in the cave.

He had slept and worked, and slept and worked, with meals in between. He was pretty sure now that he had got the hang of the thing and he proceeded confidently.

By eleven at night, after a meal and a drink, he went around the bobik, shaking the structure, bouncing the suspension. All solid. Everything that had to be greased was greased. The various grades of oil had gone in. Fuel was in the tank. He had left the seats and the floor panels out, so that he could look down at the works. The works looked as they looked in the book.

Everything looked as it did in the book. The windshield and wipers were in; lights in; doors and windows in; everything opened and shut properly. He thought he had done it.

He turned the engine over with the handle. It was very stiff; no oil circulating yet. Nothing could properly circulate without the electrics in. But the gears slotted in place. The brakes worked, as far as he could tell, jacking the wheels and spinning them. Even after he'd got the battery, hours of testing still had to be done. But nothing more could be done now.

He went out and chipped ice and made himself a pan of lukewarm coffee on the stove. Then he put the floor panels in, switched the generator off, and got back in the sleeping bag—and again, almost as soon as he'd stretched out, heard the approaching note of the bobik.

He got out and waited at the entrance; saw the flicker in the sky, then the headlights, and she was there again, bundled up in furs, pressed close to him, her nose in his neck.

She was alert now, not dazed or tired, for she had slept well. And she had news. The militia were combing the warehouses of Green

Cape. They knew he was hiding there. But Irkutsk had ordered them to look further afield. All the trucks were being searched as they pulled into road stations, and even short-haul drivers were being questioned.

She had spoken earlier to Bukarovsky, the company boss, and he thought all this was tremendous nonsense. He agreed with the militia: The Chukchi had got hold of a bottle or two. He had even summoned twenty of the warehouse staff to help with the search and call out to the fellow not to be such a fool. Nobody was going to shoot him! If they shot every driver who had funny papers here . . . He had always known the Chukchi must be in trouble at home. Why was he here instead of at Chukotka? But it would certainly take time to find him in all the warehouses.

She related this with excitement, and was disturbed at the foxlike scenting look that came over his face again.

"This isn't good news?"

"Yes. It's good news," he said, and kissed her again. There was no point in explaining now that it wasn't. He went and collected the battery. He lowered it into position and fitted the terminals. Then he checked that everything was in place, and drew a breath.

"Well. Here goes," he said, and with the hood open pressed the solenoid for the starter.

He got the first jump, and a croak, and tried again. The engine was very stiff, but it turned. At the fifth try the thing caught and roared into life. The row was immense in the cave, and he knew right away it was running too fast. The timing was going to need fixing. He left the engine running, tried the lights, the wipers. All okay.

"Look, I have to move it while you're here. I might need a tow back."

He closed the hood, fixed a seat in position, got in, reversed slowly, and braked. He tried this operation again, there and back, braking sharply. Then he took it out on the river, and drove a short distance, in first and second, and stopped. He tried the brakes going forward and backward, and made an awkward many-point turn, everything very stiff, the engine racing hard. This he did twice, left and right, and drove back into the cave.

"It's okay," he said.

"Oh, darling. Lovely man!" She embraced him as he got out, smothering him in her furs.

"Tanya." He nuzzled her, thinking how to put it without panicking her. "We have to talk a little. You mustn't stay long here, but there are a few things to say."

"I love you."

"Yes, that. But listen to me. You're going to be seriously questioned—not by the people here. Probably they're already out of it, and don't know yet. But if Irkutsk told them to look for me elsewhere, and they still think I'm here, then Irkutsk hasn't told them everything. The chances are people will fly in, senior people, professionals. You must be prepared for it. Tell me—Tcherny Vodi is the one secret place here?"

"So far as I know."

"Then that's what I've come for—they must know that. They don't know how I got here. But they know a place was prepared for me; they know the whole Ponomarenko angle now. He doesn't know why; the agent who fixed him doesn't know. I'm certain of that. But *they* know. They know there was an explosion here, and that a satellite observed it. And a few months later, I arrived. Do you understand?"

"Yes, I understand."

"Who is allowed to go to Tcherny Vodi from here?"

"I am—you know that."

"Exactly. Only you. Who drove you there?"

"Ah."

"Yes. Now remember—*I* initiated everything. I volunteered. I struck up acquaintance with you, asked if I could drive you—to anywhere, to Panarovka, to settlements. I hung onto you, made myself available, was very willing. You didn't ask for *me*. That's the first thing. Now Tcherny Vodi—could they find anything out from there?"

"Find out what?"

"Are they entitled to ask them questions? Could they question the Evenks on what happened?"

"They wouldn't get far with the Evenks."

"No." He thought for a moment. "When you left, the first time, you went to a couple of European settlements and stayed the night. What happened to the driver there?"

"They gave him a room."

"Did he eat with them? Did they get a good look at him?"

She thought. "No—he took a tray to his room, he didn't eat in the dining hall. The same both nights. He kept to himself. And in the mornings, too. I remember there was only comment on his fine hat, his fancy balaclava. That's all they'd remember—a native. They can't tell one from another. I'm almost certain."

"Okay." He thought about this. "Now, they're going to assume I had help here—that at the least someone must have helped me skip from Tchersky. They need steering away from you. You will have to mention a couple of things."

He told her what they were, and she listened seriously.

"Have you got it?"

"Yes, I've got it."

"Stay very alert. They'll be professionals. In another life I've had experience of the type. Unexpected questions come up. I wish I could think of some more for you. You'll be stuck with this, after I'm gone, and I can't help."

She absorbed what he said, and for a moment buried her face in his chest.

"Oh God, darling, sweetheart." She opened her coat and enfolded him in it, pressing them close together. "Only go safely! Please be safe. Lovely one! I want you. And we'll be together again." She drew back and looked steadily into his dark eyes. "I'll move from here. At some time I'll move, and we can be together, in another place. I love you!" She caressed his face, and kissed him. "You're necessary for my life! And you love me. Say it to me. Tell me."

"Yes. I love you," he said, and meant it. He was moved by her, and she had fallen very much in love with him. But now he only wanted her away.

She grew more practical. "I brought you more food and two flasks of coffee. I couldn't get a map. Can you manage with that?"

"Yes, I'll manage."

"Do you know where you're going?"

"No," he said. But he did. "I have to work it out, and go where I can. When I've got this working properly—it isn't anything, I can do it."

"Is there anything more you *could* want?"

"I don't know, I hope not."

"I'll come back to see. I'll come tomorrow night."

"I don't know," he said slowly, "if that's so wise."

"I'll be very careful. If it isn't safe, then as soon as I can. But I will come. If you're gone, will you leave me a sign?"

He kissed her hard, wishing her away. "Yes, I'll leave you a sign," he said in her ear.

He turned the car on the river, and got her into it and, as she clung to him, felt the tears on her face.

"Sweetheart, darling. Say it's only good-bye for now."

"It's only for now," he said.

"I love you forever and ever, my lovely lover. You know that. Say it to me."

"Forever and ever—I love you, lovely Tanya-Panya."

He watched her lights recede, and went in and had a stiff drink, and to his surprise found his own eyes were moist.

Then he lit a cigarette and looked through the book. Engine. Timing.

50

As she drove onto the main river, the aircraft passed overhead, and she saw its lights emerging through the overcast. But in the river's curve it went out of sight, dropping lower and lower.

Ahead, many kilometers ahead, unusual activity was taking place on the river; cars milling, headlights swinging.

Although it was almost three in the morning, a full reception committee was awaiting the major general of security, who was not in the best of tempers. He had slept the last hour of the long flight and had awoken bilious.

"What's this—have the fools turned out the town band?" he said, peering out of the window as the plane taxied.

Not the town band, but senior town hall staff and all the headquarters staff of the militia were tumbling out of cars and lining up as the plane came to a halt, its engines whining down. The general had a team of four with him and they went slowly down the steps, shielding their eyes in the powerful glare of headlights. In this glare the general's shoulder boards were very prominent, and the chief of militia had no difficulty in identifying him. He stepped forward and snapped off a smart salute, receiving a nod from the general.

"Are you head of the militia here?"

"Yes, General."

"You've got me an apartment?"

"Of course, General."

"Come with me to it. Which is my car?"

A fine apartment had been secured for the general, and two more, not much less fine, for his four aides, who included a colonel. In fifteen minutes all of them were at the general's.

He had brought a set of large-scale maps with him, and on the journey had ringed a number of areas. He took a glass of bismuth while casting a sour eye over these.

"The routes you sent were not so clear. On these short hops, the drivers seem to have a choice. Who determines it?"

"It depends on the load, General, and what's to be dropped off. They can stick either to the river or to the made tracks. To Ambarchik, for instance—"

"Forget Ambarchik. He hasn't gone to Ambarchik. He's gone south or east."

"General, I don't think he's gone anywhere. He's an experienced driver. He knows there isn't anywhere to go. He's a native, drinking his way through a problem. I *know* his type. When you see the warehouses you'll appreciate—"

The general halted him, with a shake of the bismuth.

"You know this fellow, do you?"

"A hundred people know him! I have their testimony."

"He's a foreign agent," the general told him bleakly. "His operation was set up in June. Khodyan's papers were stolen in June."

"General, there are many people here with stolen papers. We need skilled workers—we don't inquire too closely whether they're using stolen—"

"*His* papers aren't stolen. I said Khodyan's were stolen."

The chief of militia blinked at him.

"General?"

"Khodyan's papers were stolen at Batumi six months ago. He reported the matter to the police. Thirty-six hours later they turned up in a pocket of his suitcase. End of inquiry. You've seen this fellow's papers?"

"Of course, General. When the transport company took him on we naturally—"

"All correct, were they? Stamped? Right-colored seals, red, blue, green?"

"Certainly. Magadan papers. We're familiar with Magadan papers."

"They were copied. *Color-copied,* overnight—and properly bound and embossed, I expect, if you noticed nothing out of the ordinary. And the originals returned. That's a foreign operation. Khodyan gave us the benefit of his reminiscences. He's in Magadan, working. Your Chukchi with a hundred friends is a spy."

The chief of militia listened aghast to this, and to the story of Ponomarenko.

"There will be many things for me to look into here," the general told him forbiddingly, "but Tchersky's warehouse facilities—fix this in your head—are not among them. He's got away. These trucks are all halted?"

"Every one, General."

"Too late, I expect. I'll have every man jack requestioned, all the same. He knows of a vehicle somewhere. You've got a complete list of all those in the area?"

"All of them, General. Full details, within fifty kilometers. All surrounding areas contacted also, according to your last instructions."

"And nothing's missing?"

"Nothing."

"Well. Every one of those to be rechecked, too—*confirmed*. These short-haul routes you say he knows best—I've been looking them over. A lot of scattered developments. This one here, Anyuysk. What's doing there?"

"Various works. We had the local police check them out."

"Hmmm. And beyond it?"

"South—a few small places. They were all checked. And east, nothing till Provodnoye. Also checked—a truck delivered a load there Saturday."

"This river in between, the ice road. What's near it?"

"Nothing—the odd trapper's hut."

The general looked up and stared at him. Then he turned to his aides. The colonel was stretched on the sofa, the others in easy chairs; all hollow-eyed, but alerted now at his gaze.

"The odd trapper's hut?" the general asked, quietly.

"Tiny shelters," the chief of militia said placatingly. "Maybe three or four. Spread over a hundred kilometers—well away from the banks. For trappers. He couldn't get to them."

"Do the trappers have vehicles?"

"No, General. Trappers don't have vehicles."

"What do they have—dogs, sleds?"

"Yes. Dogsleds. Where could he go with a dogsled?"

"God knows where he could go with a dogsled! Find out! Trappers scout around. Maybe they've seen something. Go there. Cover that area. Cover this stretch from—where is it? Anyuysk. Anyuysk to Provodnoye. Volodya, I believe I could manage a drink now," he said to his junior aide. "And you—sit down. There are more areas like this. Have you got a notebook? Start writing down in your notebook."

It was well after four A.M. before the chief of militia got away but before five the sturdy vehicles of his force, their searchlights mounted on top, were off on their missions, the first of them bound for Anyuysk, and for the little tributary that branched off to Provodnoye.

In the cave, he had done what he could. A screwdriver at the carburetor, and a series of fiddles with the distributor, had brought down the revs and evened out the note.

He still didn't like the sound of it. It was too noisy. He knew he had to get it out on the track for a proper test, but was nervous about moving it at all. It could let him down after half a kilometer.

He bent over the engine, revving up and down. After all, a new engine . . . Maybe it had to settle in.

He let it run for five minutes and took it out.

He ran on his sidelights, eyes adjusting to the dark. He went toward Provodnoye, made a kilometer, tried all the gears, tried the brakes. The bobik slewed left when braked hard. And the suspension was too stiff; it would give trouble on rough ground. He reversed a fair distance, stopped, turned, went back, passed the cave. On a high bank beyond he tried out the lights. Also a bit out of true. He decided to forget the lights. They worked, high beam and low; it was enough.

He drove back to the cave. It was now 2:30 A.M., and he needed a rest. But the brakes and suspension had to be attended to first. He knew them inside out but it still took time. And another test outside. Then it was finally done, as final as it was going to be, and he got into the sleeping bag: four A.M.

But now he couldn't sleep, and at five he gave up and went into the last routines.

He climbed on the bobik and took down the block and tackle. He fixed the other seat. He stowed everything he had brought with him in the back: all the loose cartons and packing, the engine harness, the stove, all his supplies.

Then there was only the curtaining and the lighting. He dismantled the circuit—the flex, the plugs, the bulbs—until there was no light and he used the flashlight. The generator went in last.

He took the bobik out, directed its headlights into the cave, and walked in for a final inspection. In the harsh beam he could see the plug holes showing in the roof and the walls. But frost would soon cover them.

Six A.M. on his watch.

He went, and didn't look back.

By 6:30 the Tchersky militia were threading a tortuous way down the tributary from Anyuysk to Provodnoye, and cursing hard. Even with the big headlights, even with the top-mounted searchlight, it was difficult to see the bends until you were on them. The navigator was counting bends.

"Cut the lights!" he shouted suddenly.

The driver cut the lights and stopped.

"What the fuck!" he said, alarmed.

"There's a car!"

"Where?"

"A flicker. Stop the engine."

The driver stopped the engine, and they both sat peering in the dark. The navigator opened his window. Dead silence.

"You're seeing things," the driver told him presently.

"There was a flicker."

"*Our* flicker. Where is it now?"

"It's gone now."

"That's right!" The driver switched everything on again and got moving, swearing.

But there had been another flicker. Porter had cut his lights, and now sat watching those of the militia. They were moving again and he could hear the engine note. He was barely half a kilometer away. He had made it just in time.

In the dark he found a cigarette and lit it.

A few minutes more and they'd have met head on. He'd been going slowly, searching for the stream. And by God's grace had found it— minutes before.

He had noticed the stream first a few weeks ago, between the cave and Anyuysk. He had looked it up on the wall map in the dispatch depot. There it was shown as unnegotiable for trucks. From what he could see it ran from the northwest, but at some point it changed direction and meandered east. On the map he had traced the meander. It ran miles and miles, through rising ground, through mountains, to a highway. He couldn't see how it got to the highway. But it was the Bilibino highway; and above the word "Bilibino" was the sign for an airport, a major one.

He had tucked this away in his mind as a possible, a remote alternative. But now, with what had happened, there was no other. He didn't even know if there was this.

In the school atlas the long range of peaks showed up in purple, with only a general title: "Kolymsky Heights." A tremendous journey. He didn't know if a bobik could do it. And this was a Mickey Mouse bobik, untried, put together in a cave.

But if it couldn't?

He let the militia go and started the engine.

Seven

Kolymsky Heights

51

By ten A.M., with only forty-two kilometers on the clock, he had discovered why the stream was unnegotiable for trucks. No part of it was wider than two meters, and it was littered with boulders. The boulders were iced, blanketed in snow, and he had slithered over or squeezed past them. But some were not visible in the snow, and into these he had thudded as if into a wall. He was still in first gear, peering behind his lights.

He thought he must have gone halfway. On the wall map it hadn't looked more than eighty kilometers. The powerful heater kept the windows defrosted, but he could see nothing beyond the headlights.

Presently, uncertain even that this was the right stream, he stopped, got out, and climbed the shallow bank. In the freezing wind, the shapes of mountains showed, still climbing. They told him nothing, and he got back in and drove on.

A little after one P.M. a dark outline loomed ahead, and he put the lights off and got out to inspect it.

A bridge, spanning the stream.

He mounted the bank and found himself on the Bilibino highway.

It couldn't be anything else: six meters wide, leveled, a made road. The Bilibino highway. But where on it? Left must go to Tchersky, and right to Bilibino, but how far either way? He couldn't remember the position on the map. During the journey with the convoy he must have passed scores of such bridges.

Nothing was moving on the highway.

He went down again and drove the bobik up. The road ran straight, no flicker of light visible. For the first time he put the car properly through its gears, through second, through third, to top—and for the first time the bobik began to hum. It hummed through seventy kilometers an hour, and eighty, and eighty-five. He watched the needle, and remembered prizing the bare frame off the ground, remembered bolting every part of it together. *Oh, you sweet little bastard,* he told the bobik.

The big trucks wouldn't stop, he knew, just flash their lights. But there would not only be trucks. On the earlier journey, there had been the odd recovery vehicle, occasional supply bobiks. And these he had seen stopped, their drivers chatting. Well, he would have to pull off somewhere if he saw them ahead; or keep going and chance raising suspicion.

Somewhere he would have to rest. There were park-and-rest areas on the road, but he couldn't stop there. Other vehicles might also stop. No stopping at the road stations, either. He would have to get off the road. In the mountains there was nowhere to get off it. He would have to rest before the mountains—if he knew where the mountains were, if he could first fix his position.

The next road station might give a clue; but without a map even this was in doubt. The school atlas was useless. For this reserved area it showed no details; just main rivers, towns, the red line of the highway, and nothing else.

Presently he saw the lights of a road station far ahead, and he cut his headlights. As he approached it he cut the sidelights too, and coasted slowly in.

A huddle of big trucks, bobiks, a tracked recovery vehicle. All still.

He switched the engine off and opened the window. Faint music came from the log hut. He peered at it. The huts were very similar, all the early ones of wood; only a few, farther along the route, of concrete. This was one of the early ones. It couldn't be *the* earliest?

With a sinking feeling, he realized that it could be; that it probably was. He suddenly recalled that it was only after the first road station that the switchback had started. There had been no switchback yet. This *was* the first road station—six hundred kilometers still to go . . .

He got moving again, and worked this out. The clock showed 180 kilometers—the stream was more than double the length he'd thought. A lot of fuel had been used. In rough going; but the big engine was heavy on gas anyway. Even at best it gave only seven kilometers a liter—twenty miles a gallon. He wasn't getting anything like that. He couldn't make Bilibino on what he had.

The route was beginning to look familiar, and he recalled that this stretch he'd driven himself, had taken the wheel from the first road station. Under Vanya's tuition he had swung the big rig into line in the convoy. The steep climb into the high passes would start soon, and then the switchback.

And soon the first pass came, the peaks on either side no longer visible in the midwinter dark. Ahead, the ice road shone clear for miles, not a thing on it. He came out of the pass onto a straight plateau, stopped the car, and got out, with the flashlight.

A savage wind nearly took his head off. He hunched through it to the edge. Stanchions and solid railings guarded the edge. Only flanks of icy rock gleamed in the flashlight beam, and below blackness. Here he was over half a mile high, and below was a gorge. The first task.

He went back to the bobik and collected the debris—the engine harness, the block and tackle, the cans and cartons, everything that could lead back to its origin—and in three journeys pitched it over, together with Ponomarenko's lumber jacket, the mink hat, the bala-clava, the stove.

He was very hungry and he ate, and drank coffee from a flask, watching the road both ways, and then started off again.

Next would be the switchback, and somewhere along it road station number two. Another task there. And beyond the one after it, a place to rest before the mountain labyrinth. More and more the little bobik was taking the route in its stride. The jolting in the stream had done it good: the engine note settling, the eager bark yelping when he stepped on the gas. And he was making excellent time—no lumbering convoy, and a clear road.

The switchback came: rise and fall, rise and fall, a ribbon of ice but running dead straight. And presently road station number two. He doused his lights, approached carefully, and sat and watched it awhile.

Lighted windows, music faintly audible, and in the parking area a dark huddle of trucks and bobiks. He coasted slowly in and cut the engine.

From the back he collected two empty jerricans, the plastic tube, and a wrench. The trucks ran on diesel: no use. He kept his eye on the hut door and tackled the fuel cap of the first bobik. Iced up. He got the wrench to it, inserted the tube, sucked, got the siphon going and filled the jerricans. It took no time, and he was away.

Two jerricans weren't going to be enough.

Twenty liters—120, 140 kilometers. Needed more. What he had in the tank would get him past the next road station, and he'd refill from the jerricans when he found a place to rest.

Stars were visible now; the overcast dispersed. Another weather system. He'd gone a fair way. He lit a cigarette to stay awake; and, as he did so, saw a vehicle approaching, far off.

It was moving fast, not a truck; headlights coming rapidly up and down the switchback. As it neared he saw it was a bobik, and that it was slowing and stopping. They'd both dipped their lights, and now he briefly flicked his and kept going, and in the rearview mirror saw the other car had started again. They'd raised a hand to each other in passing. All okay. The other bobik didn't belong to Tchersky; some other kind of plates on it.

He suddenly realized *he* didn't have any plates.

He couldn't run into Bilibino without plates.

He worked this out, and had found a solution before he saw the lights of the next station, in a hollow of the switchback far ahead, road station number three.

He stopped on the hill above it, doused his lights, and took what he needed out of the back. Then he coasted down and went in, in the dark.

Fuel first, and he took it from a bobik. The car was backed in tight to a snowbank. Too tight for the next task. He had decided he needed only one plate, and a rear one was the least likely to be missed.

He found his target and got to work. Fixings iced solid, and he didn't bother with them. He muffled the chisel with a rag and thumped it with the wrench. In a few minutes he had prized the plate off, and had it with him in his own bobik.

Road station number three, good-bye. Five P.M.

He was making fast time, but also tiring fast. Eleven hours of driving since he'd left the cave. And the mountains would be coming up. He had to find a place soon.

He drove slowly, looking for it. If he'd left it too late, he could turn and go back to one he had already spotted. But this he didn't have to do. In starlight, from a hilltop, he saw it at the foot of the slope, a dark hollow in the expanse of white. He drove down, and took a look at it.

Barely noticeable when traveling; a little culvert with a bridge over it, one of many. In the darkness underneath was a frozen stream, a couple of meters below the road, the same kind he'd driven out of hours before. The bridge was the width of the road. The bobik would tuck easily under it.

The bank sloped gently, and he drove down, onto the stream and under the bridge.

* * *

He slept two hours there, with the heater off to save fuel. The bobik was a deep freeze when he came out of the bag, and he started the engine and the heater. Eight o'clock.

He unwrapped the bread and sausage. The hard salamis had been separately wrapped when she'd brought them. Now they were in one coarse sheet of paper. He ate, and drank some coffee from the flask; and with the flashlight took a look at the number plate.

One bolt was still bent in it. He had spare bolts in the tool kit. The whole ingenious vehicle was put together with only a few types of bolts. He sawed this one off presently, and got out and fixed the plate on the front. Then he filled up the tank and attended to a few needs of nature.

He hadn't washed much since leaving the house on Friday, and it was now Monday night. He chipped a bit of ice and did the best he could with his hands and face, and then his teeth. Then he climbed up and had a look at the road. All clear.

By ten, despite the constant zigzagging in the mountains, he had made road station number four.

He had decided to take four jerricans here. That should see him to Bilibino, with some extra in case of a detour. He hadn't seen the airport there. In the mountainous area it could be way out.

He drove in without lights, and got out with the first pair of jerricans. He filled them rapidly and returned with the second. Only one other bobik was in the parking lot—too near the hut, but shielded by a truck. He siphoned a can out of it and started the next, and stopped abruptly. The hut door had opened.

Two men, roaring with laughter, were coming out. And coming to the bobik. He had no time to get the cap back on. He hid behind the truck and heard them exchange cheerful obscenities with others still at the hut door. Then the men got in the bobik and he watched it go, across a huddle of trucks. Light from the hut door gleamed off the truck hoods, and then the door closed and he stood for some moments, quite still.

He first secured the jerricans in the car and then went back and looked at the trucks. In the dark their hoods no longer gleamed, but he went around them one after the other, and there was no doubt of it. A thick coat of ice was on the hoods. The engines hadn't been used for hours—probably not all day.

He had seen no trucks on the road all day.

He got back in the bobik and took off fast.

He had to get out of the mountains. There was nowhere to squirrel himself away here. He thought the next station was still in this laby-rinth. That would be road station number five. Only one more after that to Bilibino. He had gone almost two-thirds of the way to Bilibino. And obviously all convoys to Bilibino had been halted.

He was stunned by the revelation.

Tchersky's militia couldn't have done this—not so far out of their region, not on their own authority. Only a supraregional authority could have done it. Irkutsk had done it. Their investigators were al-ready in Tchersky, then.

And they had figured he was going to Bilibino. What other reason could there be for halting all the traffic to and from it? *From* it, pre-sumably, in case he'd already dropped off, and they wanted infor-mation. But the only reason for Bilibino could be the airport. So they'd figured that, too.

He couldn't go to Bilibino airport.

For the first time since arriving here—for the first time since leaving Japan—he was truly at a loss.

He couldn't go back. He couldn't just stop. But there was no point in going on.

Road station number five came up, still in the labyrinth, and he passed it with his lights off, not knowing what else to do.

As he switched on again, hanging in tight to a bend, a thought of a kind came to him. They could figure this and they could figure that. But there was one thing they couldn't figure.

How could they figure the bobik? It didn't exist. He'd conjured it out of *parts* that didn't exist, a phantom. And the little bastard was going better than ever, thriving on all difficulties. Since he didn't know what else to do, he let it.

52

By early afternoon the general had gone far to shaking up the mid-winter lethargy of Tchersky. He was a burly, vigorous man, and he detested lethargy. To a certain extent he could understand it here. Where he had come from, it grew light at eight and dark at four. Here it was dark all day. Such street lights as there were were on all day. The people crept about like dormice. Everything they did had to be rechecked. Everything the militia did had to be rechecked.

The first assignments he had delegated briskly, taking over the militia chief's desk for the purpose. Helicopters had gone off, driving crews were being interviewed, scores of phone calls were being made. Now, with the transport question in hand, he could concentrate on other matters.

Principal among them was what the fellow had been doing here, and *where* he had been doing it. Early on he had discovered that he had not been where he said he had been. His neighbor, his girlfriend, his workmates all said he had spent much of his time at a nearby collective. At this collective they'd never heard of him. He had not been there. But he had been *somewhere*.

A place had been arranged for him here; it was likely that cover had also been arranged. Or he had arranged it for himself. He had certainly in a short time made many contacts. In any case, somebody was covering for him *now*. That much was obvious.

He had arrived back in Tchersky at four P.M. on Friday and immediately disappeared. The man was a professional—knew he had to leave in a hurry, and before the local comedians could guess he had gone. He hadn't wasted time hiding himself. He had *gone;* out of the area, fast. This meant an air trip. An air trip meant an airport.

How, stepping out at four P.M. in this hole of a town, could he get to an airport—and not Tchersky airport, since Tchersky militia wanted him? In a vehicle. An early thought had been a transport company vehicle, but now the general thought otherwise. This artist would already have arranged a vehicle for himself.

But where? Since the vanishing trick had been performed in Tchersky the answer seemed to be, *In* Tchersky. But no vehicle was missing from Tchersky—at least, had not been reported missing, which was another matter. If the vehicle had *not* been in Tchersky, then he had been taken to it.

In either case, someone was helping him.

That was one thing. Another was why he was here at all. This was much easier. He was here to get into Tcherny Vodi. And a curious fact had emerged, one the general had only learned on arrival: it seemed he had managed to get to it.

The general had tried to get to it himself, and had found this needed special permission from the establishment. This ridiculous situation he had promptly ordered Irkutsk to deal with, and was still awaiting some action. Now he decided to wait no longer. All other persons interrogated had been summoned to his office. On this one he decided to pay a personal call.

The medical officer did not rise as he entered, and he took off his hat and greatcoat, sizing her up.

"I am afraid, Medical Officer, this fellow has duped you," he said.

"So it seems." She was screwing the top on her fountain pen, her smile frosty. "Not a common occurrence, I assure you."

"Yes. I hear you're not easily fooled." His own smile was considerably warmer as he eased his bulk into a chair. An efficient-looking person, he saw; the first he had met in the place. "I am hoping you can put me right on a few points."

Her intense nervousness she covered with an air of impatience, glancing at her watch, at the many papers on her desk. She knew the way this conversation had to be steered and the two points that had to be dropped into it. But this burly individual did not look very steerable and, as Johnny had warned, he knew his business.

She was astonished at how much he knew. He knew of the trips to Panarovka, to the Evenk herders, to Tcherny Vodi—and in detail the militia had not asked her. He had even that morning had someone interviewing Viktoria Eremevina!

He paused over his notes for some moments.

"The man has a contact here, Medical Officer. Someone is helping him. This trip to the herders, for instance—how did he come to get that for himself?"

"I am afraid I helped him to it. I couldn't drive at the time—a sprained ankle. Of course, anybody could have driven me to the helicopter. But he'd expressed interest in them, and just then was pestering me for jobs to do."

The general looked at her. "How did he do that?"

Her heart faltered.

"He telephoned me. Here."

"Did he? I don't seem to have a note of that."

"I am sorry to have to tell you, General," she said crisply, "that we don't keep an account of every telephone call here. The girls were busy, so I answered myself. I told him of my ankle and said he could come with me to the herds if he wanted."

The general continued staring.

"Where was he phoning from?" he said.

"Where from? I don't know."

"Was it a public phone?"

"I've no idea. Is there some relevance to this?"

"The relevance is where he was." The general looked at his notes. "He told various people that he was at a collective. We know that he wasn't. . . . It says here that he returned with you from Panarovka on a Sunday, and went to the herds the following Friday. That's five days in between. The source of a call during those five days is the relevance."

"Then I'm afraid I can't help you."

The general considered.

"He wouldn't have been *far*. On the other hand, he wasn't at home. But he was somewhere. . . . Let's try another tack. On the way to Panarovka you picked him up at his apartment. But it seems you didn't take him back there. Is that right?"

"Yes. Quite right."

"Did he have some other means of getting back?"

The first of the points was coming up, and she felt her pulse quicken.

"No. I drove him partway and dropped him."

"Why?"

"He asked to be dropped off."

"Where was this?"

"On the outskirts of Green Cape."

"Did he say why he wanted dropping there?"

"No. I assumed he was seeing a friend."

"Was this a residential area?"

"Well, not the most salubrious—a few sheds, the town rubbish dump—but yes, people live there."

"How far would it be from here, from the medical center?"

"I would say . . . a kilometer, maybe one and a half."

The general made a note, and frowned at it.

"A kilometer, one and a half . . . All right, so you drop him there on Sunday, and five days later he picks you up and flies out to the herders. . . . Where he stayed overnight, I believe."

"Yes. Weather. You have it there," she said impatiently.

"Did he know these natives worked at Tcherny Vodi?"

"Yes, he would have known that."

"What could they have told him about it?"

"Nothing. They know nothing themselves."

"The security aspects—guard routines?"

"Well that, yes. If it was of any use."

He pondered.

"You made two trips to Tcherny Vodi, I believe."

She nodded. "During the first I had an emergency call and only stayed to unload medical supplies—perhaps twenty minutes. The second was a normal surgery."

"How long did that take?"

"I suppose an hour and a half."

"What happened to him on these occasions?"

"He remained under guard. Almost certainly they'd have kept him in the vehicle. Security is very tight up there."

"Yes . . . Well, it doesn't seem," the general said slowly, "that he can have gathered much. But to have got up there at all was a very serious breach. Also a puzzling one . . . On these other trips, he's off work, hanging about. But this time he's back at work. How does *he* come to be driving you there? Did someone ask for him specially?"

"No. We asked for a driver. They sent him. Of course I see now he must have been angling for the job."

"Could he have known you were going there?"

"He could have guessed. They were told it was a three-day job—we group out-of-town trips—and I go regularly. Yes, he could have guessed."

"But you'd never used a driver there before."

"No. I have been fortunate enough," she said dryly, "not to have sprained an ankle before."

"Ah, the ankle. He knew about it. Tell me one thing more. You spent two nights of this trip at settlements in the area. Did he know anybody there?"

"No. He'd never been before."

"Did anybody seem to know *him?*"

"Not that I could tell."

"At both places—my officers have visited them—it seems he ate by himself, in his room. Doesn't that seem strange?"

"Perhaps it embarrassed him to eat in public."

"Or perhaps he wished not to embarrass somebody *else*. There's something funny about this. He keeps out of sight. . . . Somewhere here, Medical Officer, he has a helper. A helper with a vehicle. These places *have* vehicles—running in and out of Tchersky."

"Well, I know nothing of this, General." She had glanced at her papers again.

"But perhaps we can go into it a little. . . . He had a *vehicle* here. Or expected one to be *waiting* for him here. He knew he would be back in three days, and that his mission was over. I think that's all it was, incidentally—a look at the place, at the security arrangements. A trial run. And now he had to leave. Obviously he had made plans. But now they needed altering—the militia wanted to see him. Which meant he had to leave very rapidly. And he did. In a vehicle."

The second point was coming up and again she felt her pulse begin to pound. She looked at her watch.

"General, I don't think I can help you with this."

"Perhaps you can." He smiled at her. "Let me explain it to you. When he left you, we know he can't have gone far in the street. The militia have questioned people who were in it and nobody saw him. A familiar figure, quite distinctive, recognizable to everybody—but nobody saw him. I think because the vehicle he wanted was right there, close by the medical center. When you came into town—try to think about this—did he seem to be looking for something?''

''Well.'' She thought. ''He was certainly looking for the turning—the turning into our loading bay at the rear. He missed it once. We had to go all around the square again.''

''Did you, now? Cars parked there, I suppose. Did he look at the cars?''

''He was looking for the turning.''

''Yes. Did any of the cars flash their lights?''

''Not that I remember.''

The general remained looking at her for some moments. ''All right, so you go into the yard. And here he behaves strangely. We know he must be in a great hurry. Yet he doesn't act in a hurry. He carefully helps them unload the van. He takes in the last of the stuff. *Tells* them it's the last. He comes out, asks if you want anything more done. Doesn't that seem strange?''

''Well, I agree—it does.''

''As if he's getting everybody off the premises?''

''Perhaps. Yes.''

''Had anything come in behind you, another vehicle?''

''Not that I recall.''

''Some activity going on in the yard—someone fiddling with an engine, cars maneuvering about?''

''No, no. Nothing like that. There *was* nothing there. Just his own bobik—and the garbage truck.''

''Which garbage truck?''

''The regular one, for our waste disposal.''

''Where does the garbage truck go?''

''Well, I don't know where—''

''Is it there every day?''

''Yes, I suppose so. And now, really, General—''

She had risen, and he rose with her.

''Well, you have been very patient,'' he said, shrugging into his greatcoat. ''And also very helpful. You have given much useful information.''

And so she had, and she sat shaking, listening to his boots march briskly down the corridor. She had offered the wrong end of the stick, and he had gladly accepted it. But where would it lead?

* * *

The wrong end of the stick; but a stick. And this general, a persistent man, was not going to let it go. Where it would lead, at the end, was to the right conclusion; but that was not yet.

The town dump, just outside Green Cape, stank so evilly that the general shielded his nose. He observed that the garbage was in a three-sided compound, conveniently open to the highway of the river.

Lights were strung and he saw that the enclosed sides were occupied by sheds and cabins. Two great garbage heaps were in the middle, a tipper-truck distributing its load on one, and several natives picking through the other.

"These fellows live here?" he asked the chief of militia.

"Yes. In the cabins, with their families. Yakuts."

"Call one over."

The chief did so, and introduced the dignitary.

The man grinned at him affably.

"All well here?" the general asked, himself very affable.

"Yes. All well."

"A good life?"

"Sure. Good life. Anything I do for you, General?"

"Just looking around. Kolya thought it interesting. You know— Kolya, Kolya Khodyan. Nice fellow. Remember him?"

"Khodyan? No. Don't know this name."

"Show him the photo," he said to his young aide, Volodya.

The man looked at the photo.

"Nice photo of him," the general said.

"Yes, nice."

"Been here lately?"

"Who been here?"

"This man."

"No. Don't know this man."

And the same with the others, and with their families, the general observing that the ladies first of all consulted their husbands before disclaiming knowledge of the nice man.

The sheds, however, produced better results.

They were large sheds, used for the storage of selected pickings; and the pickings of one of them were motor parts. Doors, seats, exhausts, wheels, tires: all these not heaped on the ground but stacked quite neatly around the walls. On the ground, in the vacant center, was an oil stain, and the marks left by four wheels.

Half an hour later, the general had still not managed to discover how these marks came to be there; but he left not at all displeased.

On the way back the chief of militia explained some local regulations to him, and he had the first glimmerings of how the trick had been pulled.

Over a late dinner the general sat with his staff and explained the situation. His senior officers had been flying about all day and were tired. But his explanation was brief.

Vehicles out of use in the Kolymsky region had to have their registration plates and documents returned, and those past repair needed a certificate of destruction; vehicles must not be abandoned or left to lie about. This regulation, dating from 1962, was intended to control all means of movement in the area, and in early years had been strictly enforced.

With the area's rapid development, however, some laxness had crept in, although full records still existed. The militia had identified twenty-seven vehicles long out of use—their plates and papers returned, but without certificates of destruction. These were now being investigated.

"What is likely," the general said, "is that this man found something he could put together. And then he found a place to *put* it together. Perhaps the rubbish dump, perhaps not. They've certainly had a vehicle standing there recently. Well, natives stick together, we can look into it later. What's important now is to find a disused vehicle which has gone missing. Get a profile of it and we could be halfway to finding him."

And so they could be, he thought, settling into bed. It had been a long day and he was very tired himself. Late in the evening Irkutsk had got him permission and he had helicoptered to Tcherny Vodi. A hundred percent security there, all as the medical officer had said. An excellent woman, nobody's fool. The agent could have seen nothing— a trial run, as he'd thought. Well, he wouldn't get far. Profile of his vehicle . . .

Another thought occurred, and he reached for the phone.

"Volodya?"

His aide yawned loudly at the other end.

"Volodya—another thing. It's possible there'll be more than one vehicle missing. . . . This fellow could get at parts. The same parts don't fit all vehicles. If we know what parts he used, that also gives a profile of the vehicle. Get them moving at that transport company.

Do it now. Get them out of bed. Let them search repair sheds, store-rooms, whatever. Anything interesting, call me immediately. If necessary, wake me up.''

Two o'clock, and he put the light out.

And almost at once *was* woken up. He stared at his watch: six A.M. A moment ago it had been only two. But they were quite right to wake him. Something very interesting had turned up.

53

At two in the morning Porter passed road station number six, and ahead now there was only Bilibino.

An idea had come to him of what could be managed if only he could get through it. But it was now six hours since he had wakened under the bridge, and the mountain bends and anxiety had totally exhausted him again.

He drove slowly, his eyes sore, looking for somewhere to shelter. On the final stretch to Bilibino there would be buildings and mine workings; he remembered them. The convoy of a few weeks ago had kept parallel for some kilometers with a stream. The gold beds ran often near streams and across country. But that had been close to town, too near in. He needed something earlier, and soon.

He passed presently under big overhead cables and saw a pylon: the power line from Bilibino. It served the goldfields and some surrounding installations. He was already too near.

Fifty or sixty kilometers back the road had crossed a stream, and he wondered if he should turn and go back to it. It would eat up a lot of gas. He didn't know what was for the best and meanwhile let the bobik chug on, too tired to think.

He saw a glow coming up in the sky on his left. The first of the outlying goldfields? If the goldfield was near a stream, and the stream led to— Where did the streams lead to here? He was now far from the Kolyma. Some other river. A river south of him. Which meant to his right. If there was a river to his right and streams ran down from the left . . .

He drove on, watching the glow come nearer, until it was no longer a glow but lights, floodlights, just a kilometer or two ahead and to his left, and he knew now he had better go back. And then he knew he had just crossed a bridge.

He had crossed it and was at the other side.

Jesus Christ! He was too tired to turn. He reversed.

He reversed over the bridge and looked down at a lovely, wonderful, frozen stream, and drove down to it, and got under the bridge, and switched everything off, the lights, the engine, himself; and just sat there in the dark for a minute.

Then he got out and climbed the bank and had a look.

Yes, the first of the goldfields, not a kilometer away, the din of its machinery carrying in the air. He could even see, silhouetted against the lights, the skeletal housings of the mine lifts. As he looked two trucks lurched out onto the road a few hundred meters ahead and turned toward Bilibino.

Too much activity, and too near. But he couldn't be seen, and he also by now couldn't care. He simply had to rest.

He went down and gave himself a huge vodka, and drank it with his eyes shut. He tore off a chunk of black bread and ate it, and in his sleeping bag he ate more.

He slept an hour and woke still tired. But there was no time to linger. It was getting on for four A.M. The best time to be in town was between five and six, the dead point of any road security, but with the place just stirring into activity. He recollected almost nothing of it except that during work hours it had been a mess: slow-moving traffic, the local drivers leaning out and chatting across to each other. He wanted a clear run through, with no curious eyes looking him over.

He drank some coffee and looked at the school atlas with the flashlight. He was already off one page and on to the next.

Pevek showed up next, another familiar destination for Tchersky drivers. Still a colossal distance away; double the distance he had already traveled. He wasn't going there. Big security installations at Pevek, and big security to go with them. Yura had promised it to him, he remembered: "You'll go to Bilibino, Baranikha, Pevek, everywhere!"

Pevek was the end of the route. But where the hell was Baranikha?

He searched for and found Baranikha, three or four hundred kilometers away, in the tiniest type, a dot. But the atlas was a school one, in use for many years. From what he had seen in the dispatch depot, big loads were going to Baranikha, heavy construction in progress there. So much construction needed engineers, architects, workers, who all needed flying in. There would be an airport of some kind at Baranikha, at least a strip.

The idea had come to him while negotiating the mountain bends. If major airports were out of bounds, he could try little cross-country ones. Cross-country hopping, from one to another, could take him a long way—and he knew now he had to go a long way. And not at all the way that had been planned for him. No Yakutsk, no Black Sea, no Turkey. He had to take a route that nobody expected. And there were still some options. . . .

They didn't know how he had come in. They couldn't know how he would go out. Light-years ago he remembered the CIA man telling him he couldn't go out the way he had come in. But why couldn't he? He had come in from Japan. Why not go back that way? From Nakhodka, far down on the Pacific seaboard, ships ran regularly to Japan. One way or another he could try to get himself on one. For months now he had lived on his wits. Were they going to desert him at the last?

He looked up Nakhodka in the atlas, and his heart sank. Farther even than he thought—an incredible distance, four thousand kilometers at least. Well . . . from Tchersky, even if anyone remotely thought of the idea, it would seem impossible for him to get there. By land it probably *was* impossible, range upon range of mountains in between. But hopping it, a bit at a time? Would security be so tight at little out-of-the-way strips? If he could only get beyond Bilibino . . .

He went up on the road for another look.

Still bitterly cold, but with some change evident in the air; a sharp thin snow was falling, hazing the goldfields' lights and muffling the continuous clanging. As he watched, a truck lumbered out, and shortly after it another one, heading for Bilibino. Local field trucks. Nothing else on the road—all long-distance traffic still halted. He went down and started the bobik and got back on the highway.

He picked up the trucks after a kilometer, and stayed well behind, running only on sidelights, wipers going. Now he could see the frozen stream on his right, running beside the road as he remembered. It had come down from high ground and taken a sharp turn on meeting some rock barrier. All of the ground here was high; rich, gold-bearing land.

Presently the trucks began slowing, and he watched their rear lights turning in at the opposite side of the road. He cut his own lights, and slowed to a crawl. A big compound, evidently a processing plant, with a huge conical tip and a line of sheds, all well floodlit. He crawled nearer, and stopped out of range of the lights.

Noisy activity was going on in the compound. A trolley train was moving around and trucks were maneuvering. He couldn't see what had happened to the two he had followed, but others were slewed around and facing him, their drivers out and chatting. He had seen no trucks going the other way. They evidently didn't go back that way. They must return some other way.

When he had driven this section weeks before, Vanya snoring beside him, he had noticed little of the route, too busy keeping station in the convoy. But over dinner the drivers had told him a loop road ran through the goldfields, that if you were driving beyond Bilibino, you had to take care to avoid that road or you could get hopelessly entangled. Maybe these trucks took the loop road, at the other side of town, to return through the strung-out goldfields. He watched and waited, and presently one of them moved; and a few moments afterward, another.

He started up and followed, keeping well behind, again using only sidelights. The trucks ahead were empty and now going at a brisker pace. In barely twenty minutes he saw another glow appearing ahead, which soon became town lights.

Bilibino.

Time to move. He switched to headlights, overtook the first truck and cut in between the two. And not a moment too soon. Almost immediately the road curved, and ahead he saw a barrier strung with amber lights, and the truck in front slowing.

The barrier was down but, as they appeared around the bend, it was already being raised. The man in front had opened his window and stuck a raised thumb out as he went slowly through, and Porter did the same. He saw uniforms—militia uniforms and others he didn't recognize—and looks of mild curiosity turned on him in the light hail of snow. But peering in his rearview mirror he saw that already they had turned to the next truck, and he was in. In and sailing into Bilibino.

He remembered it only vaguely. An administrative building like Tchersky's, a cinema like Tchersky's; all the buildings—post office, supermarket, apartment blocks—built to the same design in this north land. He saw the hostel he had slept in; the goods center, the parking lot. Big trucks were lined up in the parking lot, Tchersky trucks. All still halted, no activity there. Just a little activity elsewhere: a few light trucks and bobiks trundling about town, postal vans, food vans; the odd militia car parked, cigarettes glowing inside.

He drove with his window a little open and could hear the drone of aircraft above, and saw one coming in to land, well ahead and to the right. Stay away from that area. He continued following the truck that had led him in, dazzled by the glare of the one behind. Ahead, the truck suddenly pulled in and stopped at a dimly lit hole-in-the-wall, an all-night bar or café. He passed it and pulled up himself, and in his mirror saw the other truck stop and both drivers get out and go into the place.

Shit! He had planned to follow until they turned off. If the Tchersky drivers had warned you had to take care to avoid the loop road, it evidently wasn't signposted. Nothing was signposted in Green Cape or Tchersky, either. You had to know.

He switched his lights off, kept the wipers going, and lit a cigarette. He needed a vodka himself but decided to wait until he needed it more. Five-thirty. The time was right: The town just sluggishly stirring into life, the police sitting out the last half of their shift. He'd been lucky—with the two trucks, the barrier. Would he be as lucky on the way out?

A militia car cruised slowly past and he saw, through the drizzle of snow, faces turned toward him. The wipers. He should have turned the wipers off. The car went on, but they had noted him. He couldn't stay here; they'd be around again. He waited till they were well away, switched on, and took off. He kept on the way he'd been going.

The town square passed behind him. He couldn't tell if he was on the main road; other roads had run off the square. This one had a few large buildings, apartment blocks, depot-type stores; but thinning now, dwindling. Definitely going out of town. Headlights came suddenly toward him around a bend, and dipped in acknowledgment, and he dipped his own. A bus.

POLAR AVIATION, he saw, as it passed.

Christ! He was going to the airport, after all. The road went to the airport. There would be checks before the airport.

Which now, rounding the bend, he could clearly see. It was on a large flat plate of land, slightly below, ringed with orange sodium lamps. Through the snow drizzle he could even make out a lit-up runway.

More to the point, and worse, dead ahead and downhill he could also see a barrier, and men in Day-Glo stripes, and a waving flashlight. There was no way of stopping or turning off or going back. He'd been seen. And the barrier was firmly down. He drew slowly up to it, and opened his window.

"Where to—airport?" A militia man; there were two of them, also another, in the unfamiliar uniform; all bundled up, scowling in the snow. They had come out of a hut, he saw.

"No. Loop road." He hoped to God this was the way to it.

The flashlight examined him.

"Where's your field badge, then?"

"Fuck the field badge! It's not even my job," he said, scowling. "I'm off in a couple of hours, and I win this. All through the fucking fields—for a breakdown! What's up here, no one can fix a machine themselves?''

"Where you from, old-timer?''

His number plate was being inspected, he saw.

"Road stations, way back. I'm on *equipment*. Not my job, this! Got sent up here a couple of weeks, and now every shitty number comes up I get it. Go on, send me back! The bastards *know* I'm off in a couple of hours. Do me a favor!''

As his scowl increased he saw that those outside were mellowing into smiles.

"Okay, big mouth. You know you lost a rear plate? Replace it as soon as possible. What you got in the back there?''

"Fucking tools! What you think I got? A cabaret?''

"Go on—move.'' The barrier had been raised and one of the men was waving an illuminated baton. A few hundred meters ahead he saw there was another barrier. He slammed into gear, swearing hard at the now-merry faces as he passed.

Through.

He tooled slowly downhill.

The wide opening to the airport passed with its exit and entrance signs. The only signs he had seen so far on the road. Just inside, he saw, there were more guard posts, and he sailed past and on to the next barrier, now also miraculously raised.

Then he was on his own, and the street lights ran out, and he drove on in the dark.

The road curved sharply again and forked, and he took the main branch and curved around with it; and then slowed and stopped. Was this where you got tangled up?

He reversed to the fork and took a look at it again.

There was no doubt he'd taken the major road. But was it the right one? No sign of any kind, no warning of the fork even.

A large mound of grit was dumped at the roadside before the fork, with a deep ditch behind it; evidently a runoff for the spring thaw. He left the engine running and scrambled down to the ditch. Wide enough, and no rocks in it.

He drove the bobik down, sheltered behind the pile of grit, and switched everything off. The sounds of the airport were still near: helicopters chattering, a jet warming up. They flew the bullion out, he'd heard, in ingots.

He waited twenty minutes before the two trucks came around. They passed and he watched their lights, saw them keep steadily to the broad main track. Exactly. It was the one he'd taken himself: the loop road into the goldfields. Where he would have lost himself. The through route was the narrower one.

He started up and pulled out of the ditch.

Okay. Baranikha. Three or four hundred kilometers. Six o'clock, he saw.

54

By 6:15 the general was stepping into his car. They'd asked if the transport company's vehicles could now be allowed to move. The route to Bilibino and beyond was still paralyzed. Yes, he said, on consideration. He had totally forgotten it.

They had also asked if he wanted the people ahead warned that he was coming. In no way! Catch them unprepared. The night's work had already warned them enough. Give them time and they'd soon dream up a story to account for the discrepancy.

A highly interesting vehicle had emerged—or rather not emerged—at the collective. The *native* collective, Novokolymsk. Where they'd claimed never to have heard of the fellow. As the garbage workers had also claimed . . . Well, he'd been had, and he saw it now. Natives stuck together.

The man had made dozens of journeys up and down this route. Was it likely that he'd never even looked *into* the collective—full of natives? For certain he'd looked into it, had clapped eyes on the vehicle, and had taken it away. Probably on a truck, back to Green Cape.

Which argued that he'd done it that way around: first of all prepared a secure place to work, and then taken the work *to* it. The general was beginning to get an outline of the man. Well, now for an outline of his vehicle.

They found the helicopter warming up, and before seven had landed at the collective. The row had wakened some of the inhabitants, and from them the general's aides routed out the half-asleep secretary of the place and also the individual in charge of its vehicles.

The information required was simple, yet it took three hours to get to the bottom of it.

Nobody knew Khodyan, of course—photo passed around, heads shaken. All as expected.

The vehicle was a one-ton Tatra; it had stood for years at the back of a shed used for storing fertilizers. They had noticed it missing only when the police had phoned in the middle of the night. The secretary had roused the mechanic, and the mechanic had gone out and had a look.

When was the last time it had been seen? The last time—probably August just before winter. Fertilizers weren't needed in winter, nobody had need to go to the shed. Could anybody have got into the shed? Yes, anybody could have got in—no padlocks, just this bit of string here.

A thorough search of the collective and its environs showed no trace of the Tatra. It had been a wreck, kept only for parts. Had meant to get a certificate of destruction for it, never got around to it. Had no trouble getting a new one; authorities knew this one would be turned in sometime. *Could* it be moved? Well it had been moved. Maybe some members had stripped it, shifted it, and didn't like to say. Or maybe just kids, messing about.

The general's party breakfasted at the collective and took stock of the situation.

From Tchersky news arrived that all other defunct vehicles had now been located. Only this one was missing.

Yes, this was the one. He'd hauled it away, rebuilt it with parts from the transport company, laid in a few jerricans of fuel—and had it ready and waiting in his workshop, *perhaps* at the dump. To which he had been transported, almost by chauffeur service, right from that yard. While the fools had wasted time searching warehouses, he had been buzzing away, fast, on the highway of the river.

But buzzing where?

Volodya had brought the maps, and they were studied. With a head start, the man would have taken the most direct route out. The most direct route *was* the river. The first sizable airport on the river was at Zirianka. South. He had gone south. A call to Zirianka elicited the news that its air services south had been halted for days by blizzards.

The general was pleased to hear this. On the way from Irkutsk he had flown over the blizzard himself, had flown high in his service aircraft. Now he gave his orders personally. A 1966 one-ton Tatra, farm-truck body, probably very battered, was to be found and held. Its driver, a native, perhaps traveling under the name Khodyan, was also to be held.

Yes; what registration plates, the Tatra?

The general paused. The Tatra had no plates, of course; they had been handed in. But he would have gotten himself plates. The plates, he told Zirianka, would be out-of-town plates, details unknown; but engine and chassis numbers as follows.

And the native, his description?

The general paused again.

The man would very possibly have changed his description. Hold *all* natives, he said. He would be coming immediately.

To Zirianka a long-distance helicopter was required, at present not available at Tchersky, which meant using the general's own jet. The pilot and first officer of the jet, anticipating another day of hanging about, had awakened to titanic hangovers. Further delay. The general used it to issue a series of orders.

Because of disruption to flights south, the man might try some criss-cross method involving smaller airports. *All* airstrips in north Siberia to be warned. Natives without pre-booked flights to be held until details reported to Tchersky.

Wherever he was, the man would now have out-of-area plates. All vehicles with such plates to be stopped and details reported to Tchersky.

The first order involved air control at Yakutsk, the only authority in contact with the smaller strips. The second involved several dozen calls to police and militia posts.

One o'clock when the general stepped aboard, and he was tired. Only four hours' sleep last night.

Medical Officer Komarova had also lost sleep last night. She had left late, and with a prepared story if stopped. A providential accident at Anyuysk; she had ordered the patient to be kept where he was until seen. She would see him at the earliest moment.

No activity along the main river, no watch being kept, so before Anyuysk she had turned off, driven fast to the cave, and entered with her flashlight.

Gone. And with no trace left that he had ever been here. Curtains, lighting, block and tackle, all away; no sign even of where they had been. Vapor from the kerosene stove had created new frost, bulging on every surface. No drop of oil, no stain, no scrap of anything left. Well, he'd been careful. Yet he had promised . . .

She searched with the flashlight, but there was nothing, only frost. Except one small hump that turned out to be not entirely frost. She recognized it at once, the wrapping paper from the salami, and opened the many folds for the message. No message but as she turned it this way and that something fell, and on the ground was the ring. In the flashlight she couldn't decipher the engraved motto, but she knew it anyway—"Like our love the circle has no end"—and felt the tears again on her cheeks.

At Zirianka there was no 1966 one-ton Tatra, which meant only that the cautious fellow could have left it outside, but there were eighteen ill-tempered natives stopped from boarding their flight to Druzhina. Druzhina was north, on the Indigirka River, and the general wasn't interested in it, or in the eighteen natives, after quickly looking them over.

Copies of the photo had been brought and they were passed around all employees of the airport.

Two recognized the man and four didn't. The truth was, the manager said, many such natives passed through. At flight times the place was very busy, particularly for flights south.

When was the last flight south? The last flight south had been Saturday morning, nine o'clock.

Saturday nine o'clock. Well, leaving Tchersky Friday evening he could have made it. Records were checked of that flight, and flights to all other destinations since. Numbers of natives showed up; racial identity listed from internal passports. No Khodyans.

Which meant he probably now had other papers.

All flight destinations were contacted; details of all natives given and follow-up inquiries authorized. At the same time, the local police were engaged—and had been for some hours—in a sweep of the area in search of a 1966 one-ton Tatra.

By evening, replies had come thick and fast from flight destinations, and from local police posts. All negative.

The general took dinner with his staff and reviewed the situation again. If the man had caught a flight, or even if he hadn't, he had still had to get himself here *somehow*.

If he had *come* here.

Maybe he hadn't come here.

Or if he had come, maybe it wasn't in the Tatra.

The Tatra was the likeliest, the only, vehicle they had to go on. But perhaps it *wasn't* the Tatra. Had Tchersky reported Tatra parts missing? What the devil had they reported?

Tchersky was contacted and reported that the transport company was still checking discrepancies. As yet nothing pointed significantly to any particular type of vehicle. When it did they would call in immediately.

The general decided to hang on till midnight. But half an hour later two calls from Tchersky changed his mind. The first was a response to his order for out-of-area vehicles, and it came from a strange area. A militia post at Bilibino had reported a native passing through in a bobik soon after five this morning. The man had claimed to be a road mechanic on goldfield duties, but no road station had any knowledge of him, or of his bobik.

The second related to country airstrips, and was from a source still stranger. The general took the phone himself and his eyebrows shot up. "They've found him *where?* Say it again. Spell it." But even as spelled, he'd never heard of it, and he looked around at his staff. "Baranikha?" he said.

55

For Porter, pulling out of the ditch at six o'clock that morning, Baranikha had still been far ahead. He was not clear *how* far ahead. Something over three hundred kilometers, the little atlas showed; but with mountains all the way and a twisting road it could be very much farther. In any case, he needed more fuel.

By ten A.M. he had it, and two more road stations were behind him. He had also a fantastic surprise. All the trucks were running here! Not in his direction, for he had overtaken nothing, but the other way. The road to Bilibino had been the danger—all long-distance traffic halted there. They hadn't expected him to get beyond it. But now he was beyond it, running free. And here everything was normal.

The exhilaration had temporarily lifted his fatigue; but now exhaustion had set in again. He had driven over a thousand kilometers. He was light-headed, seeing double.

Somewhere ahead and to the right a halo of light became two haloes, and one again. Then two. In the snow flurries he tried to focus. He was running beside a frozen stream but there had been no bridges for the past hour. The fuzzy light ahead showed activity of some kind; there had to be a linking track to it over the stream.

Presently, almost abeam, he saw there *were* two haloes: a floodlit aerial railway on a mountain slope above, and below it a bucket chain dumping ore into a line of trucks. He saw also that the track from this operation ran to the stream, and the highway and, thank God, to a bridge connecting it with the highway. He took himself under this bridge, leaden with fatigue, and immediately switched everything off and got into his bag.

A quarter to eleven. Two full hours' sleep, he decided.

And before one, to time, awoke. There was still half a flask of coffee left, and he swilled a mouthful around. He was faint with hunger. Plenty of food left, he saw, as he pulled the bag toward him; he had moved too fast, too continuously. He cut himself some bread, and unwrapped the salami, and looked at the coarse paper for a moment, wondering if she'd found the other one yet . . .

A lifetime ago.

He chewed his food and tried to think when it was. All Sunday he had worked on the bobik; Sunday night she'd brought the battery. Early Monday he'd left. Had driven all day, all night.

Only yesterday. And already over a thousand kilometers away. And with two more road stations behind him he must be nearing his destination.

He pulled the atlas across and found Baranikha again.

All the contour shades still purple. He traced the road he was on. A major river must be coming up. Once he hit the river, the road ran beside it straight to Baranikha—the river itself carrying on to the Arctic. He had turned north again. Now he had to fly south. Several short flights south.

He followed the pages south through the atlas. Nakhodka was so far there was no point in plotting it yet. But he saw where he had to head. Magadan first. Not the place itself but some small spot near it. Polar Aviation's flights touched down at many country stops. And Magadan wasn't so far now, maybe fifteen hundred kilometers. Two or three hops. He could make it today.

He checked out the road and in a few minutes was moving again, into snow.

Twenty kilometers along, the headlights of a convoy came toward him: a Tchersky convoy. The big Kamas flashed their lights at him as they lumbered past, and he flashed back.

Two P.M.

At 2:30 he picked up the river, pulled in, and checked with the atlas again.

The scale was so small it was hard to tell, but it looked no more than thirty or forty kilometers to Baranikha now. The color faded to green in the area around the dot, indicating some kind of valley; probably accounting for the siting of the town. The airport would be in that valley. He started up again and proceeded more slowly, looking for security checks. So far he had seen nothing, but still—his registration plate was a strange one here.

The river coiled away presently, not so straight as on the map, but the road ran dead straight. The river was now below, still to the right. It dropped quite far below, yes into a valley, widish, flattish. The high ground was to his left, fold on fold of it, an occasional frozen waterfall showing the chasms in between. The road had been built on a straight ledge of rock running between what was evidently a marsh on the right and the jagged peaks on the left.

It rose and fell slightly now with the contours, and quite suddenly, on a rise, he saw the lights of the town below. And very close below. Hazy in the snow, but not more than three or four kilometers. The road ran straight downhill to it: a toy town neatly laid out in the valley. Smoke-pluming factories; lit-up apartment blocks. And an airport, with runway, control tower, adjacent buildings, parking lot.

He sat and watched it for some minutes. There didn't seem to be a barrier. He drove cautiously down, entered the parking lot, and cruised round. No militia; no people even; just a few vans and battered work buses, all crusted with snow. He stationed the bobik nose out, put a few necessities into the grip, and picked his way across the rutted ground into the airport building.

A shabby hall, very grimy, crammed with people. His heart sank at the sight. They had all, obviously, been here a long time. Every seat was taken and everywhere people were sleeping—on chairs, benches, the floor. The air was thick with tobacco smoke and a hubbub of noise. A knot of men bunched round the check-in desk, and a denser crowd around a bar at the far end of the hall. There was a canteen there, all the tables full; card games, domino games, a man playing an accordion.

What the hell! All flights stopped, evidently. Were they looking for him here, too?

He made his way to the check-in desk, saw the flight board on the wall. A list of destinations: all times blank.

A heavy smell of sweat rose from the gang here: workingmen, many of them native, short skis and rucksacks strapped to their backs. He picked one who looked like a Chukchi.

"What's going on, brother?" he asked.

"They're giving out the tickets. For Mitlakino."

"What's the holdup?"

"No holdup. The blizzard isn't heading there."

A blizzard; not him, then. "How about Magadan?" he said.

"Magadan?" The man stared at him, and he saw now that he was drunk. "Magadan out. Everything south been out for days. And for another thirty-six hours. They laid you off here?"

"Sure, laid off. What's this other place—Mitla what?"

"Mitlakino. Work there. See a notice." The man was swaying, and was jostled aside by others returning through the crush with papers.

He pulled out of the mob and looked for the notice. It was beyond the desk, on the wall between it and the canteen. Men were sleeping here on bundles on the floor. He leaned over them and read it.

> MITLAKINO *(Chukotskiy Poluostrov)*
> Construction workers required.
> Mining experience essential.
> Union rates according to grade.
> Work permit and employment record required.
> Transport, food, and accommodation provided.

Chukotskiy Poluostrov. The Chukotka Peninsula. Way east, as far east as you could go. It was south he wanted. But there would be no way south for thirty-six hours. With this mob stuck here for days, there was no guarantee he'd get a flight even then.

He pondered this and pushed through to the bar. The bar, he saw right away, was out of hard drink: Crates of empties were stacked behind it, the two women working there in angry argument with men leaning over to see what was beneath. Some of the men, he saw, had formed tight drinking groups of their own and were taking swigs from personal bottles passed around.

The end wall of the canteen was papered with an enormous map of Siberia, and he made his way to it, trying to think what was for the best. To get as far away as possible was obviously best—but as far east as the Chukotka peninsula? Still, if it was the only place planes were flying. From there, with the blizzard over, he should be able to fly south—and to Magadan. Its supplies probably came direct from Magadan, the principal town for the Chukotka region. Better than staying here, anyway.

Mitlakino he had never heard of, but he saw its position, on the peeling edge of the map, the sheet greasily fading out by the light switch, but ringed in red ballpoint. The name itself had been hand-written in, partly on the wall—evidently nothing there yet, still in course of construction.

From Baranikha, also ringed on the map, it was a long way. According to the scale, something over eight hundred kilometers. But what of it? A direct flight would take only a couple of hours.

"What's the problem, brother?" The drunk had found him—had found him abruptly, pushed backward out of a ring of drinkers. "Greedy bastards!" he told the drinkers. "What's the problem?"

"No problem," Porter said. "You going to Mitlakino?"

"Sure going Mitlakino. Know plenty fellows Mitlakino. Good fellows, Chukchi, not greedy bastards. Listen, what kind a fellow you, brother? You not Chukchi?"

"No," Porter said. The man strongly stank. "Evenk."

"Evenks all right. Listen, you got something to drink?"

"I got something for me," Porter said.

"You good fellow. Let's have drink. Call a plane soon."

"How soon they call the plane?"

"Soon. On a board. Just time little drink."

"Just a minute," Porter said, and went to see the board, the man dragging behind him. On the board the Mitlakino time was now up, the only one up. It wasn't so soon.

Mitlakino 18:00.

The airport clock showed 16:15.

"Okay," Porter said, "we'll have a little drink. Only put your papers away, you'll lose them." The man was still clutching the sheaf in his hand. "And we don't want anyone sharing, we'll find a place of our own."

They found a place in the boiler room. The notice on the door said KEEP OUT, but it wasn't locked. The one he'd tried first had electrical flashes on it and was firmly locked.

The boiler room was hot and he helped the Chukchi off with his backpack and skis before settling on the floor and producing the bottle from his grip. It was his last bottle, only one swig gone, and the man's eyes lit up. "You good fellow," he said.

By ten to five only a quarter was left in the bottle and the Chukchi, after a little desultory singing, was nodding.

"I like a man can take a drink," he said.

"You a man can take a drink?" Porter asked him.

"Sure I take a drink," the Chukchi said.

"I take a drink," Porter told him, and glugged at the bottle. He took nothing from it but he held it up, examining it owlishly. "That's a good drink," he said. "I don't see you take a good drink."

The Chukchi took a good drink. He took all of it and showed the bottle, and smiled foolishly, sliding sideways. Porter watched, awaiting the first snore.

Yes. Out for the count. And for some hours.

It was just on five, and now there was little time.

He took the Chukchi's papers, checking to see that the ticket was there, and also the backpack and skis. He collected his grip, switched the light off, and went rapidly back through the crowded hall.

17:05 on the wall clock. 18:00 on the flight board.

He stowed everything in the bobik and drove out of the parking lot. The snow was still gusting, but now at him, from the south. He went back up the hill, to the rise from where he'd first seen the town, the river and the valley now on his left. The rock cliffs were to his right and he searched them, looking for a gap. He remembered there had been frozen waterfalls, dropping into a chasm, and soon he saw one.

He got out of the car and peered down, with the flashlight. Smooth icy bulges in the rock. No obstructions. And no sign of bottom. But deep. It wouldn't be seen for months, if then; smashed to nothing by the summer torrent.

He transferred what he needed to the backpack. Almost nothing left in the bobik's tank, but one jerrican still full. This he threw into the chasm, together with the grip. Then he took the keys out of the ignition, pulled the wheel hard over, let the brake off and pushed it backward downhill. It ran slowly away from him, ran easily, and went over easily—good little bastard, good to the end, and he watched as it simply went, vanished, without trouble. Above the wind he heard a muffled thud, and another, and then nothing.

He hitched the backpack on and undid the skis. They were work jobs, short and wide, for rough ground; the sticks bound up with them. He buckled the skis to his boots, had a look at his watch—5:25—and took off.

He was back in the parking lot in fifteen minutes, took two more to get the skis off and strapped under the backpack, and was inside the airport building in time to hear an announcement boom from the loudspeakers.

"Mitlakino—final call! All passengers for Mitlakino, Mishmita, and Polyarnik, go at once to the aircraft! Last call for Mitlakino. Departure in fifteen minutes for Mishmita, Polyarnik, and Mitlakino. Passengers go at once to the aircraft."

A knot of stragglers was still going through and he joined them. Not a direct flight, then. And something puzzling in the names. Mitlakino he'd only heard of a couple of hours before, and Polyarnik not at all. But Mishmita? Vaguely familiar.

He handed in his ticket and filed through. The plane was an ancient three-engine Yak, the short-take-off crate of the north. Inside was pandemonium, a struggling mass of skis and backpacks. Sixty or so men were aboard and he found himself crammed next to a buttoned-up Russian, evidently a professional man, lips pursed at the noisy and undisciplined natives.

"Go inside—I get off first," the man gruffly ordered, and took the aisle seat.

"Where you get off?" Porter asked him, companionably.

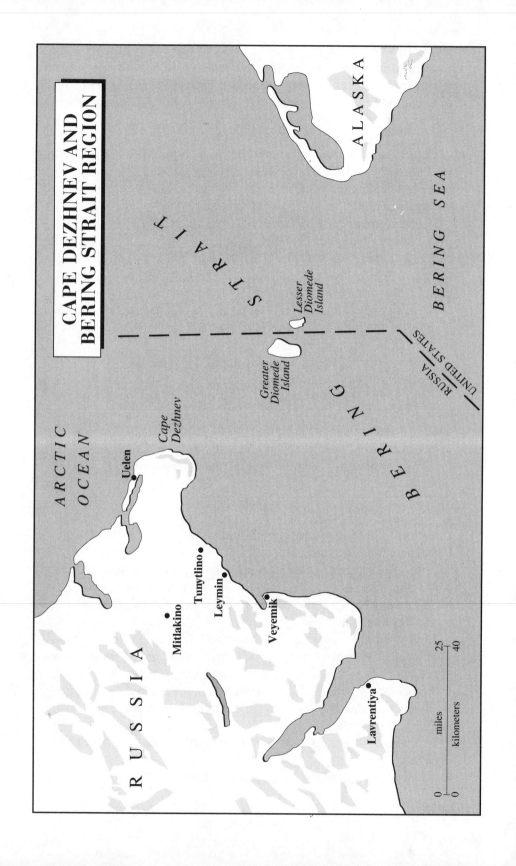

CAPE DEZHNEV AND
BERING STRAIT REGION

ALASKA

BERING SEA

STRAIT

Lesser
Diomede
Island

Greater
Diomede
Island

RUSSIA
UNITED STATES

BERING

ARCTIC
OCEAN

Cape
Dezhnev

Uelen

Tunytlino

Leymin

Mitlakino

Veyemik

RUSSIA

Lavrentiya

miles
kilometers

0
0

25
40

"Mishmita."

"Don't know Mishmita. What's Mishmita?"

"*Mys,*" the Russian curtly told him. "Not Mish. *Mys.* Mys Schmidta."

"Ah."

Mys Schmidta—*Cape Schmidta!* Last seen on the chartroom table of the *Suzaku Maru;* he'd watched a plane take off from the airstrip there, had drawn the captain's attention to it while checking the ship's position on the chart himself. From there to the mouth of the Kolyma, forty-seven hours. Now he was reversing his tracks—truly going back the way he'd come.

An idea began slowly to dawn.

"Tell me," he said humbly to the Russian, "were you ever in Mitlakino?"

"Yes, I've been in Mitlakino."

"As an educated man—excuse me, I'm ignorant—is it on the sea, the Arctic?"

The Russian thawed slightly. "Not on the Arctic, no. Inland a little. From a cape—Cape Dezhnev. The sea there we call a *strait*—the Bering Strait. You've heard of it, perhaps?"

"Ah, no."

But, ah, yes. Christ Almighty, yes! It hadn't shown up on the airport map, all peeled away there. But of course, the Bering Strait. Go far enough east and you . . . He couldn't wait to get his hands on the little atlas. He couldn't get at the atlas, stuck in the backpack with a great pile of other luggage. He waited for the first stop and the plane to thin out.

To Mys Schmidta was an hour's hop, and the Russian got off and others on, in the same confusion; then on to Polyarnik, another forty minutes, and more off and none on. And at last, with the upheavals over and the plane thinned out, he got at the backpack, and the atlas, and hungrily turned east.

Page after page, and there it was: end of the peninsula, Cape Dezhnev. End of the peninsula but not of the map, or of Russia. For the deeper knowledge of Kolymsky students the school atlas showed the boundary of Russia, and of its nearest neighbor. The boundary was in the sea, eighty-five kilometers wide at this point: the Bering Strait. The neighbors had forty-two and a half kilometers each, and the boundary ran through the middle. It ran between two islands. The Greater Diomede Island was Russian, the Lesser Diomede American. Only four kilometers between them . . .

He absorbed this and looked back, on the map, at the mainland. Inland from Cape Dezhnev, the Russian had said. Mitlakino didn't

315

show up there. Just a wilderness, with a marsh, a lake, a small mountain range. North of the cape a coastal dot said Uelen, and south of it Lavrentiya. There would be others in between. At the place itself there'd be a bigger-scale map, a work map.

Soon enough a dim haze of light below showed the place itself, with the straight line of an airstrip.

They landed on it at nine o'clock, and snow tanks were waiting to take the forty-odd men to the workers' barracks. The journey was short, but snow was now falling quite heavily.

He got himself into the last of the tracked vehicles. No one had questioned his presence so far, and the absence of the other man had not been noticed, but it was as well to see what happened ahead. As they neared the building the first arrivals were already filing in, the lead tank moving on to an adjoining shed. Again he positioned himself as last man in the mob outside. Some holdup was going on inside, and presently there were complaints and a great heave, and they were all in.

Inside, in the tightly packed lobby, an angry telephone conversation was going on. A wrong permit had been provided, and the matter was being checked with Baranikha. An official barked to the clerk at the desk that papers would be processed in the morning, and the mob began to thin. Again he saw to it that he was at the end. The men were being handed tags—for their skis and bunk numbers—in exchange for their documentation. He had his papers in his hand but was not anxious to have the name overheard by the man's comrades.

Now he felt himself on edge; time going fast. Nine-thirty. Four and a half hours since the Chukchi had taken a sleep. He could be waking up.

He gave in his papers at last—the *very* last—and was allotted a bunk and a locker. "Just dump your stuff and go right to supper. The kitchen will close."

He found his bunk, looked into the dining room, and saw that tags were being shown for meals. He went outside again.

The telephone line was coated with snow and he'd seen it on the way in. It disappeared into a plastic conduit and he traced it down the log-built structure to the junction box. With his knife he prized apart the join where it met the box, cut the wire, and pressed the conduit back in place. No more talk with Baranikha. He decided to skip supper.

56

In the air the general was in heated conversation with Tchersky. They'd garbled the story; it was obvious now. The Chukchi found at Baranikha was not the Chukchi he was after. The man at Baranikha had been found in the airport's boiler room, drunk. From his incoherent account it seemed that some other native had stolen his flight ticket and papers and flown off with them. He had flown off with a gang of native workers to a construction site. The location of the site was now providing a problem.

The name of the place was Mitlakino, and it was not on the general's maps. It was not on Tchersky's, either.

"What the devil! Doesn't Tchersky supply this place?"

"No, General. According to Baranikha, Magadan does."

"Magadan? Is there an air service from it to Magadan?"

Yes, apparently there was.

"This bastard," the general informed his staff, "is making for Magadan. He'll go south from there. Now listen," he told Tchersky, "that airstrip at Mitla—at that place—is to be closed down. Issue the order at once. Will he have landed there yet?"

Yes, he would have landed there. The plane had reported landing two hours ago, at nine P.M., and was staying the night due to heavy snow. There was now no radio contact with it, or with the small control tower, which had also gone off for the night. And the telephone line at the camp was out of order; Baranikha was still trying to get through.

"Goddamn it!" the general said. "Well, close it down when they *do* get through. That plane is not to take off, whatever the weather, and nothing else is to be let in except military craft. Contact the nearest airbase to it. Get a clear location for them from Baranikha—a precise map reference with coordinates. I'll talk to them when I land. He's bottled up there, at least. That's one thing. Now here's another." The general took breath.

"This bobik. He went through Bilibino in a *bobik*. He will have arrived in Baranikha with it. How the hell is it that a bobik has not been reported missing? What details have they given of it in Baranikha?"

Baranikha had not given any details of it. They hadn't found it—

not at the airport, or as yet anywhere in the town. They were still looking for it.

In that case, the general thought, they weren't going to find it. He had gotten rid of it; no evidence left. Increasingly it was looking as if he'd left *Tchersky* in the bobik. He might have used the Tatra to get to the Bilibino highway, and *there* snatched a bobik, a likelier vehicle for mountains than a farm truck. But there was no stolen bobik on the Bilibino highway; his officers had earlier covered it intensively, had covered every long-distance route. In which case, where had the bobik come from?

Tchersky. He hadn't simply picked one up on the way. The man was a planner. He had planned the bobik. In his workshop. Had taken some wreck there, and then the spare parts to rebuild it. Where had the spare parts come from? The Tchersky Transport Company. Where had the wreck come from? Same place. Not a Tatra. A bobik. Any number of crocks must be hanging about there—a big garage, for God's sake. But with big garages there were routines. Was this just sloppy supervision or had someone actively ... Who was responsible for such things? And who was responsible for *parts?*

"Tchersky—are you there?" The general had brooded for some minutes, only a discreet crackle coming from the other end.

"Yes, General."

"Who's in charge of bobik parts there, that company?"

"Bobik parts would be the Light Vehicles Depot."

"Do they work at night?"

"No, not at night. They lock up at five, General."

"Good. Get a key. Have the director of the place there when I land. Don't tell him why. See that my car is waiting. And have you remembered that about the coordinates?"

"Yes, General. You want them when you land."

"*I* don't want them. The *air base* will want them. Give them to the *air base.*"

Idiots!

Vassili had been very silent all night, his eyes on the TV, and his wife's eyes on him. He had known she would say nothing unless he said something; and he had said nothing at all.

Now he settled himself into bed.

"All right, what?" he said.

"Will we lose the apartment?"

"No."

"Will you get into trouble?"

"No."

"They say he's bad."

"He isn't."

"They know someone helped him."

He grunted. He should never have told her of the bobik. It had been in that romantic period when she had advised that Kolya should fuck an Evenk. He put his teeth in the glass.

"Could they find out anything?" she said.

"No."

He sincerely hoped not. He had gone through the duplicate order forms from March; delivery advices from July. His stock and deficit books had needed attention, too, and a razor blade. None of the parts showed up now. They'd never been ordered; delivery not advised; no deficits. The rumpus would come later, and he would sort it out later. If Kolya hadn't fixed him. Got himself found. Or left the bobik to be found. He wouldn't have done that. No. But Vassili was depressed. He had been used.

Eleven o'clock, and he put the light out.

At militia headquarters the general hung on, waiting for the flight controller of the air base to return to the phone.

His raid on the transport company had not been a success. A haggard director, evidently an old camp survivor, had savagely accused him of being spy-happy, of wishing a return to old times. One Liova, the manager of the Light Vehicles Depot, also an old lag, also summoned, had demanded the presence of a native storeman; vetoed by the general. They had inspected the stores, and various books, all incomprehensible. . . . A job for an expert later. For now—

"Hello, yes?"

"Okay, General. Meteorological conditions are difficult at the moment—there's a white-out."

"But you can land there?"

"Of course. What do you want done?"

"Just get him. You'll need to liaise with Magadan, they supply the place. I have no clear idea of it here—"

"I'm looking at air photos of it now."

"Ah, you have some. It's isolated, is it?"

"Yes, just a single structure. Is he armed?"

"Assume that he is. When can you be there?"

"Say 0100. I've lifted a squad of airborne now, in helicopters. You want him held there or brought back here?"

"First get him. I'll let you know," the general said, and hung up, satisfied.

A right decision to come himself from Irkutsk. The idiots here could still be combing warehouses. Upon arrival he had been two days behind the man. By issuing decisive orders—militia posts, airstrips—he had reduced that gap to two hours. Now, twenty past twelve on his second night here, the two hours had been reduced to forty minutes.

He had a drink while waiting.

57

At 12:30 Porter climbed out of his bunk, tidied the rolled-up bedding, and took his boots and the backpack. The dormitory was snoring; he had made sure everyone was snoring before even entering it for a rest.

He had heard one shift go out at midnight and another return, evidently to some other dormitory. Now the place was dead. He peered out into the lobby.

All deserted; semidark.

Behind the counter, a single lamp. In the recess by the door, the ski stack, now tidied up.

He stood quite still, reviewing the scene, and waited some moments to be sure he had it to himself. Then he went behind the counter. There was a chair there and he sat and put his boots on, looking about him. A few notices pinned to a board: work schedules; a plan showing block numbers of work areas. Nothing more. There had to be better than this, and he looked under the counter, and found it.

All below the counter was pigeonholed, and in the holes charts. The holes were neatly labeled. "Camp Plan," "Mining Works," "Geological Survey," "Topography."

"Topography" had a dozen rolled-up charts and he found the right one. They were inland from the cape forty kilometers: Dezhnev to the north, Lavrentiya to the south. In between, a curving bay showed several coastal villages—Naukan, Tunytlino, Leymin, Veyemik, Keyekan . . . Inuit villages: Eskimos.

The tiny marsh and lake of the atlas were here hugely magnified. The camp was exactly midway between them. The works were a kilometer to the west, in the foothills of a small mountain range, the chart squared off so precisely he could place himself to five hundred meters.

The islands were not on the chart—on this scale, too far out. But he knew that from midway in the bay they were directly east.

Midway in the bay . . . It looked like Veyemik. The compass bearing on the chart showed Veyemik as due southeast of the barrack block.

He dug in the backpack, found the school compass, and checked it, first finding north. North, according to the chart, should be the adjoining shed where the snow tanks had pulled in, the whole block laid out on a precise north–south axis.

He pointed the compass there, and saw it was several degrees out. No means of resetting the tinny little job, so he made the adjustment in his head and scanned the chart again.

There were three main tracks: to the works, to the lake, and to the nearest coastal village, Tunytlino. This one he examined carefully.

Tunytlino was thirty kilometers away. No track led from it to the next village, Leymin, twelve kilometers below it, but the ground looked flat. After that, Veyemik.

Veyemik was another fourteen kilometers, but surrounded by a whirl of contour lines. The place was on the far side of a creek, frozen now. . . . If he hit the coast at Tunytlino, kept the sea on the left, Veyemik was twenty-six kilometers below it. The whole journey, from where he sat now, fifty-six kilometers. Thirty-five miles.

Okay.

He slipped the chart back in its pigeonhole, went to the ski stack, and found the pair he had arrived with, tagged by bunk number. He removed the tag, hunted in his pocket for its twin—this one looped to a locker key—and took them back to the desk. They'd come out of a drawer, he remembered. In the night's confusion the desk man had hastily stuffed the papers in the same drawer. He opened the drawer and found his own papers, the tag number scrawled in one corner. He took the papers, dropped the tags in among a jumble of others, and closed the drawer.

With backpack and skis he went out through the double doors. The outer one had a simple latch and it clicked securely behind him.

Outside the wind was howling, snow blowing horizontally.

He hunched through it to the shed and turned on his flashlight. Four snow tanks, three bobiks. He looked over the best bobik; then the other two. No keys in any of them. He swore. A snow tank, then. Cumbersome; also very noisy. But nothing for it. He inspected the snow tanks, and found none of them had keys.

Jesus Christ! He wasn't going thirty-five miles in a snowstorm on little work skis, not in view of what else he had to do tonight. He shone the flashlight around and saw the snowplows—one actually out in the snow, shrouded in it. He had a look at the other. It was at the mouth of the shed, a tracked vehicle, big tracks like a tank; its shovel raised and pointing out. High, with an enclosed cabin. He climbed up and opened the door.

Keys in.

He shone the flashlight around the cabin. He had driven a snowplow before but the arrangement of levers was unfamiliar here. To hell— there was a gear stick, accelerator, wipers, lights, brake. He'd figure it out on the move.

He settled the skis and backpack, closed the door, and turned the key. It took several turns before the thing clanked hideously into life. He didn't know if it could be heard above the wind. Just move.

He slipped the gear in and moved. Got it out of the shed and well away from the building before turning right to pick up the track at the north side. In the dark he couldn't see the track. He flashed the lights briefly, but the broad shovel was sticking out, blocking the view. Just a dazzle of snow, twin embankments hazily visible ahead. Evidently that was the track, swept by the snowplow.

He drove between the embankments and switched the headlights on again. In the glare, high walls of snow passed slowly on each side and presently began curving right—east. Yes, this was it. On the chart the only track east led to the coast: Tunytlino. He ran for another minute, and stopped.

He switched the interior light on and inspected the controls. Found the lever for the shovel and lowered it out of the way. Now, the wipers going, he could see clearly—at least the two embankments he had to drive between. Ahead the lane ran straight, no signs of the plow's earlier tracks. With the heavy snow falling there would soon be no sign of his own. All to the good. The thing had no speedometer and was certainly not a racer. Still, only thirty kilometers to the coast. It was just before one o'clock; he thought he could make it in an hour, and started again. And almost immediately stopped again.

He switched off the engine; and then the lights, too.

A helicopter was muttering overhead. Even above the engine he'd heard it. A big one. There seemed to be more than one. Or was it the same one, circling to find the landing strip?

He opened the window and looked up. Through the whirling hail of snow he could see, intermittently, the hazy beam of a searchlight. The landing strip was switched off; the pilot was hunting for it. Maybe a telephone crew to see to the fault. Strange, at one in the morning. But communication crews worked around the clock. He started up again and drove on, with the lights off. From the air, he knew, he couldn't be seen, the vehicle shrouded now in snow.

He drove for several minutes, and stopped and cut the engine again. The clatter was still in the air, but distant now. The guy hadn't landed yet, or if he had was making a hell of a row, his rotors still going. But no sign of a beam through the heavy snow, and the helicopter was well behind him, so he switched on the sidelights and got moving again, pensively.

The line crew had arrived unexpectedly fast. He'd been right to move fast. The Chukchi at Baranikha would be awake by now and raising hell. He drove on, musing, the track dead straight, glaring white between the snow embankments, the sidelights for the time being sufficient.

At ten past two the first village appeared. Tunytlino.

A semicircle of shacks, their backs facing him, chimneys smoking. The smoke was coming toward him. No lights showed and he couldn't make out the sea; all frozen now, of course.

He switched everything off, opened the window, and listened. No dogs. The wind hissed only a little now, but it was coming from the sea. And the snow was definitely less. Already, from the sea, a different weather system.

A single street ran behind the shacks—a cleared stretch, at least. A path had been made from it to the track he was on, which simply petered out a hundred meters ahead, the embankments falling away. There he had to turn right.

He thought he had better get down and see how.

Coal smoke was in the air, acrid, from the sleeping houses. He crunched through the new snow, the village dead silent, and walked beyond it until the houses stopped and the cleared path ran out. Now he saw the sea. The beach shelved, a long way, perhaps two hundred meters, and the flat plain began. Utterly featureless. The Bering Strait.

To the right, everything similarly featureless. Another white plain, set above the sea. All the way along, the shoreline shelved. The temperature had definitely risen here, some mistiness in the air, a few snowflakes whirling. Between the flakes and the snatches of mist he could see a star or two. All the land flat ahead. Okay.

He turned and went back.

In the silence, switching on the engine, he gritted his teeth at the racket. Couldn't be helped. He kept the lights off, drove the last bit of track, turned right along the coast, and kept going. The mirrors— all the glass areas—were snowed up, and he leaned out of the cab to look back. A light had come on in one of the houses, but soon went out. He had been heard, but without interest. He switched to headlights and drove on.

The last few days he had slept little. But even sleepless, he seemed to be dreaming. He was driving a snowplow along the Bering Strait. Out in the darkness was America. In between, the two islands, locked in ice. All he had to do was walk there. Just get himself in position.

Leymin next, twelve kilometers.

Patches of mist, sudden squalls of snow; the weather changing every few minutes. But a night of changing drifts would cover his tracks anyway.

Just under the half hour, Leymin.

He turned inland, kept distance with the village until the shacks had passed, and returned to the coast.

To Veyemik, another fourteen kilometers. The chart had shown wavy contour lines here, but he could see no contours.

In a few minutes he came on them. The ground rose suddenly, the shore dropping below. And now on his right, snow-covered rocks, rising. The rocks became a cliff, and he was wedged between it and the drop on his left. He slowed to a crawl. No way of turning here. And no point in backing anyway. To return and go inland would mean only some other kind of contours, perhaps impassable: The chart had shown a chain of them.

He kept on, at a walking pace.

Veyemik was on a creek, so there had to be a descent to it, sea level. Whether you could drive down was another matter; it could be a precipice. Get as near as possible, have a look at the place. If necessary ski to it—not so far now. But there was the problem of the vehicle. He couldn't abandon a snowplow, leave evidence of where he'd gone.

He crawled on, peering ahead. The frozen strait was now a long way below, and the track very narrow. It could simply peter out and he'd be over the side.

And then, in a minute, everything had changed again.

The track veered seaward, a sudden squall blew in, snow spattering the windshield, wipers working double time. And gone. Calm. Flakes twirling in the air, and below, the creek. He could see it clearly, the shoreline broken, quite a wide inlet. At the other side of it, a huddle of houses: Veyemik. And a long easy slope to it.

He drove down, dropped smoothly onto the creek, crossed it to the other side, and came out behind the houses.

Three o'clock.

He switched the lights and the engine off, and got out to have a look.

To seaward, nothing—a great plain of ice, snow-covered. This was it. The islands were now due east. In the plow he could go the whole way. Except, of course, he couldn't. The thing would be detected at once. Both islands were certainly observation posts full of electronic devices. It would have to be on foot. From here the distance was greater than from Cape Dezhnev, perhaps fifty or sixty kilometers, but a simpler run, less chance of error—due east. Even with the little skis he could do it in five, six hours. Totally exposed, of course, if anyone knew where he'd gone. Time to lose the snowplow.

A stream cut down from the hills backing the creek. He'd seen it on the chart and now he could see its banks. He climbed up into the cab again, made the stream, and drove up it. The track soon lost itself, twisting and turning in the tangle of hills. He drove for twenty minutes without finding anywhere to ditch the plow: no cave, no gorge. It began snowing again while he peered. He decided to leave it anyway. No one would find it here before next summer. And time was going fast.

He switched off, climbed out, attached the backpack and skis, and was down again quicker than he'd gone up.

His face was crusted with snow, his gloved hands numb as he came out onto the creek. He poled himself across the ice to the mouth. The little broad skis made hard work of langlauf striding, but they were better than nothing. He stopped to beat feeling into his hands before taking his position.

No shelving beach here. Just the creek running out flat with the strait. The great void stretched before him. The Russian island came first, three times the size of the American and masking it completely. He had to hit the larger one and work around it before taking a position for the other. From now on, it would be dead reckoning, his bearing checked every few minutes, for in the ocean of darkness he would be totally blind. He unhitched the backpack and dug out the flashlight and compass.

He could scarcely feel the little compass. He took his gloves off and breathed on his hands and shone the flashlight down on it. He couldn't steady it with one hand, so he gripped the light under his chin and got both hands to it. Even so, the needle was hard to steady. He found after some moments that it wouldn't steady. It fluttered and swung, and fluttered and swung, ten degrees, and twenty, and thirty. It swung round the dial. He saw it wasn't merely swinging, but pulsing. Radar pulses, *some* bloody pulses, from somewhere.

He watched it a full three minutes to see if there was a pattern. The pattern was a continuous pattern: the needle, in fluttering jumps, going around the dial, around and around.

This was the position at four o'clock, when he realized he had no compass and no vehicle, and nowhere to go if he had one.

The nearest shelter before he froze was the village of Veyemik, and as he trudged there he racked his tired brain.

The first house was also the largest house. He hammered on the door, and continued hammering till he heard babies crying and shouted oaths, and presently an Eskimo stood before him in a suit of long johns.

"I stole nothing!" Porter told this Eskimo.

"What?"

"I swear to God! They're chasing me. They've chased me all the way!"

"Who's chasing you?" said the Eskimo. "From where?"

58

From Tchersky, the general was again on the phone to the air base. It was two A.M.

"What the hell are you saying?" he said.

"He isn't *there*. They've searched the camp block, they've searched the whole site. He's nowhere on it."

"But he's got to be there. What else is there?"

"Mine workings, a kilometer away. He didn't go there—at least not with a crew. They send them out in snow tanks, it's snowing like hell. Do you want the mine workings searched?"

"Of course search them. He could be hiding there. We know he's there *somewhere*. He *flew* out there."

But this was by no means so certain. The camp said it had no record of him. He had slept in no bunk, eaten no meal, been allotted no tags and deposited no papers. There were also no skis or luggage for him.

"But he was on that *plane*," the general said. "He stole a *ticket* to get on it."

Again this was not certain. Another worker might have stolen the ticket and papers—unintentionally, in the course of a random robbery. But the thief would have had his own ticket. He didn't *need* this ticket. And he certainly wouldn't have handed in the papers. Which would account for them not being there.

The general thought.

"The flight crew that's staying there—don't *they* know if the ticket was used?"

Again—no. It had been a madhouse on the plane. And no tickets had been handed in on it. They had been handed in at Baranikha. Should they check with Baranikha?

"I'll check with Baranikha. You check the mine workings."

The general checked with Baranikha and he found that the ticket had been handed in and the man had got on the plane. He had got on it but he had not apparently got off it; not, anyway, at two intermediate stops, for they had checked and no natives had disembarked. The man had certainly proceeded to Mitlakino but what happened to him there they didn't know.

"They chased me with a snow tank! They chased me from Mitlakino. Ask them in Tunytlino—a tank roaring after me in the middle of the night!"

"From *Mitlakino* you skied—from the mining camp?"

"What could I do? They'd have killed me. I've skied all night, I'm exhausted. They hate Evenks—and the Inuit too." He was speaking Inuit with the Eskimos. "The Chukchis don't trust us. In Chukotka it's only them—no jobs for Evenks."

"Well, I don't know." The Eskimo was a plump individual with a mild manner, and his house was large because he was the headman. He stroked his round face and looked from the hysterical Evenk to the other members of the household. Eleven of them gazed back with bewilderment. He studied the Evenk's face and made a decision.

"You'd better sleep now. You can sleep by the stove. In the morning we'll work it out."

"But you'll speak for me? You won't let them take me?"

"I'll speak for you. I don't understand it yet. Where do you get the tongue?"

"Up north. I worked some seasons. . . . But you won't give me up? They know I'm here. They chased me all the way to Leymin. They couldn't get past it, not on that track in the snow. But I got past it. You'll speak for me in the morning?"

"In the morning we'll see. It's still snowing. It shouldn't be snowing now. In the morning there could be fog. For now, everybody sleep—it's past four!"

It was past four, and at six everybody got up again, and there was fog.

And the Evenk, after his sleep, was altogether calmer. He was apologetic about his hysteria of the night. Maybe they wouldn't have killed him, but they would have beaten him badly. A man had lost money in the mine and immediately they had accused him—the only Evenk.

He could prove he had stolen nothing. He *had* nothing. When they came looking for him today—

"Look," the headman told him, "nobody will come looking for you today. They can't. It's a fog. And if they should, the women will hide you."

At this the Evenk showed alarm again. Why women? Why would women have to hide him?

Because the men would be away, working.

Where away? How far away?

On the ice. The sea.

Sealing by the shore? No farther than that?

The Eskimos smiled. Not sealing. Not at this season. Fishing. At their fishing station. Out in the strait. They would be out all day.

At this he showed even greater alarm. He wasn't staying all day with women. He would ski on down the coast, then. Unless the men would take him with. Would they take him with?

If he wished, but there was no danger. Nobody could *get* here in the fog. Still, if he was nervous . . .

He was very nervous, and he asked nervous questions. Could anybody follow them? How far were they going?

Fifty kilometers, they said, amused; and nobody could follow. You needed a signal. The authorities fitted it in your vehicle, a tracked vehicle. The signal told them on the island who was coming—there was an island out there. And it also guided you to your station. There was a beacon at the fishing station, also fitted by the authorities. You'd never find it otherwise. Nobody could follow—no need to be nervous!

This calmed him completely, and as they briskly set off after taking only steaming tea he showed a lively interest in the fishing. The best grounds, they told him, lay where the seabed shoaled near the islands. There were two islands there, but you couldn't go to the second, it was American. The first you could go to only in summer. The military let you camp in the small rock bays then—that's where the seals came up, on slabs.

So what kind of fishing did they do now?

Ice fishing, through holes, two meters square. You had to know where to cut. Mainly the ice was two meters thick out there but in some places it ran to twenty. You cut it in layers with an electric saw, off the car's battery. The authorities came and checked your holes from time to time, and they had to be near your beacon. The signal directed you there—see it?

The signal was an amber light on the dash which pulsed at wider intervals if they veered off course. They veered a bit to show him how it worked, and laughed at his astonishment.

It was crowded in the vehicle; eight men in it, all loudly instructing the interested Evenk. Another vehicle had set off a few minutes before them to set up camp, and a third was keeping company close beside, its headlights dimly visible in the fog.

Did people come out from the island to check the holes? he asked.

Sure. They checked your beacon too, and usually you gave them a bit of fish; they always needed fresh stuff there.

They drove over in cars, did they?

Sometimes—if recruits were being trained. They trained the soldiers in ice maneuvers. Native guys, some of them—they used them as trackers. But mainly it was in a helicopter.

They kept a helicopter on the island?

A helicopter? An army of them. See, the place was just a big hump of rock, about a kilometer long, and they'd taken the top off and made a whole landing ground up there. If they all took off at once you couldn't hear yourself speak.

Was it *that* near?

Ten kilometers from the fishing station. In summer, in the boat, you could see it from right here—not far to go now.

It wasn't far to go. And then they were there, the fishing station.

Lanterns burned at the fishing station—seal-oil lamps, on stakes, in a large square. Much activity was going on in the square. In the dense fog spectral shapes from the advance party were rigging a tent, others going around refilling the lanterns. All of them were on short skis, and now he put his own on. The backpack he had left in the village, and all he had taken from it was the flashlight, now rammed inside his anorak.

Various bits of gear came out of the vehicles: a winch, fishing lines, ropes, fish boxes. The men bustled at the work, and he followed a party of them to the first hole. Lamps burned here too and from all four sides tethered ropes slanted into the hole. The men tugged the ropes, assessing the weight in the basket traps suspended there, and each hole was visited in turn. Once the traps were hauled in they could do line work for bigger fish, they said. You dangled hook baits down through the holes; all this after breakfast.

They went to breakfast in the tent, and as they ate he asked how long the fog would last.

It depended. Snow was rare at this season, but when it snowed you got a fog. It hadn't snowed long so the fog wouldn't last long. Maybe only a few hours. You waited for the wind.

Did it affect their work?

No. Out *there* it affected them, the island. They didn't like fog. Just in darkness, they could see—they had special glasses. But in fog they saw nothing.

What was it they wanted to see?

The Americans, just four kilometers the other side of the island. They watched each other. That's what they did, while the rest of us did the work.

The men were cheerful at breakfast and cheerful as they went to work, and the headman jovially told him he could stay and help wash the dishes to pay for his keep. He shoveled snow in a bucket and put it on the stove and observed the day's chef cocking an ear.

"That's funny—there's one up there," the man said.

"A helicopter?" Faintly now he could hear it himself.

"Yes. Not one of the island's, though."

"You can tell the difference?"

"It's from the mainland. A big one, going there and back, can't you hear? No business being up in the fog."

Porter moodily cleared the tin plates and scraped leavings from the pot.

"Fat and rinds go in the basket. It's bait," the chef told him. "Hello—*they've* started up now!"

A harsher clatter was suddenly rending the air.

"The island?"

"That's them. Going up in the *fog!*"

"Where is it, the island?"

"Out there . . . What are you doing with your skis?"

He was strapping them on. They had all removed their skis as they'd sat round the trestle for breakfast.

"I'll just go out and take a look," he said.

"You'll see nothing in this. . . . The island's over *there,* past our first hole, a straight line. Jesus—more going up! Hey, stay inside the lights! It's easy to get lost. Don't go more than a hundred paces!"

"Okay."

For the first fifty paces he couldn't see the dimly lit hole, and then he saw it. At the hole the men were busy hauling in and didn't notice him. Looking back he could just make out the dim haze of the camp. He started counting again. He counted fifty, and sixty, and seventy; and looking back now could see neither the hole nor the camp. He had not moved his skis as he turned, and when he started again he kept on in the same straight line, and he also kept on counting. His paces on the skis were just about a meter, so after a thousand he had done a kilometer; the air black; the blackness now all roaring.

59

By four A.M. the air base reported that the man was not in the mine, not on the site, that no vehicle had been removed from the site, and that there was no sign whatever that he had ever arrived.

The flight controller went further. He had been growing steadily more skeptical all night, and he now said that they had wasted enough time and he wished to withdraw his men.

The general considered this. Unable to talk to the godforsaken camp himself, his communications had been entirely with this little air force shit, who was becoming a peremptory shit, and an increasingly insolent one.

"How many men have you got there?" he said.

"Twenty-four. In three helicopters. Eight-man squads."

"Isn't there one among them who can mend a telephone?"

"There's a signals staff, yes. But they're in a blizzard there. The line could be down anywhere."

"Have they tested the one in the building?"

"I'll ask them. But this is your last request, General. I will give it one hour."

"Request? What request? It's an order! You will *report* to me in one hour," and he had slammed the phone down.

But the man was right, he knew. Four hours of air force time wasted . . . And the bastard had slipped away again, it was certain; could by now be halfway to Magadan.

He decided not to speak again on the phone himself.

But when the next call came, in under the hour, he took it most eagerly, having heard where it came from.

"*Mitlakino!* You've found the fault?"

"Yeah. A break. See, they have this conduit, running into a junction box, and what we—"

"Was it cut?"

"Well, it doesn't look frayed. Only nobody said—"

"All right. You. What's your rank?"

"Sergeant, sir."

"Stay by that phone. Tell the director of the camp, from me, to check his vehicles again. Every one of them has to be checked. He is to inspect them himself, including anything they have at the mine. He will report to me personally, and he had better not miss any. Do that now. I'm waiting here; I can hear you. When you've done it I have another order.''

The other order was for the civilian aircraft on the airstrip to be inspected again. It was to be inspected from nose to tail, every centimeter of it; every seat, *under* every seat, the cargo space, the toilets, any hollow part of the fuselage.

"But stay by the phone yourself. Somebody will talk to you. If they don't talk, still stay on the phone. Keep this line open. Don't let anybody else use it.''

This was at five o'clock.

At 5:30 the director of the camp asked permission to come on the phone, and the general gave it.

"Well?''

"General, there's no actual *vehicle* missing—''

"What 'actual'? What are you talking about?''

"Not a *vehicle*. We checked them all hours ago. It's just—a snowplow isn't here. It could have broken down and the driver be spending the night at Tunytlino. They don't have a phone there, but what I'll do right now is send—''

"Tuny what? Have they any vehicles there?''

"Yes, they have vehicles. They have special tracked vehicles for going out to—''

"How far to Magadan from there?''

"To Magadan?'' There was a puzzled silence. "Well, I don't know. I would say maybe—two thousand kilometers?''

"Two thousand—''

For the first time the general was aware he didn't know exactly where Mitlakino was. Since nothing of note existed there and it wasn't on Tchersky's maps nobody had given him the location. But the *air base* had the location. He had thought the air base was near Magadan. He had thought Mitlakino was. . .

"Where the devil are you?'' he said.

"Where am I?'' the director said in a strange voice. "I'm at Mitlakino. Above Lavrentiya. Below Cape Dezhnev.''

"Cape Dezhnev!'' The general's flapping hand had summoned maps. "Dezhnev . . . Dezhnev. You mean—the Chukotka Peninsula?''

"Yes, certainly. The Chukotka Peninsula.''

"I see a lake. And a marsh, is it?''

"The lake and the marsh. Yes, General, we're between them."

"With Tuny—Tunytlino—away on the coast?"

"Thirty kilometers away. That's where I think the driver of the snowplow—"

"The coast of the Bering *Strait?*"

"Certainly the Bering Strait."

"Good God! Good God!" the general said. "He's not going south. He's going— Is that sergeant there? Give me that sergeant."

By six o'clock, the helicopters were airborne again and making for the string of coastal villages between Tunytlino and Keyekan. Their orders were to land at the villages and search them.

By 6:30 all were reporting dense fog over the coastal area. They could see nothing on the ground, and nothing of each other. They asked permission to return.

"No! Refused. Absolutely not!" the general told the air base. "They are to land at those villages."

"But they can't see the villages."

"Let them go down lower and look."

"General, I can't endanger my men or their aircraft in these conditions. You'll see on your map there are *hills* in that vicinity."

"And you'll see on *yours* there's also a strait there. The Bering Strait! Let them fly over it, a little offshore. The villages will have lights. If they get out on their feet they'll find them."

By 6:45 a helicopter had found Tunytlino.

It reported that nothing was known of the man there, but the villagers had heard a vehicle passing in the night. It had passed soon after two A.M. It had passed in the direction of Leymin.

Shortly afterward Leymin called in.

Nothing of the man there, either, and *no* vehicle had passed through.

"He's made his try in between, then," the general said. "Or he went inland a bit." He was tracing the route on his map. "Let them search both villages. But I think he went on to the next, Veyemik. From there he has a clear run, due east, to the islands. But not with the snowplow—too soon detected. He's on skis. He took them with him! But on skis he couldn't have made it yet. And in the fog . . . I think he's still there. He's either spun them a yarn or he's hiding there. He's in Veyemik!"

At 6:55 Veyemik called; and the general's heart sang.

A stranger had come in the night to Veyemik. A terrified stranger. He said a vehicle had chased him. It had chased him from the mines at Mitlakino, where he had been accused of stealing money. He had been in fear of his life and they had taken him in. Their menfolk were looking after him. Had they done wrong?

In no way! Lay hands on him immediately; subdue him, take him back to the base, keep him bound at all times! And promptly report his arrival. He would come himself as soon as notified.

Very good. One squad would remain there until the fog lifted. Then they'd go out and get him. The menfolk of Veyemik were presently at their fishing station. The man was with them.

He was where?

It took some minutes, the babble going there and back from the helicopter, for the general to gather that the fishing station was fifty kilometers out in the strait. That it was only *ten* kilometers from the first island. And that the party would not yet have reached it. They had left twenty-five minutes ago.

Twenty-five minutes!

"Go out now!" the general said. "Go immediately, don't delay! He'll slip off—this is what he'll do!"

Go where? How could they find the fishing station in the fog? The Eskimos found it by beacon. The beacon was controlled from the island. The helicopters couldn't be directed to it by the island because—

"All right. I'll manage the island. The helicopters are to take off immediately—all three of them. Sweep behind him, go due east. He's still in a car, going there! From fifty meters they'll *see* the car, even in a fog. Get them down to twenty meters! I'll call out aircraft from the island. You'll find him between you. If he tries to slip away and go left or right he'll miss the island, and he's lost in the fog. Then we pick him up at leisure. How long is the fog due to last?"

The fog was due to last, according to latest information, another two to three hours. . . . But if aircraft took off from the island there could be midair collisions—visibility was zero! The best instrumentation couldn't—

So arrange a corridor. The fishing station was fifty kilometers out? Fly forty-five. The island would be informed accordingly. Keep communication with them. He was contacting them himself immediately.

Which, immediately, he did.

From the island, after a few minutes' delay, he learned that the Eskimos' vehicles had already arrived at their fishing station. Three vehicles had been monitored arriving. Yes, island aircraft could reach the station very shortly. With the beacon, fog was not a problem.

The general asked what mobile forces were available on the island.

Twelve helicopters, he was told; augmented in winter by a company of patrol jeeps. Also sixteen personnel carriers, half-tracks, in four platoons. Four vehicles to a platoon, four men to a vehicle. Sixty-four men.

The general ordered a deployment of these forces.

The helicopters would surround the fishing station and search it. If the man had already skipped they would lift off again and support the surface force of personnel carriers. The surface force would leave at once. Six kilometers from the island it would assume its blizzard formation: the troops off-boarded fifteen meters apart. With the vehicles they would form a line of one kilometer, to sweep forward at ski-walking pace.

In case the man tried to slip back to the mainland, air force helicopters would sweep the area between. To avoid risk of collision in the fog, five kilometers would be kept between the two forces.

The fog was expected to last two to three hours. In that time the man could make a try for the American island. But first he had to find it; which he could only do from the Russian side. Was any audible signal used by the Americans in fog conditions?

No, no audible signals were used. But when the fog lifted the island was easily visible, only four kilometers away. Its masts and aerials had blinking hazard lights, and the satellite dishes were clearly illuminated.

But there was also another factor. The *island* was four kilometers away, but the international line was only *two* kilometers. On skis it could be reached in no time.

The general agreed another plan.

In one hour's time, if the man had not been taken, all forces would proceed at speed to the other side of the island. The man must not be allowed to leave it. If he made a dash for the American side he was to be brought down—*brought down,* not killed. At all costs he had to be taken alive.

While he was still speaking, urgent news arrived. The helicopters had reached the fishing station, and the man was there! He was washing dishes, in a tent, with the chef. A moment later this report was amended. He *had* been washing dishes, but at sound of the helicopters he had gone outside to have a look at them; he didn't seem yet to have returned.

When had he gone? When?

Three or four minutes ago, the chef thought. On his skis.

"Good God!" the general said. In the rapid turn of events he had been saying it repeatedly, but now he said a few things more. From two days he had reduced the gap to two hours, and then forty minutes, and then twenty-five. Now it was only three or four! If they merely *hovered* over his route, they would catch him now. How far, in three or four minutes, could he have *gone?*

60

At his second kilometer the roaring in the air was deafening and continuous. They were directly over his head now. Hovering; going on a little; hovering again.

The rotors thrashed away, a shattering row, but disturbing the fog very little. He could see the yellow haze of their searchlights. He couldn't see the machines. And he knew they couldn't see him. They were keeping altitude. And he now understood the reason why. The same reason was giving him problems.

The strait was no longer flat. Toward the center of it huge hummocks had begun to appear, windswept snow funneled between the mainland and the islands, now turned into pillars of ice. They loomed suddenly, disappearing up into the fog, very high, high enough anyway to keep the helicopters off him. But in sidestepping them he had lost his track.

Twice when the racket above had gone ahead he had taken a risk with the flashlight and shone it back to see the ski marks, had even gone back to check them. But the ice pillars were enormous, ten meters wide at least, and in pacing sideways from them he couldn't be sure he was still parallel.

Now, the ground itself was exhausting him. The stubby skis were too short, sinking into the recent snow. The row, the exhaustion, the uncertainty, had addled his brain, as he suddenly realized. He didn't have to worry about direction. The bloody helicopters were directing him.

Their job was to stop him rounding the island. They knew that first he had to reach it. Only eight kilometers to go. The two kilometers he had done in under ten minutes, despite the conditions. He was sweating under the anorak, could feel it trickling under his fur cap. He gulped the freezing fog, poled himself rapidly on, one ski after the other; still counting.

980 . . . 990 . . . Another kilometer. Seven to go.

The machines hammered and swished above his head. Hovering; advancing; hovering. Hazy blurs, bobbing there, searching. Keeping pace with a man on skis. When he was too close to the island they would have to land and face him. Or if the ice was flat, come at him at ground level. And they surely wouldn't be alone. The place was a garrison. Men could be lining up there now; a final barrier. But what else was there for him? No other place to go now.

Because there was no other place to go, he planned this one. He had scarcely any idea of it. A kilometer of rock, the Eskimos had said—and on the other side of it, the American island, only four kilometers farther. When the fog lifted it should be visible. But when the fog lifted, he would also be . . .

Well, to hell. While there was fog he had to use it—at least get himself in position. . . .

First ski within reach of the island.

Then turn left or right, to the end. And go around it and up the other side. At five hundred paces the opposite island would immediately face him. If trouble was waiting there, other noise, the Americans would probably respond with their own, which also could direct him. Even now he was only minutes away. Another kilometer had passed, the fourth. In under the hour he could be over the international line.

He was aware suddenly that there *was* other noise. Not aircraft noise. A steady rumbling ahead. And dimly through the fog saw the hazy glow of headlights; and in the same moment recalled what the Eskimos had said. There were vehicles on the island. They came out on ice maneuvers. They had come out for him.

He went flat on the ice immediately. And immediately saw a line of them ahead. In line abreast ahead, not more than a hundred meters ahead. And in the same instant, from the ground, saw that something was happening to the line. The two sets of headlights facing him had stopped and the others were fanning out. From the vehicles facing him lights began to flicker, hazy stars descending in arcs; which after a moment he translated into men with flashlights. They had jumped out of the vehicles, were strapping on skis.

He was rapidly getting out of his own skis—spread-eagled too obviously on the ice. And also out of his anorak—too visible on it. He swiftly got the white fleece lining uppermost and went flat under it. The men on skis were spacing into a formation. The other vehicles had faded into fog, only the two facing him now visible. And they too were spacing out. The men, the machines, seemed to be placing themselves fifteen meters or so apart. Lining up for a ground sweep. Jesus! He'd been right to drop. A moving figure would soon enough have been seen. He couldn't outflank vehicles. Half-tracks, he now saw, personnel carriers. But what now?

The line was taking time to assemble. Even above the helicopters he could hear the tinny quack of radio talk.

The men were stamping up and down on their skis. In padded white snow rig, he saw, hooded; automatic weapons slung around their necks. They were beating themselves with gloved hands in the biting cold. With his anorak merely stretched over him he was freezing up himself, the sweat instantly gone.

But the spacing between them, he saw, was very murky. And they would be looking, after all, for a hurrying figure on skis. If he could get them to pass him . . . He began maneuvering himself sideways between two of the stamping figures. And had not yet made it when the line stiffened suddenly and moved forward, and he went prone, skis underneath him, anorak drawn over his head.

He was just a hump of ice, he prayed. And they had only now started, not yet accustomed to the task; were seven or eight meters on either side of him.

He heard the rumble of engines, the swish of skis, and held his breath. And they were past. They'd passed. He held it a while longer before daring to get his head up and look back. Yes. Fading into fog. He buckled the skis on, got back in the anorak, and immediately set off, very fast, on the tracks left by the vehicles. And at once stopped. No! His own tracks! They'd spot them. Were certain to—maybe not right away. But *soon,* not a doubt of it. Would come chasing after him. Vehicles would get to him long before he could reach—

He turned and went back. Went rapidly, in the ski tracks, and in a minute had caught up with them, saw the flickering line of flashlights, the wide hazy beams of the vehicles. The drivers would be peering ahead. A skier *next* to a vehicle, immediately next. He came behind the man, careful not to tangle skis, and hooked him at once, one arm around his neck, a glove in his mouth as it opened. The neck he could have broken immediately, but the face as it hinged back was that of a Yakut lad, maybe eighteen, the eyes innocent and astonished.

He caught the boy's heavy flashlight and hit him with it. It struck only the padded hood and, swearing, he left the glove rammed in the mouth, and wrenched the hood back and hit him again, two solid thuds, and had him on the ice. He wrenched the gun off his neck and smashed the stock hard against the boy's temple. The tunic top was in one piece and he yanked it off him and got it on himself. It was weighted, equipment dangling at the back. He couldn't do anything about the trousers. He left the trousers, also his own anorak, took his glove, hung the gun around his neck, and set off rapidly after the patrol. In a couple of minutes he had reached it and taken up position next to the half-track.

All as before, the line swishing steadily forward, flashlights pointing ahead. He got the boy's flashlight pointing that way.

With gloves on, he couldn't feel the parts of the little automatic weapon. He'd done a course on it at the operations camp. He fumbled with it, identified the safety, snicked it off, found the trigger, and pulled. A rapid burst spat out—and with immediate effect. The flash-light nearest in the fog turned toward him and he saw the half-track driver peering sideways out of flashlight, window at the white-hooded figure now waving frantically beside him.

He was signaling with the flashlight, shouting. "He's there! Just turned—going like hell! Going back!" He put another burst ahead, saw his neighbor do the same, was aware the half-track driver had increased speed, shouting into his radio, and that gunfire was now sounding off along the line.

He let it go and turned and sped back, keeping to the tracks. Fifteen minutes at least, maybe twenty, for them to sort out the confusion, longer still for them to decide what the hell to do about it—also where the missing man had got to.

He came on the man very rapidly, still crumpled on the ice. The slender young face was solemn in sleep, mouth open, breath gently steaming. He wrapped him in the anorak, shoved his head in the fur hat. The boy's gloves had been half pulled off, and he pulled them on again. Frostbite, hypothermia—he couldn't do anything about it. *I'm sorry,* he told the Yakut.

The boy was still attached to his skis, now crossed on the ice—an altogether better pair. He quickly took them off him, with the ski sticks looped around the wrists, and got them on himself. There was a flashlight lying on the ice—his own, he saw; evidently fallen out when he had left the anorak. Now he switched it on and left it, for the Yakut to be found, and told him again he was sorry, and took off.

It had taken no more than two minutes and now he went fast, on good skis, unworried by the ice pillars, in no doubt where the vehicle tracks were leading; and after another kilometer was aware that the helicopters had gone. He could hear them well behind. They'd been called off, were now giving support to the men hunting him.

Soon he had stopped counting; no longer any point. His paces had greatly lengthened, a thousand of them now obviously much more than a kilometer. And going very much faster. In only minutes the island would be there in front of him. He could almost feel it, the solid mass of it, all his senses alert, all his exhaustion dropping away.

There would be men lined up, he had no doubt. And sensing de-vices. It was, after all, the most advanced of the electronic outposts, right on the border. The equipment would mainly face the other way, but the extremities of the place would certainly be covered. It struck him that he wasn't going to make it out on the ice; no question of simply going *around* it. He would be located immediately. He would have to get *on* it, behind the sensors, a thought that lit up in him suddenly like a bonfire.

Which in the same moment took material form immediately over his head. Amid a great whooping of sirens a flare had gone up. It arced obliquely, descending over him, and from a dozen points others instantly arced. The fog all around him became a brilliant aquarium green, shot through suddenly by a blinding narrow-beam searchlight. He skied crazily through it, waving his torch and yelling.

"Hey, hey! We're onto him!" He was panting hard. "He's doubling back there. You got the flares ready?"

"Flares? What flares?"

Behind the beam, white-hooded figures had materialized, guns at the ready. Several military jeeps were standing by, he saw.

"Christ, we yelling for them! This man moving fast—already he broke the line once! I tell you, we don't move it here, we lose him. What's the cockup with the radio?"

"Operations! Operations!" One of them was shouting into a handset. "They're calling for flares out there. They've spotted him and they need—What? Wait a minute. Who's saying this—what mob you from?" he said.

"We're all split up. They send me back—a tracker, I'm to lead a jeep there, with plenty flares for Christ's sake! Here—I go to Operations myself." He blinked around him, dazzled. "Where they keep the Operations here?"

While the man shouted into the handset, others were now surrounding the tracker. "You one of the new recruits, then?"

"Sure. Know the country, don't know too much this army. Where they put the Operations?"

He was already slipping out of his skis. In the many lights that had now come on he saw that all of them had skis strapped to their backs. The whole company was standing on a wide platform, cleared of snow, under the overhang of a cliff. A ramp, evidently for vehicles, led up from the platform, and at either side of it a walkway faded away into the fog.

"They sent back a tracker!" The man was still shouting into the handset. "Some fuckup with the R/T, he says. . . . Well, *I* can't fix up— Okay, check it out. . . . They're checking it out. You can't go up there," he said.

"Jesus Christ—they'll lose him! Is too slow here. Is slow picking me up, even! How soon you see I'm coming, man?"

"*Corporal*—you call me corporal," the man said. "And the *sensors* picked you up, animal! They're *heat* sensors. What do you understand?"

"This fucking island I understand—is why they pay me. This fellow get through, you'll see. I go take a look around the point. I think maybe needs men there—not sensors! When I fire off a few shots you know I beat the sensors, eh? I'm back four, five minutes. For the car and the flares!"

He took off at once—took off at his tracker's half-trot, and so confidently that they simply watched him. He took off along the left walkway, carrying his skis, and found it sloped upward a little, and gave it half a minute, and got off it.

He felt over the edge with a ski and found it was a fair drop now. He sat and found he was sitting on the equipment belt. The ski holster was there, and a spare magazine for the gun, and a line and pick, and a hunting knife. He eased himself off them and dropped to the ice, and got into his skis.

He skied out seventy paces and looked back and could see nothing. The sensors had picked him up at roughly two hundred meters. That was the range he had to stay inside. They had seen him go left. Now he went right. He went fast for two hundred paces and decided he had better turn in and keep contact with the island to be sure he wouldn't overshoot it.

The last twenty paces he took slowly until he could just make out the presence of the massive bulk in the fog. Then he continued alongside it, keeping contact. It took barely three minutes to reach what seemed to be the end. He went in closer, and found that it was. The great hump had turned inward. He followed its fretted shape round until it turned again and straightened out, and he knew he was on the other side.

Now he took off again, long loping paces, a hundred, two hundred, very fast.

If the rock went a kilometer, another two hundred paces would get him to the middle. But he knew now he wasn't going there. The other island was opposite—just four kilometers away, with the international line only half that distance. He could go for it immediately—a mile and a quarter! One frantic dash, and he'd be over it. Safe.

Suddenly, without further thought, he did it: left the rock behind him and headed out into the strait.

He had made fifty paces when the sirens went off.

His first thought was that he had set them off.

But almost at once a tremendous whooshing and roaring in the air told him otherwise. The helicopters were back. And *this* side of the island. Not only helicopters—vehicles, a confused uproar of vehicles, coming from the left and from the right.

But going where? Confused, disoriented, he stopped, trying to make out where.

Several events, at this time, were taking place simultaneously, the details of every one of them changing by the minute.

The general was changing them, in Tchersky.

He sat with two telephones, talking to the island and the air base. A few minutes before, the hour almost up, he had confirmed his order: all forces to be ready to transfer the search to the other side of the island. Were the vehicles in contact? Yes, in contact. And the helicopters? All in contact.

Then go.

And almost immediately, chaos, confusion, contradiction.

The surface force reported they had sighted and were pursuing a man, who had turned back to the mainland.

The island reported the arrival of a tracker, requesting flares for the pursuing surface force.

The surface force reported they had requested no flares and sent no tracker. But they were missing one man.

Hoarse now, the general rapidly took a grip on the situation. Was the tracker still on the island? Yes, he was there; with a platoon of patrol jeeps waiting on the beach platform below.

Then hold him. Hold him at once. Report *back* at once.

And at once the report back. The tracker was not now on the beach platform. Two minutes ago he had gone on an urgent mission to inspect the defenses at the north point of the island.

The general, his ears singing, absorbed this information; also, on the map, the distance to the international line. The man could be there in minutes. But not in *two* minutes.

Abandon the search.

This was the first change of plan.

All jeeps at once to the international line. Every available man to go there. The island's helicopters, the air force helicopters, the surface force—all to proceed there at speed. All personnel to disembark and form a chain, blocking access to the opposite island. The man to be brought down on sight—*disabled,* legs shot to pieces if necessary—but not killed. Imperative he be taken alive.

Moments later, advised by the island that gunfire was not permitted within five hundred meters of the line, the general amended his order.

The force would *not* now form up on the line. It would form up 250 meters before the line. But firing orders still to stand.

A minute later, on further advice, another change of orders. With all the activity ahead, the man might turn north or south. It would take him longer but still give him time to bypass a static force—the fog was expected to last another hour. Suggest jeeps be detached to cut him off before he could reach the line.

Agreed. Wait till the half-tracks arrived—in minutes now—*then* detach the jeeps. Catch the man on the ice.

But the man was no longer on the ice.

61

At first the sheer numbers had stunned him. Helicopter after helicopter, a great stream of jeeps, then the half-tracks, all thundering away out into the strait. Sent to chase after him, to pick him up before he could reach the line.

But soon he knew it couldn't be so. They'd gone too fast—just racing to block the line before he could cross. Once the men had disembarked and the little island was sealed, vehicles would be spared to hunt him—jeeps probably, zigzagging fast on the ice between the islands. He had to get off the ice.

This side of the island was deeply fretted, eroded by tides in the narrow channel. The Eskimos had said that in summer they camped in rocky bays, that seals came up on slabs then. Perhaps there was a place to hide there. He made fast work up the coast, and came on slabs, a great line of them.

They began in a heap at one side of a small inlet, and extended out like a breakwater, huge rocks, mainly flat, all iced. He skied along the line, peering for a cavity. He could see there must be gaps between the rocks, but snow had iced up a continuous wall. There was no way into the wall, and he couldn't climb it with his skis. He also couldn't tell how much farther out it went. They could be at the end hunting him at any time.

He skied rapidly back to inspect the inlet, and saw the Eskimos had used it; the beach sloped sharply upward and bits of their gear still littered the slope. A windlass for hauling boats, its tarpaulin blown open; a few nondescript humps now iced over; an abandoned lantern, hanging in an opening of the cliff face. He went in the opening, found a sizable cave, and looked swiftly around it with his flashlight.

There was a fireplace; heavy seal hooks in the roof; a rock bench for handling the carcasses. He'd seen this before in the north. Nowhere to hide here. He turned and went out fast, almost at once taking a tumble on the slope as he hit a couple of the humps. He picked himself up, looking at the humps.

Seabirds, frozen. There were four of them, caught by winter. And after the Eskimos had gone. The Eskimos would have taken them for bait. They'd fallen. He looked up the rock face. There would be an eyrie up there. In the flashlight beam a hollow showed in the pitted face, ten, twelve meters up.

No way up there, with the cave opening in between.

He shone the flashlight on either side of the hollow, and saw there had been a rock fall to the right; a jagged ledge was exposed in the cliff face there. The ledge ran above the first tumbled slabs. From the slabs it looked possible to get to the ledge; and from the ledge, the eyrie.

He went to the slabs, knowing it was a crazy risk to take. But the breakwater effectively stopped him from skiing farther anyway. He rapidly got out of the skis, holstered them on his back, and tackled the slabs.

Icy smooth, no footholds. He reached behind him for the coiled rope in the tunic belt. The plaited nylon was hooked to its little ice pick. He slung the pick, managed at the fourth try and hauled himself up the slab.

High; three meters. From the top he could see the outline of the eyrie. Still seven or eight meters above, and to his left. Hazy in the flashlight beam but with a long shadow inside.

He looked up at the ledge and flung the pick—flung it repeatedly until it caught. He tugged hard on it with his full weight: a long, long drop this time. Then he twisted the gun on its strap around to his back, and started up.

The battered rock had footholds, slippery, unreliable, but giving purchase. He walked up the cliff face, hand over hand on the rope, and when his head came level with the ledge felt carefully with his feet for a hold and swung himself up.

He knelt there a moment, released the pick, gathered the rope in his hand, and slowly raised himself.

The ledge was glassy with ice, very narrow; no room to turn. He faced into the cliff, and edged sideways along it, watching his feet.

He couldn't see the eyrie until he was at it. The cliff bulged out slightly and suddenly there was no more ledge.

He stood quite still, his arms on the cliff, and looked sideways at the eyrie. An irregular hole, very jagged; a meter wide, about the same high. It had its own small ledge, slightly below, evidently the perch from which the birds had fallen, and above it another, like an over-hanging brow.

He kept his arms on the cliff, extended a foot sideways, and lowered it to the perch. The brow above was so slight there was almost nothing to hold on to. He got a gloved hand on the icy rim, steadied himself, got the other foot quickly on the perch and threw himself in. The skis snagged behind him in the opening and he was held for a moment before he wriggled them, and himself, inside and found he was on his knees on a floor.

He stayed there panting for a while. Then he took the gun and the skis off his back, helped himself to one of the Yakut's cigarettes, and sat and smoked it with his eyes closed.

This was a few minutes after eight in the morning, and he had some thinking to do.

The Greater Diomede Island, on its east-facing cliff, is dotted with bird eyries and Porter was in three of them while the fog lasted. The first, above the so-called Seal Causeway, he decided was too obvious a place to hide in, and he didn't stay long. The second was where he hid what was in the body belt. (A half of it, for one disk was still on him when he was cornered.) The third was where he was brought down.

His account of what happened here is not totally coherent. But he knew that, although he couldn't see it, a tape recorder was running at the time and that his words, necessarily distorted, would all the same be subjected to careful analysis.

He was in this last place some time after half past nine. (The gilt-wrapped disk, containing the data, he had just hidden. He had got away from it fast; but now he was wondering whether he should bury the silver one too.) The helicopters were then still grounded but he could hear their rotors slowly turning; also the sound of vehicles, less muffled by fog now and evidently patrolling to north and south of the opposite island. From this he knew that the strait was covered for miles and that he had no chance of skiing across.

He also knew that survival on the icy cliff was impossible; that he would be trapped on it when the fog lifted, and that his options were either to give himself up or to be caught.

A jeep had turned up below at this time and he heard the crew get out and search a cave. The man in charge had shouted:

"Remember, lads, he's to be taken alive. But put a few in his legs: He's a wriggly bastard—can still make it, give him half a chance."

This had given him pause. He was to be taken alive. And he was a wriggly bastard who could still make it.

He wondered.

He had his pick and line. He had his skis, his gun.

A few minutes later he also had a fantastic view.

The breeze, already snatching at the fog, turned suddenly into a blasting wind that blew it away entirely. In minutes the air was crystal clear, and the other island stood immediately before him. It looked no distance at all—a huge skyscraper of rock, laced with lights.

Helicopters were going up and down on it, taking a look at the disturbance before them.

Before them was the disturbance facing him.

He counted sixteen half-tracks; the flickering flashlights of some scores of men; many jeeps skimming on the ice; and helicopters fluttering, a long line of them, now too beginning to lift off.

He saw three long-bodied ones thundering away, evidently back to the mainland. The smaller ones went blinking up into the sky, to land somewhere above him. The half-tracks and the flickering torches remained.

The place he was in had a low roof and the floor was covered with debris. This slit in the rock—for this was all it was—was four or five meters deep, and wider inside than out, the walls at either side of the opening hollowed in.

From the opening he observed something new happening.

A helicopter had evidently lifted off above, and presently he saw it flittering like a daddy longlegs along the coast, its searchlight examining the cliff face. As it drew closer he hid himself in the hollow by the opening and stayed there as the eyrie lit up. The searchlight looked in for half a minute, and moved on.

A little later, he saw that two vehicles were following the helicopter on the ice. Some banging had been going on, but it took him time to figure out what it was. One of the cars was a jeep. The other seemed to be a fire-fighting vehicle. It had an articulated ladder, and at each cave where the helicopter had lingered the ladder was raised.

Porter watched as, in the beam of a searchlight, a man in a gas mask went up the ladder. At the top he flung in what seemed to be a stun grenade, producing the bang, and shortly afterward a canister of tear gas—smoke streamed out, anyway. Then the man paused, head well down, before suddenly rushing the place; with a sharp rat-tat, and another pause, before he reappeared and came down the ladder.

Porter positioned himself in his own eyrie to be nearer fresh air, prepared to take a deep breath and hold it. He knew he could hold it for two minutes. The man hadn't taken as long as two minutes.

He was waiting there when it happened. He saw the walls turning milky white, heard the scrape of the ladder and the man coming up. He gave it ten seconds, filled his lungs, and actually saw the stun grenade come arcing in. It struck the low roof, bounced sharply onto his chest, and exploded in his face.

For some moments, the flash was the last thing he saw. It blinded, deafened, almost paralyzed him.

He still hung onto his breath.

The second canister he didn't see or hear. He knew it was there by the stinging of his lips and a prickling around the eyes. He was aware, through the smoke, of a bulky presence at the opening, a pig's snout emerging there. He smashed the man's head with his gun and yanked him swiftly in, remembering to rap off a quick burst at the roof. He had the gas mask off in seconds and put it on himself, exhaling and inhaling. He still could hear nothing at all. He waited some moments more, breathing quickly in the gas mask, and went out backward.

It was the trousers (this he did not learn) that gave him away. He didn't hear the order to face around, didn't even hear the warning burst chattering around his head; was aware only of the solid jolt in his right leg, that he no longer had the use of the leg and was tumbling off the ladder.

By this time he had less than two meters to fall and he landed in a heap, but with the gun in his hands. He got off a short burst with it, and saw the men standing there take cover. In the brilliant beam he had almost a flashlight picture: of the fire vehicle's driver staring out of the window; of the man at the ladder mechanism gaping at him; of the jeep, its offside doors standing open.

Two armed men had been positioned by the jeep, both now down on the ice and peering at him from underneath the car. One was yelling at him; he could see the mouth going but couldn't hear what it said. The man had his gun leveled, so Porter shot him and saw the man punched back flat on the ice; and in another soundless moment saw the other man wriggling his gun out from underneath, and he put a burst into him too.

The driver of the jeep was still in it; he now saw his legs emerging. He put two single shots near them, tore the gas mask off and yelled, "Stay where you are! Get back in!" He could just, now, above the ringing in his ears, hear his own voice, and he saw the legs go back in.

He crawled to the offside door, poked the gun in, and kept it on the man while he pulled himself in.

"Don't shoot me," the man said.

He was very frightened.

"Just drive." He had the gun at the man's chin.

"Drive where?"

"To the line—get going!"

"We can't make it. They'll blow us to pieces!"

"*I'll* blow you to fucking pieces!"

He fired under the man's chin, shattering the window.

The man was trembling very badly, but he put the car in gear, and moved, bumping over something.

He said shakily, "Give yourself up—they won't kill you. There's orders not to kill you. We can never make this."

This seemed very likely. From nowhere jeeps had come spinning—from the left, from the right.

"Go faster!"

"We're going as fast as we can."

Maybe they were. He wasn't seeing too well. When he looked ahead his left eye couldn't see the man beside him. (This was because his left eye was in the eyrie, blown out by the stun grenade.) The other jeeps were not going any faster; they had come out fast, trying to cut them off, but seemed now only able to keep pace, and automatic fire was coming from them. He understood they were not trying to hit him but to immobilize the car. The firing was at the engine, at the wheels.

And some of the half-tracks ahead, he saw, were moving. Their headlights were on and their searchlights now came blindingly on. The ones that weren't moving had also begun firing; puffs of smoke came from them, and a few meters ahead the ice began to erupt: small grenades, propelled grenades—again intended evidently just to stop the car.

The effect of the grenades was to detach the jeeps closest to him, which turned rapidly aside—giving them, so it seemed, a final lucky burst, for the car jerked suddenly and slewed, the driver wrestling with the wheel as they tilted and slithered round in a complete half-circle.

"We're hit, they've got us—give it up now!"

"Keep going!" His balance, his spatial sense had gone; couldn't tell which side was down. "Where are we hit?"

"Your side—we're all down there. See it!"

He took a look, and saw they were down. "Give it left wheel," he said, and turned back and saw the man was no longer at the wheel. He was no longer in the car. His door was open and he had flung himself out.

"Jesus Christ!" The back doors too were open, and now banging to and fro as a jeep struck them. He got his gun up and put a burst in the jeep's windshield. The magazine ran out with this short burst and he levered himself, in great pain, behind the wheel. His right knee was now in torment, no movement in the leg. He carried the leg over the seat and got his other foot down.

The car hadn't stalled, was still slowly circling, in first gear. He stepped on the accelerator, shuffled his foot to change gear, and straightened out. Two more jeeps had slammed into him and his lights had been shot out. But there was light enough, he didn't need lights; and in the frantic minutes had barely even noticed the collisions.

One wheel was dragging in the soft surface ice, and the steering was heavy. He had little speed and now was being banged again and again by the jeeps. In the brief interval when he'd appeared to stop, the RPG firing had ceased and the jeeps had closed in. But now, straightened out and on track again, he saw the grenades restarting, the jeeps again sheering away.

The moving half-tracks had come closer, their searchlights dazzling him. He saw the intention was to ram him, to catch him between two of them. He pressed the pedal to the floor, squeezed the last bit of speed and found, with the motion, the wheel dragging less, the steering coming lighter. He didn't turn away, went directly at the converging lights, waited till he was almost at them, and spun the wheel. But now, hammer blows coming from his left eye, his distance was all out, and he was jolted out of his seat as he hit the rear end of one. He clutched onto the wheel as the car lurched left, right, skittering on the ice.

His foot had come off the pedal, and he found it again, hunching back in the seat. Firing had started behind him, a hail of it hitting the rear end, low down. And ahead now, perhaps no more than two hundred meters, the stationary half-tracks were puffing at him, the ice spuming up. But they were far apart, he saw, a gulf apart, and the line of flashlights in between was wavering. They could not fire *at* him, not in the car, could only try to stop the car.

He aimed at the gap between two half-tracks, saw the men on the ice there scattering, turning carefully to fire—and he was through. But Jesus, Jesus—caught once more! Now, at the last, another wheel. The car dragged, slithered. He was through the waiting line, but crippled, two tires at least gone. And the half-track engines were now roaring into life behind him; an iron voice rasping over a bullhorn there.

"Stop! Stop while you can! You'll be blown off the ice!"

He kept going: swearing, coaxing, willing the thing to move. He was moving, moving, six or seven miles an hour maybe, the wheels churning, moving only when zigzagged. His eye, his knee, were now alight with white fire—the ice also alight, lit up, spuming with small geysers popping in front of him.

Distantly now there were other lights, racing about. The American side: surely not far now. With nothing following him—and he was sure nothing was or it would easily have overtaken him—he thought he must now be over the international line.

(In fact he was not yet over it. The vehicles behind had been ordered to remain 250 meters from the line, and this they did; a fact confirmed by watching American helicopters. But they had also been ordered to continue firing up to it, and this too they did; the subject of later official complaint.)

For the men on the half-tracks the job was now very difficult. Even at one hundred meters, RPGs could not hit a target with any great accuracy. And this target, a man in a vehicle, was *not* to be hit—at least not with a grenade—but only halted. The only way to halt him now was to hit his engine. If this could be achieved before he reached the line, men could go out on skis and get him. Probably at this time some small mortars were used.

The geysers that had been popping in front of the slowly zigzagging vehicle now came closer; and with his zigzag now established and predictable, they scored, and a cheer went up.

"Hit! Stopped him! Okay, boys, go out there."

The boys went out there, but to their consternation the target, though stopped, did not remain stopped.

The thing had landed with a whoosh, a metallic clang and a cascade of glass. The clang was the ripped-apart hood of the jeep, sections of which, and of the grenade, came through the shattered windshield and into Porter. The furnace in his head roared briefly and went out, leaving him in the dark. It had also bounced his foot off the pedal, stopping the car.

Still in the dark, he started the stalled engine again, twisting the wheel this way and that, and rocking the car in and out of reverse, which got it sluggishly crawling again.

The blast seemed to have stunned him completely. He couldn't see anything. And the shock was making him pant. The glass had exploded in his face and must have cut his mouth. He tasted blood there. The panting he recognized after a minute to be not panting but something like choking. This nightmare—quite a familiar one—he had often had. Driving a car, choking, and unable to see where he was going. He knew he must be going right, that he hadn't turned completely. When the car stuck and churned he wriggled the wheel and got it moving again, very slowly, a crippled insect, stumbling, stopping, wriggling on.

The U.S. aircraft watching from above stated that it took him eight minutes and that he halted when he was told to.

A loudspeaker told him to, in English, and presently some closer voices were bawling at him to open the door and step out with his arms raised. He opened the door but didn't manage the arms or even the step, flopping out like a bundle on the ice. Many big amplified voices were sounding off all around him, and from the island itself, and among them he picked out, weirdly, the mellifluous one of Bing Crosby, hoping that his days would be merry and bright, and all his Christmases white.

62

The medical facilities on the island were found to be not adequate for Porter's injuries and a helicopter was readied to take him 120 miles down the Alaskan coast to Nome. He was fully conscious and urgently demanding a tape recorder, which the radio room made available to him, together with a throat microphone—this last a requirement of the military surgeon who didn't want him shouting over the engine.

At Nome, the facilities were also found to be insufficient and he was jetted another six hundred miles south to Anchorage. Here, in the early afternoon of December 25, he was admitted to Providence Hospital.

Because of the festivities only a skeleton staff was on duty at the hospital, but Nome had informed them of the case and specialists had already been contacted.

The specialists drove in, and they agreed that immediate surgery was needed. The patient was still conscious but now in great difficulties. Apart from possible neurological complications, the more obvious damage was very extensive. One eye was missing; he was blind in the other; he had two shattered legs, and severe injuries to most of his upper body.

In stripping him for examination, the staff had found a body belt which he refused to give up. During the X rays he insisted on holding it himself under a protective lead apron. The tape recorder had been taken from him (the tape, after being turned for him on the aircraft, had now run out), but he insisted that he had to give some immediate instructions about it to a man in Washington.

This man could not be reached, but at a redirected number somebody promised that he would call in as soon as possible. He had still not called in when Porter, now speechless and unmoving, had to be taken down to the operating theater. By then, however, he had made his instructions understood: The belt and the tape were to be locked in the hospital's safe, and if he was incapable of speech for any length of time after the operation the man from Washington had to hear the tape before touching the body belt.

These instructions were observed: The belt and the tape went into a safe and Porter himself to surgery.

The man in Washington was his CIA escort, Walters, with whom he had established at the "operations camp" a fair working relationship. Walters was not, at this time, in Washington but in Seattle, where he was spending Christmas with his in-laws. Seattle, though well north— the most northerly city of the contiguous United States—was still fifteen hundred miles south of Anchorage.

Transport was made available, his flight cleared, and he arrived at the Providence at nine o'clock. Porter was by then long out of the operating theater, but not expected to live. His visitor identified himself, had his identification confirmed, and signed for the tape and the body belt. He had been keeping contact with Langley and was now instructed to go there at once. Langley was another three-thousand-plus miles. But by lunchtime next day, which was December 26, the material he brought with him had been duly processed. By then, however, the Providence's morgue had received its expected corpse.

The voice on the tape was a husky whisper, not always understandable, but quite understandable about the body belt.

Inside the belt was a pouch, and in the pouch a foil-sealed case.

When manipulated in a vessel of liquid hydrogen the case sprang easily open and popped out its disk. The disk was four centimeters in diameter, and the material on it highly condensed. The technicians soon unraveled the protocol and transferred the contents to a screen.

The information on the disk was known to be addressed personally, but even so the directness of the opening caused surprise as the lines began streaking, one after the other, across the screen.

"How long, dear friend—how long? I await you with eagerness. . . . "

Epilogue

The man who had been awaited with eagerness was given no name at the inquest held at Anchorage.

The medical witnesses said he had died of multiple injuries, and the military ones that he had sustained them in a vehicle that had halted, damaged, on the sea ice of north Alaska.

He had entered U.S. territory from the Russian side of the border, perhaps having strayed there in the fog. He had evidently been caught in crossfire during a military exercise, at present the subject of official complaint. For the exercise had taken place within five hundred meters of the international line, and gunfire within 250 meters of it: a clear violation of treaties.

The man was non-Caucasian. He had carried no identification and had given none. The coroner found he had been unlawfully killed, and ordered the body held until its identity was known and culpability for the death established.

The inquest was fully reported in the town's two papers, the *Anchorage Times* and the *Daily News*.

In Irkutsk the general read these reports and added them to his own for a tribunal he would shortly be attending. The Americans, he had been informed, would be producing clear and certifiable photographs of the violation. A fig for the Americans! His only regret was that he was unable to produce their agent—a counterviolation. But the man had gotten away, if only to die. He read through the evidence of the civilian surgeons again, and decided there was no doubt about that. He was dead. And nothing had come of his mission.

The *fact* of the mission was very amply confirmed, however (evidence from Batumi, from Ponomarenko, from the many forged papers). And that nothing had come of it was equally plain. Major Militsky, the guards, the Evenks—the testimony of all of them showed that. It was impossible for the man to have made contact with anybody on the mountain. And obviously he had never intended to. A reconnaissance only.

How he had arrived in the Kolymsky region was a problem, and how he had left it was another; as yet unresolved. But the action at the strait (bearing in mind the high security issue involved) was unquestionably justified. The object was to catch the man, discover who had sent him—and how. Unfortunately it had not been achieved. But the next best thing had. Meanwhile, inquiries were still continuing.

At Green Cape many inquiries were continuing.

Ponomarenko turned up and was soon appearing about town, with a variety of explanations. As was Lydia Yakovlevna, with a black eye. At the Tchersky Transport Company the inquiry into missing parts continued for weeks: ending with a new set of rules for the disposal of dismantled vehicles. Too many of them had been found about the works, and the removal of parts without signed authority was now strictly forbidden.

In these weeks Vassili relaxed and his wife also relaxed, for she knew he was no longer worried. He whistled a bit, and winked, and she thought he was himself again. And this was true, for he was. Some small problems still lay ahead, relating to his deficit book, but these were familiar and unimportant ones, very minor. The one that had darkened him had gone. For though the Chukchi had used him he knew that, at the last, he had disposed of the bobik—had not let him down, and his faith in the man was restored.

At Murmansk there was the question of a missing seaman.

Two Norwegians, who had been in transit with him at the International Seamen's Hostel, thought he had gone to the red-light district. A trawl of the girls there turned up nothing; and the arrival of his ship, some days later, produced no other evidence.

The man had not left with the ship, and he couldn't have left any other way—for his passport, his papers, his belongings, all were still at the hostel. These the police retained for three months in case he turned up floating in a dock. But when he didn't (and in the current crime wave there had been many permanent disappearances), marine agents were advised that his possessions could be sent, not at Murmansk's expense, to the ship's owners at Nagasaki.

At Nagasaki the *Suzaku Maru,* after circumnavigating the globe, was again in dock.

She had arrived, like her sister ship of the preceding year, on Christmas Day, at roughly the time that Porter had crossed the Bering Strait. At various points on his voyage home the captain had learned he would be facing a board of inquiry relating to some events at Otaru. These events he and the mate now had in good order, and the two officers appeared before the board and explained them.

Seaman Ushiba's illness had seemed just serious enough for an extra hand to be shipped in order to spare the patient deck duties. This the captain had set in hand, as Otaru radio station could confirm. At Otaru, Ushiba's condition had necessitated sedation and prompt medical care, and he had ordered an ambulance. Adverse weather reports had also impelled him to seek an early departure, foregoing a lucrative cargo of tuna—a commercial loss but necessary for the good of the ship and the voyage.

When, in the Arctic, the new hand, too, had become ill, he had stopped off the mouth of the Kolyma for medical assistance. The man had been removed to hospital, *the ship allowed to proceed,* and at Murmansk he had signed bills for the man's expenses. This was all he knew. He had acted throughout with prudence and good sense. He hoped the board would recognize it.

This the board did, and another inquiry was completed.

With all of his bills signed, the Korean seaman was of no further interest to the Tchersky Health Authority. However, a note at last arrived from Murmansk acknowledging receipt of his discharge from the Kolymsky region. It pointed out that since no application had yet been made for the man to board a ship, it was presumed other arrangements had been made and he had flown home. If this was the case Murmansk had no need to hold his papers and, unless specifically requested, would not do so.

At the medical center this bureaucratic confusion caused no surprise. But since the man was unlikely to worry *them* again, it was decided his papers need not clutter up Tchersky's either, and they were destroyed.

No record now remained in the Kolymsky region of a sullen Korean seaman, or any connection, if there had ever been one, with a cheerful Chukchi who had driven to Tcherny Vodi.

At Tcherny Vodi the new year was somber.

Before January was out a small coffin was taken for cremation (the last of the ape program), and weeks later a larger one. The administrator of the Buro was advised that the director's personal effects and his ashes need not be sent, for there was no one to send them to. Under a new director the genetic and the optical programs would shortly resume, for Moscow still held all records.

In Oxford, Lazenby, without knowledge either of the Korean seaman or the Chukchi driver, was thinking of a third character.

His mind had been led in that direction by Miss Sonntag, whose farewell party he had just attended. Her departure had been planned for June (for she was now nearing sixty-five) and a successor was already chosen. But her sister, Sonya, had fallen ill and needed attention, and now, after Easter, she would not be returning.

At the party they had reminisced a little and she had reminded him, slightly flushed over her second glass of sherry, of the day they had rummaged together through a bin and found only cigarette papers.

He thought of these papers on his solitary walk home, and of what had come of them; and of an interrupted fishing trip on the Spey and what had come of *that*. A bewildering few days . . . and a bewildering individual met in the course of them. He remembered very little of him. An austere staring face; a face as austere as a totem pole. As at that village. The one with the odd name—*what* was it, now . . . ?

Kispiox; Easter.

And for Jean-Baptiste Porteur, one further journey.

Anchorage had released the body, after a certain period, with the coroner's verdict amended from "unlawful killing" to "death by misadventure." For a misadventure it was. The deceased had strayed in fog, and in the same fog units involved in a military exercise had also strayed.

The Russians had made handsome apology, and offered handsome amends, with only a simple condition. No compensation could be paid, naturally, until the identity of the deceased had been discovered. But the identity of the deceased had not been discovered. . . .

These proceedings, too, were reported in the *Anchorage Times* and the *Daily News*.

For the journey to Kispiox, Walters had been in attendance. He had flown with his burden to Hazelton, and then had sat silently in the long somber vehicle on the slow drive to Kispiox. There he remained for some hours before returning to Langley, where he discussed the matter with the keeper of Lives.

"Well," W. Murray Hendricks said, gazing down at the file before him, "it looks to me as if we got away with it."

"I'm sure we did," Walters said. "Nobody special was there, and nobody *has* been there. No visitors of any kind. They're in the dark—totally."

Two months before, at a funeral in Anchorage, special visitors *had* been present, visitors from the Russian consulate, to convey their government's regret at the sad accident—and to examine the other mourners. But apart from the grave diggers and a Unitarian minister there had been no other mourners, only two reporters to record the burial of the unknown man; and Walters, watching from a window above the chapel.

"How is he now?" asked Hendricks.

"Coming along. You can't see a lot of change."

"He's surely changed since you saw him in that hospital at Anchorage!"

"Oh, since then—" When Walters had seen him at the Providence Hospital—a glimpse only, in the private intensive-care room—Porter had been connected up to machines and swathed from head to foot in bandages. On the flight from Seattle, Walters had not gone directly to Anchorage but to Elmendorf Air Force Base, a few miles away. The air base also had a hospital, without the full surgical facilities of the Providence; but it had some other facilities, less orthodox. A corpse had been flown in there, of another non-Caucasian male, unknown, unclaimed, a road-accident victim, a boon for Langley. For it had been decided that Porter's body, dead or alive, should not remain in civilian jurisdiction, but be removed to a more secure kind. From Elmendorf certain security personnel, temporarily "medics," had visited to examine the patient, and the order of his wrappings.

The switch had been arranged that same night, during a fire alarm that had also been arranged. The new night shift at the hospital had never before seen the badly injured patient, but were not surprised at the brain death shown on the monitors, and no autopsy had been required for the bandaged man—only his removal to the hospital's morgue, where he remained for two months until the coroner's final release. But the man in the morgue, so unceremoniously buried, was not Porter. Porter himself had been swiftly transported, doctors in attendance, to the air base, where he stayed on a life-support machine until he could be flown farther south, to another military hospital, of Langley's nomination.

"Is he able to receive proper care up in that Indian village?" Hendricks asked.

"It's what he wanted. There's a health service there, and district visitors. He's sick of hospitals. They've got some sight back in that right eye and it will improve, though he's got it covered now. His legs are wired up and there's a lot of new parts in his body. He'll be in that chair for some time. But he still has a lung—and a sense of humor. He calls himself Bionic Man."

"He's talking now, is he?"

"A little. He can write a bit, but of course he can't see and it's just a scrawl. There was a big stack of mail for him there. The postmaster will be answering for him—I told him what to write."

The letters were from colleagues and students at McGill and Victoria. Both universities had been informed of the accident—of the nonstop truck that had hit him as he stepped out of Quebec woods. From both establishments he was now on sick leave.

"Another thing," Walters said. "I met his mother up there. A strange old woman—wailing. She said she'd warned him years ago against going to college, that though he'd bring light to the world, he'd die in the dark, and it would all end in tears."

"Well. He didn't die," Hendricks said. "And as yet it hasn't ended—in tears or otherwise."

"The *light,* though . . . a strange remark, wasn't it?"

"Sure. And about that she could be right."

"Was it any use, that disk of his?"

"Certainly. Harmonics theory is brand-new. And fiber optics is an advancing field. The Russians always led in those fields—very unconventional, their science. Our people have already cracked a lot of what he brought. . . . It's a damn shame he left that full data disk up in the eyrie, though."

"Well, he wasn't going to get caught with it—knowing it would be destroyed if they tried to open it. And even here he has a solution. He thinks his Inuit friends will be able to get at it. Apparently they used to picnic there, thirty or forty years ago—parties of them from both sides of the strait, Russian and Alaskan. Then the Soviets made a base there and put a stop to it. Pretty soon now he thinks they'll be picnicking again—demilitarization, America and Russia both needing each other. But he's sure as *hell* the Russian military will never release their own data—never, ever, till the end of time. He knows precisely where the eyrie is—and that our guys on Diomede took telephoto pictures of it. He's certain the disk will be recovered and that his journey wasn't wasted. He got it out. A cure for blindness . . . ''

For some moments the two men looked at each other, silently.

"Yes," Hendricks said at last. "He did an incredible job."

And there had been another, smaller, job Porter had been concerned about. He wanted an addition made to a forthcoming book. It had been edited for him by a young woman in Prince George. He had spelled out the addition and Walters had passed it on. This he mentioned now.

"That other young woman, eh?" Hendricks smiled. "Well, he had no shortage of them. He was very attractive to women. He was married to an Indian girl once, you know—she was blind."

"I didn't know," Walters said, staring. "I didn't know that at all. We were together for weeks in camp, and talked a lot. I never understood that."

"No. Well. There's a lot not understood about him. I doubt if anybody understood him. He never married again," Hendricks said, and closed the file. "He had no real attachments, you know."

But there had been an attachment.

Medical Officer Komarova was now sick of the Kolymsky region.

From the chief of militia she heard that the villain was likely dead. Not certain—Irkutsk hadn't yet deigned to tell him—but there were rumors, and it was *likely*.

Through the winter she had observed her mother failing. And from the Evenks she knew that Tcherny Vodi's director (so a grieving Stepanka said) *had* failed: her beloved Misha-Bisha. Soon only unhappy memories would remain in this place, and she thought it well to look for another.

In June, barely spring at Tchersky, she flew west and found summer. The Karelia region needed a medical officer, district of Lake Ladoga; interview St. Petersburg. She had trained in Petersburg, knew the remote area where services were required, which had many attractions, chief among them distance—six thousand kilometers of distance—from the Kolymsky region.

A room had been booked for her, and in it she took out her ring. She hadn't worn it in Tchersky, and now she examined it again.

"Like our love the circle has no end."

She tried it on her third finger, but it was too small, and she slipped it on the little one and slept with it.

In the morning she was out early, before seven, restless in the big city. Her interview wasn't until eleven, and she walked for hours.

In the Nevsky Prospekt, still only a quarter past ten, she looked into a bookshop and wandered around it and was in the foreign section; and suddenly, almost fainting, she saw him. Saw his face. On the back of a book. She picked it up.

J. B. PORTER. *The Inuit: Life and Legend.*

The book was new; there were three copies, face down, somewhat dusty from unpacking, and an irritable assistant snatched the one from her hand, and penciled a price inside, and in the other two, and wiped them, and left them right way up.

There was nowhere to sit and she could hardly stand. She leaned against a wall and looked at the book again. The flyleaf said it was the author's latest and most significant contribution to a field already illuminated by his powerful . . .

The English words blurred before her eyes, but she read on.

In his completion of earlier studies, Dr. Porter had provided the definitive account . . . his text supplying in particular all known versions of the reverse-narrative technique of this supposedly unsophisticated people . . .

And not only the text, she saw, turning a page. There was a one-line dedication: TO AHSIB-AHSIM and AYNAP-AYNAT.

She stopped twisting her ring and wiped her eyes, and tried it again. Right to left. Yes. Yes. But the price of the book, ruble-penciled, was astronomically beyond her and she left, stumbling out into daylight.

And three months later, her mother at last laid to rest in the small cemetery at Panarovka, she left the Kolymsky region for good, her new posting noted by all relevant medical authorities—and also by Langley.

Three months more, settled but melancholy in the Karelia region, she returned one day from a trip and looked briefly through the mail that lay open on her desk. One envelope was not opened, and she paused over it. A long business envelope, the address handwritten. And unopened, evidently, because it was marked "Private." The postmark read St. Petersburg. She knew few people in Petersburg and didn't recognize this hand at all. She opened the envelope and at first could make no sense of the contents. A slim sheaf, bearing the logo "Aeroflot." A flight ticket. She had booked no flight ticket. A mistake, obviously. But stapled to the cover of the ticket, an official slip approving an exit visa; and on the slip her name and passport number, all correct. Inside, the ticket was undated, an open flight; the

360

destination, Montreal. No note came with the ticket, no explanation at all. She opened the envelope wider, and at the bottom saw it, a tiny slip of paper, a cigarette paper. A single line of writing was on it, somewhat irregular, but the Russian quite legible: "Like our love the circle has no end."

All year, with its many losses, she had remained on the whole dry-eyed. But now, the slip of paper shaking in her hand, she stared about her and found her face in a wall mirror, and saw it begin to disintegrate there. For now they came. In the end, tears. In such streams, such floods, that it was hard to tell, in the distorted image, if the face was laughing or crying; and to the assistant who hurried into the room, alarmed at the noise, it seemed, weirdly, that the medical officer was doing both.